A Necklace of Ears

Alberto Roblest

English Translation by Dillon Scalzo

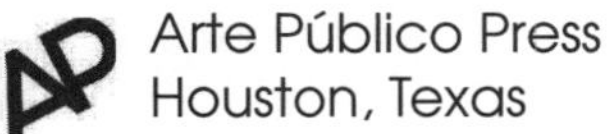

A Necklace of Ears is made possible through a grant from the Texas Commission on the Arts. We are grateful for its support.

Recovering the past, creating the future

Arte Público Press
University of Houston
4902 Gulf Fwy, Bldg 19, Rm 100
Houston, Texas 77204-2004

Cover art by Alberto Roblest
Cover design by Ryan Hoston

Library of Congress Control Number: 2025933398

∞ The paper used in this publication meets the requirements of the American National Standard for Information Sciences—Permanence of Paper for Printed Library Materials, ANSI Z39.48-1984.

Printed in the United States of America

25 26 27 4 3 2 1

To my grandmothers
To Tina for being an accomplice in my life
To my paternal family, for all the fiction in their lives
To the friends who read this work and gave me creative feedback

Contents

Part One

I throw the dice on the table with contempt, my eyes and my tongue are on the line. All the other players, despite the elegance of their clothes, have no faces. Some wear masks. It's a peculiar place, perhaps an underground gambling house, a seedy casino ... I'm unsure. I take off the necklace that adorns my neck with disgust and put it next to the chips. There are ears, somewhat blackened and dry, pierced by a wire at the height of the lobe: one after the other, twenty human cartilages making the circle complete. I feel revulsion, most certainly, although I pretend to act natural. Something has happened and I don't know what ... The dice turn in all their possible mathematical combinations—everything has a price, including the heart. The stakes rise ... only the time stands still.

1

Martina screamed first, then me. I rocked a bit more upon her beautiful body, bewildered by the sight of her face. I gave my hips a final push, slowly pulled out of her and threw myself down at her side. We both stared at the fan without saying a word. The sweat on my forehead rolled away with the back of my hand, a few kicks of my heels and the sheet hit the floor. I glanced at her out of the corner of my eye. She looked despondent, perhaps regretful, or maybe she just felt dirty. For my part it had been a wonderful thirty minutes floating in the stratosphere. She bit her lip, covering her breasts with her arm, my eyes she avoided completely. There's an old saying: *One sign to the wise is enough*, so I stood up and got dressed with little commotion. Honestly, I understood; what with her husband fighting somewhere in the Middle East and her having just traded easy passion with another man, I didn't dare do anything to interrupt her thoughts, or whatever sense of guilt might be perched there. I went out into the living room and drank the remains of the water she offered me before the ardent kisses and disruption of the bed sheet. I grabbed my jacket from one of the armchairs, my toolbox, gone cold with neglect, and eased the door shut behind me, that delicate scent of sex with me, on my skin, all the while. I couldn't help but smile.

I crossed the gardens on the way to the maintenance shed, went around the two huge halls that served as multipurpose rooms—basketball, volleyball and tennis courts. Maybe that experience was a good sign ... of course it could just as easily have been a herald of worse to come, *Who knows*? The fact is that at that moment I licked my lips, still sweet with Martina's sex, that lone rose. She was about 5'5", very narrow of waist. Her hips opened down to two perfect, firm buttocks, which were supported by a pair of well-formed legs. Her breasts weren't very big, but their shape was perfect, full and supple as fruit trees in California. Although the most beautiful thing about her was the shape of her sex: it looked like a summer flower with thick petals, hardly comparable to the lips that decorated her mouth. She was married to a soldier who had been in Iraq for at least nine months, and I had been fortunate enough to cross paths with her just as the ache became too much. She wasn't waiting for me, I wasn't waiting for her; it was pure luck and a clogged sink that brought me to her door and as soon as I walked through it, my toolbox in hand, I could sense a need that had invaded everything. You could practically smell it in the whisper of the rooms, feel its shape along the surfaces of solitary living. I introduced myself as the new employee, I "have only been working here a few weeks," but I was "ready for whatever." Oh, no job scared me, any hiccups and it was as simple as calling the manager so he could give me instructions. She smiled. I asked about the problem. We walked together to the kitchen, her ahead, so I could admire the beautiful sway of her sports pants. She pointed to the sink; dishes floated in a stagnant, green water. Surely just a block somewhere, I explained to her. She looked at me indifferently and left the room as I opened the box; I took out pliers, a screwdriver and a wrench. I disconnected the parts, introduced a wire into the garbage disposal and cleared the blockage, completely focused on my task. When she came back, she leaned against the refrigerator with a cup of coffee in her hands. Then we began to chat. She offered me a glass of water. I noticed that she wasn't wearing a bra, although I did my best not to be caught noticing; the job is the job and one has to respect it, especially when you've just started. I was three weeks in, not including the three days of training as a jack-of-all-trades; you know, cutting the grass, repairing washing machines, changing locks, windows, tightening screws and removing nails. Little fixes. From time to time I even helped the elderly neighbors with their shopping.

I asked her where I could put the waste that had been collected in the wire. She grabbed a plastic bag and handed it to me with a look of playful disgust. She was close enough that I caught the fragrance of her skin, light and warm. I took in as much as I could, looked closely at her hands, noticed a scar on her left arm. The T-shirt that covered her braless figure had the face of one of the Simpsons printed on it. I noticed her nipples were hard, but I went back to my work, ready to put the screws back in place, although out of the corner of my eye I searched her silhouette. The girl was hot, only an ascetic would have refused to look at her. The truth is that I had already watched a similar scene play out in at least two porn movies. The muscular plumber enters the house of the starlet, and within ten minutes she is already sucking greedily at his member. Nothing like that had ever happened to me, nor did I expect it to, although they say life imitates art at times, and a little fantasy helps the day go around. I'm no weakling, but I'm not a strong man with huge muscles like the men in the videos either. And Martina did not take it out of my fly to put me in her mouth, much less so. It did all happened in less than ten minutes, but only after I finished unclogging the sink, cleaning the drain elbow and replacing the gaskets.

While I worked, we talked about family, our origins and how we felt in that place in the middle of nowhere. We were both city dwellers. She told me that she was lonely, depressed and worried about a husband who could be shot dead at any moment. "I don't know if all this sacrifice is worth it. It bothers me to think that I could be widowed and helpless from one day to the next, with no options ..." I told her not to take it on that way, that nothing would happen to her husband anyway, that nowadays soldiers are very well protected with bulletproof vests, night vision goggles, satellite phones and armored trucks. She looked me in the eyes so long I thought I'd made her angry. Then she began to cry. I offered her my handkerchief and she started sobbing like a lost child. I pulled her toward me and hugged her without any bad intentions; I'm no monster, a woman in tears is something that still breaks my heart. She kissed me on the neck, then on the mouth and later, with dry eyes, she dragged me to her bedroom where we began our screaming.

2

I went into the shed, put the toolbox back in its place and went to the micro-bathroom; to bathe you have to embed the sink in the wall. I couldn't help but smile at myself in the mirror, it had been a very good morning and quite a surprise. Although, on the road you learn surprises can be double-edged swords. I just hoped there would be no bad repercussions, especially about losing the job and starting over the search for another one, in another state of this great country. Less than a month ago I had arrived in my Greyhound from Las Vegas, via Nashville, covered in a cloud of dust. I use the possessive, because I have changed cities several times in those old trucks, as I suppose a lot of people do in search of something, new or not, and someone should claim them for all they carry. I was after the job—I ended up being what my maternal great-grandfather always was after all; a migrant worker, a man in transit; perhaps until my last days, just like him. Anyway.

City: Albany, Georgia. Quiet place, friendly people.

Job: a complex where they cooked, or prepared if you prefer, the food served on passenger planes. No questions. That is, your immigration status didn't matter; you were hired on the spot, verbally.

Salary: four dollars an hour, a good deal compared to other places where they exploit us like beasts for less than two dollars a day.

I knew all this from my friend Pedro, who had already flown to another city. It was because of a fight, what else? According to Peter, a soldier had attacked him in a bar. It happens often, adrenaline, testosterone, punches, alcohol. Pedro is one of those who "doesn't let you," and he also knows how to defend himself. If he ran away, it was because the soldier must have lost.

Otherwise, Albany was passable and identical to countless small cities in the United States. What I didn't know was that, in addition to the usual, the city was home to a huge military complex with two schools, a sports complex, a training camp, a residential area and a couple of supermarkets. Something like a city within a city. In fact, the military was the second largest source of income for the town, after the factories that processed airplane food. Military personnel went to the movies, to restaurants for dinner, to the mall and above all, to the bars that were packed every night. I had never been so surrounded by soldiers in my life. I thought about leaving a few hours after I'd arrived. Soldiers produce mixed reactions in me, not exactly fear, more anxiousness, caution, distrust—that with a certain aura of violence. I don't know, it's something I have; I can't stand Sardinians, or the police, or the guards. Maybe because in all of Latin America they represent intimidation, dictatorships, covert crime, criminal association, institutional abuse, etc., etc. All the same, I went where my friend, the scrapper, recommended.

It was a few blocks from the bus station. The house belonged to an old lady with a lot of cats. She remembered Pete, although I think she confused him with an old boyfriend of hers or something. I just let her talk. She said that Peter was a simple man, modest, clean and not often given to drink; qualities that did not correspond to any Pedro *I* knew. She agreed to rent to me for a week first, with the possibility of extending the lodging indefinitely. I explained my situation; I came to do a job in the kitchens of "Cooking on Air," although it wasn't entirely a lock since I did not have a contract. She got the impression that Pete was a chef specializing in burritos and quesadillas. He had a spot in the basement with access to the backyard. It turned out to be a damp room with a small window, a single bed, a small closet, an old plastic-covered chair and a yellowed bathtub that hadn't seen bleach for several years. We went back up the stairs.

In the living room, the cats had decided to make their presence known. They stood waiting for us on the armchairs, the table, the dresser ... seemed like just about everywhere. Black, brown, white, grey and spotted cats. They looked at me with no small amount of distrust, as is their nature. Only one came and rubbed itself on my pant leg, purring about a thousand RPMs. We closed the transaction, a week and deposit in advance. She made me sign a paper and took a photo of me with a very thin digital camera; that was a new one, I must admit. She explained that it was something recommended by her niece. She gave me a key and took me through the manual. I couldn't bring in girls or friends for drinks, I couldn't turn up the volume of the radio too high and I couldn't use the kitchen after midnight. Smoking was completely out of the question. "And another thing," the upper floor, which was where she slept, was forbidden to guests—that's what she called her renters. I could enter through the front door or the back as necessary. Once inside I just had make sure to lock up properly. We stood up and shook hands. She said goodbye to me and slowly made her way up the stairs, the cats forming a trail behind her. A couple of them looked at me curiously before disappearing in the blink of an eye.

I went downstairs, closed the door, emptied my suitcase and laid down on the bed for about forty minutes. I decided to go out for a walk to familiarize myself with my new town and get something to eat. I also needed toothpaste, toilet paper, soap and a razor. I closed the garden door behind me. I walked around to the front of the house and stopped to look at the facade, memorizing the number because the house was identical to almost all the others on the block. Two floors, gabled, red brick, small windows. My eyes felt irritated; I sneezed a couple of times.

For a few years now it seemed I was becoming allergic to more things. I have nothing against cats, but something like twelve in one place is too much in my opinion. At home we had cats, Tabata the mother and her daughter, Garnacha. The latter was a super cool cat, grey with white paws and chest. Let me tell you the story of her name; she had earned it because of her father, like most everyone else I suppose. Imagine, a sweet kitten named Tabata, protected by her grandmother, wooed by the neighborhood's dirtiest tomcat, who, according to legend, had impregnated her in a state of animal rage. He was a black cat, evil, that Garnacha—an asado with nothing but bite; zero pedigree, like most humans on the planet I suppose. The whole pedigree thing, the pure breed, what a laugh. When will we humans get over our fascination with blood?

I walked several blocks, found the post office, three hardware stores, several grocery stores, a shoe store, the pharmacy, six restaurants, two gun shops and at least ten bars. A familiar sight in the several years I have been wandering this country. Mostly white people, a few black, few Asians and some Latinos. Large pickup trucks, American-made cars, narrow sidewalks and a few buses, which went around the center of the city and to other important places. The fact that there was public transportation at all was already a win, especially for those without a car, as in my case. I located a bus stop. I had to budget the cost and investigate the stop times. Downtown, I stopped at a small restaurant that didn't look too expensive. I ate well and drank two beers. Moving around a lot, you realize you only get one evening to be a perfect stranger. I paid and made my way back. The drugstore had all the products I needed, plus two bottles of water. I entered through the front door with the key that Mrs. Robbins had given me and went downstairs to my room like a ghost. A white cat jumped up on me and meowed, welcoming me.

I turned on the light, closed the door and slowly undressed, thinking all the while about how boring it was going to be, packing food or cooking it. But hey, if you have a job these days you can consider yourself lucky. Work is money, and money is just about everything: shelter, food and the rest; no wonder we write GOD on it. I covered myself with the blankets and got ready to sleep, although I only dreamed halfway.

Being in the port I see a black block floating in the sea, getting closer to land, a cube of pure granite that grows, swells, as the tide begins to rise, and the waves crash hard against the rocks. The presence of the gigantic block, the size of a ship, makes me feel uneasy. I wonder then: what does it contain? Who travels inside? How does that amorphous thing float?

3

I got up early, bathed, shaved and dressed in my best clothes, thinking about the possible interview that awaited me. I went up to the kitchen, greeted by the cats and the undeniable look that meant I was invading their physical space. But they kept doing their thing as if they understood that I would be a familiar face for a while. Mrs. Robbins had made coffee, so I poured myself a cup. I opened the refrigerator, nothing much looked back at me. Some pots with food from several days prior. Three potatoes, two carrots, an onion. Jars of jam, peanut butter, mayonnaise and ketchup. There was a bunch of canned food in the cupboard, whose do you think? A couple of them meowed behind me, as if on cue. The thought crossed my mind that my landlady might also eat that every afternoon, surrounded by her children, as she had called the felines during the tour. I couldn't find any sugar, so I drank the coffee black—strong, yes, thank goodness. I had about an hour and a half before my interview, but since I didn't know the bus schedule, it was better to hurry. I left the house and walked to the stop, the only one waiting was a black girl with a double-wheeler. We stood next to each other there for about thirty minutes, although we didn't try to make conversation. It was obvious that neither one of us was up for that. There was a chill in the air, and I hoped it wouldn't get any worse since I didn't have a coat. I looked at my shoes, they were old, although they still had some polish left. They'd been with me since about a month before I left Oklahoma City via the bus terminal. I was a little worried about what they would ask me, so I spent the rest of the wait getting the possible answers more or less memorized. Fuck I hate job interviews.

How did you get started in the kitchen?

First as a dishwasher, then as a grill cook and then as a line cook.

What is the highest position you have held in a restaurant?

Chef's assistant.

Do you know the hygiene rules that must be observed in places that prepare food?

Of course, wash your hands before entering the kitchen, wear a hat and a mask because of germs. Do not mix the meat utensils with the vegetable ones and wash them before and after use.

What do you do when raw pork has been out in the open for more than forty-fifteen minutes?

As a precaution, it should be put in the microwave to kill any possible toxins, and even washed, before putting it in the oil.

I repeated the spiel during the trip. I told myself to be sure and to answer with confidence on the test that they would surely give me.

What foods do you know how to prepare?

Some Italian food, some Mexican food and some Chinese food, which are the most common. Rice, grains, pasta.

I reviewed from memory the ingredients for rice with corn and haricots verts, the fancy green bean. I knew the recipe for chicken in sweet wine. I knew the one for spaghetti in red sauce. Becoming a professional chef was my big dream.

The bus passed through the city center, picked up a lot of people in front of the Greyhound station. I got my first glimpse of the public library—where I would become a member—and continued the stop-and-start journey, finally reaching the point where more people started getting off than on. And slowly we left the city.

The food factory was on the outskirts of Albany; it occupied a sprawling complex of twelve large warehouses, two huge parking lots and a six-story office building. The driver informed us over the speaker that he was approaching the last stop. The bus made a U-turn. The black girl, me and five others got out through the back door, which closed behind us with a snort. A group of people got ready to get on the truck, forming a perfect line. Probably the night shift. I just hoped I wouldn't be one of them. I prefer to work when the sun is out, plus I'm known to be very unreliable at night. I would have been an unlikely hire for a night watchman or a truck driver, although I do like to drive.

The guard separated the workers from the prospective employees at the entrance. The first to go in to interview was the black girl. I finished filling out the document in the fifteen minutes it took. She came out smiling. Maybe she had worked the system, appealed to the anti-discrimination law, which had been extended to the obese, to get the job. Whatever it takes for a little money, for a damn gig in this increasingly mechanized world. A rather serious secretary showed me into the office where the interrogation would take place. I sat down in an empty chair, looking around while I waited. A Latino appeared through another door, sat down behind the desk and looked through some documents. He asked me my name, where I lived, how I knew about the job, etc., all in English. I showed him my resumé, he read it as quickly as he could, handed it back to me and coldly told me that there were no positions for sous-chefs. Good ol' Peter had told me too late, or I had landed at the wrong time, one of the two. *A whole useless, fruitless trip, a move in vain*, I scolded myself… But hey, no one can see the future. The guy seemed to read my thoughts, or my annoyance at least, because he offered me a position in the butcher shop of the same company. I was almost willing to accept the offer, but dealing with dead animals is a dirty damn business. When I did, I got skin infection, rough sleep and a low feeling. So I declined, thanked him and stood up. The man looked me over from head to toe, then said he had a friend, "A contractor. He's looking at people for a position at another site. It's called The Albany MC Logistics Base." I studied the new offer; he needed a handyman, paid expenses and had a room with the rent paid for two weeks in advance.

"Are you interested, kid?" The guy asked, scrutinizing me the whole time.

If there is one thing that gives you longevity, it is the ability to quickly read and understand. You could see that he was one of those who makes a business of exploiting other people. Poor people. He was the bastard "middleman" that is never in short supply on this planet; you know, the one who counts his bills in the dark and makes good leisure of it. He told me in a low voice, "Six dollars and fifty, and that's just to start."

I was left to decide.

"Sounds good, *really*. The problem is that soldiers make me nervous." I said sincerely.

"You wouldn't be very close to them, and besides, you'd also wear a uniform and a cap. Just concentrate on your work, the rest will go unnoticed. Don't open your mouth too much—be discreet—and they won't even see you."

He knew how to sell. In a way it was like sitting at a poker table.

"What do you say?"

I needed the job. I had come from so far to earn money, and putting up with soldiers was the sure way not to go empty-handed, back on another Greyhound with my tail between my legs.

"Okay, I accept the job."

He smiled.

"Okay, I'll charge 30% of your first paycheck to get you the job. Is this agreeable?"

I looked at him seriously, I knew his trick. He was going to screw me, even though he was selling it as if he was helping someone out. I thought about how it is precisely because of that that we Spanish-speaking people do not progress in this country, because we screw over each other. I accepted. In reality there was no other choice. The Venezuelan or whatever he was, he was happy. He picked up the phone, got up from his seat and spoke to someone, although I didn't bother paying attention.

One good thing about working in a kitchen is that you always have a full stomach ... Never mind, I had already gotten my hopes up about continuing with what I thought could be a future plan: being a chef, head of a kitchen, educating my palate. The guy walked around me. "Excellent, boy. You will be given training," he said, in Spanish. "You will be in charge of maintaining the residential area at the base with another friend. The work consists of making small repairs, cleaning, cutting grass, changing switches, locks and other things—you know—servicing the homes of the military and the higher-ranking bosses who live there temporarily. Nothing too complicated."

I thought about it. I would be a gardener, a plumber and a carpenter, among other things, I was sure. It was another line of work that I had done for myself, and it was also a favorite. I had already done similar in Los Angeles and San Diego.

"Hey, I need the work," I said, also in the language of Sancho Panza.

We shook hands. I was to introduce myself the following day at the base. The rest he would arrange over the phone. "Someone will be waiting for you." I asked him how to get there. The base was also outside of the city, in the extreme opposite direction. The boss there was called Joel, and he was a Chicano. He would give me a credential with a magnetic strip and a locker key. I nodded. *No problem.* He wished me a good weekend.

I went out into the street more relaxed. I don't know, being employed always comforts me; I have the security of being able to continue putting food in my mouth and having a bed to sleep in, for now in the cat house. I sat with other men to wait for the bus, it took almost an hour to arrive. I looked at the clock. I didn't want to go back to the old lady's house, it was still early. I decided I would take a walk around the town. I would stop by the public library, stop off at a bar for a beer. We all got on in a perfect line. On the way back I spent my time looking out the window. Field, trees, one-story houses, ranches. There was a tractor working, some cows grazing, pick-ups of all sizes. You could see, in general, it wasn't a town with a lot of money; perhaps hit by the global economic crisis; by the recession that brings inflation; the flight of investments; the dying state of capitalism. Something kept it middling.

Downtown, I got off the bus and walked aimlessly for about twenty minutes. I found the public library, which was closed. The city kept to its ordinary appeal, no heavy culture or art to speak of, except for a fountain dedicated to Ray Charles. They had it rigged so the water flowed like music from the piano; very nice. There was a bench to pass the time. Carried away by my eros and excited by all the women who passed by, I thought to myself: *what tits, what ass, what legs—look at that other woman's waist, mmm.*

It had been something like three months since I had slept with anyone. In Nashville I had been close to hiring a prostitute, but at the last minute I backed out. I missed Patricia. Somewhere along the way she'd made it to the room inside where I kept my obsessions. I couldn't get her out of my mind ... despite all the harm she had done to me, despite the money she had stolen from me, despite the face she gave me when she was acting stupid. Despite even the distance. Here I was, half a continent in between, and I still remembered her. I became melancholic. I asked myself again what the mistake had been. No, the solution was to get a girlfriend ...*fuck Patricia.* Quiet environment, nice houses, plenty of women. The bad thing, though, was that there were men in olive green damn near everywhere. It was a town of uniformed men.

I entered a watering hole that seemed cheap to me. The bell above the door sounded. A couple of men turned to look in the direction of the noise. I slipped over to the bar, stopping to clock my surroundings. *Eyes in the back of your head*, as they say. I asked for a dark beer. Most of them were young men with the same haircut, although there were some older men and women here and there, also military. I felt as vulnerable as a nail in a room full of hammers. I sipped my beer slowly, not wanting to appear like I didn't like company. And I was doing just that, when a soldier approached to refill his jar—it was that kind of place.

"Ordinance," he told the barkeep. The amber liquid purred out easily. While he waited, he turned and greeted me with a nod. I responded in kind. They served him his beer and he started up a conversation, in Spanish no less. Turns out he was from Phoenix, but his parents were of Guatemalan origin. He made it clear he wasn't out to be a big hero; he was actually going to war because he needed the opportunity to pay for an education, to gain citizenship. He liked guns, of course, adventure, and if he stayed alive, he could build a future for himself. "But only if I stay alive," he made clear. We talked about Latin America in a general way. "The truth is, I don't know much," he confessed, although he didn't rule out a visit to Colombia and Argentina, "where they say the women are beautiful—*big* tits." He secretly admired Che, especially for his bravery and honor, although he had never told this to any of his soldier friends. We ended up drinking three beers together, the last one accompanied by a chubby girl who would be shipping out to Afghanistan in a few days. She was a freckled, simple-minded girl—and a compulsive drinker—who got into a dispute with my friend about whether an airplane was capable of destroying a Bradley tank. I said goodbye to them, paid and quietly slipped away to the exit. The minute I hit the sidewalk I took a deep breath, smoothed my hair and continued my Albany walk-through toward the cat house. The cinema was showing two new films. I looked at some shop windows, passed other bars, other shops. Once I was back at my accommodation, I really thought about whether I could last more than six months working at the base. Well, the contract was signed. *So be it, things are what they are*.

4

I knocked on the door. It was the second knock of the afternoon. The house was located in the area designated exclusively for high-ranking military men. These houses were larger of course and were characterized by having "a Californian style;" red bricks, gabled roofs; a larger garden, porch and garage. Apparently, the bathroom faucets were leaking and needed to be changed out.

I rang the doorbell twice, discreetly. I heard footsteps, put on my stupid smile, the same one we all had been advised to wear consistently, the friendly face of the service provider. A black woman about six feet tall and almost as wide opened the door. She was really big, although she smelled good. She wore expensive clothes, gold jewelry and a smile as white as a toothpaste commercial. She let me in, but not before pointing to the mat where I had to wipe my boots. It was an elegant house. In the dining room there was a table with twelve chairs and display cabinets with porcelain dishes, decorated plates and cut-glass goblets. There were leather armchairs in the living room, and its walls were adorned with imitations of great artists such as Leonardo, Monet, Van Gogh. There was also a collection of old pistols, rifles, knives and medals in leather cases, probably her husband's decorations. They were "just passing through," as I understood. I dragged my boots across the mat three times and turned to look at the lady; she must have been about forty years old, perhaps a little older, although she was wearing makeup like a younger woman. I followed her. Out of habit, I looked at her rear; it was huge, wide, barely contained in the blue tights she wore. Rolls of flesh, impossible to hide, poked out like tufts of hair in a beanie eaten at by moths. All this despite the girdle under her clothes. She smiled at me. It was clear that she intended to be sexy, but she was not successful. We entered the bathroom, quite large by the way, but with just enough space to contain the big woman. Everything seemed oversized—the sink, the floor, but above all the mirror. I sat my toolbox on the floor and was about to open it when I felt first a blow to my head and then a strong slap, which left me breathless. I closed my eyes and fell into a deep hole.

I am in the cemetery. I have been here before and I look at everything around me in detail, from the simple cross stuck in the ground to the elegant graves. The pantheon is full of candles, which crackle in the same rhythm. I look for my grandmother. I see her sitting on a very white tombstone. She calls me. I slowly sit next to her. First, she scolds me for not watering the plants in the hallway at home, for arriving late. I have no excuse, I simply cannot speak, I am mute. She talks to me about the candles and why she must change them constantly, since burials have increased. She tells me about a young woman who brings flowers every morning; she talks to me about the spirits, about the Holy Death, about this, about that, while we walk among the graves. My grandmother speaks slowly, with emphasis. She begins to tell me about her brother Ignacio, who was a ghost in the revolution. But he was also a spy, and he doesn't remember if he came first as one or the other. Ignacio, who went crazy crossing the walls, who collected old books, spoke legends, sayings and tongue twisters. Grandma stops at a humble grave and lets out a phrase: "What matters is preserved." Suddenly my old lady falls silent. She dives into her past, splashing around like a young girl at a family reunion. Her face changes, it's clear. What I see in her eyes are fragments of time. I put my arm behind her and hug her, resting my head on her shoulder. "Wake up, son," she says. I hear from afar. Wake up ...

I opened my eyes. I was handcuffed to a large bed, hand and foot, and completely naked. My head hurt; my eyes kept rolling. I found my bearings with difficulty; a dim light illuminated the space. Music was playing at a low volume; it seemed to come from somewhere else. It was only then that I realized that a muzzle was covering my mouth and a pacifier-like object with a pleasant texture was holding my teeth. *What the fucking hell* ... I think, as I can't scream for help; I'm scared shitless. I'm also ashamed of my exposed nakedness, of the helplessness of confinement. I suddenly remember the last minutes before the attack. I'm definitely in that fat woman's bed. It's a big room with red curtains, a huge flat screen TV and another gigantic mirror. A collection of penises of different sizes gleam on the dresser, smeared with grease. I think the worst. Imagine the scene: there's one at least the size of my arm. I pull on the chains and try to scream, "Fucking fat woman!!"

She came in, wearing a mask and a tight two-piece bikini that barely covered a pair of enormous breasts.

"Hi, daddy, look who came ... Your tamer."

The truth is that I don't like black women. I'm not racist or anything—the ones who drive me crazy are Latinas. And blondes. But brunettes don't arouse any pleasure in me, and even less a desperate woman of those proportions. I even like Chinese girls a little. I don't know, I guess every man has his own preferences and nothing can be done to set him against that. She came with a whip, with black boots that reached past her knees. She walked around the bed, eyes on me all the while; she swayed this way and that, trying for sensual, although that act seemed ridiculous in the position I was in. I wanted—needed—to get out of there as soon as possible. I came to my senses. *There is no point in screaming*. I was at her mercy.

She stood up on the bed and showed me her big ass, then her bust, from a few inches away. Nothing. I mean, my penis had no reaction, as if I were watching paint dry. No part of this excited me. She tried again, this time opening her panties a little, and rested herself on my face. I thought she would pee on me or something, expecting the worst. I felt truly helpless, small. Her private parts were hairy, very hairy, and coarse. Maybe she thought that my penis would spring up like an inflatable yard decoration, but there was still nothing. I remained as flaccid as if I were doing math, cutting my hair…This offended her, no doubt, as she jumped out of bed, disappeared for a moment into the next room and returned with a bottle of pills. Without smiling, she wrenched off my muzzle. I tried to bark an order, even throw a punch at her, but it was useless. My gesture only served to allow her to throw a handful of pills into my mouth, which she forced me to swallow. She squeezed my nose and placed her hand over my mouth; for lack of air, I choked and swallowed. The bitterness of chewed pills followed, and the knowledge that my throat was being torn. I knew it by the taste of blood.

5

I showed up at the base to meet Joel, my supervisor. He was a short and arrogant guy who took pleasure in treating everyone badly. He read me in as we walked. "I dislike mistakes, so save them." Every Friday we had to give him some signed sheets with the number of calls attended to during the week. Repairs could only be done at his express order. To be paid, the customer had to sign a sheet once the service was completed. "It's the way we know you work." Saturday was taken as overtime; a dollar and a half more was paid by the hour. Cleanliness, a good attitude and efficiency were valued above all. We entered a workshop. It had everything; from shovels to make holes in the ground to hammers and nails, to mini tractors that were used to keep the grass cut. He asked me if I knew how to drive, and I said of course, no problem. And really, I have been driving since I was very young—I even had a red Camaro suited for an action movie when I lived in Las Vegas. He took me to a map on the wall. The Base included: two supermarkets, an elementary and secondary school, offices, a library, a gym, tennis courts, a bowling alley, swimming pools and fields for outdoor activities. And for fishing, it even had an artificial lake. There were three smaller workshops for customer service, but he called them "units." I would be assigned to the residential area, basically to answer repair calls, but also things like cutting the grass, trimming tree branches, changing out light bulbs, etc.

There were areas restricted to military personnel, and woe be to us if we dared step into those areas. He handed me a pair of pants, a blue shirt and boots. I would have to go myself to request a bar code and get my photo taken with a lieutenant in charge of that, in order to obtain an entrance pass.

"Number thirty-two is your locker. Welcome to the Security Services Association. The changing rooms are on this side; change, I'll wait to take you to your unit."

"Thanks," I said, and headed toward the changing rooms. I liked thirty-two—I have a thing for numbers, although I'm not good at math. I put on the company uniform and looked at myself in the mirror; it fits us poor people, no matter what. "Sergio in his new costume," I said mockingly to myself in the mirror. I put the cap on my head, to complete the picture. I adjusted my features. "You go changing from clown to acrobat all your life ... what the hell, man." It was just another job. Food, shelter, beers. I rolled up my personal clothes and put them in my backpack. I found Joel scolding a woman, who was in the middle of cleaning the floor very carefully. I waited until he finished reading her the riot act. I tried to stay out of his line of vision, hiding in the shadows, until he saw me: "Okay, new guy, follow me."

We crossed a soccer field, passed a gray building, a parking lot, more offices and finally arrived at the residential part of the base. It was a group of two or three hundred houses, a normal neighborhood, except that this one was installed in a military complex. Joel told me that this would be my assigned work area, supposedly because my English was less bad than others. On a small hill, apparently artificial, there was a prefabricated rectangular cabin. We headed there. The maintenance unit was located about three hundred yards from the main entrance of the complex, where there was a surveillance module with two MPs inside. On the way, he repeated to me that there were areas on the base that were exclusive to the military. The contractors, that is, us, had to follow the same rules as visitors and friends of the residents. We were all subject to inspection by the Military Police upon entering and leaving the base, and at any time we were ordered.

He knocked before pushing a half-open door. A man dressed like me came toward us, coiling an electric cable. His name was Antonio. I was told we would each cover a shift, sharing a desk, a bathroom and maintenance equipment. We would help each other if necessary. He would be in charge of the first few days of training, since he had been on the job for two years; we shook hands. The supervisor scolded Tony, that's what he called him, for not cleaning the pruning shears and not keeping the tools in order on the wall board. The other apologized and ran to tidy things up. Before leaving, the boss told me to report immediately for the identification process, and to come see him at the end of the day; "Something to do with your documents." I nodded.

Once we were alone, Tony warned me not to expect classes, training and all that stuff. He told me about how to do things on the base, because sooner or later I would be on my own. I told him not to worry, I had once worked in California as a plumber, "…and I also know a lot about electricity. Also, I'm a good driver." The guy congratulated me and shook my hand. He pointed to a cart, like the ones they use on golf courses, although this one was painted blue and had a metal box attached to the back.

"It's the way we get around the base and move our gardening and plumbing stuff… and since you can drive, that's your cart. It has three speeds and reverse. Doesn't carry much, but it's better than walking like a donkey."

I gave the blue cart a once-over and got in. Two-seater, a small 500cc engine, looked like fun. "Fun?" he repeated, "well, the next call is for you, brother."

Antonio went to a worn-out chair and turned on a mini television with a remote. The color on the picture was faded. There was a soap opera already in progress. "Las ruinas del amor" (The Ruins of Love), a typical cheesy bolero, although this one had new cars and actresses dressed in the latest fashion. From the beginning I understood that he liked *novelas*. Sometimes he watched them all afternoon when there weren't any calls. I sat down in the other dirty chair next to him. A couple of minutes of commercials went by. He seemed a little antsy, but when the story restarted it kept Toño enthralled. The plot was the same as always; the thief girl finds love with her boss, who seduces her, gets her into trouble and cheats on her. The phone rang, Toño threw it to me and I barely managed to catch it. "It's for you. Don't worry, if you can't change the lock, you call me, or you come find me. Oh, another thing, don't leave the key in the cart, and don't lose it. It's the only copy. And remember, between you and me it's one thing; with boss Joel it's another."

6

I yawned. One of the neighbors had given me a book: *Strategies For a Landing*. It was one of those books used in military schools like West Point or the School of the Americas. That morning I had attended the call of an old captain named Thomas. One of the doors had been locked from the inside and the room couldn't be opened. I replaced the lock and gave him two keys. At first this captain seemed arrogant to me, but little by little he softened until he showed himself to be likable and kind. It was a rather technical book about what the landing of troops was like during an invasion. I didn't understand why he had given me such a book. Perhaps because we had talked about the local library and the quiet pleasure of such a place. I got bored and stowed it in my backpack. I yawned again. I was waiting for the bus to take me back to the city. A shiny car, really nice, although not new, screeched to a stop. The glass lowered. Maybe someone after directions or something, but no.

"Hey you, come here," she said. At first, I thought she was talking to someone else. It took me a while to react. I turned one way, I turned the other; no one, it was just me sitting there.

"Hey *you*, come here," I finally recognized her. It was Martina. She began to move her index finger, hurrying me along. I walked as if pulled by an invisible thread. The vehicle turned out to be a classic metallic blue Mustang, really beautiful up close. It had wide tires, special rims.

"Hey, how are you?" I said, smiling. It was a pleasant surprise. The thought crossed my mind that she might hate me, that maybe she had a gun and would shoot me right there on the sidewalk.

"Get in," she ordered.

I looked at her for a moment, walked around the car and got in next to her. "Wow, beautiful vehicle ...." *You're beautiful*, I thought. In other circumstances I would have planted a kiss on her mouth, but we were at the base gate. Plus, we hadn't spoken a word to each other after "our thing." I had to tread carefully.

"Seat belt, sir," she beamed, then the car took off.

I fastened my seat belt fast as I could and put my bag at my feet.

The Mustang roared onto the road. She accelerated hard, passing a trailer and several cars. About ten minutes of tense silence passed; she turned on the radio but immediately turned it off again. She finally turned to me and said: "Excuse me ... for the last time."

I smelt trouble. I responded cautiously.

"Me too ..."

She gave me a serious look.

I had to check the temperature of the water. I said: "I never forced you to do anything, right? Besides, no one is gonna ask, and I'm not gonna tell. I need to keep my job. I'm the man with the least money in the world right now." I said the latter in case she was thinking of suing me.

Martina took off her sunglasses, smiled and said, "Not because of what happened, but because I made you feel bad. I didn't speak up at the end. I acted like a young girl."

I took a deep breath.

Martina continued, "That, what happened ... was good. At first, I felt bad, but I realized that there are basic needs of the body and one of them, as much as sex, is the affection that comes with contact ... and you were very sweet."

I kept quiet. What was I going to say? *Affection?* I had gone to unclog the kitchen drain, according to the order signed by her. Everything else had been pure luck.

"It was a surprise for me too. Maybe I should be the grateful one; you are a very beautiful woman."

"Thank you ..." she put her hand on my knee, "but give yourself some credit."

I smiled. I was a guy regaining some luck at least, yes, but that's as much credit as I allowed myself. This time I was the one who turned on the radio.

"Hey, by the way, where are we going?"

"Oh, sorry, I didn't ask you, I'm going to Walmart. Is that okay?"

I lowered the back of the seat, already feeling comfortable. "Yeah sure, let's go." This time I leaned over and kissed her, first on her cheek and then a quick one on her mouth. She turned to look at me again. If there wasn't a problem, there wasn't a problem.

"Careful, stud, I'm driving," she said, putting her sunglasses back on.

I breathed a sigh of relief, my spirits aloft, somewhere up in the clouds overhead. "By the way, who's car is this?"

"It's Lee's, my husband. The idiot who's been away nine months and has no plans to return ... anyway." She pushed the pedal down. She sounded resentful, spiteful. Her look wasn't much better.

We found a spot in one of six parking lots. We took the elevators down a floor, grabbed a cart and dedicated ourselves to the favorite of twentieth-century American pastimes: *Buy! Accumulate! Turn money into things!* The place was packed. You'd think they were giving the products away. It was all a type of socialization that a large number of consumers suffer from, according to what I read. The mega store had a buildable shelf for Martina. She put simple things in her cart as well; soap, toilet paper, food, beer and wine.

"Which beer do you prefer? It's Sergio, right?"

She knew my name.

"Yes, Sergio, like my great-grandfather. He was an Italian who for some reason ended up in Mexico; even he never knew the real reason. Many say it was because of his grandmother, others say it was because he was doing well in the grocery business and was able to get a store in the center of Hermosillo. Some others say it was because he had decided to change the sea for the desert.

"Err-mah-see-yo." She held her lips at the end as if she were about to whistle.

I took out my phone. "Here it is." I showed her a map of Mexico. "*Hermosillo*. In Spanish the 'h' has no sound."

"Cool."

Someone had left message. It was good ol' Pedro, saying hello and checking in.

"What beers do you like?"

"Hmm, let me see, let me see. These. I like dark beer ... and white women." I whispered the last part into her ear, close, so she could feel my body temperature. Martina raised her shoulder and smiled flirtatiously. The dark glasses made her look like a Hollywood starlet, a current kind, dressed in faded jeans, sneakers and a white blouse. I noticed that she kept a certain distance between us, but she didn't seem bothered by my wooing.

We finished shopping and took our place in one of the long lines formed at the checkout. It was a torment. We must have changed positions about a hundred times. Martina finished flipping through a magazine and I got tired of seeing the women around me. I focused on the clumsy cashiers, slow customers and cheap merchandise of suspicious foreign origin. In the future we will be remembered as The Era of Cheapness, just as today we understand the Dark Ages or the Renaissance. The time of junk in clever packaging.

We loaded the trunk, except for the beers. Martina suggested taking them in the back seat. Before starting, she made me open two cans so we could share a toast.

"Just roll up your window, I'll turn on the air conditioning. That's one of the benefits of having tinted windows; we're going to do what I did with my high school friends back in the day."

"What was that?"

"Burning gas around town while we drank beer with the radio at full volume."

"What town is that?"

"It's near Michigan." The car stopped at a red light.

"Do you miss them? Your friends and family, I mean."

"Sure, and that's part of my problem ..." She took a long sip of her beer, set off the click of the turn signal and got ready to get on the highway. "I know a place we can go, it's a small lake. We went there sometimes when we first got here, you'll like it."

"Okay, wherever you want. I'm *all* yours." I put a horny emphasis on it.

She turned to look at me and ran her tongue over her teeth.

"Okay. Do you like classic rock? Could you stand Guns n' Roses?"

"Oh, I like rock a lot. I know them. Put it on."

The slit swallowed the disc and soon "Welcome to the Jungle" started playing. She turned up the volume and sank her shoe on the accelerator.

The lake turned out to be a place as peaceful as it was beautiful. You could even rent boats. I took my position behind the oars.

"Can you row?"

"Sure, I was a gondoliere."

"Really? In Venice?"

"No, in Las Vegas."

"Las Vegas?"

"Sure. They have that one casino there, like a tour of the world: Venice, the Eiffel Tower and so on. They even have an Egyptian pyramid. Of course, I would like to go to the real Venice. Never been there. One day ..."

"Don't worry, I haven't even been to Vegas ... but I did live in South Korea for a while. It was when I was real little." She said it with the face you make when you remember a happy time. "The truth is that I didn't leave the base all that much."

The splash and glug of the oars broke the tranquility of the place. I felt the muscles in my arms start to heat; I had forgotten all the effort that moving a raft takes. She took two beers out of her bag and opened them like an expert, then looked me in the eyes and grinned. We toasted again. She pointed out some bushes along the bank. I have to say, I was truly enthralled by the place. I landed the boat in a shadow and raised the oars. Martina laid down at the bottom of the boat. She closed her eyes I mean I guessed she did; they were still hidden under her dark glasses. Or maybe she just stared at the sky, absorbed. The boat rocked gently, lulling us. We stayed in silence for a while, listening to the sound of the birds, all the nature around. I looked into the distance without thinking about anything. Martina took off her shoes. She used one of her feet to caress my knee. I took off her sock, her bare foot soft as a river fish in my hands. It had a beautiful shape, with long, delicate toes.

"At the base of the foot we have a lot of connections with the rest of the body, did you know that?"

"What do you mean?"

"See, our nervous system is like a tree that grows inside us, and it has roots and branches just like that. Our feet are where our nerve endings come together, and they can be relaxed if they are massaged properly. Do you feel it?" I squeezed the sole of her foot.

"Oh, that's so nice."

"There I am massaging your liver. And here? Your back."

She raised her legs over my legs. She peeled off her other sock with her toes. Now I began to really give her a massage, which I heard somewhere is like an appetizer for an orgasm.

"Oh, that's so nice. And where did you learn this?"

"In Las Vegas. My girlfriend was a massage therapist ... among other talents."

"She sure taught you something. What else have your girlfriends taught you?" She lifted her glasses and looked at me coyly.

My eyes found her breasts. Her nipples looked hard, practically blooming. Even a blind man could see that she had not been touched in a long time. I massaged her back, her shoulders, her legs, her thighs… and finally that warm place between her legs. By the time I returned to her toes, she was asleep. I left her in peace, and I took pleasure in the view; her, of course, and all of those trees, the mist floating over the water, the sky watching it all in silence. I could see a fisherman in the distance, and beyond him, another. The mountains lay covered in green in the background. A tranquility invaded me that I had not enjoyed in a long time. I had definitely had my fill of the desert. I looked at the water, noticed life continued below too; a small turtle swam from stone to stone and stayed there long enough to miss him a little, when he finally disappeared from sight. I closed my eyes, leaving my peace at the mercy of life. I laid down next to her and slept.

I felt her fingers on my face. My eyes opened.

Martina had taken off her glasses. She looked at me, bright and amused. Maybe it was because of the open mouth that I usually slept with. We were face to face, a royal and a servant. But she was a queen I could love. The husband must be fucking crazy; leaving luxury like that abandoned...*Damn, what an idiot*.

We touched each other's faces. She began by running a finger over one of my eyebrows, then over the other. Back and forth. I repeated the same action on her face. We were touching each other like that, back and forth, until the kisses came. First were light kisses, whispers, brushing lips. Little by little they became more solid, then open, then wet. My hands found her breasts, squeezed her buttocks, her legs. We stopped only to agree that we would not have sex, because some game warden or ranger could come by surprise. We decided to leave, knowing it was necessary, besides it was getting cold. We sat back down in the boat chairs facing each other.

"When we were kids, we went with my father to a place called 'Estero las Jaibas.' That's where how I learned to row. There were estuaries, when the Gulf of California was filled with water, and that was truly beautiful, like a big lake, but salt water," I said. Martina put her socks and shoes back on. I mentioned my sister and my grandmother.

We returned the boat to the rental agent. I paid, was handed a tax-deductible receipt and my driver's license, left as collateral. We returned to the Mustang hand in hand. We agreed to go to my place, arrived in no time; the return trip is shorter when it's painted with excitement. Martina parked a ways down, so we stroked a little sidewalk in the spreading dark. Like two thieves, we snuck into the yard where Mrs. Robbins planted catnip for the cats and other plants that made *her* happy. I quietly pushed the door open, Martina following me close. We crept the steps to the basement. I closed both doors along the way; the one to the hallway and the one to my room. One of the cats, the one that had become my friend, jumped out of bed when Martina dropped onto the old mattress with a giggle. I pressed a finger to my smile, *Everything had to be low volume*. I threw myself down next to her and we undressed. She captured my mouth and I sent one of my hands low, caressing curly hair, the slickness at the heart of it. My penis began to grow, to fill with heat. I began to kiss her breasts, to put them in my mouth, to suck at them delicately. I kissed her hard, dragged my tongue from her mouth to her navel and flicked it around, tickling her. I moved again, put my face between her thighs and began to lick the soft of her. She shuddered. I lightly bit the flesh of her sex. A strong perfume began to impregnate us, a smell of the sea, of a lake full of life. I slid into her, wanting it—needing to be a part of her completely, before we lost each other. Time passed in positions, and with a spin I was on my back; she danced on top of me, first looking into my eyes, then leaving me to watch her hair rasp at her back. I went to my knees, the slope of her waist and hips driving me crazy. My hand spread on her back, right where her wings should be. The roundness of her ass bounced against me. We finished, don't ask me when. When I found her, she was leaning on my face, sweating, fighting for breath at my ear.

"You make me feel beautiful ... I had forgotten what a good fuck feels like."

"I love you, too."

"Don't be confused," she said, through the teeth and past the smile. "I'm not crazy. You and me, we're just getting to know each other."

"And you're married," I laughed. She slapped at my chest. "Don't worry, I know the rules. Plus, explanations are unnecessary. Besides, I'm the one on cloud 9 ... You fascinate me."

"Yeah?"

"To be honest, you feel like a gift; the way you smell, your moans. You're a gift, maybe even from heaven. You make me feel like my good luck's come back."

"Ah, one of those romantic Mexicans. You're just missing a rose between your teeth and a sombrero. Hehehe."

We drank water from one of my backup bottles, went back to bed and started a new round of kisses. This time for a voyeur; my cat friend came around like a pervert to smell our feet and heads, before throwing himself unto my friend's sneakers in a small frenzy. Martina and I melted, said nice things to each other until sleep defeated us.

7

"Come in, come in," a man in a wheelchair told me.

I crossed the threshold and waited. He slammed the door shut with panache. He couldn't have been over thirty; he was blonde, good looking. He spun the chair around on its axis, agile with the strength in his arms and big shoulders. He was almost breaking out of his green army shirt. I followed him toward the bathroom, where the defect was. The house was like any other in the Al; a standard living slash dining room that had space for a table with four chairs, two loungers, a medium-sized flat screen TV, a coffee table, a small bureau and a pedestal lamp. The walls there had random posters, a bunch of framed photographs lined a bookcase built into the wall. There were two not very large bedrooms that could fit a double bed, a desk with its chair and a table for a TV or books. The bathroom was also standard, if not basic, although this one had special fittings in the shower and near the toilet where metal tubes had been installed so that the man could maneuver with his arms. He pointed out the problem; the toilet bowl had come loose. I placed the toolbox on the floor, squatted down and pulled out a wrench. The four bolts jittered.

"Once upon a time, I would have done it myself, bro, but ... fuckin' war, man," he said, as if he needed to give me a reason.

I smiled. I imagined with legs he must have been a big son of a bitch. "Sure," I managed to say.

The stumps of his legs showed where his skin had been. There was a color between pink and violet in the tissue, as if he'd been on fire. It read in a familiar grotesquerie, like a map of warfare itself. He also had a scar on his angular face, crossing from his left eyebrow to the middle of his cheek. The half-soldier, or "What's left of me, bro," as he said once or twice, wheeled away to let me work. I decided to add thicker washers to increase the sturdiness. I had to search, but I finally found them in an odd compartment under a bag of nails. *Sharing a toolbox with another person is a real joy,* I thought. Country music jangled in from the living room. The guy must have liked the company. *I neither like nor dislike country myself, quite the opposite*. A Mexican president had said that once. "Damn Mexican politicians, you have to keep an eye on 'em." I removed the bolts one by one. The wrench was hardly necessary. I put in the washers, tightening it all up solid. When the handicapped man appeared again through the bathroom door, he was smiling. I was almost done. He carried a basketball in his lap. Despite everything, he seemed like a positive, upbeat guy, and a lot more fit than most people with two legs. I finished up by checking the metal rails for any wiggle, synching everything. He studied me while I put everything back in place, took off my gloves and squared the toolbox away. I stood up with the intention of leaving.

"Ready, mister," I said proud of my work.

"Aww, for real?"

"Like new."

He looked at me and said, "Can I offer you a beer?"

I shook my head. "Thanks, but it's against the rules. Drinking with clients, I mean."

"Nobody'll find out."

"Even still ..., thanks but no thanks ... Should be a lot sturdier now." I added with a nod to the toilet.

"Do you think I'm a snitch?" His face was serious, even his eyes seemed to be a little more blue.

"No, of course not, but ..."

"In the fridge. C'mon, brother."

I looked him in the eyes. It was obvious he wasn't taking no for an answer. "Okay, just one."

"I hope you've tightened that shit good, cuz if I fall, I'll charge you for the body I'm missing ... *Hehe*!" He turned around and sped for the kitchen.

I washed my hands, grabbed the toolbox and followed. I found the man waiting with two beers on the table.

"Take a seat, friend," he said in Spanish. "I'm Terry, by the way—Second Corporal, Mobile Land Company."

I set my box near the door and sat. "My name is Sergio, nice to meet you."

He nodded and we clinked beers.

"Where are you from?"

"From Hermosillo, Sonora."

"That's north Mexico, right? There's a desert?"

"Yeah, the Altar Desert. On this side it's called the Arizona Desert, but it's the same one. Covers *a lot* of ground."

"I hate deserts—I can't even tell you. Shame the whole planet's gonna be one of 'em someday not too far away."

"It's possible, the way we're living."

"Possible? It's already happening."

"Deserts aren't my favorite either, but you learn to find your shade, if you know what I mean. When we were kids, my father took us out to collect cacti for our garden—my mother liked them. We watched the sunset, too. Sometimes, especially at the beginning of winter, we went to see the colors at a place called 'El Pinacate.' Later in high school, out with the gang, we'd go there when we wanted to shoot, or drink, or smoke. Grandpa took us bighorn sheep hunting."

He shook his head. "It seems like you had a good time. I'm from a Texas desert, maybe that's why I don't like them."

"From Texas? Like Tex-Mex?"

"Yeah, that's why I know some Spanish. When I was a kid, all our neighbors were Mexican Americans. Hell, my first girlfriend was a Latina. The most I know are bad words. *Puta*, *pinche*... *pendejo!*"

"Haha! I understand, those are the easiest to learn. The first word I learned in English was *fuck*. *Fuck this*, *fuck that*."

"Nice word, isn't it?"

"Fuck yeah! Cheers, Terry."

"Cheers, Sergio. Wait, you have anything against Tex-Mex?"

"No, on the contrary. The food's good; spicy ... sweet. It's a good fusion."

"You *better* not, it's my favorite."

I noticed his tattoos for the first time. I didn't want him to think I was looking at his legs, so I kept my eyes on his face, on his big hands. He had a wedding band and an earring in his left ear.

"Do you want to know how this happened to me?"

I looked into his eyes. They were very blue.

"Only if you want ... I'm not the curious kind. You're a war veteran and I respect it, and that's enough for me."

He put both his hands on the table and drummed his fingers. He leaned back.

"I'm going to tell you anyway. Because I'm over it, but it wasn't easy. You know, I've gotten used to the idea that my legs ran away from me. It comforts me to think that they're still in the desert, jogging up and down those mountains. You follow me?"

I nodded, although I really didn't know what he was talking about.

"It was in a dusty village near Basara. Routine inspection, something simple—that's what we were told. It looked like the remains of a hut, but it was earmarked as a possible enemy lookout post ... it was so fast—even when I see it, I find it hard to believe. You learn that a minute can make up a whole eternity. Out of all of us, all five of us, the only one left is me. Two of my buddies were killed instantly, the explosion, you know? One more blew his brains out a few months later, after they told him he'd be blind the rest of his life. The fourth fell into such a deep depression ... the drugs consumed him, first his liver, then his stomach and finally his kidneys. He would wake up in the middle of the night screaming, see his comrades disintegrate over and over again. He died waiting for a donor, although by then his brain had gone to shit too."

We drank, Terry with his eyes fixed on the amber.

"Did you know I hate doctors?"

I shook my head.

"Well, I know a few things, like how in this country they don't work for patients; it's the labs and insurance companies, not us."

"The motherfuckers—they fix one thing, and then they make you sick with something else. A friend of mine had a simple skin infection; he was given so many antibiotics that he became immune to all of them. And in the end, you know what cured it? An *indio* remedy based on mud and lemon."

"I don't believe it."

"I swear."

"Sons of bitches, the only thing these bastards want is money, and since they're thick as thieves with the damn pharmaceutical companies, the more shit they put in your body, the more they earn."

"It's disgusting. I'm sorry about your friend, I'm sorry about what happened to all of you." His eyes turned a watery blue.

"Fuck it! Occupational hazards, bro. If you're a carpenter you're gonna smash your fingers every now and then, *qué no?*"

I took a sip from the bottle. I didn't really know what to say. I saw myself in his place for a moment and I shivered.

"Have you ever killed anybody?"

I looked at him strangely. His question seemed a bit out of place, even for the mood of the conversation.

"Yeah sure, mice, mosquitoes, cockroaches ..."

"No kiddin' around, I'm saying something real."

"How do you mean?"

"Just that. Have you killed someone?"

I squeezed the beer bottle, nervous. It was a strange question, especially for a stranger. He didn't seem like he intended to incriminate me or anything. I lied anyway.

"No, not really ... I mean, thank God."

He stared at me, sorting me out. He pursed his lips and said, "Well, pretend it's the same thing, only the body is bigger." He grinned.

We were in the silence that followed when we heard the lock. A door opened and closed again.

"It must be Regina," he said.

A beautiful blonde appeared in the kitchen, straight from heaven. She wore shorts that showed off shapely legs over a pair of high boots. A checkered shirt was tied around her waist. She placed a couple bags with groceries on the sink counter and turned to look at us. I couldn't help but take her in from head to toe. She was a real beauty. Terry turned to me. I couldn't hide my nervousness, and as a reflex I raised my bottle and took a long sip. *Pretended she doesn't exist*. I put my eyes on the table.

"Hey, guys, what are you up to?"

"Knockin' back some cold ones. What else can you do these days?" was Terry's response.

She gave him a kiss. He wrapped her in his muscular arms. She extended a hand to me.

"Sergio, from the maintenance team. I'm the new guy, low man on the totem pole."

"How long you been in?"

"This is my third week at the base. I came to fix the toilet."

"Thank you, Sergio, that is very kind," she said in her melodious voice. She could have sung soprano for a choir of angels.

I avoided looking at her breasts, or anything else for that matter. I concentrated on her face. She had deep green eyes, framed by large brows. Her skin was like mother-of-pearl, zero imperfections. I wanted to be respectful; Terry was a nice guy, and I didn't want to offend him in any way. Much less to make him jealous or even give him a hint that his wife had impressed me so terribly. Regina broke free of Terry's arms, went to one of the bags and took out a bag of chips. She emptied some onto a plate and placed it in the center of the table. She opened the refrigerator and looked over to her husband. "Can I have one?"

"Of course, honey. Sergio, can you hand me the bottle opener?"

I took the bottle from his hand and uncorked the beer in one movement.

"Ah, your friend is an expert." The three of us laughed. Regina showed a beautiful set of very white teeth while she thanked me.

"Well, guys, cheers!"

"Cheers," we said in unison and drank.

Regina began to put the groceries on the shelves and arranged the dishes in the drainer. Terry looked at the food with disdain, looked at me and when he saw me shrug my shoulders he said, "Come on, honey, are you gonna feed junk food to an athlete like me?"

"Ha-ha, no! I brought real food, just wait."

Regina opened the refrigerator again. This time she pulled out a box and showed it to us.

"Are you kidding me? *Microwave* food?!"

"It's real food, not all microwave food is bad, honey. Look, it says it right here."

"Are you going to believe what the damn package says? They fed me better when we were in the desert."

"No way ... this is organic, I swear. At least that's what it says on the back."

"It's part of the marketing; they want you to eat shit. What are you thinkin'?"

Regina ignored his comment, unpacked the contents and arranged them on a plate. On another dish, she arranged some vegetables and sprinkled a sauce on them from another package. Terry pulled his chair over and hugged her from behind, resting his head on her back. For the first time I felt sorry for the man, this was unfair. From the way they kissed when she turned around, you could see they loved each other. She looked at him tenderly, with a smile, patted his head and gracefully slipped away with two agile jumps toward a drawer, where she took some cutlery. Terry brought napkins to the table, a small bottle of hot sauce and a sleeve of bread. I finished my beer; it was time to leave anyway.

"Well, Terry, thanks. I'm leaving."

"What do you mean you're leavin', friend?"

"Yeah, I have a couple waiting. Two calls left."

"You can't leave yet," said Regina. "There's enough food for the three of us. I mean, hell, we could feed a whole village!"

Damn, besides being pretty and kind, she had a good sense of humor.

"No, thanks, I can't. I don't know if it's in the company regulations, but it doesn't seem right. Technically, you are my clients. I'm off." I stood up.

"Come on, friend, don't fuck around. No one is going to say anything to anyone."

"What if my boss finds out?" I addressed myself to Regina.

"Who's going to tell him? Terry?"

"Yeah, I'm gonna tell him you drank all our beer and ate all our food, you greedy Mex!"

"Yeah, yeah, like in the Goldilocks story. A brown Goldilocks." I smiled. "But no, that's not right. Besides ..."

"Bah, don't be so hard on yourself, boy. You never say no to a delicious microshit meal."

Regina laughed. "Don't think we always eat microshit either, I just didn't have time to cook."

"She's an expert in spaghetti with meatballs."

"Ah, don't listen to Terry. I cook pretty well considering no one ever taught me. I have what they call, 'quite the repertoire.'"

"Sit down." Terry ordered. He opened the refrigerator and took out three beers, placing them on the table.

The microwave oven began to beep. I sat down while Regina set out plates, glasses and cutlery. I uncapped the beers for my part, and Terry made room for the hot plates. Regina sat between the two of us.

"Do you want to say a prayer or something, Sergio?"

"The truth is that I don't usually do it, but if you do, it's fine with me."

"No, bro, this house has no faith. If there was a God, there would be no war."

The three of us looked at each other. Regina was the one who spoke "Let's eat then."

It was a mix of chicken, mushrooms, onions and spinach in a dark sauce.

"It's not so bad for microshit food, as Terry says, huh?" She gave me a devious smile.

I looked to Terry, then back at her, in cahoots. "No. I tell you, it tastes *organic* and everything."

Terry squinted his eyes at us playfully. "Yeah, yeah! not bad for instant food."

"No, Terry, it's not instant. Someone... somewhere cooked it for us and put it in the freezer for us to enjoy right now."

I didn't want to comment on the way the food was prepared, since in Regina's version a chef cooked it delicately in a pan, like in a restaurant, and then placed it lovingly in the freezer when it was finished. In the unedited version, there were huge containers in a warehouse where people put cut and peeled vegetables, mixing it all with artificial flavorings in accord with computer calculations. It's not for nothing that the food industry is one of the most clandestine on the planet.

"And you, do you cook?" Regina asked.

"Yeah, of course."

"What? Rice and beans? Beans and rice?" Terry said with a mouthful.

"Yeah, among other things. I worked in restaurants for a while, first in California and then in Las Vegas."

"You've worked in Vegas? Really? And what's it like?" She bounced in her chair.

"Well, it's fun for the ones with money, for the compulsive gamblers or for the famous people; for the rest it's like any other place to live and work." I remembered Patricia, my stripper girlfriend. I remembered my obsession with winning a million dollars from the damn slot machines, my luck with the dice.

"Lots of famous people?"

"Tons."

"And what is your specialty?" asked Regina.

Finally, the answer I'd practiced for the interview would have its time to shine.

"Some Italian food, some Mexican food and some Chinese food, since they are the most common."

Terry and Regina looked at each other, amazed.

"You should cook for us one of these days, bro."

"With pleasure, of course."

"Really?"

"Of course, just to work the cobwebs out."

"If you want, we'll buy the ingredients ... and we'll help you, of course," Regina said.

"Okay."

"In Iraq, one of our cooks was Latino. He made some delicious food."

"You guys are good at cooking, right?" Regina asked. She got up and came back with more napkins.

"Not really, I had a friend who could burn water," I said thinking about Pedro.

"And did you take a course, or did they teach you at home?"

"Well, not at home so much, but my grandmother and my mother were very good in the kitchen. I liked to watch them prepare things. My grandmother had her own herbs and spice garden. That lady would make you whatever you wanted in the area of Mexican food. If she'd written a recipe book, she would have become a millionaire."

"I love Mexican food, as long as it's not too spicy, of course. I'm not really into *chile*, unlike Terry. He'll put it on almost everything."

"In Texas, if you don't eat *chile*, they tell you that you're a faggot."

"Well, peppers are one of the basic ingredients of Mexican food, but not everything is spicy. There are some dishes that don't need it."

"I'm better at Italian food, but Terry makes better grilled meat, and he is the *king* of hamburgers. Right, Terry?"

"It's a matter of having the charcoal just right and dark beer on hand."

"He wants to put beer on everything too, even waffles." Her laugh was lovely.

"It gives good flavor, adds a little color, and she always wants one more. When we have a cookout, you can give me your opinion."

"Speaking of beers, do you want one more?"

"No, Regina, thank you. I have to get back to work. And I even told Terry I would just have *one*."

"He's convincing that way. Did you like the chicken, baby? It's not so bad, right?"

"I loved it," Terry said. "Did you go shopping here on the base?"

"Would you believe it, they opened a new store, near my work."

"Where do you work, Regina?" I asked.

"Starbucks. It's around the corner from the public library and it's only been open for three months. I'm making out like a bandit."

"There used to be another coffee shop in the same place, a 'real' one, but people prefer Starbucks these days. I don't know why, maybe because they put sugar in everything."

"Come on, the coffee isn't that bad, Terry."

"I understand why you defend your business; they're your bosses."

"It's true, Sergio. The coffee isn't that bad, right?"

"Maybe a little watered down for my taste ... and expensive," I said, preferring the good coffee from Veracruz.

"If you come to my place, I promise to give you the good stuff," Regina said, winking at me.

"Thanks, I'll take you up on that."

The three of us smiled.

"What I don't like about those kinds of places is that they're always pressuring you to drink quickly and leave. For me, a café is a place where you can read the newspaper in peace, smoke a cigarette calmly and talk to people," Terry said.

"Everything changes, darling ... besides, nowadays they only smoke in cafés in novels."

"And in my memories."

"We can't hold on to the past. That's impossible," Regina said.

They exchanged glances with each other. I knew that to them, the phrase contained a heavier meaning. I used the opportunity to stand up.

"Well, thank you for the good food, the beer and above all for the hospitality. The trust was nice too. I'm out."

"*Mi casa es su casa*," Terry said in his Americanized Spanish and smiled broadly.

"Thank you."

"Come on, we'll walk you to the door."

I grabbed my toolbox, extended my hand to both of them. Terry gave me a firm squeeze; Regina gave me a kiss on the cheek. Her perfume was sweet.

"Why don't you come to the basketball game this Sunday? We're playing against the technicians. We're going to beat them, so you can come by and cheer on the carnage."

"Terry is the captain of the team, don't you know. They're undefeated." Regina put her arm around her husband's back proudly.

"Come out. You're gonna to have a good time, bro. There'll be cheerleaders... their legs go all the way up—"

"Terry ..."

"If I'm free on Sunday, I'll see you there, but it also depends on whether there is a bus."

"Of course there will be. Since it's an event open to the public, they are required to have a bus back to Downtown," Regina explained.

"Don't feel obligated, Sergio. If you can't it's not a problem."

"Oh, and don't forget, you promised to cook us something, remember?" Regina pouted.

"Hey, a promise is a promise. We'll talk on Sunday."

I crossed the front garden, started the cart and drove fast to the phone booth. I hoped Toño could come help with the other errands; he had been lazy lately. I was answering almost all the calls by myself, and it was exhausting. On the way, I felt admiration for that couple, for the love they showed each other, but above all, for having overcome adversity and finding a way to live happily with the consequences of the war.

8

I rang the bell and waited for Captain Thomas Thomas to open the door. We both agreed that we would help the captain empty his garage. Either he was hungover, or one of the soap operas he couldn't miss was on. *Fat, lazy asshole*, I thought to myself when he was nowhere to be found. It was extra work, a little more paper to chase after. *Dollars before everything, maybe even God*. The captain opened the door and the first thing he said was: "You're late. What the hell ever happened to honor?"

He read me the riot act with a warm grin. We had been on friendly terms for what seemed like a long time by then. Toño and I had already done the work of cleaning his basement, and in gratitude gave me at least three more military books. He didn't seem to read anything but.

"I'm sorry, Captain. I was waiting for my partner."

"Come in."

We went straight through the house to the back door. The garage door was open, practically bursting with all kinds of things. Seeing it made me want to run for cover.

"Lots of stuff as you can see," said the captain, scratching his head. "It's impossible not to accumulate. Imagine, ten years living in this house."

"I can see, I can see ..." I studied the matter; no less than four hours of work.

"Of course not everything goes to the trash; I'd like to donate some things, give away others ... If you see something you like, you can keep it."

"Thanks for the offer."

"Where would you like to start?" he asked me.

I took another look.

"How about we empty this area first, Cap ... unless you have another suggestion?"

He walked from one side to the other, thought for a moment and said, "It seems the most viable tact, right?"

"At least there's the two of us."

"It's a shame about your friend. Damn, between the three of us it would have been faster."

"True. Maybe he got sick or something."

"Sure, the enchiladas didn't agree with him. Ha! Lazy ass."

"I know."

"Okay, we'll sort through the mess as we go, make it easier to decide what's trash and what's brass."

"Excellent, Captain, you're in charge."

I climbed a mountain of objects as best as I could. We started clearing. There was so much of it, a pain from purchase. It all struck me as a close look at the horrors of first-world consumerism. There were three or four units of everything. Unusable air conditioners, old televisions, cassette players, fans without buttons, lamps of various make, radios, speakers, coffee tables, broken vacuum cleaners, plastic Christmas trees from various eras, beach chairs, rugs ... on and on. My calculation was correct; it took us a couple of hours to remove the junk from half the garage, another two hours to put some of it in order in the garden area and another hour for a final separation of everything. We made three groups: what was unusable, the trash; what the captain would donate to a second-hand store and what could possibly be sold at a garage sale, or through the internet, this last idea being mine.

While we worked he told me about his dead wife, his two children; Marian lived in Canada, and Dan was serving an eight-year sentence for assault in a Texas prison, where the penalties are harsh, I found out. It is the state with the most death sentences per year in the United States. He lamented having little contact with his cubs, as he referred his children.

He talked about his years in the army, his trips to different parts of the world, saying he loved Hawaii in particular. He would take some objects and stare at them at times, as if they were covered in memories. I told him about my Mexican origins, about the city of Hermosillo, about my stay in Las Vegas. We got a little closer and he told me, that all his life, he had secretly had a thing for Asian women. It turns out that he had been in love for many years with a Korean woman, she was married to a friend of his who died in combat. But between what people would say and the respect he had for his wife, he never dared to take a firm step to have something with her; it was an indecision that he regretted with all his soul.

He spoke of the sadness of being a widower, of how difficult it is to grow old and end up alone. We drank three beers, and he offered me some reheated pizza. After lunch we worked a little more. The trash went by the garbage can, the sellable stuff went into the house and we covered the donations with an old tarp. He looked at me with satisfaction and patted me on the back. We agreed that we would need one more Sunday. In the second part of the garage there was an old six-piece living room set, three rusty washing machines, a disassembled ladder, chairs of various kinds, tools in wooden boxes, paint cans and cardboard boxes lined up against the wall, saws ... and on, and on. There was also an old Cadillac under a dusty, plastic cover; you could see the grill.

"What model is it?" I asked.

"It's a classic. It was an anniversary gift for my wife. She had already been diagnosed with cancer ... I stupidly thought that a Cadillac might make her forget a little about the pain."

I remained silent, walked over to the car and lifted the cover a little. It had a metallic color, between green and blue.

"We took a ride to Ocean City and another to Washington, DC in that car."

"Does it run?"

"It should ... I don't really know. It's been about six years since she went in and it hasn't been started for at least two, almost the same amount of time since I opened the garage door."

"Really? Maybe the engine has already seized."

"I hope not. I'd like to give that car to Dan. As you can see, there's not much to leave to either of them. Marian can keep whatever she finds of value in the house, you know, her mother's jewelry, some paintings, Grandma's watch ..."

"Why don't we see if it runs?" I suggested.

"Do you know anything about mechanicking?"

"Yes, a little. It's one of those things you learn in this country."

"How long have you been in the country?"

"Something like seven years," I lied.

The captain unzipped the cover of the car. I focused on moving some things to clear the door. At three we uncovered the vehicle. It was shiny, impeccable. Not a single scratch on the bodywork. I was awed.

"Wow, it's gorgeous." I couldn't hide my amazement. I peeked through the window. The interior was made of leather, and the dashboard could have been from an old space vehicle. "The important thing is the engine."

The captain got into the car. He opened the glove box, moved the gear lever, pressed the pedals, tried turning on the lights. Dead.

"To start with, the battery is useless. That's a cold fact."

"It must be. Two years without moving a car is a long time, Captain. Let's hope the pistons aren't stuck. Or the gears."

The captain pulled the hood latch. It opened with a pop.

"Let's hope it works, because if not, Dan will be left without a car."

I unlocked the latch and lifted the hood. The eight-cylinder engine was somewhat dusty, dry. The captain stood next to me.

"Now *these* were cars, real engines, not that plastic crap of the so-called cars made in China."

"Yessir, this was a tank," I agreed. It really was a nice old car.

"There is no car today that weighs three tons. I mean family cars, like this one was in its day."

"True, it also has a particular line." I never tired of admiring it.

"How do we know if the engine works?"

"Let me see something, Cap," I said. I put almost half my body under the hood. I grabbed the belt and managed to turn the crankshaft.

"It's a little hard, but it turns. That's a good sign. We'll have to change the oil, and the spark plugs before we start her up and wait for the valves to work ... Buy a new battery, of course."

Captain Thomas closed the door of the vehicle, looked around the garage and said, "You're right, boy, we have to get it running. There's no point in it being left to die here."

"We can spend some time with the car next Sunday, if you want."

"Sounds good to me."

"Just one thing. Why don't you ask one of your friends to take you to charge the battery during the week—buy oil, spark plugs and other spare parts?" I lowered the hood.

"To be honest, kid, I don't have many friends left. The few that survived have had to move to nursing homes, because they can't take care of themselves ... and the rest of my acquaintances are dead or in the process."

"Bah, don't be so pessimistic, Captain." I gave him a pat on the back. "Next Sunday you'll have a working Cadillac, be able to go on a trip."

He smiled. I found out his eyes squinted when he was amused. He said, "What a surprise, you even turn out to be an expert mechanic."

"Well, not an expert, but I know some things. Before I wanted to be a chef, I studied cars."

"Let me ask the neighbor next door or her husband for a favor. I don't get along very well with them, but we trust each other, and we have the agreement to help each other out if necessary."

"Once the battery is charged, the rest is simple."

"Say no more."

"Captain, let me wash up. My ride leaves in about thirty minutes."

"Yes, yes, of course. The kitchen, let's go."

We set off together. At the sink he turned on the faucet and put liquid dish soap on my hands.

"One of the main reasons why I'm cleaning is because, just as in a campaign, one should never leave obvious traces of habitation, so should it be in life. It could be used to track us."

I didn't understand what he meant, but I said, "Interesting perspective. I like it." I finished drying my hands. "Ready, Captain. Next Sunday we'll finish cleaning that garage."

"It's a deal. Just come early, okay?"

"Sure, sure."

"Now then, how much do I owe you? Doesn't the company you work for cover it?"

I looked at him, a little concerned.

"Remember, Cap? When I spoke to the bossman Joel? He told me that we could only help you empty the garage on Sunday or in our free time ... The company doesn't cover those kinds of expenses."

He smiled, I understood. He was testing me. If they see you've got a face like a mariachi, they're going to want you to sing, you know?

"I understand, I understand ... I was just asking," he searched in his wallet and handed me two twenty-dollar bills. I took them with a little confusion, looking him in the eyes. *Surely, he wouldn't be trying* not *to pay me*.

"Next Sunday, I'll give you a little more, don't make a fuss. Besides, we already agreed; if something sells, you'll get a percentage of that, too."

"Okay, but we're clear. On Sunday, new work, new money. This doesn't cover both Sundays, okay?"

"Of course," he looked at me mockingly.

"Fine, see you then."

"See you ... and thank you, young man. *Vaya con Dios!*"

9

It was about three in the morning when I woke up feeling the paws of Little Ocelot. I had named him that because he was half tabby. Now that's what I call friendship at first sight; we liked each other right away and spent the nights dreaming together. He came to greet me almost every night, it was rare that he didn't. Of course my landlady had her favorites, the main one was a white cat, quite fat, so spoiled and lazy he didn't leave her lap. And the other, a gray cat with a white chest, thought she was the queen. She was aggressive with the weaker cats. I figured out soon enough that Little Ocelot was one of the least regarded in terms of Mrs. Robbins' feelings and preferences. They say that cats adopt their owners, and soon he became a regular in my space. I got up, peed and when I came back, he was coiled like cooked shrimp in the warm place I had just left. I smiled.

"Now then, just go over there." I stroked his head, and he meekly let himself be pushed aside. I wrapped myself around him and felt him leaning back into me. He began to purr again. I slept a little more, got up at six. I put on my clothes from the night before, tidied some, picked up the cat and we left the room, making sure the door locked. I said goodbye to my friend. This time I decided to escape through the garden. I climbed the steps of the slope, went around the house and out into the street. I could've had coffee with Mrs.

Robbins, but I wasn't in the mood that morning. I bought a coffee at the 7-11 instead and walked to the bus stop.

I arrived at the base early, since my plan was to leave a few hours early. There was a movie playing in the town that I didn't want to miss, an action movie, you know, busty girls, blood, car flips and gunshots. I changed into my uniform and decided to make a second coffee, even stole some cookies from Toño's stash. There were two calls, one from the wife of a commander who wanted the curtains changed. The other, at the home of a handicapped man and his wife, no specific time. Toño had told me the gossip. A bomb had torn off both of the soldier husband's legs and now the poor man was moving around in a wheelchair. The phone rang. It was Joel, the manager, looking for Toño; he had received a letter from immigration, and he told me to inform him. I hung up. I sponged the bathroom, cleaned the dust off the shelves and took the trash out to the dumpsters. I filled some buckets and watered the bushes and flowers. I picked up the empty beer bottles and cigarette butts from the back of the cabin that someone had left the night before. The two-car parking lot behind there, which nobody used, was the ideal place to drink a few and fuck your girlfriend once the sun went down. It was a blind spot for the guards at the entrance, a good hiding place. For some reason I remembered Patricia again.

I used a wet rag to wipe down our Golf Course Cadillac, as my partner had christened it, and washed its tires with soap. Toño had been reporting late, so I answered all the calls alone. I even attended to an emergency. It was two in the afternoon by then. I had to go back to the cabin for fuel. I parked the vehicle in the covered area. Antonio had arrived, the television was on. He came out buttoning up his uniform shirt and greeted me: "Hello, Sergio, what's going on?"

"Nothing, Toño, just getting back. Some crazy people cut down a tree at the entrance to the tennis courts and I went to replant it." I unloaded some shovels and took them to their place.

"How was your morning?" he asked.

"Normal, apart from what I told you."

Two gaskets, a jammed lock.

"What about the tree?"

"Some fucking kids cut it down last night, probably drunk."

"Uh-huh."

"There was only one life-or-death situation. At least that's what the voice on the recording called it. What do you think it was?"

"I don't know."

"To get the neighbor's cat down from number seventy-two. The bastard climbed a tree and once he was up there, he panicked and started screaming."

"The house where the neurotic girl lives with her grandmother? The crazy redhead who treated us like we were retarded when we went to repair the gas pipe in the kitchen?"

"Exactly. The bastard scratched me, look. I already had him in my hand, when the ... coward jumped again." I was about to say "fat," but Antonio was quite chubby, and I didn't want to hurt anyone's feelings. Although, truth be told, Antonio's obesity didn't seem to bother him. He always went home with bags of junk food, especially on Fridays and Saturdays, when he would devour three to five bags of trash by himself in front of the small, old television mounted on the shelf next to the toolboxes, paint cans and extension cords.

"I usually like all cats, but that cat in particular seems as unpleasant to me as its owner."

"I agree," I said.

"That cat was eating the little birds last summer. In fact, he didn't even eat them, he just killed them, the bastard, and left them on the ground as if they were prizes. I told the lady what I had seen with my own eyes. One morning, I asked her to please not let him out for so long or so early, just so the new birds could fly, etc. She didn't listen, or I couldn't convince her, and she didn't even believe that her cat was a trickster, a coward who runs crouching when he has to confront the parent birds."

"Bastard. The truth is that he wasn't even very high up in the tree. It's just that the fucking cat was scared shitless, froze and cried. This is the second time I've taken him down from the same tree—the same branch."

"The oak tree on the corner of this street with General Patton?"

"The same one. By the way, the captain asked me if we can help him empty the garage on Sunday."

"Are you talking about the old man with the same first and last name? He lives in one of the houses that Ana Graciela, the maintenance lady, cleans."

"What Ana Graciela?"

"The short, dark-skinned Colombian woman, kinda masculine with a nice nose? She cleans houses with two other Latina women, the 'Maid Easys.'"

"Do the three of them ride around in a white cart?"

"Yes, they do. They clean the houses of the retired people."

"Oh, yeah."

"Sometimes they pass by the front here and look this way."

"Ha! Really? I know who you're talking about, she's the youngest. She has a very pretty nose, nice tits—small, almost perfect. A little minx."

We laughed.

"So ...? One hundred for the whole job; half and half. What do you say? Fifty dollars for a few hours of work." Toño looked at me, scratching his belly.

"Damn captain, he always wants to make us his slaves. Why doesn't he put the PM idiots to work? They spend whole days dozing in the guardhouses. Last time he threw some bills in our faces like we were whores."

"That's not true, although it is true that we worked a lot. But he paid us what was agreed to."

"Damn old man."

"Besides, bro, it's Sunday and a little extra money is good for us." It was true. "And, as far as I know, there aren't any soccer games going on, or are there? And you go to church on Sundays real early, right?" I asked Toño. "If you want, we can do it after that."

"Okay. But you negotiate with him. I'm not going to open my mouth," he warned.

"Okay, I'll deal with him. We do the work, and we don't listen to him much. Let him order us around for a while, what the hell."

"Okay, around noon."

"Yeah, buddy."

He sat down in front of the TV and offered me some junk food.

"Thanks, man, but I brought lunch. And the old lady with the cat gave me cookies as a thank you."

"That old lady always wins the baking contests."

"What contests?"

"The cooking contests that are organized at the base. She took two of the biggest prizes last year, chocolate cookies and anise cookies. You should have seen the amount of food; we kept a large part of what no one ate. We had breakfast feasts for more than three days. Our refrigerator was full for the first time."

"That's cool ... well, I hope they organize it this year, because that cooking thing interests me."

"The contests usually take place where the outdoor basketball courts are. Do you know where they are? There are tents with tables and chairs, stands selling stuff and different activities. It's all one big party, like everyone is part of one big family. At least two military bands play, there are dance contests and the general in charge of the base gives a great speech. In addition, the military does something they love: giving each other medals, especially for heroism."

"Of course."

"Hey, what's pending?" Toño asked as he emptied his first bag of scrap metal of the day.

"One window needs to be replaced, Custer in number three. I've never been there."

"The manager told me the clients are new to the neighborhood."

"Uh-huh."

"Another person, also handicapped and a little crazy."

I haven't told you; Antonio was Honduran. He had been living in the United States for more than fifteen years, although his English was limited, and he hardly opened his mouth unless it was absolutely necessary. He preferred to listen. Toño was an obedient man, the model immigrant that everyone likes; calm, quiet, a consumer of junk food—both food and ideology. He was good guy, solitary, reserved and thrifty, always dressed in jeans and plaid shirts when he wasn't wearing his uniform. Round face, mustache, thick eyebrows, wide nose, heavy belly. That's Antonio, a guy incapable of awakening low passions, inciting violence or generating the slightest suspicion.

"And... uh, what about wet the T-shirt contest?" I provoked him.

"No, it's not what you think ... it's a family thing. The kids play basketball, volleyball, the grandmothers come over and everyone eats ice cream or chocolate cake. Wet tits ... man, you're crazy."

A somewhat Machiavellian idea occurred to me. *How about stealing the recipe for some chocolate chip cookies?*

"How often do you see Ana Graciela? Where is she assigned?"

"She and her friends are cleaning an old man's house; he died about a week ago. They're going to sell the house, or rent it, I don't know."

"The little house on the corner of MacArthur Avenue and Earl Blaik, like you were going to the grocery store?"

"That's the one."

"They are there now?"

Toño looked at his watch and said, "They should be. Do you want to go see them?" His face lit up. "We could pretend that we're checking the water taps."

I took stock; maybe I underestimated him.

"Attaboy, Toñito! You read my mind."

Toño smiled like an idiot; sometimes he made strange faces, which in the frame of his round cheeks made him look like someone with downs. I changed my shirt. Toño bathed himself in cheap cologne and rinsed his teeth.

"Don't get so worked up, bro. I don't think you're going to kiss them," I snapped. "You *or* me."

"You never know."

We got into the cart and headed toward our meeting. Just as Toño had anticipated, the white "Maid Easy" car with the logos on the sides was parked outside.

“So calm down, Toñito. Are we good? It’s all just a coincidence and we gotta check the water key housing and the door locks.”

“Should we go in with the toolboxes?”

“Of course, if we’re going to put on the show it has to be complete.”

“You got it, dear Sergio.”

“Don’t jump into conversation immediately or try to get on their good side. Moderation and patience; otherwise, the bird takes flight.”

“You even turned out to be a hunter.”

“I know what I’m telling you.”

Toño smiled and tried to suck in his stomach. I put on my dark glasses and took off my stupid cap, which was part of the uniform I hated.

“You remembered the key, didn’t you?”

“Of course, of course. You think I’m that stupid ... I have something here,” he pointed to his head. “Don’t kid yourself.”

When we were at the door, Toño knocked timidly anyway.

“Open it with the key,” I told him.

Two of the girls were cleaning the carpet with a machine. Ana Graciela was in charge of removing stains from the glass of the garden door. They had a radio on, at low volume.

“Good afternoon, girls,” I said in Spanish with my best voice.

“Hello,” the two girls in charge of the carpet responded in chorus.

Ana Graciela waved at us. They looked less upset but more hurried. Maybe because they hadn’t finished paying for the car (Toño would gossip to me sometimes). They were people with initiative, hard workers.

"We came to check the water taps and put the gaskets on the windows," my companion said, unable to hide his nervousness.

"Hey," I said, "we've seen each other before, haven't we?"

"Yes, we've seen each other before," said the eldest of them.

We introduced ourselves and chatted a little. I took a quick but clear look at my new friends. Carmen, a woman in her fifties, Esther in her thirties and Ana Graciela in her twenties. Carmen hadn't seen her children in person for fifteen years, but she called El Salvador to speak with them every weekend. Esther was a single mother; she had been in this country for ten years, by way of Ecuador. And Ana Graciela, who came from Bogotá, had been in the country for five years and had big dreams.

I pulled Toño into the kitchen, made him open the toolbox and we began our "inspection." Fortunately, he liked Esther, so there was no problem. I explained the next step to him with signs. I went to check the door near the window where Ana Graciela cleaned and offhandedly started chatting with her. She told me that one of her uncles had died in a bombing. That he had studied, like me, until halfway through high school, and that, like me, he had emigrated to the United States due to a combination of social violence and economic hardship. She told me that she had been living at Carmen's house for a year now, and that the small business, the website and the home delivery pamphlets had been *her* initiative. I congratulated her. She asked me questions. I told her about how Hermosillo had become "Terrorsillo" because of the shootings in the streets at all hours of the day; the kidnappings, the murders, the decapitations. I also told her about the fire in my house, about the "accidental death" of my father as the police report had it. I told her about how, since I left Mexico, I dreamed of my grandmother more than ever. Ana Graciela mentioned "Collateral deaths," the euphemism they use for all hostages killed by police incompetence. We were silent for a moment. I continued to dismantle the lock, and she continued to clean the windows with newspaper.

We changed the subject. She was the first to speak; she said she danced very well and that she loved to move her body. Toño had already settled down next to Carmen and Esther and seemed content. I put the lock back together, turns out there was no problem with it. We approached the group. Ana Graciela wore the same work clothes as the others, so I couldn't really see her figure, although I could imagine it. Toño, Carmen and Esther were gossiping and eating cookies, seated on the floor. Esther was talking about an old manager, a supposedly very exact and demanding guy, who had been accused of molesting a child, and how they had found a bunch of photos of children having sex and other atrocities on his computer. Toño took the opportunity to talk about a guy who had been caught fucking donkeys back in his town one night by another guy, who later turned out to be gay. Everyone laughed, although I didn't think there was anything really funny about either story.

I picked up the radio and discreetly pulled Ana Graciela into another area of the house, a large, windowless room behind the kitchen. I placed the radio on top of a paint can on the floor and asked her to dance. She seemed amused, bowed and took my hand. When the song ended, Ana Graciela went to the radio and looked for a station with something she liked. She jumped up on her feet and began to move sensually. I approached her and we moved to the rhythm of a very tasty *cumbia*. During the commercials she explained a couple of steps to me, which I failed to comprehend, and when the music started up again, we got a romantic one. She raised her shoulders. I respectfully put my hands at her waist, and we began to dance slowly. It was less a romantic scene than a sweet one. Two figures in work uniforms dancing during work hours to a romantic melody inside an empty house with a battery-operated radio without enough volume.

I liked her eyebrows, her lips.

We heard Doña Carmen yell out; she called her by name. We stopped, she with a small, disappointed smile. She snatched up the old radio and ran gracefully to where the others were waiting. I watched her in slow motion and ultimately came to the conclusion that the girl had a thing all her own. I thought about asking for her phone number, making a date with her, inviting her to dance more ... A woman who knows how to dance drives me crazy, maybe in a past life I was part of a troupe of dancers, a tribe of real body-movers. I caught up with the group and we continued talking for about an hour more before we said goodbye.

I did ask Graciela her for her number. On the following day, we saw each other, and I invited her to dinner. We went out again, and a week later we went to bed; we kissed, we breathed each other in, and it was wonderful. It didn't last long, though. She had a boyfriend in Chicago. He arrived a month later and she acted like nothing had happened. I didn't exist, removed like grime with a newspaper. It comes that way sometimes.

10

I arrived at the base like I did every day, although this time I wasn't coming to work, but to the basketball game between the Kangaroos and the Leopards, the latter being the team my friend Terry played for. There were two lines, one to buy tickets and the other to enter the stands. Regina and Terry had dropped off two tickets at the cabin during the week, though I was coming alone. I thought of inviting Toño, but the truth was that my workmate bored me after a while; at heart, he was just a very basic, quiet man. The line was considerable. There were entire families: parents, children, grandparents, grandchildren. Couples, too, lots of them. Soldiers, military personnel or those related to them. There were groups of men in wheelchairs, the occasional journalist, all at a party atmosphere. I felt a little strange in my role as a civilian, in the middle of all those people.

Seats 124 and 125, mine, were downstairs. The ushers showed me where I could sit. I was almost in the center, between the two baskets, a good view without a doubt. The place began to fill up. Two steps down, Regina and two other women appeared, they wore the Leopards jerseys. They were carrying rattles, trumpets, pennants. Before taking a seat, Regina turned her head and our eyes met; we smiled, greeted each other discreetly. She made a sign to me, which I understood: *We'll see each other later.* She sat down next to her friends.

It had been at least three years since I had been to a game in person, a hundred-dollar bet in Las Vegas. The Celtics lost to NY. In Vegas you can bet on everything—it's all about the money. I once won fifty dollars betting that a guy would eat twenty more hot dogs than his competitors in less than ten minutes. Next to me sat a dark-skinned man with a giant bag of popcorn, his two chubby children in tow. On the other side sat a kid, the seat meant for Toño in between, where I put my jacket and my duffel bag.

The players began to emerge from the tunnel in two lines. The cheers, the clatter, the whistles, the hurrahs and the American anthem sounded. Terry's team wore a green uniform, the Kangaroos wore yellow. On one of the screens I saw Terrry himself. Regina and a group of people stood up and applauded. From time to time, people stood up when their family or favorite player appeared on the screen. One of the Kangaroos began to spin his chair quickly, suddenly stopped it and held it almost in the air on one rim for about a minute. We applauded. One of the Leopards tried to do the same, although he fell short. We applauded anyway.

The players began passing the ball to each other and shooting baskets, warming up; the opposing team did the same on their side of the court. While this was going on, the cheerleaders began to lift their legs, shake their butts and motivate the spectators with their cheers and sexy choreography. Twelve young women in shorts and T-shirts doing sensual movements. "*Buum Buum,* go go go, take it!" Of all of them, the one who fascinated me was a girl with black hair, very white skin and deep blue eyes that flashed at the crowd. she was a fantasy of legs, breasts and hard buttocks. They were all tall, with long limbs; if there was still an American dream, it must be those dolls. The boyfriend of one of them was in the crowd, and they began to blow kisses to each other, kisses that the other men tried to catch, without success. I threw myself at one, but it reached her recipient meters behind, a soldier with glasses and a happy look, lovesick with the pretty cheerleader.

A whistle pierced the air, everything seemed to fall silent. The baton-twirlers turned their backs to the public and a referee appeared in the center. The two team captains came in their chairs and sat arm in arm. The referee threw the ball into the air and started the game. They were agile players, with big hands and strong arms which they used to work. Terry got the ball, used his team for an imperceptible exchange. They threw the ball back and forth a couple more times and advanced toward the opponent's backboard. Terry and another teammate stayed to take care of the house, while another of their teammates scored the first of twenty baskets on a pass.

I began to get interested. The other team wasn't made of pushovers, so they scored back at their opponents in about four plays. The opposing team's cheerleaders jumped in the air and began to do somersaults while being applauded by their admirers. The Leopards formed a circle, exchanged information and prepared for the attack. They advanced slowly at first, then suddenly, in a change of strategy, they accelerated the passes and Terry scored from under the rim in an elegant move. We all stood up and applauded. Regina gave a very long holler and dragged the rattle in the air. Terry raised his arms and high-fived with his teammates. The cauldron was lit, and they started to play seriously. Fast balls, accurate shots. It was the first time I attended a basketball game where the players moved on wheels. The truth is that I was awed watching them play. I followed the close-ups on the screens, the hands trying to snatch the ball, the sweaty faces of the players and I couldn't think of anything else but the courage and bravery of those people. I stood up to applaud when the first half ended. I left my jacket on the chair and got up with a bunch of people, some heading to the bathroom, others to buy a soda or something to eat, like me. I heard my name. It was Regina; we agreed to meet in the lobby. The kid next to me blew his horn in my ear and for a few minutes I was deaf. I turned to look at him with harsh eyes, but he took refuge in his father's arms. I remembered that my wallet was in the pocket of my jacket; I put it in my back pocket. I asked permission and left the line. I went down the steps, down a hallway, down some more steps and found myself in the lobby. Regina was there waiting for me, drinking a soda.

"Hey you, you look so different when you're not wearing that horrible uniform!"

"Thank you, thank you. This is the real me."

"Of course ... What do think about Terry's team?"

"They are definitely superior ..." I said like an expert. "I mean, it seems that they have a better concept of team play."

"Do you think so? I thought that you Latinos didn't like anything but soccer."

I smiled.

"Of course soccer is the king of sports ... but we're not that closed off. Especially when it comes to sports. You know, I personally played basketball in high school."

"Really?" She paused a moment. "It's good that you came. Terry will be so happy when I tell him."

"He already saw me. I think ... if not tell him thanks for the invitation. And seriously, Regina, I'm enjoying it a lot."

"Is the cooking thing still on, or have you changed your mind?"

"Of course it's still on, let's make a plan. In fact, tell me when it would be good for the two of you."

"I'll let Terry answer that question, but I don't think there'll be a problem. He only has an appointment with the physical therapist in something like a week. Their next game, win or lose, isn't until a month from now."

"They're going to win, you'll see."

"They deserve it; you don't know how much they've trained. Terry has got it into his head that he wants the national trophy at home... and if everything goes well, to participate in the Olympics."

"I'm with him! Terry gets what he wants ..." My friend's wife was a doll, really, and I couldn't help but make a play on words, a glance at her firm breasts.

"Did you come alone?"

"Yes, the friend I invited couldn't come at the last minute."

"So what, no girlfriend?"

"No, not yet, but let's see if one of the Leopards' cheerleaders wants a taste."

"Cheerleaders? Yes, of course, I'll ask them." She laughed her lovely laugh.

"The girl with black hair and blue eyes is gorgeous."

"Which one? Samantha?"

"Samantha. Is *that* her name?" I was interested, "Is she your friend?"

"Well, not like my close friend, right? But yes, we're friendly."

"Do you happen to have her phone number?"

"Yes, of course, of course, *and* her address ... don't you also want her measurements? Ha! You men are such dogs."

"Gee, if you could introduce her to me, it would be a great help."

"One of these days," she beamed.

"Don't kid yourself, I'm just playing."

"Sure, sure." She drank from her water bottle and said, "I'm heading back, see you later in the week."

“Go ahead and think of something. Remember, I’m not a certified chef, maybe one day, but I know how to use my ingredients, that’s for sure.”

“Mexican food! Terry loves it, and I like it too but ...”

“Not when it’s too spicy, I remember. Okay, Mexican food it is.”

“My friends are waiting for me. Bye.”

I stood in line, ordered a lemonade. When I got back to my seat my jacket was folded on in the lap of a woman. She was about forty, although not bad looking. She was waiting for me with a big smile in Toño’s chair.

“Hi.”

I sat down. “Hi,” I said, taking my jacket and putting it over my legs. The cheerleaders were moving their bodies, kicking in the air, swaying their tits.

“My name is Candice.” She held out her hand.

“Nice to meet you, Candice.” I shook it and took a long sip of my soda without taking my eyes off her.

“I’m sorry I took your seat, but I saw it empty, and I said to myself, *It’s a good seat, I don’t think he’ll mind ...*”

“Sergio, my name is Sergio.”

“Nice to meet you, Sergio. Candice Slack.”

“The pleasure is mine.” I glanced at her. It was obvious she was there for me, not for the seat. Her little skirt displayed tremendous thighs; one leg crossed over the other toward my knee. Her high heels barely held on with her toes. I took in the tight blouse, the studied movement of her hands. I smiled. She was a typical cougar on the hunt. I used to love cougars, I must confess, but that was years ago. I had a girlfriend named Maritza, at least ten years older than me, back in San Diego. I moved into her apartment. Another was Agnes, a Sonoran to whom I owe my life, you could say. Mature women are a whole separate chapter in the lives of many men, not to mention mine.

"I've seen you talking to Martina and Regina, and I wondered what you're talking to them about?"

This time I read her face more carefully. The little vixen had been watching me.

"Well, both are clients. I work at the base, and I have done repairs in their houses," I explained.

"Repairs?"

"Yes, home repairs. Plumbing, carpentry, gardening, electricity, etc."

"Homework?"

"Yes, of course, it's part of my work at the base."

The game restarted with the Kangaroos in the lead. They soon reached the opponent's court. There was a ball rush, and the referee whistled twice. Terry took the ball, advanced with two passes deeper into the enemy court and shot from a considerable distance. The ball circled the hoop a few times and finally went in, causing the crowd to cheer. The Leopards returned to the middle of the court and regrouped.

"So if I called you, would you come to my house?"

"Only if the boss deems it necessary, something that needs to be repaired in an emergency."

"Would it have to be an emergency?"

"A *home* emergency, something that needs to be replaced or serviced. For a real emergency, please call the MPs."

"Well, huh."

She looked at me with an incredibly mischievous face. She was telling me something that I couldn't understand, or rather I was pretending not to understand. I took a second glance at her. Good legs in flashy shoes, big tits in an expensive blouse. The lady should do some exercise, eat better and use expensive creams. My penis spoke through me, telepathically, sent her a message, which she understood completely. We smiled.

"Yes, it's a very simple procedure; my boss sends me to the service call, I arrive at the house and service what needs servicing, the client signs a form once the service is done and I get served a paycheck."

"Oh, I *see*." She turned her head as if looking for someone. "I'm going to call that boss of yours."

"I'm here to serve you, Candice ... for your home needs."

She gave a small, low laugh. "You're so nice, Sergio."

The Leopards scored again, and the crowd roared to their feet. We both stood up automatically.

"Take care, Sergio. My lock will need *servicing* in the near future," Candice whispered in my ear. She excused herself and disappeared.

Well, that was some introduction, I thought, grinning. The flirtation had done me good, boosted my self-esteem, sent my ego spinning. It seems incredible that ego is so important for the spirit, as much as luck, to go on in life.

The game continued with some good back and forth between one team and the other, until the end. The Leopards managed three unanswered baskets in a row. In the first, Terry intercepted a ball and gave them the lead. Then came two free throws and an offside that allowed them to score one last shot before the final whistle. The Leopards circled up and hugged, all of us fans in attendance celebrated with joy at the finish. Terry and the rest of the Leopards lifted their hands in the air. The crazy guy did another three-hundred-and-sixty-degree turn on one wheel. They had played like true champions. *That's why they're undefeated*, I thought.

Applause, photographs, the press, the final cheer, the anthem, the apotheosis of the game won, the pass to the nationals; all followed. The players' wives came down to the field of battle to greet them with the kisses and hugs they had earned. The Kangaroos came in a line and shook hands with the winning team, then with each other, more than one exchanging jerseys. I saw Regina and Terry kiss while they raised the team's flag. They looked happy. I tried to get their attention, but it was useless. They were swallowed up by the crowd. I went out to the parking lot with the other commuters and got in line to board the bus back to Albany.

11

I woke up in the company golf cart, dressed as if nothing had happened. In fact, it was the morning cold that snapped me awake. I was parked under a tree near the area where the artificial lake was, half hidden in some bushes. The keys were in the ignition. My first impressions disconcerted me. What was I doing there at that time of the morning? How had I gotten to this place? I went over the events of the previous night. I touched my penis, and it hurt. Under my shirt I smelled of sex. The image of that fat woman riding on top of me against my will hit my mind like a sledgehammer. In fact, my wrists and ankles hurt too. I pulled up my pants. The chain mark was still visible, just below my shins. One of the marks had blood on it. I remembered everything ... something, perhaps. What should I do? Report her? I concluded that it was useless. Everything was against me. I was a Latino with no influence, she was the wife of a high-ranking military officer, a friend of the general in charge of the base. The place of the incident, inside his house and within the jurisdiction of the military police ... I cursed the hour that I answered the call from that fat rapist ... What bothered me most was the fact that I had served as a human dildo. She had mounted me after the fist of Viagra in my mouth and used me as her toy .... I remembered the toys; I flexed my rectum in alarm. It didn't hurt, that was a good sign. I got out of the cart and examined my ass in more detail; normal and painless. At least all the damage had been in the front. According to Captain Thomas Thomas, and the experts at West Point, it was very important to cover the rear. I tied my boots and started the cart. I felt low. I returned to the cabin, took a shower and dressed in clean underwear. It was then that I began to feel beaten, mistreated, abused... *raped. For being so damn naive*, I thought to myself. I thought of slaves and hostages—people who had been mistreated, whipped, beaten up and insulted—with contempt. Now I was one of them. I threw myself on the carpet. I closed my eyes, tried to relax and almost immediately fell asleep.

I am in the desert, on a very large cactus, vigilant. Maybe I am a bird, although it is something I cannot see. My eyes cover 180 degrees; I see the particular cacti of this desert, the Saguaros. These are then an army of mummified and silent men. Another strange thing, there is no sun above, no clouds. There is nothing, just a blood red sky. Sand in swirls and silence, petrified, mortal.

I woke up restless from that dream, and from the fact that I was hollowed by the rape I had been subjected to. I tried to imagine the faces of the fucking lawyers when I told them that I accused the wife of a national hero, holder of three stars, with rape. Not only would they laugh at me, but they were capable of turning the tables on me. Maybe I went to jail for rape on a massive sentence; at least five to ten years of purge without appeal. Being Mexican in the USA is a fucking pain.

I put some skin cream on my battered dick. I made breakfast stark naked, washed the dishes, cleaned a little here and there. I didn't know much about scarring in that area of the body, but I figured It would be at least two weeks without sex. I ease my underwear back in place and put on my pants, careful when putting on my shoes. I avoid walking too much, pretend to be sick for a couple of days and take advantage of the opportunity to rest.

I turn on the television. I wait for Toño, although I don't tell him a single word, especially since he is such a gossip. I ask him to cover me for at least three days—he owed me at least a couple of favors, the bastard, and now it is me who is feeling unwell. I check my phone messages, there is one from the manager, another from Mrs. Robbins and one more from Martina. *Do I tell Martina?* I call the landlady; she says that Ocelot has been locked in my room and is crying. I ask her to throw a slice of ham under the door. Toño arrives late, eating some spicy peanuts.

He owned an old Tercel which, at certain distance or time, asked to stop to take a break, that or demand water. It heated up worse than a pressure cooker. There was no repair for the old thing; it was old, that's all, overworked. Toño had paid too much for what they call in English, a "lemon," with a good body, good suspension and a pristine record player. Sometimes at the end of the day, Toño would wash it, polish it and feel like a complete man. His Spider, as he affectionately called it, represented savings, comfort and status to him. Toño loved the intimate moment in which he would turn up his favorite song at full volume and realize his American dream on the interstate toward Albany. The car, with which he would find the mother of his children and go on his honeymoon, even if it blew black smoke, was magic to him. The Spider had "...stopped three times and needed oil and water," he told me. I didn't make any comment, it was unnecessary. Toño was in love with the damned old car and used it as promise; like those who marry a grumpy woman. When I suggested he sell it for any amount of money he could, he got offended.

As soon as he was in his uniform, I asked him where he had gotten the box for a hundred television channels. He smiled like someone who claims to have outfoxed them all. Lilith, one of the elderly neighbors, had given it to him, along with a two-year subscription. I revisited the image in my mind of the little old lady with the white head who sometimes brought us pasta or reheated chicken.

"So she's stuck without a television?"

"No, she got a two-for-one offer. I don't know if two are the boxes or the subscriptions. But either way."

"Cool."

"If you want, one Sunday we can come watch the game with some cold ones behind closed doors."

"Okay, I like the idea."

"Plus, I have three extra channels of soap operas and like, five of movies, including one porn."

"No, that's great," I said so as not to discourage him. I really didn't give a damn about the hundred channels and the porn. I put my hand on his back. "Toño, I need to ask you a favor, bro."

He turned to look at me and grabbed his chin: "Yes?"

"I need a *big* favor."

"I owe you two favors, right?"

"Yes, but I'm collecting without reason, or anything like that ... yesterday I hit my knee, and I think it got infected. I need to rest."

"Really? That sucks, bro. How many days?"

"Starting tomorrow."

"It's Tuesday, right?

"Yes. So I wouldn't come on Wednesday, Thursday—or Friday either. But I'll be on the ball next Monday. If you want, all that week, if there aren't many calls of course, I'll cover for you, and you can take advantage of all those days to watch soap operas and eat shit."

"Don't insult me ... It's all good."

I went for my backpack. He saw me walking hunched over and half dragging my leg. The pain was in my genitals and walking like that was the only way to avoid friction with my pants. I still felt my hatred for that rapist bitch.

"Does it hurt?"

"You have no idea."

"Get well! I can do favors too; if Joel comes, I'll tell him that you're on a mission at one of the houses, or that you took one of the old men shopping."

"Awesome."

"But with this favor I pay you the two I owe you."

"Okay, two-for-one. How'd you ever get so lucky, buddy? I really appreciate it. See you next week."

We said goodbye and I slowly left the base and crawled to my house, still as I could be on the bus ride. *Fat, abusive whore*. I felt truly terrible. It was bullshit. What I kept asking myself was: *How had she transported the golf cart without being seen across Patton Street? How had she put my clothes on?* Suddenly it occurred to me that the rapist might have had help from someone. When I got home, I felt I had accomplished an enormous feat. I entered through the garden door, threw myself on the bed and slept for about twelve straight hours; the same hours during which my grandmother sent me a message in the form of dreams, some of them were difficult to decipher.

12

I finally answered Candice's call; I had already made her suffer enough with two stand-ups. Since I didn't pay attention to her messages on the office phone the first few days, she started calling my boss until he sent us an ultimatum. I even sent Toño in my place, but she was holding out and sent him back with swear words. When a woman has a mission, there's very little in the way of human power that can make her change her mind. I finally got to her house, prepared. I knew that the supposed broken water key was fake, so I didn't even bother to take down the toolbox, but I did take condoms. The tool was going to be me, well, at least a part.

This Candice wasn't all that bad, of course, even with the years on top of her; she swam, exercised an hour a day at the gym—and meditated, I later found out. Her husband was a major with a medal for valor, but a premature ejaculator, whom she periodically cheated on. I learned this last bit of information from Martina's mouth; they had overlapped in at least two of the same bases. On the first occasion they had been next-door neighbors, so they knew each other from a fairly intimate basis. According to Martina, she chose men who did not represent problems—inexperienced, single ones, widowers, domestic employees, not very bright guys. I found the matching door number and entered the house.

The curtains were closed, the lights off, but there were about twenty candles everywhere, strategically placed, and flowers scattered on the floor. The smell of lavender incense draped in the air. She was only wearing a transparent robe, blue high heels with very thin stems and her hair loose at her shoulders. She greeted me with a long, wet kiss and slowly undressed me. I let her do it, while I touched her nipples and spanked her. We rolled on the flowers. When she took off my pants, she kissed my abdomen, my pelvis and put my member in her mouth faster than I expected. Just like that. Suddenly I stood up, lifted her by the hair and threw her over the back of the couch, penetrating her from behind. With a single push I found her depth; she let out a cry of pain, which little by little turned into pleasure as she melted. Deep, hard thrusts on the way in, slow movements on the way out. I lifted her leg over the backrest and gave a strong circular push, she turned to look at me tenderly, bit her lip. Her nails dug into the upholstery. I stayed inside of her and began to kiss her back. I ran my tongue over her ears, her shoulders, caressing her tits. We changed position and rhythm, this time I moved at a fast pace. She began to pant. I felt her vagina tighten over my penis, saw ecstasy her in eyes as she let out a cry and rested her head on her arms. I took a breath. I had a little more gas left, so I threw her down on the flower bed and I gave her another turn, her legs resting on my shoulders. She helped guide me into her. This second round of thrusts started slow, slow as blues. She scratched my back ... What followed from there were three or four sexual positions approved by the Kama Sutra; screams, saliva and sweat; kisses of course, lots of kisses; caresses all around and onomatopoeia unintelligible in our languages. Two and a half hours later we looked into each other's eyes lying side by side. Candice seemed to reveal her true age and being.

"It was amazing!" she told me with her eyes full of pleasured tears. "I came four times; I've never felt so good in my life!" She kissed me and said, "What's your name? Sorry, I forgot."

"Sergio, the serviceman."

"Oh, that's right. Nice."

As usually happens, once the flash of desire had passed, we were two strangers. She was the unsatisfied wife of an active member of the US Army, and I was a little Mexican with a face like a penis and ears like two big balls.

"Well ... I think you have to go."

I understood. I sprang up, got dressed and walked toward the door. I felt like a whore who had had a handful of bills thrown in his face. I heard the small scrape of a pen on paper. The saddest thing was that it was nothing but a way of working toward her signature. It felt vile, like pure blackmail for having seen me talking to Martina and Regina. I discreetly took my phone from where I had left it, pressed play and watched a little of the sequence of events I had recorded.

"Well, now I'm the one who has this." I showed it to her, snatching up the page while her eyes were caught and her mouth hung open. "We're even."

"But ... what?" She looked mortified; of course she didn't expect the little Mexican might have a plan to get leverage of his own. She sat down on the bed covering her breasts with an arm, mute. Now she would play the harmless victim.

I tied my shoelaces and fixed my hair in the mirror. I turned to look at her with disdain. *Slut*. She hadn't even offered me a glass of water. *Of course she had fallen out of the theater*, I thought, and I said before leaving, "I'm not your toy anymore. That's it, no more calls. We owe nothing to each other ... What's *your* name?" I said and I winked as I headed to the exit. "Hello and farewell, queen. *¡Qué Dios te bendiga!*" I shouted and slammed the door.

13

As we had previously agreed, I went to Captain Thomas' to empty the second part of the garage. I put aside what I was going to keep: a base lamp, a mini fridge and a massage machine. *When you don't have anyone to give you a massage, then you're at least going to have a way of massaging yourself,* I remember thinking. It looked almost new, and it worked. Everything worked. We drank beer again and ate more reheated pizza. Apparently, the captain had a habit of ordering pizza over the phone every Saturday.

He explained to me: "When you get old you decide to stick with certain habits. At a certain age, it's hard to form new habits. You'll see for yourself."

When we were about to finish our second beers, an old man arrived, walking with the help of a cane. He was an ex-lieutenant; they had been together in the first Iraq war, and he was a grumpy guy. He arrived in an old pickup truck with a rusty bottom that was barely hanging on, a smoking wreck. He parked in the driveway. The soldier got out of it spitting. He had five liters of number forty oil, eight platinum spark plugs, a condenser, plus gasoline and oil filters. Also, a new battery.

"Hey motherfuckers, what's up?!" he shouted at us. "Give me a hand."

The captain stood up slowly and walked to greet his contemporary. They hugged.

"In the back," he said to me, emphasizing with his thumb, signaling my capacity as an employee.

The truck had Florida plates from two years ago. Surely the old man only used it within the perimeters of the base. There were two boxes and the battery. I made two trips.

The grumpy guy was a know-it-all. At first, he wanted to direct me, but he soon realized I was the better expert on cars, and besides, I wasn't very given to listening to nonsense. He complained about the weather, about the price of beer in the supermarket, about the teenagers leaving the basketball court on their skateboards, about the girls, "...almost children!" who were tanning in their mini bikinis in the pool area and how there would be no increase to the lousy pension he received. But above all, he complained about how racial minorities were taking over America. They let me do my thing and went to sit under one of the parasols recovered from the garage; another one sat next to the trash.

I replaced the old spark plugs with the new ones; cleaned the engine base and the carburetor injectors; and changed out the old battery and cleaned the starter cables. The whole process took me about an hour and forty minutes, during which the captain and his grumpy friend were reminiscing about good times spraying chemical agents and torturing suspects. Of their escapades with prostitutes, soldiers and arrests. I got under the car with a container to take out the old oil and replace it with the new. I turned the screw under the crankcase and the old, burnt-smell oil began to glug, slowly at first and then more fluidly. I lay down on the floor as long as I could to wait for the engine to drain. I took a look. The damn Cadillac looked impeccable even under the chassis, and if it weren't for the dust and old oil, you would think it had just come from the showroom.

The grumpy guy had done something for the CIA, a logistics job. He began to boast about things that few people would do. Cutting off another human being's fingers, hanging him by his testicles sadistically or tearing out his teeth with mechanic's pliers. Neither of them were old men for whom one should open the office door with tenderness; they were both lazy bums. I kept listening to them from under there, where I briefly closed my eyes. My ears went empty ... I imagined I would get up from the floor with the Cadillac in my arms, holding it high, then I would spin it twice and throw it against the garage, breaking it into pieces with a great crash. I saw myself kicking the old bastards, smashing the chairs and the sunshade ... I heard sounds again.

I opened my eyes, saw the eight-cylinder engine on my face; I was still lying under the car. I smiled to myself. Something was happening to my imagination, lately I saw myself in dreams or at times like this, doing unbelievable things. Things so real and clear that they seemed to me they did happen in a past time, or in another life. I waited until I saw the last drop of oil before returning the screw and the gasket to their places. I manually added gasoline to the carburetor. I put the key in the ignition and gave it a turn. It stuck a little, but on the third attempt it got there, throwing out wisps of smoke from the exhaust. I pressed the gas pedal several times, pumping it. The old car purred for a few moments and then, little by little, the rhythm of its engine became more regular. The captain jumped with joy and patted his friend on the back when he heard his car breathing, roaring. The pair of old men became two kids again, playing with hot blood in wrinkled skins. The torturing know-it-all said that the valves in the engine were making noise. Maybe that was true, but I didn't give his comment much care. As far as I was concerned, the job was done, the engine was running. The most unpleasant thing about the guy was his tone of voice, his obvious despotism. But well, you learn that with soldiers, sometimes it's better to act dumb, truly clueless, and smile at them. They have been taught to be hostile. "Ready for a ride?" I said to both of them.

"Yes, sir."

"Go on, I'll drink a beer while I wait for you. I think I deserve it."

I nudged Captain Thomas into the vehicle.

"Of course, of course," he said, fascinated, gripping the steering wheel. He closed the car door with a smile. He stuck his head out the window a little and asked me, "Are you sure you don't want to come?"

"No, no, you go. After all, I have my own Cadillac parked right there," I pointed to the golf cart.

The know-it-all ex-torturer took the passenger seat.

"You're missing out, kid."

I went to the table under the umbrella, grabbed a beer from the cooler and sat down in one of the four chairs in the set. I wiped my sweat. I took stock of the lamp I had decided to keep. *Very good condition*. I already knew the place it would occupy in my room in the cat house, next to the chair outside the bathroom. I would put the small refrigerator behind the door and keep beers for when Martina visited me. I looked back at the empty garage. It had been quite a bit of work, but I was consoled by the thought of sixty dollars in my pocket. I had done the mechanicking for fun. For a moment I felt at peace with myself; luck was definitely returning in its full flow. I thought about Martina again; I would invite her to spend the weekend with me. I smiled to myself: *luck is everything in life, for sure*. The luck of not having died, of not being crazy, or crippled, or a prisoner. But also the luck of finding a job, money, of women, of health, of good humor, of good food.

"You can be born rich, but if you have bad luck, you lose everything; or you can be very poor, but if you have luck, everything is possible," Pedro's words. In cities like Las Vegas everything depends on that factor. I had seen guys in a limousine one day, then standing on the street asking for a coffee the next. I raised the bottle. Martina smiled at me once more; I was remembering the last time we had finished making love. In the end, the change hadn't been so bad, neither had the work at the base. I congratulated myself. I considered myself a lucky guy. Maybe not the kind of luck that wins a million dollars on the first roll of the die without even knowing how to roll, but the kind of luck that can keep you playing without having to leave your underwear, or worse—your pride—behind.

I finished my beer when the Cadillac reappeared. The two old men were laughing, the car was running perfectly and I was a genius in both their opinions. They hadn't been able to leave the base; their licenses, plates *and* driver's, had expired. I cleaned the grease off my hands with gasoline, packed my things and approached Captain Thomas for my pay.

"Well then, see you later, gentlemen. My bus is about to leave," I waved as if I was in a hurry.

The captain stood up, led me out to the street, reached into his shirt pocket and handed me a folded envelope containing my money. I looked inside discreetly, the agreed upon three twenty-dollar bills and a little something extra was there.

"Young man, thank you for the car. Just between us, I was thinking of sending it to the junkyard."

"Nah, it's a beautiful car, and your son is going to be happy as soon as he sees it."

"I know, I know ... I'll get the new plates in a few days."

"Good idea."

"You'll come for a ride, right? Do you have a license?"

"Yes, from Nevada, *and* it's valid," I joked.

The captain smiled bashfully. "Let's not talk about it anymore. Listen, I don't think they're going to let you get on the bus with that lamp and that refrigerator, so as soon as the new car has plates, I'll take you home with your things."

"It's a deal," I said and walked to *my* Cadillac.

I went to the cabin. The thing about the bus was fake, the next one wouldn't be there for another two hours. The truth was that I didn't like that torturer, and I didn't think it was prudent to sit down and listen to his stupidities. Come on, even for us who are paid to walk around with a smile, there is a limit. At least Captain Thomas Thomas was ashamed of what he had done; I had heard it in his voice, the way he tried to change the conversation here and there. I took off my uniform and, in my underwear, I sat in front of Toño's television. The door was closed, the curtains were drawn. I flipped through the channels available to us and found nothing but banalities.

Personally, I don't give a damn about celebrity gossip, the bank accounts of British royalty or reality shows that are nothing but empty calories for idiots. I opted for an old cowboy movie, but that soon bored me. In the end, it landed on a music video channel. I stood up and went to the hiding place where we kept a small bottle of rum. Either Toño replaced it or I did, since we both always felt like a drink at the end of the day. I poured myself a glass; we had three, two for appearances and one for booze.

I returned to my place in front of the television, when there was a knock at the door. *Shit, shit. What do I do?* I could just not open it, technically it was Sunday, and that day was not a working day; it was not my obligation to answer. They knocked again, this time more insistently. Maybe it was The captain for one last thing, or maybe Martina had seen me in the area, although that was wistful thinking—but sometimes lovers do wistful things. I thought about it. I wished for the latter with all my heart. It turned out to be nothing of the sort. It was a neighbor I had never seen; she had removed a light switch in her home and now held it in her hand, at a loss for how to re-install it. She didn't seem surprised to see me in just my underwear, but I did feel embarrassed for her, so I half-closed the door: "Sorry, sorry! Caught me changing!" I said and ran to put on my pants.

She came in behind me, closed the door behind her and looked at me like ....

"Hi, I'm Jaire."

"Nice to meet you."

I was born with the good grace of knowing how to read women. Of course there are difficult women, the more complicated ones, but I almost always understand their messages; the little hidden enigmas, or who knows what the hell to call them. Isn't that a gift? I'm not saying it's something only related to pulling panties down, it goes beyond that. It's a kind of sensory connection, let's say. There have been plenty of women in my life with whom I've never slept, but that connection remained; platonic friends, some cousins, aunts, coworkers, neighbors. And my grandmother, the best of all women... It was possible that I had been a woman in another life, as Patricia had once hinted, but that was in an attempt to screw me.

The woman looked me up and down. *Jaire*. Maybe I did recognize her ... one of the neighbors ... she was a short Asian girl, but with perfect proportions, a real fortune cookie, holding a message inside. I still didn't understand what the fix was. One thing was clear, though. She had picked up something between Candice and me; something intimate, through the window of her kitchen maybe. *That's right, they're neigh-*

bors. She had probably seen me talking with her at the game as well, had connected the dots ... I had to figure out if she was looking for money in return for her silence, or something else. Her English wasn't perfect, either. She circled around me a few times as I adjusted my pants and zipped up my fly, sizing me up. This allowed me to see her fully as well. She wasn't bad at all; the yoga pants glued to her body made her look sexy. I noticed something else. She wasn't wearing underwear, or a bra. Her blue blouse hung on her shoulders with three buttons undone. I thought of Asian girls as hot, yet fragile. She would be the third exception on my list, I had decided. I took a step forward and blocked her way, now in a manly mood. I turned the lock. Everything happened behind closed doors.

14

When she found out I was sick, Martina was quick to show up at the cat house. She brought flowers, chocolates, a bottle of wine, pastries and kisses. When she insisted on making love and I refused, I had to tell her everything that had happened. It was the hurt look, the confusion that made me confess, for fear of her running out and that being the last moment between us. She listened to me with wide-eyed astonishment. She got very upset, sprang up and walked around the room three times. She felt offended for me. She threatened to report fat Vanesa to the MPs, to the general himself. I told her that I had thought about it too, and that every time I had come to the same conclusion: it was useless, maybe even dangerous. I pulled her close, she hugged me. I made her swear not to do anything. I reassured her; I was grateful to still be alive, to still be a virgin, "as far as my anus is concerned," I said, trying to make her smile. She looked me straight in the eye.

In a fit of annoyance she stood up again and reproached me for a certain cooperation in the fat woman's little act. She was wrong, I told her. Now I was the offended one again. I told her to go to hell. After all, I didn't have to explain myself to anyone, much less to her. The decision to not say anything had been made. She sat down again and apologized. She lifted my blanket and saw my poor, irritated penis. She relented, a few days without sex wouldn't hurt us. She smiled. She kissed me, first on the forehead like a child and then on the mouth. We both apologized. I told her about my days off work and she suggested a trip to Atlanta. I accepted but told her I needed at least two days in bed ... alone. Reluctantly, she got the vibe and offered to bring me books from the public library. I asked her to go up and drop off the box of chocolates to my landlady before she left. "Makes a good impression." She had promised to make me chicken soup, thinking I had a stomach ailment and fever.

"What if she asks me who I am?"

"Easy, you're a friend from work. She also knows you visit; I think she heard us or something. I had to tell her about you, as a coworker, of course."

"What if she asks me questions?"

"No, it's not her style. Besides, she's half deaf, half blind and forgetful."

"Okay, I'll bring up the chocolates. I'll tell her that you have a stomach bug and a fever. Tomorrow, I'll bring you books. Any preferences?"

"Yes, anything but erotica or self-help books."

"That's it, I'm out," she said with a smile she tried to fight. "You better get yourself ready, because we're going for a walk this weekend." She lifted up my blanket again and said to my penis, "Feel better, sir, and take care. Goodbye." She blew him a little kiss.

"Thank you, thank you," I said. "He sends you his best regards."

Martina smiled. She gave me a long, passionate farewell kiss on the mouth that almost broke my vow of chastity. I readjusted with a grunt.

During those days of reading, meditation and chicken soup I recharged my batteries. I slept a lot and reflected a lot. I even picked up some guilt and thought about breaking up with Martina; what we were doing was not right and unfair to a certain third party fighting in a war, while I took advantage of the loneliness of his wife, of the distance between them.

For three days I spent time in my room alone, my doors closed and my balls hanging out. I didn't see her, I missed her ... That was a bad sign. On Friday, after lunchtime, Martina arrived at the front door. She brought a cake for the landlady, gourmet canned food for the cats and a new shirt for me. Her overflowing energy was felt throughout the house and even Little Ocelot, *Tigrillo*, who is quite aloof, ran upstairs to greet her. She chatted for a moment with Mrs. Robbins. I heard the clicking of her boots on the wooden floor, then the steps. She appeared in my room. I closed the book I was reading, looked up. She was truly stunning. She smiled at me and literally threw herself onto me. We kissed and caressed each other, but even though I was almost completely recovered, I didn't want to take any risks. I asked her to wait a little longer, maybe one more day, but continued to kiss her, tugging her bra away from her breasts. Resigned, she stood up, straightened her clothes and asked me to do the same. I packed a small suitcase, dressed in big underwear and baggy pants. We said goodbye to my landlady and went out as happy as two little kids cutting school. She opened the trunk of the Mustang and I placed my suitcase next to hers.

"Fuck, why have you brought so much?" I said jovially.

"Just what is necessary. What if there's a place to swim at the hotel? And if we go dancing?"

"Okay, okay ... see, that is another thing that differentiates us from you women."

"I would say, it is not that we are different, but more cautious."

Martina took the driver's seat. We left Albany and drove late into the night. We talked about a thousand things, we laughed and even sang a couple of songs. We stopped for dinner at a truck stop with a restaurant, which turned out to be quite good; I devoured a steak with salad and potatoes, everything tasted heavenly after my recent diet of bland soups. Martina drank a beer, I settled on a large coke. We agreed that I would drive the next leg so as not to leave her with all the work. I paid, and we went out and looked at the full moon and the stars for several minutes, Martina telling me the names she knew. Hugging each other cheek to cheek, we saw a comet fly by and our skin prickled. We didn't say anything, but we both knew it was an omen.

I adjusted the driver's seat to my needs and we returned to the highway. I told her about how I had driven since I was a kid, because my father had entrusted me with my grandmother and relegated me to certain things; taking her to church, to the cemetery to visit my grandfather, shopping here and there, all in an old truck assigned for the use of the house.

Finally, at the last part of the trip, Martina fell asleep. My hands were on the wheel, Martina's face laid on the headrest and the whole of the landscape was covered in an orange light. Near Atlanta, the sun peaked over the horizon. I was dying for a coffee. I stopped at a gas station, took the opportunity to fill up the tank while I bought two lattes. When I returned, a serviceman was cleaning the windows. He told me that he had already checked the air in the tires. "Ready to roll!" I gave him two dollars and my loose change as a tip. When I got into the car, Martina was still sleeping peacefully. She didn't wake up until I put the coffee cup near her nose; she smiled as soon as she opened her eyes. It's the best way to welcome the day, smiling, and I was glad it came to her that way. She settled into the seat and took the cup with both hands. She asked me where we were and how many hours she had slept.

I started the vehicle and moved while we made plans. We would keep the car in a secure garage, Martina didn't want to risk being recognized. She tried to explain the importance of the car to her husband and all that. I stopped her dead, putting her at ease. I agreed to keep the car safe, no risk of it being stolen. It really was a jewel. But more importantly, I didn't want to get her into trouble.

We changed places again. She kissed me on the mouth and we got moving. We approached downtown, stopped at a mid-range hotel and were told about a garage there, it was monitored 24-hours a day, safe. Now, without a car and free of responsibilities, we spent the rest of the morning taking in the city. We looked at corners, climbing stairs, crossing streets; we looked at graffiti, street names, tall buildings; stopped at facades, shop windows, kissing. We stopped at a window display, saw a nice dress and agreed it would look pretty on her. We ate at an Italian restaurant; she ordered breaded shrimp and potato soup. I had pasta and tomato soup. She told me about her father, an office soldier for forty years. Of her brothers, one was a blue-collar policeman and lived in California. The second brother had ended up as a bodyguard for a politician; he was abusive and mistreated his wife and children, just as he himself had been abused by their father.

"My father used to have it out for him. He punished him for anything, maybe for being rebellious ... One day things changed, and *he* started to abuse my father."

I thought about saying I was sorry, but in the end, I didn't say anything. I hate abuse.

"In my case it was different ... well, I can't deny a Catholic mother and what that implies; repressive, moralistic and not very consoling."

"Of course ... and what was your father like?"

"I'm proud of my father. He talked to me, he argued with my mother. She got to the point of attacking us, hitting us. For a long time I stopped talking to her, especially at the beginning of her illness ... but soon after I forgave her. One has to forgive one's parents to be at peace with oneself, don't you think?"

"Yes, you're right."

"My father was an atheist. He thought the government was nothing but a gang of official thieves in cahoots with each other. He didn't believe in the state, or in the Mexican police. But most important to me, he was a man who suggested and didn't scold; he let you be."

"I like your father," Martina commented.

"Although of all of them, my favorite was my grandmother, a very special and wise person. She never abandoned me."

"I didn't know my grandparents."

The waiter came and put the bill on the table. Martina took the black leather booklet with the receipt. She opened her handbag and said, searching inside: "I've forgiven them all, including Lee." She hurried to a wait stand to pay.

We left there and walked arm in arm, acting like new lovers; enamored with each other, in total reverie. We stopped to listen to a street musician, a violist who made his instrument cry while he closed his eyes, inspired. I threw five dollars into the open violin case. In the glass of a gun shop we stood looking at a large collection of pistols. *What is the sinister attraction that men have toward weapons?* I asked myself silently.

Martina came up behind me and bit my ear very gently. I got excited and took her by the hand toward the hotel. We barely waited to cross the threshold before we threw ourselves into each other's arms. She tore off my shirt and I helped her take off her pants. I slid off her panties and we rolled on the bedspread of the king-sized bed. When I was naked, I found myself with a huge erection. The damage had almost disappeared, but I had to be careful. Martina was achingly wet, so without much preamble, I found her with a single slow and sweet push. She moaned and began to kiss me. The dance became slow, fast, up, down, from one side to the other, our minds, our wants on merging together. I wanted to enter her not only with my penis, but with my whole body. We were sweating, we were enjoying, and a combination of scents—sex and her perfume—increased our pleasure.

We rolled over, Martina on top; her eyes were on mine when she said: "Hit me."

I gave her two slaps, rather soft.

"Harder."

"What?"

"Hit me harder."

I moved around, finding her deeper again, giving rhythm instead.

"Mm, I love it," she whispered in my ear, where her tongue soon followed.

"I love you too, Martina. You're so ... so sweet," I managed between heavy breaths.

"Hit me for real."

"What?!"

"Hit me, you little bitch!"

I pushed her aside and stood up from the bed, offended.

"You're crazy, I'm not going to hit you, not even to make you come!"

"Don't you like hitting women or are you just afraid that the police might take you?" she said coldly, sinisterly.

"I don't like hitting women, not like that. I'm not wired that way. At home I was taught that women are to be respected and protected."

She covered her breasts and leaned back on the cushions. After a few minutes she said: "I'm sorry ..."

We lay down again face to face. I caressed the scar on her arm. With one finger I followed the line of the wound from beginning to the end. She looked at me guardedly and said: "It was a fall," but there was no honesty in her voice, just justification.

I understood. Maybe it had been in service to one of those orgasms she was really after ... a painful one, but I refrained from making any comment. My finger ran over her eyebrows and down her nose to her lips. The beautiful lips; each of Martina's lips.

"And the scar on your back?" She seemed worried, so I helped her a little. "Part of the same fall?"

"Yes," she answered.

Another lie. Lee was an abusive husband, like Martina's father and brother. Martina and her husband had met in high school. They dated for two years and then married, madly in love with each other. For Lee, the army had been the only option to support a wife and a son on the way. The war was in full swing and the demand for young men willing to die bravely was high. In less than six months he had donned a soldier's helmet, a rifle with two hundred bullets, several grenades and stepped on a plane bound for the Middle East. Lee found something in the war. Contrary to what Martina hoped for, upon his return he did not resign, but rather prepared for promotion to lieutenant. There were more trips, longer, some together, but so many absences in which Martina had changed and thought a lot. Military bases followed, countries, people, temporary friends who also changed along the way. Martina, Lee and little Lee had lived in Korea, Dubai, San Diego, Virginia, North Carolina and other places. It was in one of those cities that little Lee caught a bacillus, which consumed him in months, before the impassive gaze of doctors who advised her it was a very strange virus for which they could find no cure. Two years had passed since his death and still the memory of the boy made her cry. Lee's violence had increased since the death of the child. He indirectly blamed her. She had come to develop and accept a certain taste for beatings and abuse during sex.

"You know, I never told anyone about this."

I hugged her.

"It's sad when one abuses the other. There's no turning back, respect is lost," the therapist who took me off the meds told me that.

"Drugs?" I asked.

"I started taking them when my little boy died."

"I'm so sorry, I really am."

"I've wondered and will always wonder, what the fucking virus was that killed my son. When I recommended a criminal investigation, the MPs laughed at me and suggested I go to the psychologist. That's how I ended up stuffing myself with drugs."

"They're beasts, they don't know any other cure."

"I have a theory; someone who was jealous of us at that time poisoned my child with something they gave him to eat, or drink. I don't know if it was at school—one of the teachers, a neighbor or one of Lee's girlfriends, or *their* boyfriends, I don't know. I've racked my brain trying to guess who would be capable of such cruelty."

"It sounds sick."

"How come the damn virus wasn't detectable until the very last moment? How could a bug created in an Iraqi lab end up in my son's body?"

"Maybe someone with access to the army labs."

"I thought the same thing, but the truth is that I didn't want to cause a bigger problem, affecting Lee's career. I mean, it was just a suspicion after all. There was a man, he was always looking at me with lust in his eyes. He was an insignificant guy, a nobody, and only later did I find out he was the guard of the Bioweapons National Program labs. I thought about telling Lee, but what could I hope to win? What if he killed the guy? What if someone else ended up in the cemetery and another one ended up in jail? What if he accused me of infidelity? Either way my child would never come back. The guy became obsessed with me; he followed me with his dirty looks, he harassed me ... although he never approached me directly or told me his intentions."

"You're a dream ... I can see how anyone could become obsessed with you."

"You're a little fucked up," she smiled. "You scare me."

I smiled back: "Don't worry, I'm not that kind of person. If a woman doesn't let me in, I understand. I just turn around and look for another, and that's it. I've never harassed a woman in my life; it's not my style."

"I hope so."

"And you never thought about another person? I mean, someone more closely related to Lee."

"Yeah, I thought about that too. And yes, there was a woman in the same unit as my husband, in Iraq. She definitely could have had access to those kinds of laboratory monsters."

"What about her?"

"I'm sure they had an affair. I'm also sure that she always thought that Lee would be happier with her than with me. At a party I saw them kissing."

"And what happened?"

"I blamed him for it, but he denied it flatly. In fact, to please me we moved base, and that's why I'm here."

"Which doesn't mean that they don't continue seeing each other."

"Of course. That's what I told *him*."

"Have you ever thought of hiring a private investigator?"

"It would have been impossible for a civilian to investigate anything related to the military. It's a world apart; it has its own rules, its own law, its own way of doing things. Anyway, I'm sorry ... maybe the healthiest thing is to forget everything, like the therapists suggest."

"Have you tried to get pregnant again?"

"Yes, but nothing. Maybe I just haven't had any luck, maybe we need more time, maybe our chemistry isn't the same anymore ... It's something from nature, maybe it's a sign that I won't be a mother again." A tear ran down from her eyes.

I wanted to drink her tears, to help her bear this sadness.

"Don't take it like that."

"Some women lose the opportunity, that's just life."

"You're still young. There are so many hopes left to you."

"I don't know what to think. I'm cured of resentment, I do know that, mainly against God. Cured of hatred against people who seemed suspicious to me, of the crushing love I had for many years with Lee and my lack of interest in him, of ... regretting everything I didn't do."

"That's good, that's important."

"These last few weeks have been really special, Sergio. I feel like I'm in a bubble, a safe place."

"Me too. You've given me back my confidence, not only in myself, but in luck. It's something I thought I had completely lost in Las Vegas."

"Are you ever going to tell me what happened there?"

"Someday ...," I gave her a smile. "I don't know for sure what happened, really. I only know that it was something very serious, something that I haven't put into perspective yet."

We were silent for a few minutes.

"Being with you fills me with peace." She said it softly.

"Just that?"

"No, silly, but it's something different, something unknown. I feel like a young girl ... maybe because you inspire a lot of confidence in me. Maybe because I've never been unfaithful and, suddenly, I discover it's not so bad."

"Just *that?*"

"I've lost the shame I felt the first time, the sense of guilt."

"It's a hard but important thing to learn, to not be afraid, especially when you're helpless."

"Do I seem like a helpless woman to you?"

"No, you seem like a beautiful woman with a great future just ahead of her."

"Really?"

"With all my heart. There's divorce, you could go back to school, maybe go back to your town or move to a big city where you can look for work and be independent. You can fall in love again, I don't know ... Maybe you could run away with me."

"Hmm, thanks. I'll think about it."

She kissed me. I bit her lip, touched her nipples and said in her ear: "I've picked up some Kama Sutra recently. Now just close your eyes and relax, abandon yourself to the sensations. We're going to enter the 'Temple of Tenderness.'"

Her giggle sounded a new wave of pleasure while the outside world went dark.

15

I would finally get a chance to cook at Terry and Regina's place. Fajitas were the order of the day, that with *chayote* salad and three cheese quesadillas. Terry himself had gone through the list of ingredients a week before. He arrived after lunch time, in a wheelchair with a motor, fat tires, lights and a horn. It took me by surprise. I was reading in the bathroom when I heard the knock at the door, then my name. If there's one thing I dislike, it's being interrupted while I'm in the john. In fact, shitting is almost a sacred act, when it's accompanied by a good read. I grumpily threw down a book by García Márquez, I don't remember which, wiped my ass and went out to see who the hell was messing around. When I opened the door, my friend greeted me with a big smile.

"Terry! How are you, man?"

"*Sergio, ¿cómo 'stá*?" he said in his Americanized Spanish. He extended his hand to me.

"Good, good. Wait," I said. I went to the sink in the corner and washed my hands with laundry soap, the same one we used to wash rags and cleaning fabric. We shook hands.

"I went to the game. Did Regina tell you? Congratulations."

"Yes, she said. Good game, wasn't it?"

"Yeah, man, great, the last part was total suspense."

"We beat them up, but they deserved it. They went around saying that we were a piece of cake, and that they had the game in their pocket."

"That's what the sons of bitches get for being loudmouths."

"It's better not to go around saying anything, because later it will come back to you, and you're screwed to the wall."

"Besides, you end up looking like an asshole. Congratulations again, Terry!"

"Thanks, bro."

"I understand the game placed you as regional champions, right?"

"Indeed, we're going for the cup."

"Yes, sir, that's how it's done."

"What do you think? My new acquisition," he said, referring to the chair.

"Damn, bro, now you're in a Mercedes."

"Of course. It's aerodynamic, ergonomic and automatic, with turn signals and ... listen to this." He honked the horn.

"It's very cool."

He turned it around. If it hadn't been a wheelchair, I would have been able to say it was pretty.

"I prefer my competition chair of course, but from time to time you have to take it easy, don't you think?"

"Of course, of course ... what the hell are you doing here, anyway?" I put my hand on his shoulder. He chuckled.

"Regina has it in her head that you're cooking for us soon. She says you promised again on the day of the game."

"Of course, I'll be happy to cook for you. In fact, I can give you some recipes if you want, too."

"She's going to love it. When? Give me a date, so that woman doesn't bother me."

"How about Sunday?"

"Are you talking about Sunday in five days?"

"Yeah, Monday is a day off for me, so that works, but ... what about you?"

"Sunday ... Sunday ... sometimes we go to Savannah, to see Regina's half-sister. But I don't think this weekend ... Let's do it!"

"Okay, Sunday it is then. Do you like fajitas? Flour tortillas? Guacamole?"

"I love all of it, especially with some good *tostadas*."

"Buddy, get ready for the most delicious fajitas you've ever had in your entire life."

"Haha! Give me a list then."

"List?"

"Of ingredients."

"Ingredients?"

"Sure, to buy them. We're not going to let you spend money on something like that."

"No, man, if I'm going to cook, I'll buy everything."

"Don't insist, bro, you can't give *and* prepare ... besides, here at the commissary we have better prices, and pretty good quality."

It was true. Also, those bastards paid me like misers.

"I see your point. Next time, when you cook your incredible burgers, I'll buy the meat."

"Done."

"Lemme write it down then." I entered the office, grabbed a pen and paper and wrote down the ingredients. I went out to where Terry was waiting for me.

"Excellent, that's it. Sunday. I suppose you drink tequila, right?"

"Tequila and beer, vodka and rum, anything ..."

"Good, because I have a tequila there that you'll like."

16

On Sunday I woke up calm; I shaved, bathed and removed the hairs from my ears and nose. I cut my nails, put on perfume and left the bathroom naked, with the intention of returning to bed. I have a routine of getting up at six o'clock, rain or shine, working or no; it's a bad habit acquired in all my years as an employee. Tigrillo was already waiting for me, you know, in that expectant way cats have mastered. We had adopted each other. We started a conversation.

"How are you? How you been?"

Tigrillo responded with a meow and lifted a paw, showing me his claws. From the bookshelf, fitted with fruit crates I found on the street, I took one of the two cans of special gourmet-style food that I had bought the night before. "Gutties, chicken livers, and other giblets, probably artificially flavored." Each can cost fifty cents more than the food the other cats ate. For the price, I assumed it was better. I opened the can and sniffed.

"If it's not better, at least it's better packaged. Try it, brother, this is how to the other half eats. Come here. Do you notice the difference?"

He licked his whiskers. We were really solid comrades; it wasn't for nothing that I had won his company and trust. I stroked his little head while he greedily gobbled up his delicacy. Then I left him alone. I'm an individualist in the same way as cats; I don't like intrusion. Still wet, I got under the covers and started reading. When I got up two hours later, the cat was laid out on my back. I stretched and yawned pleasantly. He got the message and hopped away.

I dressed slowly, rubbed deodorant under my armpits and tied my shoes. I looked at the photo of my mother from the train station, when she was young. The one of my sister hugging Carlos, her husband and my lifelong friend, on their wedding day in Hermosillo. I remembered getting drunk, dancing, singing, screaming. It was a special day in my faraway Sonora. I grabbed an apron, rolled it up and put it in the duffel bag. I left the room, closed the door behind me and went upstairs. The old lady was watching her third Sunday TV show. She had made pancakes, she told me. I glanced at them in the pan; they looked like pale, shapeless, ugly flour beasts. My landlady had no talent for cooking, poor thing, but I thanked her anyway. I accepted a coffee and watched TV in the living room with her for about thirty minutes. She made comments about this or that actress, or this or that story; she was an encyclopedia of banalities. You know, junk material with which to make easy conversation. She told me about the neighbor. The brunette next door had apparently gone into the garden to steal basil and mint. Curious, I asked how she had discovered that.

"From the footprints in the mud," was her answer.

I was surprised by her Boy Scout knowledge. Maybe all the absent-mindedness was just a screen, or maybe too much television was affecting her. We continued gossiping. Another of her tenants, who rented the room under the stairs, was about to leave. He asked me if I knew him. I replied that I didn't. Apparently, the guy was an aeronautical designer and had been there for a contract at the same base where I worked.

"Do they design airplanes at the base?" I asked.

"Of course; airplanes, tanks… they say that downstairs they have a bunker the size of a parking lot full of sophisticated weapons. There are even several submarines."

I stared at her; false or true, there was always the possibility. Two of the cats began to engage in a fight and rolled on the floor growling. My landlady, without delay, scared them away with one of the water pistols that she always had at hand. "Don't do that, Mateo, he's your brother."

The cats were all named after the twelve apostles and only she knew who was who. I was tempted to ask her why she had named them that way but decided that was a conversation for another Sunday. I went to put the cup in the sink and said goodbye to her before leaving the house and locking the door from the outside. I had arranged to meet Regina and Terry at the Ray Charles Plaza, it was a common reference. They were picking me up after noon. I plugged headphones into my phone for the walk down the street. I am a good walker, even more so if there is music in my ears; it makes me feel like reality is a movie.

Regina arrived alone, honked the horn twice. I got into the car without headphones or sunglasses. She wore faded jeans and a pink blouse. She gave me a kiss on the cheek, and I returned it. She told me that Terry was sorry, he hadn't been feeling well that morning. They had already bought everything; it would be a wonderful afternoon. She also thanked me for cooking for them. Another couple was coming to the party, it would be the first party at her house since the "New Terry," that's what she called him. We talked about the game, the meaning of the victory and how important it was for her husband to feel that he was part of a mission, a project. We entered a gas station, where she parked at one of the pumps. Through the rearview mirror I saw her insert a credit card. I got out of the car, took the hose and inserted it into the gas tank. "Fill 'er up!" She smiled. Regina took her receipt, and we returned to the car.

"I saw you talking to Candice on game day," she said.

I was caught off guard, I didn't understand the tone of that.

"Candice? What Candice?"

"The woman who came to sit with you around the second half."

"Ah, the lady."

"Lady? Now you call her lady? I saw how your eyes wandered to her legs." She gave a devious little laugh.

"Well, it's true, she has nice legs, but going from there to anything else would be exaggerating. Besides, she came to introduce herself, I didn't know her."

"You didn't know her?"

"I swear."

"But it seemed like you were close."

"I'd never seen her before in my life."

"Well, anyway, I will tell you one thing: be careful. Not only because she's the worst, but because the husband is crazy, and I don't know what he'll do if he sees you hanging around his cougar wife."

"That's exactly what I thought, she's a desperate cougar. When I got back to my seat she was already there, in the one next to me, smiling."

"You don't have to explain anything to me. What I do know is that her maniac of a husband is not going to listen to your excuses for a minute. He is a very talented ex-green beret; good at what he does. He is active as a counterintelligence trainer and teaches at different bases."

"Wow. Rambo is too small, is he? I repeat, I'm not interested in the cougar, so I don't give a damn about the crazy one. I love the cheerleader, remember? Your friend, what did you say her name was?" I asked.

"Samantha."

"Yes! Man, the most beautiful blue eyes I've seen in my entire damn life. Damn."

"I told her about you, I told her that you are her number one admirer."

"Ha! Number one admirer? Really?"

"If you hadn't disappeared the day of the game I would have introduced her to you."

"You're kiddin'"

"Of course, it wouldn't have been hard for me. It's a matter of saying, *Look, I'll introduce you to so-and-so*."

"Really? That easy. What did you say to her?"

"Well, that you were her biggest fan, that you were Mexican, that you liked beer and that you were a chef. She loved the latter because she doesn't even know how to cook eggs, according to what she told me."

"Chef, as in *Chef?* Well, not yet, right? But someone really good at seasoning."

"Of course, and a piece of paper doesn't necessarily tell what you feel you are."

"Did you really tell her I exist?"

"Of course. You do exist, right?" She pressed at my shoulder. "Don't come to me now saying you're a ghost!"

I closed my eyes: "Maybe ... maybe."

Terry's teammate Scot and I didn't like each other. At first, he tried to make me feel like a simple potato peeler. Regina had to intervene and make it clear that I was also a guest, but that didn't change his arrogant attitude. The truth is I'm very pragmatic, but I know when my glass is full. He was a racist guy, you know. There's no shortage of them, not even among the disabled. I took it easy. I didn't want to cause problems, really, and much less with the hosts. Regina helped me cook; we got into a good rhythm. Another woman put oil in the pan, walked around the house a few times, drank coffee and went outside to smoke cigarettes. When dinner was ready, it passed without incident. I participated in the conversation almost as a non-entity. I concentrated on eating, watching them and joking a little with Regina, a little with the other woman, who turned out to be a bundle of nerves. Besides the nicotine, perhaps another reason why she seemed so excited was the amount of coffee she drank, almost compulsively. From her arrival until her departure, the only thing she drank was coffee. In the end, Regina suggested they take me back to Albany, but I said thank you, I preferred to wait for the bus from the base so as not to put anyone out. Terry tried to intervene but finally accepted my decision. Scot and his wife said goodbye and the four of them left through the front door. For a moment, I was alone. I looked at the photographs. Terry with legs, a tall, good-looking guy, in a suit like a high school prom date. Terry stood with other soldiers in front of a helicopter. I heard the door close, and they came back.

"What's up!" Terry shouted. He had noticed the tension between Scot and me.

"Nothing, nothing."

"Thanks for the food, delicious," said Regina.

"It's a pleasure. I like to feed others."

"We appreciate it."

"Somewhere I read that cooking is a very old rite, you know better, but yes, it is a gift that not all of us are given ..." said a drunk Terry, a little red in the face.

"I like to think of it as a gift to share."

"Hehehe, don't be cocky, asshole. Come on, let's go for one last beer." We headed to the kitchen, Regina went to the stereo and put on some new music. Terry opened the refrigerator and handed me three beers. I looked at my watch, I had fifty extra minutes before my bus. He gave me the bottle opener. Freddie King blues was playing. I opened the three bottles and Regina appeared in the kitchen. She also looked half drunk, happy. She stopped in the doorway and started dancing for us. Suddenly I stopped seeing her as the kitchen assistant from a few hours ago, or the confidant sister, or my friend's wife ... Her dancing looked clearly sensual, even though she wasn't dressed provocatively.

"Dance with her ..." Terry told me, moving his head toward Regina.

I hesitated a little. Terry insisted again, and Regina was already waving me over. We danced for two songs. Out of the corner of my eye I saw Terry look at us with envy. I noticed the sadness in his expression. Regina seemed to notice it too, as she stopped, and we went to the table next to him. We toasted. For the first time of the day, I noticed Regina's smell. It was nice to have her so close. Our eyes met. I sat down.

"Hey, Terry, cheers!"

Regina excused herself and left the kitchen heading for the bathroom. Terry approached me and said confidentially, "You like my wife."

I jumped in my chair.

"Geez, what are you saying?"

"You like Regina, right?"

"You've had too much to drink."

"You don't want to fess up to it, do you, bastard? I saw you ogling her."

I stood up.

"Time to go ... take care, bro. See you later." It was starting to get dangerous; it was better to run away. As the saying goes: *It's better to run there than to die here*. I left the kitchen, took my windbreaker from the coat rack at the entrance and said goodbye to Regina as she left the bathroom.

"Regina, thanks for everything, see you later. I already said goodbye to Terry. I remembered, my bus will pass soon. Good day tomorrow."

"Same. And remember, you owe me some recipes, eh, don't forget it."

"Never."

Tequila makes you see ghosts, shadows, immaterial characters that tear off their clothes, crazy people who crash into padded walls. Surely, I would see them again in a few days and everything would be as if nothing had happened. I left their house, crossed the fields, left the base and walked to the shuttle stop. The humidity was stifling, risen to such a level that it was brave just to stand there listening to the buzzing of crickets, mosquitoes and other insects, plus the song of certain nocturnal birds. The image of Regina dancing that sensual dance against the door frame continued to fire in my frontal neurons. At what moment had my eros met Regina's? My thoughts did not get back in order until I and three other people got into the bus, sat down and began to enjoy the air conditioning. I rested my head on the glass and closed my eyes. The rocking of that ship crossing the night in darkness lulled me. I fell into a deep sleep.

17

Once again, I feel like I am coming out of a nightmare, a bad trip. Without shoes, with torn clothes, with a damned worrying amnesia. My fists are sore, as if I had hit someone. Blood on my shirt, on my torn pants. With a bad feeling, with a sour taste in my mouth, a pain in my chest. I find myself lying on the sand, in a fetal position trying to keep warm, to withstand the morning cold. I don't understand how I got here. I feel like I have a hangover, but I haven't had a drop of alcohol in several days. I make the decision to stand up. I do it in three steps. First, I sit on the dry ground, I breathe deeply trying to gather enough strength. I squat down and with a last push I manage with difficulty to stand upright, like the first man. I suffer a momentary dizziness; I close my eyes and cross my arms as if I were hugging myself. I recover and open my eyes; the desert surrounds me; I am alone in that immensity. It's not until I'm standing up that I notice something is hanging from my neck. I feel it, and the texture disgusts me when I touch it, so I proceed to take it off. When I have it in my hand, I jump back and throw the necklace forward, as if it were a snake. I'm surprised. I take three steps and look at it in detail. They are ears, one after the other, human ears, threaded onto a thick metal wire at the height of the lobe, a dozen of them, forming a necklace. I feel disgust ... A damn necklace of ears? Are there perhaps six men without ears walking down the street? Or are they dead? And if they are dead; first, who killed them? And second, who ripped their ears off of their skulls and for what purpose ...? My bad feeling is not unfounded, something has happened, something serious, my inner self tells me, someone who has seen everything. I try to remember, with all my strength. I don't remember anything, not even fragments. I feel chills, I imagine tearing those ears off my victims' heads like a savage. I look at the sky, the sun is about to rise, and it will start to heat up until it becomes unbearable. The best thing to do is to get going. I look back at the necklace of ears and feel the urgent need to get away from there. I start walking. Why have I taken the ears as a trophy? What dark reason has led me to keep those body parts and string them on a wire? And worst of all, why have I hung them around my neck? There is a very bright full moon, it spreads across a grey road, from which weeds sprout through the cracks in the ground. I deduce it is a dawn in outer space. I detect a strong smell of vitality; it is as if life is emerging everywhere in a magnificent way. Where have I been, or where do I come from? A group of Saguaros, each no less than a hundred years old, surrounds me.

Part Two
(Las Vegas—The Past)

I roll the dice with all my hopes, my beliefs and the photograph of the grandmother who did magic. The dice loaded with all the images of the future. The cubes spin, hitting each other in the air, in all their possible combinations. I raise my intuition to heaven, I entrust myself to the sacred and I hold my breath at the moment when they hit the wall of the gaming table where they bounce, and in a last spin, they fall unscathed into the area where the chips representing money rest in piles, and everything that had stopped starts moving again, except for one die, which continues to spin and spin, forcing me and all the players to keep their breath in a thread ... Here is luck; the waitresses going from one side to the other carrying drinks, the combined sound of the roulette wheel, the gaming machines and the chips falling on the tables, the voice of the croupier who stretches the bets, the cries of the other losers, of the few winners, the adversity that no one expects. The dice spins, and it is my face on different occasions; all the "I"s who open their eyes every morning, the one who bets and feels butterflies in his stomach while throwing the dice in the air at an unusual speed.

While we let the dice stop, and the faces of the men regain their features, let's go back in time and let the man in front of the mirror of bathroom X, of place X, recognize himself, among the flashes of light from another day in his race against time ...

18

I just threw up. I have a terrible taste in my mouth although I have nothing left in my stomach. I am a little dizzy, holding on to the sink, with tears in my eyes ... I don't know who I am. I search inside my jacket, find an ID in the inside pocket and read my name. It is as if I heard it for the first time, it simply does not sound familiar. My face in the reflection does not manage to fit with the one that looks at me from the ID. There is blood on my knuckles, but I discover it is not mine, since there is no pain and the stain dissolves with water. I am afraid because I do not remember. My shirt also has blood, but I am not hurt anywhere, I check by feeling myself; I have some scratches, a small swelling on my right cheekbone, another on my forehead. I take off my jacket, my shirt and put the latter in the trash. I am left in my undershirt. I look again at the photo on my Nevada driver's license. There is no doubt about it, the guy in the photo must be me; two, three years younger, with longer hair and a thinner face, but it is the same one who watches me from the mirror of the public bathroom, at least that is what I want to believe ... It is possible that I suffered a blow to the head, I think, and hence my strangeness ... Maybe during the drunkenness my vision became clouded, my personality changed or the damn alcohol washed away my memory, who knows?

I refresh my face again and put on my black jacket again, zipping it up to my neck. I clean my muddy shoes, some stains on my pants, more blood. Finally, I smooth my hair and dry my hands with paper. I go through a door, another door. I come out of the bathroom to a place with dim lights, a blue atmosphere and rhythmic music gallop by a woman who, on the pole in the center of the stage, moves sensually for the pleasure of other men. They all drink, lick their lips and throw dollar bills every time the dancer shows them her beautiful backside, her perfect tits barely covered by a tiny bra. The woman grabs onto the pole, rises in the air and hugs it with her legs. She lets herself fall on her back. It is then that I recognize her. It is Patricia, the woman with whom I sleep and share a house, my girlfriend. Her short brown hair covers part of her face, and I remember why I love her ... Now the stripper smiles, blows kisses into the darkness before she starts spinning on the pole, spinning, spinning, spinning ... Like the dice on the table ... Like the planet and the solar system ... She spins like the breaded fish she tossed from the frying pan into the air to cook on the other side in a kitchen where other men cut vegetables, wash soiled dishes and move with prepared dishes back and forth at a nervous pace; everything is shadows, beams of light passing by ...

I roll over and wake up; I open my eyes, shake my head from side to side. It takes me a moment to get my bearings, to figure out who I am. I jump to my feet, pull back the curtain; the glare of the sun comes through the window and forces me to close my eyes again; it must be midday. I find myself several miles from an Egyptian pyramid, an Eiffel Tower and a few blocks from an instant wedding church. I am in Las Vegas, or rather, I work in Las Vegas to be exact. I live surrounded by money brokers, dealers, moneylenders, thugs, drug dealers, nightclub owners and of course corrupt politicians—one cannot escape them—rubber judges, pawnshop owners, bodyguards, dancers, spies, actors, drunkards, users, mobsters, showbiz people, policemen, petty drug dealers, comedians, thieves of all kinds, prostitutes, pimps, loan sharks, developers and off-course lawyers, among other smart guys; and the occasional one who is scared to death, hungry, lonely, but what does it matter? In "Vice City" this fauna is normal; everyone is a voter, and the majority are citizens of this country. What other fauna could surround me? Beyond the indispensable gamblers, caddies, taxi drivers, bellboys, cooks, doormen, chauffeurs, onlookers, waiters, chambermaids, lucky girls and one-night stands. Of course, we cannot forget the private investigators, the newly rich, the retired; the corrupt third world people who are fond of gambling, blondes and coke; the models and photographers, as well as doctors who are experts in prescriptions for hard drugs, the porn producers, the money launderers and other takers; as well as the foreigners who add their grain of sand to the flavor of the city as they come and go. Among these, there are various types, the most common are those who, dressed in shorts and Hawaiian shirts, go into the casinos to look and spend the obligatory twenty dollars on the machines, naively looking for their first million. Or those who, armed with theories of quantum physics, come to prove that gambling is not a matter of luck, but of knowledge. Many are the typical Japanese experts in numbers and equations, Indian computer geniuses and Germans masters in the theory of possibilities. There are also others who wander around and cannot be missed; Arab sheiks and sultans who own the oil in their countries, the princes, dukes and other blue-bloods who live at the expense of their citizens and have never worked, or the ex-politicians living the crazy life, among other rich people of various flavors and colors. Together, sometimes side by side; the amateurs, the deluded, the believers in voodoo, Christ or Buddha and other cults and sects of various inclinations, entrusting themselves to their god; the god of luck, god via the banknote; *in god we trust* and in no one else, they pray while they throw the dice, throw the cards or watch in a daze as the marbles spin in the roulette wheel. "Help me, God, with this one and I promise you that I will change." Of course, among the tourists not all are rich and religious, otherwise we should mention the dealers, the freeloaders, the fortune tellers and the frauds ... in short, my neighbors.

An example, the man next door is an actor, and like me, he works in the entertainment industry. He's a free agent, works in a major casino, and I've seen him dressed as Elvis, Burt Reynolds and even Darth Vader. I tell you, one night I almost had a heart attack; I was half drunk, I parked the old ride, and there was nowhere to go but three blocks ahead. I was walking home, thinking who knows what nonsense, you know, watching my steps. When I turned the corner and Darth Vader appeared, I almost shit myself, not because of the stupidity that he imposes, but because there are a lot of crazy people around here too, right now there are two serial killers working the Downtown area; the fact is that I was paralyzed, I didn't know what to do and I would have probably died if it weren't for the fact that from the metal head came out a: "Good night, neighbor, see you tomorrow ..." in the cavernous voice of the king of the dark side, wanting to be friendly. I raised my arm, and he did the same, even my drunkenness went down.

Damn, only in this city of neon and air conditioning, without which you can't live. In fact, people get out of their cars with air conditioning and run to get into the gigantic refrigerators of the establishments; the sun kills. The truth is, we should be grateful to Las Vegas for the environmental destruction, better yet, we should charge them for betting with our lives and gambling on the roulette wheel. Can you imagine the energy, the cost of water, electricity and ozone layers that are needed to keep these gigantic casinos cool? It's no exaggeration—they say that with the amount of neon lights used in this mecca of destiny in a single day, the main cities of Central America could be kept lit for a whole week, or an entire area of Africa. In fact, if you come to Las Vegas during the day, you will find a pale and raw city, like a whore without makeup after a night of too much sex, or a drunken gambler lying on garbage bags the next morning after losing everything. During the day it is a senseless city—others would say that all of them are—but this one in particular is not a place for normal people. More than half of the population sleeps during the day, like vampires; and another quarter avoids daylight as much as possible, because of a heat that fries ideas. So everyone lives in artificial environments, freezers and under thick curtains.

At first when I arrived, I had no respect for this place, not the slightest. You're going to tell me that this happens with all cities when you first arrive, and it all depends on how long you live or have been living there before you start to hate or love the place. Maybe you're right, but this city is nothing more than a facade in which its inhabitants are shadows. Needless to say, it has the record for blondes per capita; the world record for artificial flowers as well—just take a stroll through the lobbies of the hotels and restaurants; the record for the use of makeup—okay, just a little behind California—as well as the record for hair dye and other transformation greases. Of course we take in the billboards, the artificial lights, the slot machines; and of course the shows, the best in the world without a doubt, as the song says. There are some for all budgets and tastes. They can range from very harsh girls modelling the latest fashions and babydolls, to juiced wrestlers—two huge Japanese elephants attacking each other—and from there to cock or dog fights in clandestine places, passing through wet T-shirt contests, or massive orgies, where anyone who pays their entrance fee can participate.

The point is to pay money and have fun; arrive the next day, free the night. Las Vegas is the city of night par excellence, where even love and other feelings are nocturnal, like its women. Take the case of another neighbor, she's an old lady named Adria, and if you see her in the light of day it's horrifying, but as soon as night comes, she's young again, as if she were Dracula's bride or something; even the skin on her neck stretches. I don't know what she does, but she sure rejuvenates; maybe it's just because she's a witch, although she's not the only one, I swear. Another one I know, she even gets up from her wheelchair, you'd have to see it to believe it.

Anyway, what I wanted to tell you is that Las Vegas is a strange place, no way to argue with that—since its birth; they say it came from a grain of sand, just like popcorn in a microwave. It is well known that Las Vegas was built by the mafia. It is a city that pays homage to money. It is the product of a drunkenness by Bugsy Siegel, founder of the Flamingo back in 1947, when it was christened Sin City—*The* City of Sin, although for many it is a more than fascinating place, an oasis in the desert from which rich people have been made. I am not so sure yet; I like to bet, but apart from that, in my opinion everything is lights, cardboard and scenery, in fact Sin City is quite ugly, given that, as I said before, it is a city to be seen at night, when it transforms into something else and is really spectacular, unique; everything is happiness, there is music in the streets, even the breeze blows and the palm trees wave overhead. They also say that cities resemble their inhabitants and vice versa. I say this because in the same way, we also look washed out, sleepy and sad, although perhaps the real reason is because we live at night and sleep almost all day; because we share our lives with people who don't sleep enough and stay up late, or are constantly exposed to artificial light, especially neon that turns their hair grey. Sometimes I have the impression that Las Vegas is a mirage, which disappears every morning under the sun's rays and reappears at night with all its noise, its cars and its varied people; mainly fools who come to try their luck, beautiful women looking for the old millionaire, swindlers—of both sexes, gambling and betting addicts, alcoholics in the process of losing everything, crazy people, roulette riders. Here we are all gamblers, all of us, including those who are not betting, or watching out for the house not to lose, that's what our lives are all about; betting, risking fate and luck.

As for me, I am an aspiring chef, but sometimes I am a free entertainment person like half of the population of this city, where one half pays the other to laugh at their expense. I have done everything. My first job in the performance field, immediately after working as a hot dog maker on a cart in the Downtown area when I had just landed from Los Angeles, was under the Mickey Mouse costume outside the Disney hotel. An easy job if they say so, but I would like to see them six hours a day under the intense sun, inside several layers of fiberglass. Not only because of the sweat—you end up soaked—but because of the lack of visibility and the isolation in which you find yourself, carrying the rigid and heavy head of Miguelito. Almost three months as a mouse—in a job that began as a substitute—and two more as a dog, in the Pluto costume, until one day I fainted, just like that. Sunstroke was the doctor's verdict, a week's rest, lots of water, and Disney didn't even say thank you; another Pluto was barking and waving his hands when I returned to my post. Afterwards I worked in a kitchen in a big hotel, part-time, as a dishwasher. Later in a gardening company, from there going on to be head of box stackers in a warehouse, but also a bricklayer and messenger. I returned to the kitchen, this time as a grill assistant in a casino. How did I end up in Las Vegas? If I told you I really don't know, you wouldn't believe me. I opened my eyes and there I was, although I like to think that I came to Las Vegas to improve myself, because according to what I was told, some of the best chefs in the world are here. I think I have a talent for cooking. The person who put it into my head to be a chef was my friend Pedro, whom I met in Los Angeles. He noticed that I was good at mixing ingredients and that the results were tasty.

"Having a way with seasoning is a unique gift, brother, and even more so if you perfect it. With that you can open many doors and become someone, especially in this country, where people like to eat." Let's say he convinced me.

The Las Vegas thing is also Peter's idea, I suppose; he worked part of the year here and part in LA depending on the flow of tourists. Even today, he says that his Inca blood does not allow him to settle in just one place. Peter turned out to be a very active and somewhat bohemian man, who also liked to play the guitar and read. Thanks to this friend I understood many cultural aspects of this country, such as the love for shopping, fascination with serial killers and hard tits, like balls. I clarify; I was a little lost before I met him.

At one of those unforgettable parties that were organized at his house, a guy, Ross, approached me and told me that I could get a job with him, if I was up for it. He gave me his card; he was a manager for several people in several cities, and I didn't call him until he saw me in Las Vegas. He connected me with an entertainment company, they gave me the nickname *Freelance,* and they started sending me to parties, soirees, stores and openings. At first, I liked the name, it even seemed romantic to me, although I soon discovered that it meant doing everything when you can and charging with a fee receipt. Also, they only pay for the hours worked per minute earned, not a second more, and the doctor is on the employee's account, not to mention if he dies ... *What the fuck?* Freelance, free worker, is what they say proudly in Spanish. Free from dying of hunger he will be. The first job through Ross was spinning an arrow-shaped sign on the sidewalk for a real estate agency. Others followed. One memorable one is a job that I did on my birthday, let me tell you.

19

Those of us who toil in the entertainment field know that days off, for us, are also days of work. The job was to compete with others ... an everyday thing. That morning I got up earlier than usual, even though it was Sunday. I did a set of squats and a set of sit-ups, and I didn't have breakfast, just water, something like three glasses. I was going to a cooking contest where I was one of the participants. Unlike other competitions, I didn't need a helmet, special gloves or a coach. I was going to a dinner, but not exactly as a guest. It was an eating contest with others, to have fun with fried chicken wings, marinated in buffalo sauce according to the package. The contract was very clear, and it looked like most of them today: If I died during the competition, they wouldn't pay for anything, not even for the cremation; nobody forced me to do such an act and the after-effects were my problem—this meant that if one of the damned wings was rotten or something worse, they would take no responsibility. In another of the clauses it was written that I had to wear the names of the sauce, the wings and the contracting company on my chest, back, head and shoulders—for the not inconsiderable sum of thirty dollars an hour—and the worst thing was that if I won first place, the trophy would go to the company, and Ross, with fifty percent.

Damn, that philosopher sure did say it: we are nothing. I don't know if I told you, I've been doing everything in this country for several years; from parking cars and being a target at fairs, to jumping naked into a pool full of beer; receiving the pie after the party; or being the one who gets the bucket of water thrown on him when he walks through the door. All this besides being a bricklayer, a mechanic, a carpenter, a gardener and a messenger. Necessity is a bitch, and dreams are possibilities, if you focus hard enough, according to my grandmother. Until that, I consider myself quite optimistic and I'm always waiting for a change.

Being a chef was something relatively new in my mind. I was tired of working in anything, especially as a clown. It's more than the truth, of course; I was without a wig and makeup, but at the end of the day a damn clown. But not a Fellinesque clown, because I hate melodrama and tears. I'm a clown who takes it easy, tries to get through life and smile; fuck hard, eat better and wait for the change in damn luck, although sometimes I get very angry with myself and especially with those who hurt me. What else can I say, how can I justify myself? That it's not my fault, but fate, luck and circumstances? That when I was little, I wanted to be something else, and I was full of dreams? That's why I went to high school and wanted to go to college? That violence came to our city and then to my front door? That it's the fault of the Mexican presidents—and their friends—who are as incapable as they are mediocre and who have looted the country? Well, yes, maybe all that is true, without a doubt even, because I'm a guy who saves and worries about what happens in this world of clowns without big noses ...

One thing I'm proud of is that I've never stolen or raped. In case you're interested or want to add something to this story, I have a false name in this country and my Social Security Card is also false. I'm from Hermosillo, yes sir; funny, little name, a town destroyed by the same people as always, although now linked to drug trafficking. Anyway, let's go back to the past. I'm dressed and bathed. I turn the lock twice on the door of the shared house and go down the steps. I get into my old car, turn on the radio and immediately blast the cooler. I head toward Fremont Street, the other clowns behind their windows watch me intently as they pass me by. I come with a blank mind, although you may not think I'm prepared. I'm a born competitor, don't forget that, and this is my big day; I didn't eat yesterday, I didn't have dinner, or breakfast. I also bring a Melox and another vomit-reducer, as well as olive oil, so that once inside, the fucking wings that await me come out smooth. I also carry a thermos with a special tea prescribed by my friend Lola for such purposes; she uses it when she gives blowjobs and wants to dissolve what has accidentally passed through her throat. Lola lives in one of the rooms in the house where I rent and she is also Latina, although from the Caribbean. She arrived on a raft and says that out of the twenty only she and two other women survived the sharks. I prepare to swallow, swallow and win ... I plan to use all my skills and hopefully my stomach won't abandon me. The truth is, I'm worried about the rent and if there's one thing I'm afraid of, it's being homeless and having no livelihood. A famous writer once said it; all Mexicans have a Macario inside of them, and that's what I'm relying on, plus the enzymes in the tea that I hope will work. Anyway, wish me luck and hold on tight because I'm carrying a bullet and have my incisors sharpened.

I parked the car in a space between two enormous limousines, like a suppository. What I mean is that I drive a small, half-beaten Japanese compact car, which I have to buy tires for, align and change the oil for, if I want it to pass the inspection, which will come in a month. I bought the car from a dealer, my friend sold it to me himself, and he worked for an insurance agency that specializes in accidents, that is: they recycle useless junk once they've been given a makeover; among the screwed up, the blacks, the whores who have fallen from grace, the single mothers, those who live on welfare and the Indians. I adjusted my tie and tucked my shirt back into my pants. At the entrance of the mansion there was a large security presence, not only police and bodyguards, but it seemed to me that even the secret service had gathered there. I got in line and put on the badge given to me by Ross the night before.

"What can I help you with?"

"I'm here for the contest."

"What contest?"

"The one with the wings."

"Wings ...? What the hell are you talking about?" the giant responded from behind his dark glasses. Another guy, no less big and no less strong, came to us.

"What is it about?"

"Look, there's going to be a contest to see who can eat the most wings and I'm one of the contestants."

They exchanged glances.

"I'm here to entertain these people, man, it's that easy."

"Okay, through the back door."

"Why? I'm one of the contestants."

"I don't give a damn, only the guests and the important people can get in here. The rest enter from behind."

"A contestant isn't important?"

"Look, shorty," I felt the second big guy's index finger poking my chest, "it's not like you're on the fucking Tour de France and we're your fans, you heard the lieutenant, only VIPs and special guests come through here."

"But it's just that ..."

"Are you deaf? You're wasting our time, if you don't bring us an invitation and you're nobody, you should move your ass to the back door. There you can fix yourself ... or do you want us to accompany you?"

I looked them in the eyes, insulted them without opening my mouth and headed very forcefully to where I was indicated. I hate the privileged, although I hate their mastiffs more—fucking brainless, muscled and stupid people. I got in the line for the back door. Besides the waiters, there were musicians, dancers, maids, cleaners, stagehands, magicians, acrobats and wing-swallowers. There were six of us in total: a giant with a shaved head, a black man with a big belly, a Chinese guy who looked like a karate champion, another skinny white guy with an idiotic face, another one with a big mustache, who must have been Russian or something, and me. It seemed like a big party. They made us take off our shoes, take our coins out of our pockets and take off our belts, and we had to go through one of those machines that are found in airports, casinos, fancy restaurants, schools, banks, government offices and almost everywhere, supposedly dealing with terrorism and spiders; the sleeve, the rich being afraid of the poor, nothing else.

Two more policemen with dog faces, but these ones in uniform, scanned me up to my ass. I put my shoes and belt back on and took my coins out of a plastic box. They made the bald guy turn around four times, even though he was supposed to be there, and he explained: he had two metal prostheses, one on his knee and another one at shoulder height. I saw him getting fed up and it would have been a good idea not to let him in; in the end, he was the one who was the most annoying. Those of us from show business were taken to the dressing room, Ross was waiting for me.

Each of the six wing-eaters represented a company. They made us wear overalls, caps with logos, hats and big bibs with the name of the company. Reluctantly I followed Ross' instructions and told him to go to hell when he told me that I should go on stage doing somersaults. For a few fucking dollars they want me to show them my asshole. I took out my contract, the jumping and somersault thing wasn't stipulated in the paper and I let him know that. Nowadays it's harder for them to think I'm a fool and be too clever with me. One has to put up with enough shit in this business without putting up with more. I learned from Peter; everything can be lost except pride. Ross walked away offended. And finally I was left alone, in front of a large mirror surrounded by spotlights. I tried to concentrate, this thing of going on stage is not so easy, sometimes you have to be a damn actor. I entrusted myself to Santa Muerte. I closed my eyes and thought of Macario, of the hunger of millions of Mexicans who eat only half a taco a day, and of the hundreds of malnourished people that globalizing policies generate year after year on the planet. My stomach seemed big, enormous like a ball; I heard it growl, entering into communication with my brain. Suddenly I felt a very great hunger, from centuries and centuries of scarcity and need, I began to levitate and feel my intestine, my kidneys, my—that was when my employer returned.

My time had come; the third call, in these matters, is the moment when you jump off the diving board into the pool. He insisted once more on the subject of jumping and doing somersaults, but I didn't even answer him. I just gave him a murderous look which he understood very well, and he didn't say anything except a blunt: "Good luck, boy, may the force be with you." I stood up and walked to the exit, not forgetting that it was just a Sunday job and in three hours it would be a thing of the past. I went to the podium and sat down in a place assigned to me, while praying to Macario, patron saint of the hungry. Through a slit in the curtain I could see. There were about two hundred people, all sitting in garden chairs, under a sky-blue tent and an atmosphere scented with orchid perfume. It was an ideal scene. The waiters served drinks, snacks and instrumental music floated in the air. It even seemed like a party of decent people; if it weren't for the fact that I knew everyone. A man came and lifted me from the chair, told me to hide and come back when he heard my name; I would no longer be the master of ceremonies. I did as I was told and stood behind a false wall, where the other clowns were ready for the show.

The Chinese man was sharpening his teeth. The white man was doing squats, moving his arms and head. The black man was rubbing his belly with cream. The curtain of the proscenium was drawn back and the master of ceremonies jumped on stage with a smile from eyebrow to eyebrow, told some bad jokes, greeted the most powerful in the audience and finally introduced us, always exaggerating a little. The bald guy turned out to be an international Olympic champion in swallowing greasy wings; the Chinese guy a rare specimen from Beijing and a survivor of the Maoist cultural revolution; the black nephew of the butcher Amin Dada and the other two, I don't remember, finally me, a Mexican who escaped from the famines in Chiapas, the hunts of the Minute Men and the border patrol. They all turned around, jumped and did somersaults, except for me, since it was not specified in the contract. "Fucking boring Mexican," I heard someone shout and I answered to myself: "Fuck you. Motherfuckers ... I've had enough work from you." I bowed and sat down in my seat.

"Place your bets, choose your horse, each one of these gluttons is really hungry and they will devour each other when the time comes, I swear! Look at them! Aren't they scary? They are hungry beasts, devil dogs that when the bell rings will leave nothing on their plates ... Look at the teeth of that Mexican; they are not those of a Chihuahua, nor those of a California farmworker ... no! They are those of Pancho Villa, the Chupacabra, Zorro ... Now look at the Chinese, isn't he impressive? It is the very mouth of Genghis Khan and his cronies ... As for the black man, those white teeth are those of the slave who rebelled against his masters, of the rabid slave, not of the noble Uncle Tom ... nooooo! And what about the Russian? He is none other than Stalin's secret son, the one who was fathered in the steppes and raised by hungry wolves. And the skinny one? He fills his legs and arms when he can't fit anything else in his belly." Applause! Because these six animals, these beasts with steel jaws are going to finish off those enormous Ferdinande brand chicken dogs, against them our champions of this morning will fight ... Applause!"

Everyone applauded and the presenter jumped up and down motivating those present: "And now, to make it more difficult and entertaining, let's call one of the police officers to this podium, so that he can handcuff them, because these animals don't need hands to carry out their task, that would be like serving them a dish at a buffet ... no! These beasts don't need hands, because their mouths are the only thing they need to butcher an entire animal, two, a herd of elephants if we let them ...! Applause to these mouth-men! Thank you, officer. Handcuff them behind their backs, just to see what they're capable of ... Applause for Lieutenant Stanley please!"

More applause and cheers; there were people shouting at the Chinese, the Russian, the black man, but no one at me, perhaps because I avoided doing somersaults, although I didn't need to because there was Macario sitting next to me, with his hand on my shoulder encouraging me: "Eat, son, eat."

"Okay ... everyone ready, on your marks, get set, go! The clock is ticking."

The bell rang and I buried my face in the dog dish, trying to get a couple of wings in my mouth, chewing quickly but being careful not to bite the bone. I heard my bald show partner crushing them with his damn jaws, as if he were turning them into dust. More than a snout it was a damn blender, although I didn't flinch, that motivated me and I began to swallow the meat and some bones, although unintentionally, as if they were damn aspirins. Two hundred dollars is a lot of money, ask the hundreds of Latin Americans who cross the border every day, the Cubans who risk their lives on barges to reach the coasts of Miami, the Chinese packed in industrial containers, the Pakistanis in the false bottom of airplanes, the Filipinos hidden in the engines of ships, the Africans imported like cattle and the whole third world in general dying of hunger and misery; two hundred dollars is a dream. You don't know what can be done with two hundred dollars in your pocket, ask in Colombia what an amount like that sounds like, in Iraq, in Tijuana ... two hundred dollars behind a display case, like the carrot tied to the donkey that moves the world and makes the economy turn, the damned earth from its very axis, two hundred beautiful green pieces of paper with Franklin's face, the illusion, the ideal to reach ...

I lifted my face once I had finished my first dog dish, and took a breath, like a marathon runner. I felt the buffalo sauce all the way into my eyes, which began to scream at me, but I paid no attention and buried my face in the second dog dish full of cloned wings. My closest opponent, the bald guy, also lifted his head from his dog dish like a Doberman and turned to look at me with disdain for a moment, while they picked up the empty dog dish to be replaced by a full one. I noticed his hatred, although I didn't give it any importance and I felt Macario pat me on the back, urging me on. I began to stop chewing, the damned wings fell into my stomach like coins in a damned piggy bank, where they fluttered around. I lifted my face again and asked for dog dish. I heard the Chinese guy on my left side make a guttural sound and then the sound of vomit exploding on the floor.

"The Chinese guy has been disqualified, a round of applause for such a brave opponent from the land of Confucius. It was no use closing his eyes to the poor guy, hahaha!"

I heard the damned announcer in the distance, and a new wave of laughter at another of his bad jokes.

"Our black friend, he seems very civilized, maybe he has become too accustomed to using cutlery, look at him, he is still in the first dog dish! What's wrong, boy, have you forgotten your manners ...? Cheer up, the audience expects more from you, a round of applause for our black competitor, he seems discouraged because he was expecting bananas."

More laughter, it seemed like our host was a bottomless barrel of racist jokes.

"Look at the scrawny white guy, he has also lost ... Remember, you must not raise your head from the plate until it is completely empty, our friend with the number three is disqualified. Five is also out! We only have left, Yupa Yupi! the Mexican Gonzales and here, our strong and trained mister wings world, champion of champions, scourge of chickens and son of Putin."

More laughter and applause.

"Let's see, the Mexican devours one of our delicious, well-packaged and ready for breakfast, dinner and any time, Ferdinande wings, while the other one sticks two in his snout, watch them devour. It's incredible the way, or rather, the neat style of our number two participant ... Oh oh, the Mexican begins to turn purple, he can't seem to take it anymore, watch him making the superhuman effort to defeat his opponent who is ahead by about thirty of our delicious and well marinated Ferdinande wings, within everyone's reach and the envy of the best gourmets... This is battle, gentlemen, this is winning and losing in Las Vegas, *this* is competition. And what better prize than our unique and special Ferdinande wings ... The countdown begins when we only have two opponents left, capable of completing this Ferdinande wing marathon and when our number two competitor has a few pieces left in his dog dish to defeat our Mexican, who has fought like the best, cheers to our Speedy Gonzales, come on hurry up boy ... Come on Mexican, we know you're hungry, you can make the effort, remember the Aztecs, who if they had known our wonderful Ferdinande wings would have surely stopped eating the hearts of their enemies. What's wrong with you? ... Look now, number two has taken advantage of the small oversight and has moved ahead, that's for sure, and now he's very close to taking home his two hundred dollars and this beautiful trophy, the pride of any competitor, sponsored by light wings, Ferdinandeeee! Two more wings, bro, two more, that's it, you got it ... there it is, that's how it's done."

Out of the corner of my eye I saw my opponent raise his head and smile at the crowd.

"We have a winner, unbelievable ...! The Mexican hasn't even noticed, his face is still stuck in his plate, although it doesn't make sense anymore, but he's still obsessed with finishing what they've served him, wow, this race is unique, that's for sure ..."

I raised my face, my head was spinning and a feeling of disgust was hovering over my being like in red shadows, because of the buffalo sauce in my eyes. I saw how they raised the hand of my show partner, whom the people applauded and cheered. With difficulty I stood up like an automaton, felt my hands loosen behind me. I got down from the podium and, with long strides, I ran to the bathroom. I closed the door behind me and fell to my knees, now sticking my face in the shitter. My insides contorted, I felt myself bleeding, but through my snout; I expelled the disgusting, greasy, transgenic and poor quality Ferdinande, *bruuuuuuu*, motherfuckers, *arrgggghhh!* I gulped air, *bruuuuuuuuuuu! fuck!* I was able to breathe again, but now with more work, the bone of a fucking wing was blocking my throat, the air was going away. I stuck-in two fingers, I don't know how—in desperation—behind the tonsils that were in pain. I located the Ferndinade bone and managed to pull it out from where it was lodged with a lot of pain, *son of a bitch bone! Go to hell! bruuuu, cough, cough*. I wretched. *Bruuuu*, more vomit, now through my nose, *coughcoughcough*, I threw up a clot of saliva, this time out of the toilet, on the wall, where pieces of bone, blood, skin, I don't know what, saliva and pain, of course, dripped down. No denying it, it hurt me to the core. Fuck, but I breathed again, something important don't you think? I grabbed some toilet paper and blew my nose with difficulty. I felt dizzy, the paper had a slight smell of roses, a series of disgusting things came out of my nostrils that I prefer not to describe in detail in order to spare you.

I leaned against the wall ... maybe it had been stupid to swallow the whole fucking wings without a thought. All for the money, because for money one is capable of swallowing shit by the spoonful. In the mirror my face was completely orange. I turned on the faucet in the sink and washed my face with liquid soap from a blue bottle. I cleaned my nose with water, my eyes, my hands, I took off my shirt and threw it in the trash. I took a breath; second place, it wasn't so bad after all. I was unintentionally screwing them, since the contract didn't mention anything about second place, or the commission, since the money was all mine. I smiled in my pain. I would drink enzyme tea, the rest of the taffy I was going to throw out the back door of my mouth in the next few days. I would make myself a salad with lots of olive oil. I straightened my hair, looked at myself in the mirror again. I opened the door, I had to smile, that's how winners do it, the charros, and long live Martin Urrieta, bastards! My manager was waiting for me outside, my manager according to him, although he was not the one getting me these ridiculous jobs.

"You won second," he said dryly, perhaps because he had lost fifty dollars. He handed me the suitcase where I had my second change of clothes; a clean shirt, pants, cologne and other concoctions. I took the thermos and drank a big gulp of tea; I know what this is like, it's not the first time, well, choking on a chicken bone. I have to stop with these shitty jobs, otherwise one day I'm going to die. I have to look for something better or more stable for the fucking weekends, but what? The only industry that pays well is the entertainment industry. What would you do? Last time, in the previous contest of the greediest, they were tacos, supposedly Mexican, quite experimental to my taste, with mustard inside and other unidentifiable garbage, *arrrggggh*. Can you believe it? Fucking Frankenstein tacos, nothing else. On that occasion we had to wear sombreros and toy guns on our belts. There I did take first place. Two hundred and two tacos, although just two more than the closest of my competitors, another Mexican of course. They say that there is no worse enemy of a Mexican than another Mexican, especially when it comes to tacos. It helped me that the bastard didn't know how to count, but he was a pain, you could see the hunger in his eyes... After that I hated tacos for more than two months, let's see how I'll do with the chicken. You work for what you can in this unequal world, not for what you want ... Although nothing pays as well as making others laugh. Just do the math, fifty of the prize, plus my fee of twenty an hour, seventy dollars! Damn. For less you can get your enemy's head served on a platter in Michoacán ... Macario congratulated me, while I finished getting dressed.

"That's winning, bro, a clown who takes risks and makes people laugh does well, the king would say so." That Macario is funny; I'm almost sure that in the movie he takes some hallucinogenic mushrooms, but I don't remember well. And that in addition to the four kilos of chicken that he eats in one sitting, what a hunger. Dammit. That López Tarso takes the cake—that was the name of the actor with the face of a sly Indian who played the role in the movie. Anyway.

They said my name over the microphone, and I went to collect my prize from the hands of the oldest clown, the racist announcer who was about fifty years old, dressed in a navy-blue suit. Once I had the check in hand, I said loudly in his ear while still smiling at the audience, "Fuck you, piece of shit ..." That's how we get along. I mean, that's how the rules are in this entertainment industry; if you don't talk you don't survive, and in the case that they don't like you and you don't defend yourself, they put you to clean the bathrooms. The two of us, we laughed, hugging each other in the snapshot.

The big guy in first place looked at me contemptuously, I returned the same look and kicked him with bad vibes. It was only then that I realized that he was at least twice as big as me, especially on the sides, a long, bald tractor with a terrible appearance. They made us stop together for the photo. When I stood next to him, I came up to his shoulder. A couple of hostesses took pictures next to us and a supposed reporter with a drunk's pulse and a freeloader's appearance asked us stupid questions. I said goodbye to the crowd, received some applause and left behind the tent. I claimed to feel bad, and I really did. My manager came over and said that we should talk in two days, he had a great offer for me ... I didn't want to know anything about food, was my answer.

"No, not at all, it's something better, you'll see ..." Of course, asshole, that's what I've been hearing since the first day at your company; I didn't even dare to ask him if he was sure of anything, it was that he was humiliating himself a little more and more.

I went out into the street, put the key in the ignition and stayed there for a few minutes, thinking while I downed half a bottle of Melox. *The thing about the handcuffs wasn't in the contract*, I thought, *aha, that was the mistake*. You see, one has to be involved in everything, because if not, you'll eat it. My serious mistake, damn it. I would have refused... but a philosopher of show business once said it: "Once you're in front of the public, nothing matters anymore; if they ask for your skin, then you give it to them, at least until the next show, if you want to survive." Racist, son of a bitch ... How much did the politicians who organized the event give him in bribes for seeing us suffer ...? Motherfucker. "Bad luck this time, bro," Macario told me, adjusting the passenger seat belt. I turned on the radio and put it in first gear. It's paradoxical, don't you think? Coming to the desert to seek luck, the oasis where everything is sand, the good luck abiding in chance itself, abundance in the midst of emptiness ... damn. I accelerated, entered the highway a little over the indicated limit and then I had an epiphany; I would fulfill my dream of being a chef, perhaps a famous one with my own restaurant, a show on television ... well, dreaming costs nothing.

And well, things don't happen by themselves, one thing always comes with another, or vice versa.

20

The other thing was Patricia. I met her one morning after having spent the whole night awake parking cars and arranging coats in the dressing rooms of a private party at an exclusive casino. An incredible place, with a landing strip and a helipad, one of those unique places that the rich love; remote, hyper-secure and discreet. On the surface it looked like a simple country house, although once inside the place grew to twelve stories underground, and like most large casinos it included a hotel, bar, pool and spa. It was called "The Atomic Shelter" and was part of the "International Five Star Hotels" chain, which managed six other casinos, including "El Cosmos," my job for the week. As usual I arrived on time—in this culture it is important; "When in Rome, do as the Romans do," my grandmother used to say, and I like to follow her recommendations as much as possible. I stopped at the guard's booth, showed my ID and the car's permit. I managed to find a spot and parked the car in the first underground parking lot, assigned to permanent and temporary employees. I walked to the elevator, the door opened on the fourth floor. I went to the substation, at the window I was given a maroon suit similar to those worn by hotel bellhops. The manager that night gathered us in a room with round walls—I later learned that it had been part of the observation tower of a truncated project where they planned to sell seats to tourists who wanted to see the atomic bomb experiments.

There would be thirty of us, men and women, already dressed as bellhops and ready to serve the VIPs of the night. We were the weekenders, so we would cover the vacant positions. The guy in charge assigned them to us as we stood in front of him. He sent me and three others to the coat room.

"Of course it is a delicate position, because of the bags, wallets and other valuables, you know?" said the guy, finishing. "So, in the end of your shift you will be subject to inspection by a guard ... okay?"

"Yes," we answered, not very convinced. When you are poor, they suspect you are a thief, although it should be the other way around.

At "The Atomic Shelter" all transactions were carried out with tokens; they could be used at the gaming tables, at the bar or at the slot machines; the same for receiving and returning clothes, as well as for our payments. At the end of the day, we would be given a number of tokens, which we would exchange for cash, depending on how many clients we served. In Las Vegas, many things work with tokens. I have paid for food, drinks, company and even the laundry with tokens. The point is that once the job was over, I changed, and they searched me. I left the parking lot; the sun dazzled me. It was Monday, very early in the morning, and I was walking around with three quarters of my salary on me, the other quarter I had lost playing dice before leaving a couple of hours ago, already a client. Even though there were employee-only bathrooms, employee-only restaurants and even elevators for the staff, as if they were ashamed of us, we could gamble as much as we wanted, as long as we weren't on work hours and weren't wearing uniforms. I was thinking about my hundred dollars lost at craps when I left the dirt road and got on the highway.

I had promised myself not to gamble anymore; either I was unlucky, or the casino was rigged. I have had my streaks.

I decided to forget it for good, even though the reality was that I hadn't been able to contain myself. I'm like a fat guy on a diet who always ends up choking on half an extra cake. A porn addict visiting his favorite page at midnight, what do I know ...? I felt hungry. I decided to go to the cafeteria at the "Nevada Inn" where I was a regular because it was located across the street from my weekday job. The city seemed deserted. I got green lights. Something had happened at The Venetian, as there were a bunch of police cars parked outside the casino. I clicked on my signal, turned onto Flamingo Road and parked on the street, almost putting tokens in the meter instead of coins. I walked down the sidewalk and entered the Nevada. Once inside, I went to the restaurant area. I was craving some eggs with ham and cheese. Rolls and black coffee. I can't function without a strong morning coffee. As I told you, I was one of the regulars there, and it would have been just another day if it hadn't been for Patricia's presence. When I arrived, she was already at the bar with half a *milanesa* and on her second coffee. Karla, the girl who was working at the bar greeted me with a sing-song: "Good morning, good *morning*!"

"Hello Karla," I answered jovially.

"How's your morning going?"

"Great, my dear, I can't complain." She smiled big.

"That's great."

"How's work?" It was her turn.

"Nothing very special, a convention and the national meeting of the baseball leagues in a private casino."

"The second sounds interesting. Did the players come?"

"No, not at all. The ones who came were the bureaucrats from the teams, the ones in suits who are in the offices, speculating with the money. We never saw each other." She looked at me with interest; made a gesture of approval and sweetly asked me: "The usual?"

"Yes. Karla, thank you, only this time with potatoes."

"As you wish."

Karla was a good person; kind, regular, accommodating. I sat down and looked up at the television. Somewhere in the center of the country a man had entered a church with a machine gun and killed twenty people. It was on all the channels: "Another act of unusual violence," said the television presenter who dramatized a little and shed a few crocodile tears.

"'The same as always?' Do you eat the same thing for breakfast every day?"

I listened to the voice next to me. I turned. A seat separated us at the bar. She was a girl who was undoubtedly pretty, with a good body and a bad girl attitude, the latter being the trait that caught my attention the most. I looked at her, studying, and answered: "I come here because they cook well, the food has good ingredients and the price is reasonable."

She put the bite in her mouth and attacked again: "The question was if you eat the same thing for breakfast every day, not if it is cheap or tastes good."

Interested, I looked at her closer. I liked her poise and her way of provoking. Besides liking gambling, I have other bad habits, including a taste for angry and arrogant women; in my country they abound, and I loved at least three of them, among others a cousin on my mother's side, secretly of course.

"It goes without saying, but with different variations according to the menu; sometimes with potatoes, sometimes with ham, with—"

"I don't know if I could do that every day. It's boring, don't you think?"

I liked her eyes. She left the cutlery on the plate, picked up the coffee cup and took a slow sip, all without stopping her cool look at me.

"Oh well, I also come here because it's close to the hotel where I work; it's over there, the one with the 70s spaceship entrance."

"El Cosmos."

"The very same."

"Where the waitresses are dressed like, in space suits from different eras?"

"Exactly ..."

"And what do you do? Are you a waiter, a caddie ... do you take out drunks or cheat women?"

"None of that. My thing is food."

"I chewed in the air looking at her breasts and imagined me biting them."

She liked my mimicry and smiled.

"Cook."

"Yes, that. The art of food."

"Ha, don't be so arrogant."

Karla arrived with my order on a tray and placed in front of me, scrambled eggs with ham, fried potatoes and cabbage with mayonnaise. A steaming cup of strong coffee and toasted rolls in tow.

"Enjoy, Sergio, I'll come back later to tell you what your horoscope says."

"Mm. Thanks, Karlita, I'm really hungry. I didn't have dinner last night."

"Very bad, very bad. Come on, start, it's going to get cold."

"Yes, that's what I say, *The basis of life is food*," Patricia intervened, putting a piece of meat in her mouth.

Karla and I exchanged glances. I turned to look at Patricia and closed my eyes; sometimes I think that was my first mistake, playing the punisher of a torture expert.

21

I woke up at four in the afternoon. I went out to get some breakfast, faced with an empty refrigerator, and bought some toilet paper and toothpaste. I was at the checkout to pay when a front-page story in the Vegas News stunned me: my former manager, Ross, had been caught with several underage girls, exploiting them. I picked up a copy and paid. It described in great detail the intricate network of pedophiles, human traffickers, artists' representatives and police officers involved. After six months of investigation, the FBI had unraveled the web of complicity, criminal associations and links between them. Most of the girls were recruited in Mexico and Central America under false promises, ranging from work as babysitters to offers in the world of modeling and film. Everything seemed very legal and decent, until Tijuana, where the victims discovered their condition. Three safe houses had been searched with more than two hundred girls guarded by former Mexican and border police. Among those involved were high-ranking officials of the Baja California government, immigration agents, artists' representatives and owners of entertainment companies. In addition were a transportation company, a modeling agency and an internet pornography site, of course, active-duty police officers, drug dealers and mobsters.

I arrived home, unpacked everything, put some instant soup on the stove, and sat down on the couch to continue reading. Ross had been caught by surprise by the feds at home, where three thirteen-year-old girls were on their way to another location. They had found him in bed with two of them; they were drugged, and one more was tied up with chains in the bathroom. Another four safe houses had been seized in the Las Vegas area, along with others in California and Arizona. Ten of the little angels were in custody, although other birds had flown away. The affair stank, and already the politicians were preparing to disassociate themselves. Ross and his cronies were charged with rape, pederasty, deprivation of liberty, kidnapping and breach of trust among other offenses. I remembered Ross, his wide smile, his ringed fingers, his gold chains and his cheap pimp attitude. The last straw was when, without warning, he wanted me to participate in a private masochism event. I flatly refused. I've never been interested; I'm one of those who think that love should not be mixed with violence.

"They're girls, it's about hitting them a little ...," he tried to convince me with his coral voice.

"And what if they want it the other way around?"

"Well, you let *yourself* be hit a little."

I remember looking at him incredulously. I couldn't believe what he had just said.

"The women are already inside waiting. The light is kind of dark, so you won't really see anyone, in case that worries you ... Besides, I know you're a good performer and you won't leave me with the audience waiting ..."

He was a rat. I grabbed the black latex suit he was holding out to me with one hand and threw it in his face.

"Fuck you, Ross, you son of a bitch! I've done a lot of things with you, but accepting to be sexually abused? Never, you bastard!" It was the last time I saw him. I was glad I had gotten rid of him. The guy was very manipulative, with a voice like a Judas and the lips of a snake. I remembered what it was like to humiliate yourself for a little money. In life you come across all kinds of people you have to fuck with. Once I was a witness at a wedding, dressed as Elvis Presley. The bride, a forty-something woman in her third marriage, had become obsessed with that idea. Part of the fantasy was that she would spit on me, but as that didn't work in that church, it turned out that the groom, already outside, gave the king two punches. That is, my nose broken for a few coins.

I sat on the terrace drinking coffee in shorts and a T-shirt. For some strange reason, I remembered my grandmother's music box, almost intact, one of the few things that had survived the fire in Hermosillo. According to the story, my grandfather had given it to my grandmother for a wedding anniversary. It was an octagonal Italian box made of white cedar, from which a ballerina rose from the bottom, spinning around its axis to the rhythm of the music. As the music ended, the doll's spins also decreased, until it stopped in the center. I tried to remember where I had been. That led me to think of Gaby, of Carios. I felt nostalgic for my house, for my land, for my family, for what could have been and was not. Did I tell you? Other things that survived the fire were a smoked mirror, a dictionary and a soccer trophy from when I was in high school. Gaby also found some keys that had been lost for a long time, they opened all the doors in the house ... I put my left hand on my chest and sent my loved ones a hug across the distance and across time. At the first opportunity I would call Gaby on the phone. Paradoxes of existence, aren't they? The house was gone with all its doors and the keys appeared; the mirror ended up blackened with nothing left to reflect and the dictionary was the only surviving book of all the books accumulated by my father ... Maybe one day I would return to Sonora, maybe when everything was forgotten, when there was no longer a price on my head.

22

Another day, another morning, but the same life. I crossed the avenue and went to have breakfast before going to sleep. There was Patricia, sitting in the same place. She smiled when she saw me.

"Same thing," she said, pointing at the contents of the plate with her knife. She was indeed eating *milanesa*, potatoes and salad, the same as the previous time, although her comment was clearly a joke.

"You see, it's not always bad to repeat," was my response in the same sarcastic tone.

"Hey ... I was convinced by your story about the good ingredients, the seasoning of the place, the friendly waitress who reads your horoscope and blah, blah, blah."

"Sure, sure. I took off my jacket and rolled up the sleeves of my shirt. I had just started working as a gondolier.

On television they were showing another massacre, this time in a high school. Three boys had burst into the event hall with sawed-off shotguns: the reason, their virginity intact. The death toll was ten people and many wounded. The reporter had obtained a copy of the security footage. In the grainy image, the assassins can be seen entering the place wearing masks of different American presidents; Nixon, Bush 2, Reagan, Clinton. They wear black trench coats, baseball caps. From the stage they bow to the audience and then they shoot in all directions. Commercials.

"Have you tried the atomic cocktail?"

"No, but it sounds like it's going to blow your ears out, or something like that."

"Something like that. Imagine, it has vodka, cognac, sherry and champagne."

"What a beast. Who the hell wants an atomic explosion in their head?"

"I tried it last night."

"And how did it go? Aren't you radioactive?"

"Of course, that's why I'm having the same thing for breakfast."

"You can see it. You *can* see it."

"It's a drink from the fifties, when they were experimenting with nuclear bombs right near here and tourists came to see the explosions."

"I don't believe you."

"Yes, I swear."

"Fuck, they were really idiots."

"Hello, hello ..." Karla came across the bar from me. "Same thing?" she asked with the order pad in the position of someone who is about to listen and write.

I turned my head and looked her in the eyes.

"No... not this time," I said.

Karla lifted her glasses and looked at me strangely.

"Give me a breaded meat, with potatoes instead of onions and tomatoes."

"What happened?" Karla asked intrigued, as if I had broken some rule.

"I just got the urge. Besides, she eats so well that it made me want it."

Karla wrote in her pad and adjusted her glasses again.

"I eat well, what is that?" Patricia gave me a flirtatious look.

She was very flirtatious, she did it with grace, maybe not entirely natural because certain learned attitudes were noticeable. She made the most of the big eyes, certain feminine manners and funny pouts that she knew how to make, I confirmed it later.

"Yes, seeing you eat inspires eating. I mean, when you eat, I get hungry ... or something like that."

Karla closed her notebook and left without understanding anything, there were days when that happened to her.

"And by the way, why did we end up talking about atomic bombs and all that stuff?"

"Ah, I was wondering who the hell comes up with so many stupid things, like those damn cocktails."

"I'll tell you who, the guys from the marketing departments, who can sell you anything, are capable of associating two opposites in a positive light. What fucking association takes a delicious drink, like I believe the daiquiri is, and combines it with an act as stupid and irrational as exploding one or a hundred atomic bombs?"

Patricia stared at me, in astonishment this time.

"Don't tell me that the thing about the kitchen was fake and you're actually a science teacher."

"No, not at all. Someday I'll be a famous chef."

"That's right ... I like the confidence with which you say things."

"Do I really seem confident to you?"

She raised her eyes from her plate, turned her head and looked at me once more. I should have guessed that when I asked her that, I was giving myself to her all on my own; she opened her hand and like a miniature doll I entered there. Her eyes enchanted me, her body without a doubt.

A month later we were living together. She managed my bank account—one of them at least—and I put up with all her bullshit, mistreatment and insults. Not only did I pay the rent and cook, but I became her voyeur, her bodyguard and her driver. Sometimes I wonder why I put up with so much.

Why deny it? Getting married is exciting, nice I suppose for many people; when you find the right person and follow certain rules, but that wasn't my case. I would have liked to of course, although things are sometimes different. With Patricia, I didn't just strip myself physically, but like an onion with its layers removed, I was left without skin. I didn't hide anything from her, I even told her things that I should have kept to myself. For example, that I had started having sex at a very young age and my first experience had been with an aunt when I was eleven years old.

She was a twenty-year-old relative, with big eyes and even bigger tits and wide nipples and lots of hair from her navel to the middle of her ass. A wide ass, which she forced me to lick while she sucked my penis, so that it would develop and grow to a good size once I was a man, she said. At thirteen I was already having sex not only with my aunt, who got married a few years later and I never heard from again, but also with two of my older cousins when they visited us, and with a servant of my mother. Beautiful afternoons of sex, in which I sometimes fucked up to five times a day, all of them secret trysts; either in the bathroom, in the closet, between the curtains in the living room or on the carpet in the bedroom. One of my cousins ran away with a rancher and the other went to Mexico City to study at the university. During those times, for a while, I thought of nothing else, it was my favorite game and the best way to pass the time. I came to distinguish between one pussy and another, between the taste of the honey of the four women who were fighting over me and between the effect of a strong and fast thrust and a slow and deep one with a circular movement.

My undisputed teacher in all this was Juana, the assistant in the store. She was twice my age and had a lifetime of experience in sex, since she had been a prostitute from a very young age to support her family, like a lot of women in my poor country full of satraps. When they all disappeared, little by little, my affection focused on this woman with dark skin, Indian eyes and a robust body who held me with her powerful legs while she gave me instructions. Everything was fine, until my grandmother, who had rescued her from who knows where, began to suspect her other duties at home. My grandmother had taken Juana in as a stepdaughter and she stayed with us until grandma discovered that I also occasionally visited the room where she slept. One afternoon, when I came home from school, Juana was no longer there. I cried for her departure, secretly of course, because secrets in Mexico are kept under the bed, like pornographic magazines accumulated over several years. That was until I started having girlfriends, always older.

I repeat, the only thing interesting to me until I was sixteen was sex. As a sport, as entertainment, as a case study: Julita replaced Juana, but unlike the latter, this woman was old, fat and smelled bad, so both my father and I kept our distance. He became a regular visitor to the brothel in town, as did I, between masturbating and winning over ugly girlfriends who would open their legs easily, some of whom I got during my hours at "La Picolina," where I served them a little more rice or gave them a little extra orange, in the sweets, behind my grandfather's back first. And then, when he died, behind my father's back.

I told Patricia all this and more, because she thought I was naive. Also, I thought that was done in marriages, although she used it all against me later. I also told her how when my mother died, from an eternal illness, my grandmother took care of us despite her age. In those years, until his death, my father concentrated on working like a real madman in the store. On Saturday nights he played cards with his friends in the back, once the metal curtain was down, and on Sundays we went for walks like a normal family, of which Gaby, my sister, was the joy.

I gave myself to Patricia, and I thought she would do the same, until I learned everything little by little. She was not from Arizona, she did not have three brothers as she had told me, but an older sister with whom she had no contact, and her father had not been a celebrated archaeologist of Indian tombs, but a truck driver who disappeared when she turned six. Her mother had died of alcoholism, and from a very young age, she had learned that "two tits move more than two wagons," as my grandmother would say, and that men are hypnotized faster with the eye of the ass than with a smile. She had three versions, all different.

Why did we get married? To be legal and receive a better salary at work as a citizen, to save better, but also for health insurance, and I suppose to make sure that I would be in debt to her forever. Papers in this country are the best thing that can happen to any immigrant of any origin. This is perhaps the only good thing that Patricia did for me, and I thank her for it, despite everything else. The ceremony was one of the most common in vice city; a cocaine-addicted judge who apologized twice during the ceremony to fill his nostrils with powder; a sleepless pianist who listlessly hit the electric organ and a part-time priest, who placed the gold-plated metal rings on us. And to seal our commitment, a tongue kiss, which was bitter because the night before we had gone on a spree. Our witnesses, as in many cases, were strangers: a fat guy to whom we gave twenty dollars and a black woman with a face like Tina Turner at sixty years old. In Las Vegas, I got used to the nightlife and strong drinks, dealing with drunks, gamblers, lucky girls and frauds. Apparently the easy, fun, express life. But I would say difficult, risky, slow and false, like our marriage, which lasted less than two years and left me with a deep wound. Not to mention the bankruptcy. There is a saying that what happens in Las Vegas, stays in Las Vegas. I would say that it is false. What happens in Las Vegas, follows you wherever you go and sometimes for the rest of your life.

23

When Patricia appeared, I had some money saved, a small vehicle and a shared house with Peter. I was what you would call moderately happy—honestly, I have never been completely happy, I suppose like most human beings on this planet. It was a city full of injustice and cynicism, but let's say I was floating with my head above water, and I was the owner of my time and emotions, in general, without many complaints. By that time I had already found a taste for the city. I am very easy; a few months are enough for me to fall in love with the place. The first few months I would park the vehicle and walk along Las Vegas Boulevard, fascinated. Of course my favorite pastime was seeing the women, some of them simply divine. Extravagant people. Not to mention that it was not unusual to find girls on the sidewalk in a hurry dressed like showgirls on their way to a show; Playboy bunnies; fat men dressed as Elvis Presley or Blacks in Michael Jackson costumes. I would stop at some corner and entertain myself watching the fauna. Groups of men in tailcoats holding hands with girls covered in evening dresses and sneakers. Clowns, acrobats, jugglers. In less than an hour, it was possible to see at least three famous people; leaving the luxurious hotels, descending from their enormous limousines, hiding behind dark glasses and hats. I had never seen a limousine the size of an extra-long trailer, which according to Peter could fit a swimming pool and a compact movie theater.

My first few months, without entering the casinos, I had fun. I stood in front of the facades, lit in the spectacular illuminated marquees. I looked at the advertisements, and sometimes, I went in to drink a beer or to put ten, fifteen dollars in some machine. This was more of a pretext, since I went in to cool off from the scorching heat before I went back to observe, recording everything. I stopped, dazed, to watch the elegant roulette players; the drunks who pawned even their shirts on cards; those who, as if insane, cursed in front of the monitors with virtual greyhound and horse races. I have a lot of respect for gambling, and a bit of fear to be honest, but I like it. Two people in my family were inveterate gamblers, a brother of my grandmother and a distant cousin of my father, both ending badly. The first one shot himself in the head and the other killed his daughters and his wife, with whom he bet. After that he went crazy.

I don't know about you, but my blood boils, especially when I'm winning. That's why I try to control myself. Of course I have won, not big of course, but something and that is why it is dangerous, because the mood of a winner is as intoxicating as the feeling after an orgasm with a pretty girl. I have won up to twelve thousand dollars at dice. I think I have always been lucky with dice, and here in Vice City that can be worrying. For that reason, and nothing else, I tried to stay away from gambling as much as I could, until Patricia appeared. She didn't care about my reasons and made me play like her little rooster. We had some very good streaks, no denying it, but I wore myself out. I left my luck in her hands until she consumed it all. From the beginning she sold me the idea that she was my talisman. That our joint luck could achieve big numbers. At first, we did well. I won at kino, at roulette. I compiled enough to buy a used car, designer clothes and rent an apartment for the two of us. We won at horses, dogs, cockfights and boxing matches. I felt like a lucky man; with a red Camaro, money in my pocket and a beautiful woman like the one behind me who whispered magic numbers in my ear. It was true, we made a good couple and according to Patricia; it was a matter of the stars, the zodiac signs and the proximity of the moon to the planet. Sometimes we both thought of the same combination ...

Many things wore out, one of the first signs was that the numbers no longer matched. Our favorites, like twelve and twenty-seven, began to lose; thirty-three, which began as an erotic joke and then became a magic number, didn't come out either. I must confess something, I am lucky, but not great luck, rather mediocre luck. Not bad enough to have a piano fall on my head from above or sink me into an open drain; nor good enough to get out of poverty. I'm winning, I start dreaming and raising the stakes, until I reach a point where I start losing and then I walk away ... like a petty thief with his small win. Once, a few weeks after I met her, with three thousand in my pocket, she started flirting with another guy, and then I got two bad bets. I didn't even get half of it back and I ran away from the bar wondering what had happened. Patricia's presence was like that of a guardian, who protected me for about nine months, until the angel showed the other face.

In Las Vegas, Medusa cut her hair, and all the vipers were reincarnated into people, people like Ross, like Patricia, like the mayor, like many other heartless individuals.

24

From the first day, my favorite casino was NY-NY, which is nothing but a panoramic view of New York City, and it's mind-blowing; all those buildings replicating the Big Apple. It's a huge place inside. I have taken photos next to the Statue of Liberty and next to the Brooklyn Bridge, even confused my brother-in-law Carlos, who got the idea that I was in Manhattan. Another simply spectacular place is "Cheops," where the waitresses dress like Nefertiti and there are real sarcophagi in the reception area where they also display authentic parchment with the legend of a pharaoh. Of course everything here is a joke, like the city itself, where there is also an Eiffel Tower and a Venetian canal, where, by the way, I worked for several months. I dressed in a long-sleeved striped shirt and a little black hat. While rowing on the lake I sang in Italian "*Oh sole mio, la vie en rose ...!*" My sister Gaby would love to see the Eiffel Tower one day, "... the real one of course," she confessed it to me in her last postcard.

In Las Vegas, the only person who never tried to rip me off was my buddy Peter, whom I initially met in LA at a laundry. You know the maxim that the poor are the same everywhere. It turned out that I didn't have enough quarters. The manager, a fat woman with a bad attitude, wouldn't change them. I saw a guy; he was reading an English magazine although he was obviously Latino. We got into conversation. We went outside to smoke while our soapy clothes tumbled in the machines, became friends almost instantly, before the time on the machines was up. We went back to move the clothes from the washer to the dryer; dollar fifty. While this was going on, Peter told me about a trip to Machu Pichu.

"Tremendous energy you feel up there. If you ever have the chance go, you won't regret it."

I told him about my experience at El Pinacate and my entrance into the desert, my exorcism. "I changed planets or times, I don't know. Something happened to me there, something I still can't fully digest, even though it happened several years ago."

Magical places are unique, we agreed. Peter had been in this country for twenty years. He worked part of the year in Los Angeles and the other part in Las Vegas, especially in the summer during peak season. Patricia took me away from him for a while and even tried to poison me against him, telling me that I had grown away from him. Of course I didn't believe her. In Las Vegas, before Patricia, Peter and I became brothers. He knew several tricks: like where to get food stamps, discount coupons on clothes and entry to free events. In addition, he was part of a network of casino employees. They had a pact to give each other discounts or simply turn a blind eye to certain tickets to a show when they could; charge two instead of four and things like that. "If we at the bottom don't help each other, then who will? Especially us Latinos who have been really screwed in this country." I completely agreed.

His job was to be a waiter; setting the table, the cutlery, speaking nicely to the customer; he had learned to carry three plates on each arm. "In this city people come to spend money, bro, you know? Whatever they ask for, do it, and fast, if you want a good tip." At first, he was surprised to see me in Las Vegas. He asked me if I had a girlfriend, a house, friends, a dog that barked at me. *Nothing ... and sometimes I feel super lonely, you don't know,* I told myself in all honestly. When he found out that I lived in a sixth-floor hotel and was tired of sharing a house with twelve people, and that I was about to complete three months in the city, he suggested that I move into his house, "Paying rent of course." I accepted, I was already fed up with the filthy little hotel where every night you could hear people fucking behind their pillows.

"And why do you ask me about the girlfriend? Do you want to get rid of one?" I asked.

"Hehe, Mexicans are so nice; they have the full favor, right?"

"I mean, if it's possible, it wouldn't hurt me."

"What I have is a fiancée and she has friends, none of them is a beauty. It's the truth, but well, maybe some of them meet your expectations."

Pedro was quite a character, just like me, violence had sent him out of his country. Emigrated from Peru, when Shining Path was up to its tricks, he had entered the USA as a refugee. At the university he had received death threats and had to disappear for the sake of his family. Another of the stories he told was when a car bomb had exploded as he turned the corner on his way home. "Just as you hear it, bro; one more minute and I wouldn't be here. The force of the damn explosive managed to knock me to the ground, but I was fortunate not to be hit by any metal fragments." He hadn't finished his degree of course, and he felt a deep resentment toward politicians in general, particularly those of his homeland. In this country he had learned not to question, not to be a busybody, when it was necessary to be a chameleon. He was one and put on camouflage.

Through him I got a job in kitchens and left the difficult world of performance-circus-humiliation-comedy-show business role-play and theater. The opportunity came when in the kitchen of the restaurant, where my friend worked part-time, they fired a guy who was caught spitting on a diner's food while he was taking it to the table. "The idiot was on camera bro. You know these guys like to watch us, so there's the kid spewing phlegm and hiding it in the sauce ... Close up capture of him laughing, they even wanted to send him to jail ...."

Because it was my first time working in a restaurant, they opened a part-time position for me washing dishes, "to start like everyone else," said the head chef. There was no way I could turn down the job. Pedro had recommended me, and to be honest, I was pretty much strapped for cash. Two weeks looking for something in the world of entertainment, without Ross' baton now ... and nothing. Of course, the savings went between feeding myself and paying my share of the expenses to Peter, to whom I told my situation. Without hesitation he interceded on my behalf. A month later the opportunity to start as a waiter in the same restaurant came up, but I was honest with Chef Esteves and decided to wait until they opened a position in the kitchen; I was more interested in learning to cook. That's how I started my career in this creative area of culture, as I like to call it, my true profession. I discovered it when I realized the implicit art of mixing substances and educating the tongue. Talking with Chef Esteves, I came up with the plan to study to become an international chef and later ask for a job on one of those cruises so I could visit many cities. Cooking and having a good time was what I wanted. "Having raw substances and ingredients and transforming them into a tasty dish made by you is something that fills anyone with satisfaction." Esteves' words. They say that people don't change from one day to the next, but one morning I realized that doing insignificant jobs wasn't going to get me anywhere, much less betting on dice. On the other hand, if I became a chef, I could have prestige, work and reach a dignified old age, something that was starting to worry me.

Peter's apartment wasn't very big, a small bedroom and a living-dining room, as well as a kitchen and bathroom. The place was nice, I told him, but sleeping on the couch was like being a visitor and I didn't like that, especially when my plan was to settle down for at least a couple of years in Las Vegas. What's more, the problem wasn't the accommodations, but a certain minimum privacy. I didn't have much money, but I had enough to put up a couple of screens and give some privacy to the area that would be "my room."

"It's different if you see my feet, or my head, than if you see me naked, don't you think? It's a bit embarrassing, both for me and for you."

"True ... what if you want to masturbate?"

"Haha! It usually happens."

We moved the old and heavy leather sofa to a corner, on one of the rugs and rearranged the other two chairs and the coffee table aside.

"Right Peter, two screens and this little space to enter. What do you think? This is how this other space looks for watching TV, sitting on the individual sofas. Come on, it's not for dancing, but it can be a small multipurpose room."

"Damn, you're an artist at arranging, bro. Did they teach you that at school?"

"Ha, ha, ha. I'm thinking what if one day I bring a girl. That way at least I know no one is watching us; this thing of seeing each other is not my thing."

"If you want, we can rotate."

"Rotate what? The girl?"

"No, the bedroom! Six months I'm in and the other six you're out here, keeping up the place."

"Really?"

"Sure, if the rent is half."

"I like it, that's camaraderie." I extended a hand.

He took my hand and bowed like in the 18th century.

"The chair is incredibly comfortable," said Peter. "It's leather as you can see, the inheritance from the previous tenant."

"Did you know him?"

"Yes, an Argentinean who escaped from the dictatorship. When the country returned to democracy he went back. He transferred it to a previous renter, and then he transferred it to me; the chair came with the package, you know, nothing comes alone. The owner of the apartment is a lady, she was a waitress at the Stardust, super cool."

"It's a deal."

We sealed it with a handshake.

"Just one thing, don't just disappear like you did in Los Angeles. Are we ...? What happened?"

"Bah, it's a long story, I'll tell you someday."

"Okay. At least don't forget to say goodbye."

"Sure, sure ..." I said, evaluating the space in that small apartment. "Where would you buy some screens at a good price?" I asked him.

Peter smiled.

"I know exactly where, it's a huge store where they sell a lot of things, a few real antiques, but old things in good condition, nothing Chinese. I worked part-time there when I first came to Vice City. They have a lot of things, they're from old people who die and don't have anyone to leave their belongings to, from hotels that go bankrupt. The owner buys lots of stock month after month. Everything shows up there. That mirror on the wall is from there, that vase and that Van Gogh."

I walked to the Van Gogh, the reproduction was worn, eaten by the sun; must have been many years old behind that obviously cheap frame. But it was Van Gogh, and he was still one of the geniuses of painting within everyone's reach.

"Cool, bro, we should take a walk. Recycling things is the best thing that can happen to this world."

In the restaurant kitchen we recycled almost everything, not just product packaging and jars. I imagined my space with decorated Chinese screens.

"We could use a small table here and a small lamp for reading on top, don't you think, Pete?"

"Of course. We'll find something nice, you'll see. We'll go tomorrow; they open at nine."

"No more talk. Where will I put my clothes?"

"There are two small closets in this room," I followed him. "In this one I have some junk that I can put in the trash. As you can see, it's not big enough to store a wardrobe, but it's decent.

I laughed to myself. Peter sounded like a real estate salesman. Needless to say, we shared not only a house, but memorable moments. One of our favorite activities during the week was going to the hotel and casino pools to have a drink, see women and swim a little. We would sneak in, drink at half price and get a taste of the luxury that money offers. Peter's network of friends was quite large. You had to arrive at a specific time, through a specific door and stay in a specific area of the pool without attracting too much attention. We went to concerts, the circus, to see comedians. When we were free, we would drive to California, other times we would dress up as elegant guys, go into a casino and walk around courting women, especially the old ones—not too clear in the head—they are the ones who come loaded with money to go crazy in Vice City. One time we ended up sleeping in a two-bed room with a countess and her twin sister. The next morning we took turns in beds to see what faces the blue-blooded old ladies would make, but instead of shocked faces they seemed to enjoy the joke and so we were there for three days, jumping on beds doused in cheap champagne, Chinese food and pizza.

Peter didn't believe in God; he hated the Spanish for what the murderous conquistadors had done, and he thought that politicians were the evil of everything in this world. Like me, he loved women, although today he is married and a faithful husband. By the time Patricia appeared on the scene, I was also part of Peter's network of friends, and I knew several secrets, like he had already had two girlfriends. One was a Nicaraguan consumerist in the wide range of the country, junk products, junk food and junk culture. The other was a Colombian with a beautiful ass, who only thought about banalities and money. Her name was Andrea, she built dreams in the air and had unoriginal fantasies. "Entering one of those places and sitting at the bar makes me feel rich for a moment, and I love that ..." she used to say. "One day I will return to Colombia with a suitcase full of money." With one I lasted two weeks and with the other, especially because of the beautiful rump, a month. There were also two maids, one a close friend of Peter's fiancée, the other a Facebook friend. By the time Patricia crawled into my bed, I was free of Ross, driving a used four-cylinder pickup truck, fresh from an ice-sculpting class taught by an expert dessert chef, and had begun living alone in the apartment full-time since Peter had decided to move in with his girlfriend in Washington, DC.

25

Through Pedro's network, I bought tickets for a concert, tickets for a dance and booked a room in an expensive hotel for two nights with champagne and all the trimmings, just to impress her.

"Hello, handsome," Patricia said, just out of the bathroom in her underwear and T-shirt, and in one swift movement she got under the covers where my arms were waiting for her.

I looked at her. That's why a pack of men were chasing her, others were paying to see her and the rest were sighing as she passed.

"How are you, beautiful?" I answered.

"Cold. Hug me."

Patricia settled between my arms and legs. There was no light between us; we were that close. I remember thinking how lucky I was to have a female like that.

"I have three days free in front of me, to do whatever I want."

"Mm, that sounds dangerous. And what are you thinking of doing?" I said.

"I'm open to listening to proposals," she said, smiled and gave me a passionate kiss.

It was our first date without clothes, our first weekend together, and I was fascinated by the hot body I had seen spinning on the pole. That was perhaps one of the most beautiful weekends of my life, I think. I even thought I had fallen in love with her, although later I learned that women like that never belong to just one man. It's true, from the beginning I knew she was a desired and sexually fluid woman, a woman very aware of her charms. What I didn't know was that she was also a liar, that she was ambitious and manipulative. *Nobody changes*; it's a very true saying. A bad queen for whom I not only lost all my money and savings, but also forever the trust and luck in women. But hey, who understands the heart? She made me joyful like a puppy, but all the same she kicked me out of my own apartment, she kept the savings destined to pay for culinary school, and I managed to be a puppet.

The first clue that I didn't notice was the sale of the big sofa in the living room, the same one where Peter and I took turns sleeping. One day I came home, and it was gone. At first, she said she had lent it to a friend, because she slept on the floor. Later she told other friends that she had sold it as an antique. In another version of the story, she had gotten rid of it to set up her studio through a company associated with public charity. In yet another, it was a piece of junk full of fleas.

We usually despise those who love us, who care about us and make an effort to please us. So we go through life, devaluing selfless affection when it is offered to us; perhaps because we are too used to things costing and nothing being free. *If I had stayed with the Colombian ...* On the other hand, those who treat us like donkeys, we love them more; it is a form of hypnotism between human beings, and I fell for it. I cooked for her, cleaned the place where we lived, was her driver and when she wanted money, she took it from my account. Later I opened another one, which by some miracle I managed to save, thanks to Peter's advice. At first the sex was a marathon, soon after she reduced it to a limp, as well as the baths together and the romantic outings, we mostly went out for work reasons. In the end I found out, she had a rich boyfriend who invited her to expensive places; an old man of course. She had met him in one of the clubs where she gave shows; some of those places were really degrading. Needless to say, Las Vegas has its touristy part in Downtown, but like every city it has its places for the locals; the filthy and seedy bars, the poor and sometimes illegal casinos in the slums, the betting houses set up in private homes. The barracks for dog and cockfights. The Las Vegas that doesn't appear in the movies, the sordid part of a sordid place that was very well lit and had a good mood.

We slept during the day. Around 4:30 she would start cooking and we would eat about six. We would talk about nonsense; about the news, about friends and about things that happened to other people. She preferred it that way, she almost didn't like to talk about us, much less about the future. Sometimes when we had different shifts, we would barely see each other, we would give each other a soft kiss on the lips and she would go back to sleep or I would, depending. After eating we would shower, get ready and go out together. I would drop her off and sometimes pick her up. Going to dinner at five in the morning was normal for us, having a drink at eight a.m. was a regular thing. Patricia knew a lot of girls with problems, noisy little homosexuals and mean-looking guys who were regularly outside the clubs, casinos and bars. Among the butterflies that surrounded her, there was one, Sharon, who made me feel sorry for her. She was beautiful, but as stupid as they come and had the worst self-esteem I've ever seen in anyone. Her agent exploited her like crazy and we suspected he was using her to make hardcore porn, although she didn't cop to it. She took Oxy regularly for pain, according to her, and carried a valid prescription with her at all times. She ate like a bird. Patricia had taken her under her wing and sometimes she would sleep, fried, on our floor. after selling the couch—this is the real version—she set up her rehearsal studio. One of her filmmaker friends gave her two lights and a blue background to take pictures, although that's another story.

I felt sorry for Sharon, so I cooked her delicious things I learned from Don Estevez, and she appreciated it. Patricia got jealous. She was perhaps the first woman I made fall in love with food. She confessed to me that eating my stews was better than having sex. She was my third platonic love after my cousins, Marilú and Fernanda. I didn't touch her, although I did see her naked. She would get into bed with us while we were sleeping, and at least a couple of times she would burst into the shower while we were bathing. It's not that she was ugly, on the contrary, but she seemed so fragile that she produced more of a filial love in me. I think we both understood it, there were flirtations on her part, on my part, but we both knew that sex would end our friendship. Once she told me, in one of those phrases she used to say, some silly, others very interesting: "When I chew your food, I eat a part of you." Or: "Sometimes I see you as someone who penetrates my palate." Patricia would look at her disapprovingly and laugh, sometimes she was cruel. "Don't say silly things, silly girl, and eat ..."

If I had had more resources I would have helped her, although it was difficult because of her propensity for bad decisions; for keeping nefarious people around her. I didn't know that she put on a show with Patricia from time to time until much later, when Sharon had disappeared from our lives. Some said she married a rich man who paid for her rehabilitation, others said she ended up as a street prostitute, still others said she died of an overdose in a hotel. I found the video by chance in a folder on my computer, and I watched it all. They had a cameraman. Patricia and Sharon were kissing and undressing each other on a chair where they ended up fucking, screaming. I recognized the place; everything had been filmed in the corner of the apartment, the same space that had been turned into a studio. The cameraman should have been me, but it was someone else; the bitch brought men into my place, which filled me with rage. She brought others in while I worked in my kitchen. She produced her pornography for money in my house and had fun with her friends at my expense.

One thing, I think I already told you, my luck was better than ever at that time. Every night she would be behind me, cheering me on, kissing me on the mouth, whispering little things to me, making my opponents jealous, provoking them. One night I made five thousand dollars in three bets. Contrary to my rules I continued betting and went up to eight thousand dollars, but I fell again and went up for several hours; that night they gave us a room in the casino and all the champagne we wanted. We were like two parts of the same talisman, she told me after making love for two hours.

26

How did I end up living with Patricia a few weeks after we met? How did she convince me to marry her? I suppose it was because of her statuesque figure, the wonderful way our bodies fit together, or her pussy with big lips that sucked me dry; not only the principles instilled by Grandma, but the soul itself ... How did she come to manage my bank account? I don't remember. The truth is that I swallowed all her dirty tricks, her mistreatment and her snubs one by one, because I really came to love her like no one else. At the beginning of our relationship she was a very nice person. I was heartbroken about her being orphaned at twelve, about the kind uncle who took care of her in exchange for sex twice a week. About the alcoholic father murdered by another drunk with a weaponized beer bottle. About her sister with six children from an abusive husband, to whom she sent money. About her desire to leave the hustle environment and start studying, about marrying me if I gave myself to her. I don't know how much was true and how much was a lie; what I am sure of is that the witch did something to me, there is no doubt. I don't say the witch thing in a figurative sense, either. She used magic, voodoo and herbal medicine. Don't you believe in that? I didn't believe it either until I lived it.

One morning it took me a long time to stand up, it was as if a tombstone was blocking my way. My breathing stopped, I started to sweat, I was buried in the mattress up to the springs; I was conscious, but I was motionless. It wasn't until she appeared in the bedroom and spoke to me that I came to, gulping air as if I were emerging from the bottom of a pool. Other times I started to get stupid, that is: things fell out of my hands, food burned, I headed toward something without remembering the purpose, I bought unnecessary things, I was very distracted when naturally I am not like that. What convinced me was when I discovered, looking for a birth certificate among old boxes and under some rags, two dolls. They were rather crude dolls, made of cloth with pieces of clothing and hair. They were tied separately, with needles stuck in their hands and feet, gagged. I observed them in detail. I discovered that one of them had my hair, the pieces of clothing tied to it came from a lost change of clothes. It was a shock. I didn't quite understand, it seemed partly a joke in bad taste, partly a prank, but also something more macabre. Thorns sprouted on my spine when I fully realized; one of those little dolls *was* me. Who was the other one?

That needle in the back of the doll was the reason why my back hurt, the other one in my chest was the reason why I had a sore throat. I was frozen, the woman I lived with had me under a spell. My first reaction was to complain to her, to make a fuss, to put the gypsy in order. I thought about killing her, I was that scared. I thought a lot; there was no doubt, she was operating miles ahead of me. It irritated me not to suspect that she had her little stash, her alchemy, her sexual smells, the damn dolls and her ritualistic bullshit. I was very upset. I have never touched a woman with my fists, maybe pulled her, shouted at her, but I never hit her, I don't know how. Besides, my parents were very strict about that. I still remember when I was young, no one speaking to me for a week, it was the punishment imposed for hitting Gaby. The voodoo dolls were the straw that broke the camel's back. I wanted to squeeze Patricia, grab her by the neck like a chicken and tear it apart.

That discovery made me realize my hypnotic state; it was like taking off a blindfold. I began to put two and two together, to discover a lot of games and manipulations. That fucking Patricia had been playing with me the whole time. I decided not to say anything, to play along. The bitch came back very calmly, we gave each other a lazy kiss on the lips, she put on her house clothes and began to pour herself a drink. I looked at her out of the corner of my eye, studying her. How was it possible that a western, North American girl turned out to be a total fucking witch, with knowledge of *toloache* and voodoo? I was friendly for the last time and served her food. She smiled at me with that smile that had melted me in the past; the same one she used in her rituals, probably. I smiled back, I didn't want to arouse suspicion. By the time this happened, I had already done some things that I morally regretted; I had entered into a draining relationship, and from being jealous I had gone to being a voyeur. I wasn't going to tell you about this scene, but here it goes.

27

I finish masturbating, the floor and my hand slick with an oily shine under the dim light. In the background the panting of Patricia, who is being fucked by two young men with big cocks like animals. What had excited me minutes before now hurts me deeply. It is a moral issue of course, something that is affecting me more than I thought when I started the game.

However, I must admit that I was guilty of that damned petty situation myself. I was never more confused; it was an aberration. The fact is that I didn't get erections if I didn't see others having them. Patricia was delighted of course, especially if she saw me suffer, she was a filthy and increasingly degenerate harpy, although I loved her like crazy; I got sick. It wasn't necessary ... all those bastards, damn it. She convinced me to change the rules, I don't know why I accepted.

We were at the bar; it was our second honeymoon. We had been drinking since early in the morning, and by dinner time I was feeling sloshed, but also excited ... She insisted on inviting a woman she met on the way to the bathroom to our room, she told me. She got her way; it was a fun, sex-filled night, but a difficult, reproachful morning. Then she brought up the subject of men. If two women had been fun for me, how about the other way around? Over the next two months we were intimate with other people on at least ten occasions. On one of them, I kissed a guy while Patricia played with us. She introduced me to threesomes and partner swapping, and our sexual fantasies stopped being that and became reality. If I hadn't loved her, maybe it wouldn't have been so difficult.

I wiped my hands with a dirty towel, crossed the threshold of the bedroom and listened to Patricia's muffled moans and the slapping of the three bodies. Once I had discharged my libido, I clenched my jaw to avoid the nausea that this scene produced in me. I entered the kitchen. I opened the refrigerator and grabbed a beer. Naked as I was, I stopped at the threshold and watched the three of them move in unison, as if they were one beast. One penetrated her from behind and the other enjoyed her sweet lips. The mirror showed me the image of Patricia with her eyes rolled back in her head at the attacks of those two animals. They pushed as if they were lifting weights in a gym. They began a new kind of dance and the men alternated positions; it stank of body, of ass. I crossed the room again and went to the door of the porch, I couldn't take it anymore.

I grabbed my underwear on the way to the terrace. I lay down on one of the wicker chairs, looking at the mountains in the distance. I lit a cigarette. I felt bad ... After all, morals and ethics are what keep us in working order. I knew it, and I had broken with both of them, driven by that slut. I let myself be brainwashed and manipulated.

I took a second drag on the cigarette. I was suffering; it was hard for me to admit it, but I was suffering abysmally. I had the feeling of someone who has jumped out of a plane and doesn't know how to open the parachute. I blew the smoke out of my mouth as if I were letting out a last sigh. I held my head. I had already been warned, not all damned sexual fantasies should be carried out, you always have to leave something to the impossible.

We had agreed to meet to go to the movies. I found her talking to a young blonde, apparently, he had lost a lot of money in bets. According to him, he bet on everything; Greyhounds, horses, football, wrestling, baseball, kino, two flies if they fought, whatever. In winter he rested, and usually, he traveled to her parents' house in California, where he took advantage of the opportunity to surf, he loved it. I finished my second glass of gin. During all that time I didn't talk, nor did I make any comment. I pretended not to know her, although I noticed I had an erection. It was strange, seeing her talking so close to that guy gave me great pleasure. She wiggled, laughed, looked provocatively at that unsavory blonde, showed him her legs. I adjusted my penis under my pants, seeing her there like any other female looking for a male without my direct participation, was a new experience. I raised my glass and went to sit next to her. The blonde reacted angrily.

"Hey, friend, the girl and I are together! Move!"

I smiled and said, "The girl is none other than my wife, in case she hasn't told you."

The blonde looked at her strangely. It was she who spoke.

"Okay, okay ... it's true, but we're fighting, so pretend he's not here."

"But I am, you understand?"

"You're not here," she said coldly and froze me with her gaze. Then she laughed and tipped the glass all the way down, she looked drunk.

I turned to stone, speechless.

"*Ciao bello*," she spat at me with the worst of her faces. She approached the blonde and whispered in his ear. "If you want to come, follow me." Patricia adjusted her skirt, letting the blonde see her wide and well-proportioned rear, which she moved hypnotically until she went out the door. The blonde stood up. He took some bills out of his pocket and threw them on the bar, then ran to the door. I knew where they were going, so I drank my drink calmly and waited for the commercials on television. *They say that fire is put out with fire* ..., I remember thinking. *How about cynicism with cynicism?* I paid and took a bottle of tequila with me, hiding it under my clothes until I got home.

When I opened the door, my wife was kissing the blonde, who had already taken off his shirt and pants. They both looked at me strangely. Patricia, surely wondering why I had dared to come up and not wait until that faded wretch came out forty minutes later. The blonde seemed to see it as some kind of a joke. I showed them the bottle, I knew there wasn't a single drop of alcohol at home. My wife broke free from the other's arms and came to me smiling, with her arms open, she looked really drunk.

We went to the kitchen, my hand open on her wide buttocks. The blonde came behind us, the drunkenness had diminished. He had his shirt in one hand, his pants on. He seemed upset, perhaps thinking he was a clown, so I handed him one of the glasses. The three of us drank hastily and refilled our drinks. Patricia looked flushed. I went to the stereo and put on some blues. I took her in my arms, and we began to move rhythmically. She looked at me somewhat confused from her drunkenness, perhaps evaluating my mood. I didn't open my mouth, a serious mistake.

The blonde put his shirt back on, perhaps a little disconsolate because I had ruined his party, and was already walking toward the exit, when Patricia called him and he came to join us. The blonde began to lick her legs, while I pulled her dress off her arms. She looked shaky, wet. The blonde took off his pants and shirt again like an expert. I left them playing for a while, dancing. I went to pour myself another drink.

My wife kissed him tremulously, then she withdrew from him. The blonde lifted her up and I could see his erection, he had a rather small penis. He put her on the chair and began to poke at her pussy while he jerked himself off. It looked very hot. For my part, I took off my clothes and went to sit next to Patricia, she greeted me with her mouth open. She looked me in the eyes, this time I didn't understand her look. She herself was the one who reached for the lamp and turned it off to remain in darkness. You can imagine the rest. In the end, we both possessed her, the three of us kissed.

I'm not going to deny it, that first time was a bit strange for the two of us, especially the whole scene after. The guy sneaked out an hour later when Patricia began to cry, supposedly repentant. I also acted ashamed. Today I know that she lied, because behind the scenes she made me do things and took decisions that seriously affected me. For more than three days after that encounter we spoke little, always with the light off, without touching each other or touching the subject, which began to grow like a wall between us.

As we all know, once an effect is unleashed, the most that can be done is to belabor the cause. The fact is that nothing was the same between us again. The couples' clubs, the bars, the cruises, the alumni meetings, the sexual colloquiums or the private orgy parties at very high levels were not a surprise anymore. Neither were the couples who exchange their wife for the wife of the member, the friend or the gym buddy. All that is normal today, in fact, there are thousands of swingers on the planet who live without problems for years and sometimes for life, raise children, love each other, etc. Patricia wanted to drag me into that, fortunately she couldn't, perhaps due to my inevitable burden of Catholicism, my complexes, I don't know ...

The fact is, that at the point, I didn't enjoy it anymore. It wasn't that I suddenly became moralistic, but as soon as I looked away, she was already sucking off the first guy who came along; she missed a couple of weekends supposedly working in a private casino, earning very well. For Patricia it was all about money. She said things like: "They gave me a beautiful room, all for me, alone ..." She showed me her pay, a bunch of twenty-dollar bills from inside her wallet. One night of drinking she told me, looking me in the eyes, that she liked to give pleasure to two men at the same time, she realized, she loved it. She felt beautiful. Being loved by two men at the same time was a supreme act ... I begged, insisted, implored for things to return to their original course, but it was impossible. The last two months with her were the longest and most painful ones in my life.

I heard Patricia scream; it seemed like they were about to finish their little game. The damn beer tasted like cyanide. Those animals never tired, one of them started howling like a wounded dog. I covered my ears. It was terrible to feel helpless. Who knows the reason, but the fact is that as soon as she touched me, I was already ejaculating, *mmm,* like a fountain, it was ridiculous. I saw her walk naked around the room and *boom*, she left them there.

The last straw began when I stopped participating in the games and she seduced me enough to watch and jerk myself off, while she writhed in the middle of the men, always willing and within her reach. It was as if I were watching a three-X movie, just for my eyes and with the woman I had married. All that, all those guys who came and went every weekend. I suffered the most during that time; it was a martyrdom that I came closer to every day. Just looking at the faces of the new men who would fuck Patricia was torture.

One Friday afternoon I found her sweating with three. I couldn't stand the scene and went to the cinema to watch an action movie, just to forget. When I came back, she was preparing dinner, like any other normal wife in the planet. One thing I must say, in a way she protected my place in front of her friends, acquaintances and clients; none of them stayed overnight at our house, nor did they sit at our table to eat and neither did any of them wear my clothes, not even my bathrobe. At first, they went on and off, sometimes they had a beer, but it didn't go any further, and thank goodness, otherwise I don't know how I would have endured it ... You might wonder if I didn't want to kill her. Of course I thought about it, to murder her while those pigs were fucking her. You think not? Because I'm not made of rubber. However, deep down, I just wanted to go back to my traditional marriage, as far as possible toward normalcy.

I heard the door close. I assumed the two guys were leaving. Thank goodness, Monday and another quiet week ahead. I took a sip of my beer; the siren of a patrol car broke the quiet of the afternoon and moved away until it disappeared. I heard noises in the kitchen. The door to the porch opened and when I supposed I would see Patricia in one of her stunning robes, a naked guy of about twenty-four years old appeared, with dark skin and average build. He had one of my beers in his hand. He sat down in one of the armchairs. We greeted each other with a nod. I observed him. He looked well-endowed and in good shape.

"I hope you don't mind, I took a beer from the refrigerator."

I looked into his eyes. I thought if he could mount my wife, why couldn't he drink one of my beers?

"No problem." I said.

He looked familiar. It was not perhaps the first time I saw him at home. I tried to remember a little. I had seen him around there on at least two occasions. Something was wrong. That was against the agreement. No regulars, or the same men. Why was that clown sitting next to me? What was that bastard trying to tell me, stroking his reddened penis like a dog cleaning itself? The guy was strong, although he didn't intimidate me; I'm good with blows, especially when I want to give them. I glanced at him out of the corner of my eye, he looked thirsty, he was still sweating. *Anyway*—I thought—*let him drink his beer, then leave*. I felt disgusted. I drank the rest of the liquid in the bottle and placed it on the table between the armchairs. The terrace door opened again, and Patricia's face appeared. She looked radiant, really beautiful and I couldn't help but smile. I loved her, those men could have her for a day, a weekend, bite her, suck her, ejaculate in her mouth, but that beautiful woman was mine—she slept with me, lived with me and we shared that apartment. Those beautiful almond-shaped eyes, that voice that burst into laughter and said my name and charmed me, belonged to me.

"Want another beer, guys?" she said now, smoothing a curl over her face.

"Yeah," we said almost in unison, which bothered me a little. What was I doing? I looked at my watch, it was time for the guy to leave ... I suddenly thought either he was a fucking cynic, or I was a double idiot. Although, on the other hand, I didn't want to bother Patricia, she looked so good, so splendidly beautiful that I didn't do anything else. Anyway, one more beer, *then* I would kick him out.

Patricia came back with two open bottles, chewing something. She was wearing a very short blue robe, it covered her just a little above her thighs. She handed me a beer, another to the guy. She sat on my lap and pulled me in with her arms:

"I love you," she whispered in my ear, kissed me with her lips closed and caressed my penis under my underwear.

"I put on some pasta, and I'm going to make a salad ... I'm hungry as a lioness," she said and gently bit my ear. all those cuddles in front of the guest never ceased to surprise me. She kissed me again. I hugged her waist, kissed her on the cheek, she smelled like sex, like a satisfied woman. I watched as she glanced at the guy, whose penis was starting to grow again. Patricia separated her legs a little, she wasn't wearing panties. She smiled, stood up and went to the man to kiss him on the mouth too. He extended his arms to attract her, but she playfully let go and then said something that I didn't quite understand, or that I didn't want to hear clearly.

"I made some space in the closet ..." She walked to the door to the kitchen. "Lloyd is staying to eat with us," she said, this time looking me straight in the eyes.

I almost threw up my mouthful of beer.

"How? What?" I choked.

The guy blew her a kiss, while continuing to stroke his cock. I shook my head, I still couldn't catch my breath, my hands were shaking. Patricia adjusted her robe, turned to look at us, this time as if her gaze could cover a very large area. She sighed and said: "I am the happiest woman in the world ..." She smiled again, winked at us and disappeared through the door to the kitchen.

It was with that bastard Lloyd that she ran off with. I had shared a wife for something like fifteen days, until I found the dolls in the attic, until I got tired. In any case it was too late; I had already given him all my money, auctioned off my Camaro and lost my pride. She borrowed the money from me to supposedly pay off a debt to the mafia. Don Cellucio, her boss, had made her sign a contract blindly. It included exclusivity, and she had been discovered doing things for another "company." The point is that she had to pay for her mistake in cash. If she didn't make the payment, they would break both her legs or something worse. With the sale of the car and most of my things, which she also auctioned off over the internet, she and her boyfriend would make about twelve thousand dollars in cash, plus a credit card that she maxed out, along with two overdue rent notices. When I tried dice, I discovered that I had also lost my luck.

Bad company brings bad company, the saying goes, and I don't know to what degree Patricia got involved with the mobsters, because if you don't know, the casinos don't only belong to hotel chains, big entertainment corporations, Wall Street investors and "decent" people like Hugh Hefner; but also to shady characters related to prostitution, drug trafficking and money laundering. Elegant men who live in mansions, drive expensive cars, have political connections and an armed wing for difficult cases. In Las Vegas it is not frowned upon to be a mobster, in fact there is a museum of the underworld where the gangster Bugsy Siegel, owner of the Flamingo, is the main star. He is considered a visionary. The fact is that she didn't pay the mafia. She said that I would pay them.

One morning, I was awakened by the barrel of a gun on my forehead. They were Don Cellucio's men, and they wanted their money. No matter how much I told them I didn't know anything—and I got tired of explaining to them that I had given her the money for the payment—no matter how much I tried to convince them, it was of no use. The two big men didn't believe me, they forced me to get dressed amid strong pushing and slapping. I had to go with them, but not before they turned the apartment upside down. In the car, one of them sat with me in the back and kept pointing his big gun at my chest. We entered through the side door of the casino, Don Cellucio greeted me in person.

"In addition to the money, I want the videos of the mayor's son having sex with a friend of hers."

"Videos? The mayor's son?"

"She also made a video or took photos of one of the city councilmen," said a second big man, lieutenant of the old boss.

"What the fuck are you talking about?" I managed to say.

"Don't play dumb, asshole, you and the other faggot who lives in your house are accomplices."

"I swear, I don't know anything ... and I'm not a faggot."

"Now you deny it?"

"I work in a kitchen eight hours a day and sometimes at night."

"Everything was done in your house, by my order."

I couldn't even explain to them that I had been deceived, used, manipulated, and that really, I was just a poor innocent cook in the hands of a witch.

"I don't know anything."

A third big man came and hit me so hard he knocked the wind out of me and made me choke.

28

In Hermosillo, violence arrived in the blink of an eye, knocking on the door of my house and entering with guns drawn. First it passed like air, settled on us like an amorphous cloud and finally fell on us like a thunderclap. It was a spiral of evil that came out of its container, like the demons living in Pandora's box, and it devoured us in its curved walls. The violence, which few of us knew about, unloaded its heavy carry, cut down the palm tree in the oasis and went into the water with boots and all.

My father, Gaby and I were having dinner, Doña Julita serving us, when we heard gunshots. Dining together was one of the few traditions we kept from the time when my grandmother was still alive. The first thing we thought of was the typical drunk celebrating his birthday with fireworks. We realized it was a battle when the shots increased in intensity. Then we heard the sound of an explosion. My father forced us to lie under the table and ordered Doña Julita to turn off the light. The four of us crawled into the room between the dining room and the stairs. The shots began to sound closer, and the glass in the windows shattered into fragments. We heard screams, car engines, screeching tires.

My sister burst into tears and my father hugged her. Julita began to pray next to me in a low voice and took my hand. Doña Julita was the lady who worked in our home, since my mother fell ill with cancer, and she helped my grandmother in her bed during the years in which time consumed her. After about forty minutes of the shooting battle and tension, there was a deathly silence, during which we did not move.

The first to stand up was my father, crouching down he returned to the dining room and looked out onto the street through one of the windows. I followed and stood beside him. Outside everything was red, as if the white light of the street-lamps had been replaced by the red light of a disco. Some cars were burning, there were dead people lying on the asphalt. We heard the church bell, the sirens of the patrol cars and then the sound of the city slowly coming back to life. Like other neighbors, we went out into the street and discovered with horror some ten men hanging from the streetlamp posts. The drug dealers, in a theatrical display, had spray painted the lights red. The victims had the same message painted on a piece of cardboard hanging around their necks: *We were you, the shadows will come to end in the landscape, and the cowards will die of terror, because fear reigns in this world, prepare to pay for it.* All of them showed signs of torture and were half naked. There were also other dead people, next to cars with the engines still running; it was a grim scene. My father could not hold back his tears and hugged us, as if he sensed something worse was about to happen.

Carlos Alpizar, the neighbor and my sister's boyfriend—behind my father's back, of course—approached us and my sister ran to hug him. Carlos was a good person. We had known each other since we were children, and we were lifelong friends since he lived next to us.

The news of the "takeover" of the square, as they called it, occupied not only the front pages of local newspapers but was also national news on television; the radio commentators chewed it over for several weeks until they tired of it. The war continued for several months in our city. Every night there were shootouts in different streets, neighborhoods turned into battlefields with burning patrol cars, dead people, chases, crashed cars and the sound of machine guns. "Long Knives" versus "The Men of the Middle Ages" was what the warring gangs called themselves. Other dead people followed, hanging from pedestrian bridges, not only members of one side or the other, but also police officers, journalists and public servants. The escalation of violence seemed to have no end and became an everyday occurrence. An expert from the University of Sonora said in a radio interview: "The problem with violence is that when one thinks it has reached its peak, it always surprises us, because there are always new ways to honor it." Dead people hanging from lamp posts and trees, turned into heads separated from bodies, hands and arms piled up on the awnings of cars, outside the municipal palace, at the entrance to the church and on the benches of the main avenue, containers with eyes, tongues, penises and testicles, internal organs in pots outside the police station. Sheer panic. Kidnappings, extortion, revenge and vigilantism was also happening. And although the city and we, its citizens, tried to lead a normal life, the cloak of night reminded us that these were different times, and we had to be cautious and hide.

As if by agreement, the moment the sun set, the war began. People stopped going to parties, for a drink, to the movies, to serenade their girlfriends; they simply didn't leave their homes. The violence was a dark cloud in the sky, and blood claimed victims. That is how the city became a wasteland of shadows, where the only thing that flourished was the fear of others, the total fear that does not forgive, that corners.

During that period there were a couple of national scandals: the photograph of the state governor having dinner with the head of the new bosses who were ravaging the area, "Los

Cuchillos Largos," and the other, that of the state beauty queen, Miss Carmen Delgado, detained at the border with more than half a kilo of cocaine in her personal suitcase. The lady turned out to be the lover of a powerful businessman from Kino Bay. The scandal grew in size and revealed that the investor lent his facilities to the drug trafficker to make shipments and store long weapons sent from the United States by the DEA. An admiral was also involved, along with the mayor and part of his administration.

The crescendo of violence included the appearance of thirty bodies in the municipal dump, "arranged" on the dunes of waste. "A piece of art," an important critic in a specialized magazine would dare to say. The corpses were made up, dressed in different ways, some naked, with half their bodies buried in the garbage and half their bodies in the stinking, open air; as if they were performing a play, a mortuary play. Among them was the body of my cousin Fero. They had dressed him in a suit and tie, just as I had seen him when he left high school. I never saw him dressed like that again because he was a bit of a bohemian. Fero, the cousin who hated suits, was there in "that performance"—the critic continued—wearing a navy blue one. Also among the naked men, two magistrates appeared with their faces disfigured; they had been recognized only by their fingerprints and DNA. There were of course journalists, whose hands had been cut off, four police commanders dressed in bras and panties, and so on. The five women in this stunning theatrical act had been raped. Everyone wondered about the meaning of this absurd staging, "a nihilistic work" concluded the art expert.

Two children, four elders, two doctors, three beautiful women, a priest, two filmmakers, two clowns, the lead singer of a northern band, four foreigners, a poet, three students, five peasants, two teachers and a hairdresser. Thirty corpses perfectly arranged. The magistrates had been found face down, as had the priest, so only their legs were visible with their socks pulled up. Three of the women had been buried with their shoes on, high heels. Of course it had been planned, it was not like dumping a body on the side of the road. This was the work of a group who had a plan. Maybe the mastermind behind those crimes was an installer, the critic commented again in a second article, or the son of a drug dealer with aesthetic tendencies.

The press had arrived at the dump thanks to an anonymous call. The police arrived later, after the press, as always. One of the reporters from the evening paper had received the call in the morning while he was drinking his first coffee. The voice of a woman with a *chilango* accent had given him the news. The commander could not believe what he was seeing. Among the rot and waste that the city generated, there were those people. In short, that barbaric act had a message. "What happens when crime becomes symbolic?" The critic did not stop. What was obvious is that this was nothing but a return to the Middle Ages. What relationship could there be between a pedophile priest and a student with excellent grades? The police could not understand.

From one day to the next, the violence changed like a salamander, metamorphosed. The square was taken, the people knew when rough and provocative, arrogant and threatening men appeared in armored trucks, from which they took notes and looked at us all with contempt. They turned out to be the rent collectors for security services, as they called their type of extortion. Through the church bell they summoned the merchants of the first square of the city, that is: from Sufragio Efectivo No Reelección Avenue, to Luis Encinas Johnson Boulevard, and from Jesús García Avenue to Rosales Avenue. Instead of the kindly priest on Sundays, a sullen man welcomed them and, without preamble, told them that they would have to pay a fee if they did not want to lose their business, or a child or a wife.

There were complaints: "Under what law? And with what balls?" said my father.

"With the balls of steel," the guy answered, and ten of his accomplices cut cartridges in unison.

The fee would be monthly, and any delay would be paid with punishment, or with payment in kind. Don Marcos, the owner of the hardware store, told them that he would not participate, that he would speak with the commander of the military zone because it was clearly illegal and ... I can't say more, he was knocked down by a rifle butt in his attempt to get out to the street and almost died. They had a month to get the money together, was the ultimatum. Everyone left, upset and offended, by such a display of abuse. Finally, the guy told them the names of their children, wives and other relatives, as well as their addresses and activities. "We've got you bastards on file." Big offenses were paid with death, it was that simple, they were in charge now and anyone who opposed them immediately became an enemy. It was simple math.

My father made the first three payments, was a little late with the fourth and by the fifth, he was fed up with the blackmail he was subjected to. He began to suspect that the criminals intended to take over the store—his life's work, our inheritance. "La Picolina," the business my grandfather had started, was taken over by my father with almost the same enthusiasm. I was supposed to take it one day, since I was the oldest and a male. For the second time, I saw my father dejected, dejected and sad. I had only seen him like that when my mother died. For the first time in his life, selling the store and of course our house above it crossed his mind ... The problem was that my father was not very easy to manipulate, and he secretly summoned the neighbors; he made them see that their situation would not end, a letter had to be written to the president of the republic. The letter was drafted, signed and sent to the post office early in the morning ... However, the letter was intercepted, and my father was summoned to a meeting with the mobsters. He was the third signer on a list of fifteen people.

When he returned from his meeting, my father dusted off grandfather's hunting rifles and loaded his pistol with bullets in the closet. He made arrangements to send us to Guanajuato with one of his first cousins, Aunt Carmela ... but there was no time. What my father didn't realize was that he was up against a huge arsenal and the system as a whole. Two nights later, the store caught fire ... Three guys managed to sneak in through the bathroom window and sprayed about ten liters of gasoline.

I've always had a good nose, and that night I smelled something burning and I jumped up when I discovered what was happening. I alerted my father, Julita and my sister. My father grabbed the suitcase where he had all the official documents, birth certificates, passports, property deeds and asset declarations. He always had that suitcase at hand, ready, as if he had always waited for that moment. He grabbed the gun too and pushed us toward the stairs. I managed to put away my wallet, my IDs and a double frame with a photo of my grandmother and another of my mother ... Cancer again; this time in the form of a fire caused by groups of men capable of anything.

Before opening the door to the street, my father made us wait and came out with the gun in his hand. He had barely taken three steps when he fell down, he had been shot dead. Gaby screamed and tried to run toward him, but I stopped her. I took her hand tightly and we went back up the stairs with Doña Julita. I remembered a way to escape via the roof. When we got to the laundry rooms, the fire was already coming out of the windows into the patio; there was smoke, and the crackling of the flames was deafening. I heard the siren of the firemen and the police. We ran with luck because as soon as we crossed the door to the roof, a flame entered through the stairwell.

I looked Gaby straight in the eyes, she looked horrified. I calmed her down. There was a trick. The dangerous part was walking on an L-shaped platform practically over the walls of the two properties, up to a tower, on top of which the neighbors had a water tank, and from there, down a metal staircase to the garden of the Alpizar house. To my surprise, Julita did everything with a lot of courage. Coughing from the smoke, we got to safety as best we could. We burst into the neighbors' living room with a look of terror, I suppose, given that Carlos' mother came to comfort us. She covered Gaby with a blanket. We waled into tears.

The image of my old man being shot down by those thugs; his perplexed face, the grimace of death and the surprise of the moment. I fell. I fell in slow motion. I wiped my tears and went to the front door of my neighbors' house. I opened it slowly, the black trucks had disappeared, the firemen were already spraying water at my house which was consuming itself in flames. I went out into the street; the police had also arrived. Behind me, the neighbors followed, my soul cringed and my scalp tingled from seeing the flames coming out of the front windows of the house my family had lived in for generations, since the arrival of my great-grandfather from Italy. My sister's heritage and mine was turning to smoke and ashes.

I ran to where my father was lying, knelt down beside him, lifted his head and held him. I closed his eyes. I couldn't stop crying. I barked at the sky: "Where is the damn law in this fucking country?! God, demon, whatever you are, where is justice?!" My tears fell on his face, I looked at the gun on the ground. I took it and put it away in my pockets. My pain tasted like ashes and bile. Doña Julita and Gaby came toward us and knelt down, in a sea of tears as well. My sister threw herself on top of our dad and stained her forehead with his blood; it seemed as if she herself was bleeding. Her uncontrollable crying broke my heart, and I hugged her. People surrounded us whispered ... I wiped my eyes. I remembered a lesson from a teacher in voice school: "Head held high despite everything, and above the abuse." The Red Cross people arrived with a stretcher and put my father on top, my sister on another; she couldn't stop crying. The three of us got into the ambulance. Doña Julita fainted and a paramedic helped her regain consciousness.

The morning caught us in the hospital, I saw the saddest dawn of my entire life hugging my father's suitcase. With a universal emptiness expanding in my stomach I saw my mother in the photograph where she smiles languidly from some train station; my grandmother in another snapshot, but she in front of "La Picolina" when she was still young. I ran out of tears. My sister appeared again in the waiting room, she looked dejected, just free of the sleeping pill; she came dragging her feet and sat next to me. We didn't say anything to each other, we were two lonely souls sitting in that waiting room, without hope. I snatched my father's death certificate from Gaby's fingers and put it inside the suitcase, next to the photograph of my mother at the train station. Whatever we had in that suitcase was everything we had, that and perhaps the still smoking ruins of our house, three blocks from the historic center of Hermosillo, Sonora. Carlos came through the door. He saw us and sat down in the chairs behind us without saying anything, out of respect for our pain. A doctor made a sign to us. I stood up and forced my sister to do the same. I left the suitcase with Carlos. Gaby and I, arm in arm, walked to where they would take us to our father's body. When I saw my father lying on the cement slab, I felt fear and anger, a great rage with the taste of formaldehyde that dissolved in my mouth and was difficult to digest. I felt dry, without tears. Gaby burst into tears again. I pulled her to me. She hugged me and rested her head on my shoulder.

"What are we going to do?"

"Don't worry, we'll figure it out."

What followed this were formalities, a quick wake, a sad burial attended by a lot of strangers and a slow emotional recovery while my anger increased day by day. Our neighbors treated us very well and welcomed us into their house. They put my sister in the bedroom of one of the daughters, and they gave me a small room on the first floor, next to the kitchen. During the months it took us to recover from the shock, my sister and I talked a lot. We agreed to sell the remains of the house as land, that money would be used for her education. In my father's suitcase I also found the deeds to another piece of land, the papers for our old pickup truck and a bank account whose beneficiaries were us; not much money really, just enough for a down payment for a house in the outskirts of Hermosillo. Gaby suggested renting an apartment, buying furniture ... or just visiting Aunt Carmela in Guanajuato as my father had planned. When Carlos heard this, he decided to talk to his family.

He told them that he loved Gaby with all his soul. He wanted to marry her as soon as possible, because the love was reciprocal. One Sunday, Carlos Alpizar, Sr. spoke to me about his son's intentions for my sister; they were asking for her hand, and in the absence of parents, that honor fell to me.

I accepted immediately. The bride and groom agreed to marry within three months to avoid gossip, living under the same roof without the holy blessings was not acceptable. I told the Alpizars that before the wedding I would move out of the house. Mrs. Alpizar said it wasn't necessary because they considered me a son, and Carlos' father finished by saying it would be an honor to have me there. They were wonderful people. My sister couldn't be in better company.

The truth of the matter is, I felt like I was superfluous, but also that I had been freed from a great responsibility. I was alone, that was obvious, so I had to think for myself and make a change. And part of that change was to stop being passive and dependent. To hell with the good citizen who pays the extortion on time, the tax on the crooks, the timid person who doesn't complain about abuse or the helpless person who prefers to keep quiet and suffer in silence. To hell with the all-powerful criminals, to hell with the system ... I had never been one to let anyone else do it, and I resented the *montoneros*—bullies. I was expelled from high school more than once, and on a couple of occasions I was taken to the hospital, once for a broken nose and the other for a broken arm.

I would take revenge, it was a moral obligation, it was my right. I would never be a victim again. Maybe after that I would make other plans ... An executioner should die like an executioner.

During those months, when the Alpizars were busy preparing for the wedding, I identified those who had set fire to my house. I followed them and found out about their activities. All the merchants paid a fee, from the established ones to the street vendors, from the store to the newsstand. All of them, without exception. Some activities that were considered nocturnal became daylight activities, such as drug dealing and prostitution. I learned about many things, including the opening of several gentlemen's clubs, where the girls were none other than the young ones kidnapped from Hermosillo, forced to work under threat. The owners of the places were pigs. They came in to eat wherever they wanted, to drink, and if they wanted someone's wife, daughter or niece, they took her by the waist, used her and then threw her into the stream like garbage.

The burning of "La Picolina" served as an example of what could happen when one did not obey, and the other terrified merchants prepared to catch up on their payments. "El Perro," my father's murderer, and his henchmen appeared to be happy with life, proud. They were my immediate enemies, I concluded. At my father's grave I had sworn to take revenge and make them pay for their crime. In the absence of institutional justice, the other, the one that is taken into one's own hands. As the saying goes: *An eye for an eye and a tooth for a tooth*, and I had my eye on them. I even came to know the brand of cigarettes they smoked.

I had no military training of any kind, but what I did have was knowledge on how to hunt. I learned it from my grandfather. The three of us practiced it, including my father. He would say that I was a natural hunter, as my grandfather's father had been; a surgeon's pulse, eagle eyesight and the sensitivity of a feline. The first rule of a hunter: patience under penalty of losing the prey; the second, that the animal never sees you, until the last moment. I had hunted ducks, rabbits, deer and even wild sheep. Once a mountain cat, but never four fat thugs who had to pay for their crime. Carlos offered to help me, he would drive for me, if necessary, but he would not dirty his hands with blood, it was not his style.

"I'm not a coward, my friend, but I wouldn't be able to sleep at night."

He was good with computers, so I suggested he help me gather information about the killers. We forced ourselves to watch a lot of detective and mystery movies, conspiracy and spy shows, like *Morgue* or *Crime Scene*. We learned a lot, there were seven-hour days glued to the computer screen. We made plans. We agreed then that he would be the official driver for the operation.

He brought his family's five cars to the table, so we used different ones to spy on them. The pigs were not very creative and repeated the same routine day after day. For reasons of strategy or not, they lived very close to each other, in the same neighborhood. They would meet up for coffee and then go off to the stores to collect the money from their terrified victims. At mid-morning, they visited their chief leader. We assumed this because they went to a huge ranch guarded by men who were armed to the teeth. We also managed to see inside the wall thanks to a satellite image, which Carlos acquired through his research. That place was a paradise, it had a lake, a forest, an artificial waterfall, as well as a mansion with two swimming pools, a tennis court and a zoo.

Don Pepe, the boss, was the owner of that stunning place in the middle of the desert. He was a powerful man in politics and business, untouchable by everyone, a man of respect and care. He was the boss, everyone, without exception, was accountable to him. We saw the mayor, the commander of the military zone, the president of the chamber of commerce, mobsters like "El Perro" and the other leaders of "Los Cuchillos Largos" come out of there.

In the afternoon, "the pack," as Carlos had baptized "El Perro" and company, would eat at some bar, collect more payments, visit friends and finally, at night time, would go into any one of the brothels. El Perro was nothing more than a sub-boss whom the other three brainless men obeyed. We also realized that El Perro and his thugs were limited to the area of collections, that there were other cells operating. From those in charge of negotiating and distributing drugs to the small-time vendors, to those handling the Chinese merchandise sold by the street vendors. Other cells were dedicated to credit card issues, others to the brothels and so on. Each thug boss reported to the man who owned the walled house; El Perro and the others functioned as the concessionaires. Thanks to the GPS installed in the vans, we were able to draw up an activity diagram. We had them.

Killing the first one was very difficult, I hesitated a couple of times, I could not make myself pull the trigger ... I sweated, my hand shook, but I gave myself courage. I had to wait for a third time. I shot the guy who had emptied the gas cans inside the store. The guy was not very tall, but of heavy build. The bullet struck his forehead as he left his house, just as they had killed my father. It was a whole project practiced and reviewed ad infinitum. I went up to the roof of the Bahía Kino hotel, where I registered under a false name. I paid in cash wearing a mustache; I stayed there for two days. Grandpa's rifles turned out to be in good shape, but they were antiques. A few weeks after, we drove to Tijuana to buy a hunting rifle with cash. A Candor rifle, expensive, that fit my needs and was enough to kill a bear at a distance of 1,600 meters. It had infrared precision telescopic sight, and best of all, the rifle was assembled in parts and fit into a metal briefcase. A beauty. I felt no remorse, perhaps maybe some euphoria.

Carlos followed the second man via GPS for a week. I stationed myself on the roof of an abandoned mechanic's shop, so when he arrived at the 7-Eleven to buy coffee and cigarettes, I blew him out of the parking lot. The first two were easy. In order to kill the other two, I embarked on a whole messy odyssey. The day the second bear was killed, someone had seen my truck near the shopping center and, without hesitation, the judicial police came for me and subjected me to an interrogation. They didn't touch a hair on my head, to be honest. Strange, right? I told them what I knew. The story of the extortion and how, thanks to my good sense of smell, we were still alive, how I had woken up before the flames consumed everything. They asked if I had seen the faces of the perpetrators on the day of the premeditated accident, and I said no. Although, of course, I had seen their faces, sometimes I woke up with them looking at me in my dreams, setting fire to "La Picolina" again and again. They showed me photos, I didn't know who the guy was, and I didn't know anything about it; that was my statement, and I stuck to it until the end. One of the policemen tried to intimidate me, but it didn't work. The truth is that they had no evidence, no murder weapon, nothing. Indeed, I had been to the mall to buy a T-shirt, I showed them the receipt. Once the interrogation was over, Officer Dávila accompanied me to the street, walked a little with me and then made me stop under the shade of a tree.

"You know what, kid? I don't care what you're doing, what they did to your family was a disgrace."

I kept quiet.

"I knew your grandfather, a very fine person ... Anyway, good luck. Remember, despite the appearances, there are still decent policemen on this side."

We walked half a block more and stopped in front of my old truck. I took the keys out of my denim jacket.

"Let's talk, in a few days," he suggested. "Another thing, I left you a pair of bulletproof vests in your pickup as a gift, when you get home don't forget to take them out, and what's more use them ... like socks, every time you go out. This has become a war zone."

29

I almost emptied the savings account investing in my revenge. I justified myself to Carlos: "Come on, it's not like I'm spending money on clothes, expensive shoes and partying, I'm doing justice." Of course Gaby never found out; adjusting to being an orphan and keeping up with her studies took all her time. Carlos lashed out, saying that not only was it irresponsible of me, but I was endangering my sister and his entire family. "In any case I'm taking my share, and I don't plan on taking a cent from the sale of what's left of our house ... It's a matter of honor. Besides, those pigs have as many enemies as the entire city of Hermosillo. I'll disappear once I've fulfilled my revenge," I told him.

We returned to Tijuana to buy more weapons, this time two pistols, cartridges and a set of grenades. Carlos seemed frightened by my transformation; I had become a resentful animal. I ran several kilometers a day, lifted weights, kicked and punched a boxing ball in the backyard of the Alpizar house. All I could think about was the death of El Perro and his second in command. They themselves were aware and alert, I would dare say frightened. They knew that someone, with very good aim, wanted to nail them. They now traveled in three separate trucks with ten heavily armed men guarding El Perro. It was impossible to get close to him.

While this went on, I dedicated time to exercising and preparation. I decided to move to the Alpizar ranch with the pretext that I was interested in animals, pasture and country life. I wanted to practice shooting with the pistols. Don Carlos said he had no problem, that maybe it was a good idea, especially before the wedding of his son and my sister. In any case, they thought I was a strange young man who had been consumed by the shock of the tragedy; maybe what they said about me was partly true. I still had nightmares of my father being shot, I was still filled with rage knowing that two of his killers were walking around town in broad daylight.

I loaded the old truck with a suitcase of clothes, tennis shoes and boots, and another where I kept the pistols and the cartridges. The rifle I had used to deal with the first two pigs was hidden among the charred ruins of my house, in a secret place. If they caught me with it, my revenge would never be consummated and I would go straight, without trial or anything, to the penitentiary to rot for life, or to a mass grave.

I spent almost four months in the ranch. I ate well from the hands of the manager, who later became my friend. She was a widow with whom I shared a bedroom from the second night. Doña Agnes was her name and she got along well with the five laborers and the administration of the place. She carried a rifle inside the property and did what she said. Her husband had died about a year and a few months before, and she had a twelve-year-old son who was quite withdrawn. Her husband had been the foreman, but since his death she had assumed that role, quite successfully according to the bosses, and that is why she continued to work there. On the ranch, in addition to animals, they also grew cacti, mainly for decorative purposes, a business that Clara Alpizar herself managed. From the start, I told Agnes that I liked target shooting, that I had gone there to practice and to get in shape. I gave her five thousand pesos because I did not want to depend on the expenses assigned to her. At first, she did not want to accept the money, but I explained to her that it was my contribution for being able to eat her food, live there, use the bathroom. The only thing I asked of her was her silence if the Alpizars ever asked about the guns. She took the money, rolled it up and put it between her breasts. She did not question me.

Agnes was older than me, about ten years, and what happened, I hadn't planned it, and it hadn't even crossed my mind when I met her. I arrived at the ranch very early in the morning, introduced myself and we talked almost all day. She showed me the bathroom, took me to my room and everything was fine. It wasn't until after midnight on the second day that the hot-blooded woman slipped into my bed and fucked me wonderfully. She spent a third night and a fourth. Before a week had passed, I was sleeping in her room, which was larger and had a bathroom inside. She treated me like her husband, and after each erotic session she claimed to have been reborn. She insisted on teaching me things and telling me legends.

"They say that many, many years ago, what is now the desert, was a jungle of very tall trees and thick vegetation, where large animals lived and made homes, that the climate was cool, and it rained often."

"Says who?"

"That's what they say, nobody knows. There are no signs of when that changed and it stopped raining, or when the big trees and vegetation were pulverized to form this immensity of sand."

"What are you talking about?"

"When you're inside me, I sense an old spirit in you ... like another being that's not you. Have you thought about that? Do you know?"

"Just don't fall in love with me, Agnes, okay? It wouldn't be fair."

"You don't believe what I say, maybe because you don't believe in yourself, but you're inhabited by something."

"Not someone?"

"No, by some *thing* ... that's why you seek revenge."

"Don't give me esoteric stories."

"Maybe you should pay more attention to what your heart tells you."

"And do you know how I could do that?"

"By entering the desert perhaps ... deep inside, until you find yourself ... and face it."

"Face what?"

"I don't know, whatever is necessary, it depends on the relationship with silence, with fear ... with nothingness."

"It seems complicated and dangerous."

"It is, but I don't see any other way. Maybe your conscience wants to tell you something."

"I've been told about that. I thought it was necessary to be under the influence of some drug."

"Are you talking about peyote? Not necessarily, it's a matter of talking to the spirit that lives there."

I looked at her, she seemed completely convinced of what she was saying, like someone who professes a religion and speaks about it with great respect.

"Sometimes you speak to me in Russian, Agnes, but I like you."

The truth is, I didn't know anything about entering the desert. One afternoon she showed up with a cage full of birds, all grey. I asked her the reason. Her answer was that I couldn't train properly if I continued shooting at motionless cans. I told her I couldn't kill all those birds; maybe half, a few, three, four. She looked at me seriously. I told her I liked birds, their song and everything they represented, because they are a fundamental element in the food chain. Agnes left her gun on the nightstand and prepared to take off her boots while she listened to me. Barefoot, she walked to the bathroom and before closing the door she said: "So forget about your revenge, kid, start saving for your funeral."

Her comment hit me hard, I don't know if I was more offended by the kid thing than by the funeral comment. The next day, well, I aimed for the birds; she insisted so much and I had no other option.

"They are common and ordinary birds, there are a lot of them," she said again in a serious tone.

"So that's why I have to kill them?"

"Not because of that. I'll tell you why, two fundamental reasons: it prepares you to shoot moving targets, and two, if you're going to kill people, you must learn by killing living beings."

Her logic surprised and terrified me.

"Also, you have the advantage that the bird is not going to draw a gun and shoot back."

I killed about forty birds, some of them outright, others I let live, out of pity, or because they were very naive. There was one bird, with some kind of skin infection, that after I had shot at it three times without hitting, came back to stand on an adobe wall next to me, as if it wanted to sacrifice itself.

Agnes shared some hunting secrets and helped me better adjust my aim. Without telling me, it was clear she was worried that I wanted to confront professional killers. I was honest with her and told her that I had already killed two of them, although, she apparently didn't believe me.

She had an idea, which she didn't share with me until we were in Nogales. Maybe because she thought I would reject it. It was a two-hour drive and another Agnes showed up; a woman with a very good voice and grace for singing, an independent woman, a woman with compassion. She took off her jeans, boots and camisole, and walked out the door of the house wearing a pretty, flowery dress, her hair down and loafers on her feet. She looked attractive, but she quickly got into the truck as if she didn't want anyone to see her dressed like that. She hurried me as if someone was waiting for us somewhere.

We crossed the border without a problem, we both had active passports and visas. Agnes knew where they sold what she was looking for, it was the perfect opportunity to get it. We went into a mall and parked in the shade. We found the place on the second floor, right between a tattoo shop and a comic bookstore. We stopped in front of a blonde guy with a beer belly. We were looking for a paintball gun game to train ourselves with, and Agnes spoke up. The guy jumped for joy. He sold everything from uniforms to real heavy weapons, like AK47s, RLS rifles, vests, virtual simulators, night vision goggles and grenades—of all colors, of course. The guy liked us, showed us weapons and let us use several "toys," as he called the paintball guns, in the back of the store, where he had a whole target shooting kit set up. I shot several guns and decided on a squad. He also let me shoot a real machine gun, even though it was out of our budget. Pulling the trigger on that instrument made me feel invincible; not only the sound of the gun, but its power, the continuity of the burst; I understood why any guy could feel like the most intimidating being with hardware like that. I had a ball. The blonde buy thought it was a good idea to train me with paint guns; it was like a game of killing someone else, only with colored bullets. "That's what wars should be like, painting us, the painted ones are the losers," he said and smiled. I thought it was strange for a weapons dealer, but well, the world is full of contradictions.

We loved the boutique, that's what the blonde called it, and we promised to return. While he was wrapping our order, I took the opportunity to ask him some questions. Among other things, I found out that in the USA shooting with colored guns is considered a sport. That security groups use colored guns to train their personnel. That there were international competitions, and even private clubs where bets were made. Agnes bought a lot of ammunition of various colors, a revolver and a set of guns, plus two eye protectors. With our package in hand I suggested we drink a beer and eat hamburgers, taking advantage of the fact that we were on this side of the border. She loved the idea.

As we had agreed, Agnes started shooting with me. She was agile, strong. She was a good shot, and several times left a mark on my chest, or on my side. We had a good time, play-shooting each other made us horny, so after each shootout, we ended up rolling around in bed furiously. My aim definitely improved tenfold, my reflexes, not to mention my physical appearance, too. At the end of the first month I was already an expert with the rifle, a weapon that has not stopped being my favorite. One of those afternoons, lying inside the cabin, which was at the end of the property, Agnes made me look her in the eyes and said: "You do know that we women like to talk about delicate things in bed ... right?"

"Yes, I know."

"Then let me speak to you truthfully and ask you a question: once your revenge is complete, what's next? Will you turn into a bully?"

"No, of course not."

"So?"

"I don't know, one step at a time."

"Do you think you're ready for revenge?"

"No, of course not, but I'm preparing myself to the best of my ability."

"Are you preparing for something big, or do you just want to be strong and athletic?"

"I'm not kidding about what I told you."

She looked at me seriously and then said: "I can connect you with a Chinese guy, he works for the drug dealers."

"Why the hell would I want to meet a Chinese guy?"

"So that he can teach you to fight, to defend yourself better."

"I know how to fight," I said proudly. "At school, I was on the boxing team."

"What you do is sport, it's not fighting."

"For now, but I know that when the time comes …"

"At that moment it won't be of any use to you. Sports are for watching, there's a referee, lights. The other thing is for surviving and you must play dirty."

I looked her in the eyes, she was right.

"What do you suggest?"

"That you forget about revenge—"

"Never, how can you ask me that?"

"Wait, that or I'll introduce you to this Chinese guy, he's a master of karate and other martial arts, and a very interesting person."

"Really?"

"He's great at the art of kicking, and you could use some lessons."

"And this Chinese guy you're talking about, how did he get here?"

"He trains the drug dealers' troops, like I said, on a ranch around here."

"Really ...? And how do you know him?"

"As you know, the ranch's business is cattle, and I've sold them several heads, very discreetly."

"Cattle? For what?"

"They have to feed the people who come to train; no one leaves, no one enters until they're finished. Also, they have to pretend that it's a cattle ranch; I've lent them animals to graze in their fields too."

"The Alpizars don't know about that, I suppose."

"You guessed right, they don't live here. Besides, it's better for us to get along with them, they're neighbors and well ... the thing is that I know him, he's my friend, let's keep it at that. Do you understand?"

"Of course."

"What I do know is that he owes me favors, I can ask him to give you some advice, a couple of classes."

I took a breath and looked her in the eyes: "If he's a drug dealer, I'm not interested."

"First of all, he's not a drug dealer; second, he works for the opposing cartel, not for the ones who harmed your family."

I thought about it for a few minutes, maybe she was right.

"I'd have to be very discreet. The truth is that I don't want to get involved with those guys."

"Of course, of course, it would be here on the property and with all the discretion in the world. I think that's what he's going to ask of me as well."

"Sure."

"Come on, it's not like you're going to be an expert in karate and martial arts, but it will help to know what they know, right? A month, maybe two of training with this guy won't hurt you."

"Of course, of course. And how much would he charge, or how would it go?"

"Don't worry, I'll take care of that."

I was silent for a few minutes.

"I hope you're not mistaken."

"Not at all. If there's one thing that the years give you, it's a certain wisdom. Now go to sleep, tomorrow I have to go to an animal auction, and you have to get up and run before the sun becomes unbearable."

In the same half-ruined cabin that we had turned into our love nest, Agnes sent me to meet Chian Ho. He was waiting for me outside, alone, and if I hadn't known he was a dangerous guy, I would have said he seemed like a harmless man. I saw how he studied me too. I introduced myself.

"Are you Agnes' nephew?" he asked.

"Yes," that was the farce, we had to play along.

"She tells me that you don't know how to use your hands."

"Let's say I know a little."

The Chinese man laughed and took off his dark glasses. He put them delicately inside his jacket; he was wearing a light, white linen suit, and a little Cuban hat.

"Yes...? Attack me."

I looked him in the eyes.

Chian Ho took several steps back, stood firmly on the floor and waved a hand, inviting me to hit him. Just like that, without further ado.

I raised my guard and approached him with the intention of landing a jab to his jaw, but before my fist even got close, the Chinese man gave me a kick in the shin and another in the stomach. I fell to the ground.

The Chinese man laughed and laughed, amused.

I jumped to my feet and, swinging my fists. I launched into the attack, but the action was repeated, and I fell to the ground again, this time from a kick to the side and a slap that entered my defense with unusually graceful ease.

He laughed again; he couldn't stop laughing, he doubled over. This time I didn't try to get up and from the floor I held my hands in the air.

"Okay, okay ... mercy."

"You should apologize first, look at you raising your fists at me."

"You're right, I'm sorry ... Wait, it was your idea."

"Fists are not raised unless you are sure of winning."

"Okay, I'm sorry again."

"Master."

"I'm sorry, Master."

"What you do was called boxing and it is no longer used ... Think, what happens when you only use your fists and forget about your legs?"

"It becomes more difficult to win a fight."

"No, what happens is that you only use one part of your body, and you leave the other half immobile."

"Well, not completely, your legs are used to jump, give momentum to the blow and ...," I tried to argue from my position on the floor.

"The way you fight, you expose yourself to any opponent. The fact that the other uses all of his limbs to hit puts you at a disadvantage from the start."

He held out a hand to me and helped me stand.

"We'll have to focus on how to use those lower limbs of yours."

"I'd appreciate it."

"Agnes says you run, that you're very athletic ..."

I nodded.

"That might help, although you need to get to know your body again, understand how it works and what relationship it has with gravity."

He made me stop next to him.

"Have you heard of yoga, Thai Chi ...?"

"Yes, of course. My sister goes to yoga classes, she says it makes her very happy."

Chian Ho made a salute, then a hand movement in front of his face and opened his legs, turning on one foot one hundred and eighty degrees.

"Repeat this movement with me."

I did it, as close as I could, although in the movement I almost lost my balance.

"Good, good. Don't look at your feet, look forward. Do it again."

I tried, although this time it went pear, and I lowered my hands completely.

"The hands and arms follow the legs. It's a single impulse."

"Okay. How about this?"

"Better. Since you lower your hands, here, you're already lifting your leg, here."

"Okay, I lower my arms, move my leg and raise my knee ... I think I understand now."

"I'm going to give you five basic movements, the same ones that you are going to repeat for several hours without stopping until you perfect them. Tomorrow, at this same time, you will show them to me, and I'll give you another five movements. Once we have completed a series, we will start hitting."

I tried a second movement, in this one, it was the trunk that turned throwing a fist forward.

"Concentrate, boy, Agnes tells me that you plan to carry out justice. That should be your objective while you practice."

"How do you do that?"

"What? Concentrate?"

"No, practice with the mind to do justice."

"If justice is for revenge, concentrate on that, or on the pain that brought you to it."

He gave me the series of five turns and I practiced them until I learned them by heart. I didn't know until much later that the second movement was the beginning of a deadly kick to the liver area.

I embarked on a routine, running, shooting, horse riding, squatting, push-ups, practicing Master Chian Ho's movements and certain ranch activities, such as feeding the chickens and goats very early. I hadn't thought about entering the desert yet, but it was like a call, and I couldn't get it out of my head. Perhaps it was the product of the idea planted in my mind by Agnes or because of a legend mentioned by my grandmother; it was becoming an obsession. I had heard at home that the desert holds secrets not accessible to all men. When my father was alive, we visited a magical place called "El Pinacate," for many it was the entrance to the vast Altar Desert that continues beyond Arizona and is one of the hottest areas in the world. The site houses about twelve enormous, deep, perfectly circular craters, which contribute to its beauty. It is like a lunar view, quite unique. My grandfather insisted on the energy of the place, and when we traveled there, he made us all lie on towels on the desert floor and look up to the sky, with sunglasses of course, and sunscreen. When I think about it, I imagine it could have been a good cover for a rock album.

One afternoon, without much thought, I drove to Caborca, where I stayed overnight in a dingy little hotel that had been in the area for a long time. The next day I had a frugal breakfast, bought two oranges, three apples and nuts, and bottles of water. I drove down Highway 37 to Puerto Peñasco, which had gone from being a pleasant, quiet fishing village to a tourist town with hotels and bars, not to mention the haughty tourists who treated everyone like servants. I bought sunscreen, aspirin, a compass, some canned food, batteries for my flashlight and a plainclothes hat. I parked the van in the parking lot of the El Pinacate Visitor Center.

When the van was closed and I was ready, I called Agnes. I left her a message explaining my decision, without trying to sound too dramatic. I also told her that if I didn't show up in a few days and didn't make it to the wedding to please tell Gaby and Carlos goodbye for me. I strapped my backpack on my back, put on my hat and started walking.

The evening fell, and at one point it was so dark that I had to turn on my flashlight to make my way through the depths of the night. It was a very long journey. I lay down next to a Saguaro, drank a whole bottle of water and slept for a few hours. At dawn, I encountered death for the first time; it was in the form of a very poisonous scorpion, which almost ended my journey. A few centimeters from my right hand, the insect closed its pincers, and I sprang up. The earth moved on its axis. The sun was heavy above me, and I was bewildered and not at all prepared for such an undertaking. I gave up on squashing the little animal and questioned my decision ... for a moment I thought about going back, but I remembered the message I had left on Agnes' answering machine; I would make a fool of myself. There is a Dutch saying that goes: "Whoever is outside the door has already started part of the journey."

It was my first day face-to-face with the desert. How can I describe the experience of fear, of death? Of desolation? I would be lying if I said I agreed with someone who swears that life passes by like a photographic succession. The truth is, you don't remember much, it's part of the pact. What I do know is that when you come out of the experience, you are another person. In my case, it was not until seven days later, when Agnes and two of the laborers found me half naked eating cactus, ten kilos lighter and covered in mud. I have vague memories of those days. What still keeps me awake is the confrontation with a beast, which chases me, and I run terrified trying to climb a gigantic dune in which my legs sink up to my knees ... When I come to, I am in an hourglass about to pass through the neck, between the two spaces of time.

30

My mouth is dry, my thirst is painful, the idea of going into the desert has become an abysmal stupidity. I am lost, I have used up all my water, I don't know where I left my backpack with all its provisions. I walk, but I don't advance, at least I don't think so. When I come down from a dune with weeds, on a hill, I find a group of people. A girl with a bloodstained dress looks around in disbelief, she has the expression of someone who has just woken up from a dream. The same thing happens to a young man who is missing part of his scalp, and to a guy with a hole where his heart once was.

I realize they are dead, even though they think they are alive. A woman wearing a housewife's apron picks up her bag from the ground, paying no attention to the hole in her stomach, and walks around in a perfect circle in the space of her grave. I stop, stunned; I have found a clandestine burial site, four meters below where I am. I sit on a rock to watch, taking a break. Perhaps the whole desert is a wasteland of souls. A man with a bullet hole in his temple searches through his briefcase with a worried expression, like someone who has lost a folder of valuable documents. Each dead person has no notion of the other next to them. Even a pair of men buried back-to-back, both with their faces disfigured by blows, touch each other but do not seem feel each other. I'm a few steps away from a massive grave that opens to the ground ... that, or it's all a product of my thirst and I've started to hallucinate. I open and close my eyes in order to get out of the trance, but when I try to return to reality, those people are still buried together, in that space in the middle of nowhere.

A pale girl with elegant features seems to be the only one who has noticed my presence; she calls me, smiles and gestures for me to go to where she is and sit next to her. She really is pretty, I think, although I shouldn't believe what I see, my intuition warns me, it's a bad idea to enter the place. I stand up, the best thing to do is to leave, go around the grave and get away as soon as possible. I take a few steps, in another blink of an eye, two vultures come and make their presence felt, they stand on some rocks and look at me. They're not there for the others, they're there for me. A few minutes later an eagle appears too, perching itself on a saguaro. For a moment I want to think that there is a meaning to it, but the birds don't take their eyes off me, especially the two scavengers, who if they catch me will drag me for a while until they are sure I am dead, and then they will start pecking and tearing me apart with their claws, just like I once saw on the Discovery Channel. Fear takes hold of me. Am I living the last moments of my life? Is this some kind of test? I have to calm down. I am definitely at a crossroads ... Either I overcome it, or I abandon myself to the birds; the eagle will come for my heart, that's what they like the most, and the other disgusting ones will come for the rest; they will slam me on the ground to break my bones and devour me more easily ... I cross the neck of the clock.

That's when I decide to urinate and drink my urine. I take off one boot, stand up and concentrate with my penis in my hand. Seconds pass, minutes, hours, a comet flies by. I finally manage to get some urine, something like a quarter of a glass. The liquid is hot, not at all pleasant, but my body needs it. It's incredible what a little kidney water does. I come to my senses, I must find a way out of the desert, I have not come here to die .... I must fulfill my revenge to see El Perro crawl and ask me for forgiveness; see my sister dressed as a bride, celebrate with my friends, say goodbye to Hermosillo. The very red sun on the horizon is gigantic, the afternoon is falling.

I have reached this point, another day, this time before ascending a dune about a hundred meters high. It is a petrified wave in this sea of sand and I am a surfer, with lips full of blisters, skin lacerated by the sun. Suddenly I realize I have been here before. Have I walked in circles? Past and present intertwine their hands, this is me. I must be not far from the Altar Desert, or at least I hope so. I look around: on one side the mountains, on the other the vast sea of sand. I see what I have seen. The distant sandy hills taking on a beautiful blue hue. I take a step, my foot sinks into the sand almost up to my knee, when I step back and pull out my leg, a yellowish snake is coiled on my limb. I am about to scream, but a part of me opposes that reaction and I turn to stone. I know that with any sudden move the reptile will sink its deadly teeth into my being. It looks at me, I start to speak to get his attention and distract it. I put my arm behind my leg and manage to uncoil it, with my hand, I hold his head. Suddenly I realize, everything is still part of the test. I move at a surprising slowness, I myself am amazed, the snake barely notices when I put it on the ground. Slowly, I take a step back and we look at each other, the viper shakes its rattle and moves its tongue, it shows it to me threateningly. Weaving, it walks away without taking its eyes off of me, it is evident that neither of us trusts the other. I step back, afraid of running into the rest of its family and retrace my steps a little. A saguaro, a few meters away from me, snaps in my direction.

"Very few are capable of heroic acts."

It is simply impossible that the great three-armed cactus is talking to me.

"If you intend to go to the center of the desert, that place does not exist, nobody knows it. Neither our friend the bighorn sheep, the coyotes, the foxes or the deer have been there. Neither do sparrows, woodpeckers, pigeons, quails or roadrunners. In fact, not hares, turtles or rodents ... Maybe the scorpion by mistake, but no one else."

I look at the cactus, it must be at least a hundred years old. That's what its tree trunk and thick spines say. It's at least a meter and a half taller than me, a beautiful specimen. I approach it, I walk around it, looking for its mouth, its lips, something that tells me which is the front, and which is the back. Where did that voice come from?

"They say that in the very center of the desert there is a small oasis," the saguaro continues, "also known as the fountain of youth."

I sit next to it, slightly under its shade. It says something again. The cactus' voice resonates throughout its body, and I pick it up not only through hearing, but also through touch. In fact, I don't know how we are communicating with each other, but we are.

"The only problem is that the center is not exactly in the center, and it also moves. It is one of the lost craters of 'El Pinacate.'"

This time the Saguaro seems to move its arm from the center of its body. I find it imposing. The voice of the cactus fills me with peace, it is not an understanding, it is a feeling. It is as if time had stopped although night falls in the process.

"What is that about the crater?" I do not receive an answer.

An army of saguaros surrounds me imperceptibly. They are having a conversation in an ancient and strange language that I do not understand, it is a murmur. I find myself in a state of pure contemplation, it seems to me the most natural thing that all those cacti, moving their arms and nodding their heads without a face, exchange messages. A turtle realizes that it is not in the way and slowly crosses the stage. I get very drowsy; I cannot hold my eyes open, and I sleep. I dream that I have arrived at the same point. I have walked in circles, it is another day, another morning. I lift my face, the thorns are making the big saguaro I've been talking to bleed, the cactus seems to stoically accept its punishment. I look around and the landscape of saguaros is like a field of bleeding Christs under a red sunrise. My grandmother is sitting in her rocking chair and tells me, while she is threading a roll of black thread with which she is knitting a sweater: "Son, we are surrounded by traps and lies, do not believe everything your eyes see, they may be mirages. Walk to the mountains and protect yourself against psychic powers; you are not just the spectator, but the subject who performs the action. You are a dual being."

When I open my eyes, I am naked. I am not thirsty, I am not hungry, I am lying inside a rock formation, it is a crater of blackened stone. I jump when I realize the change of realities. I try, as I have been doing, to open and close my eyes to get my bearings ... But then I can't open them anymore, I feel so desperate; I try to separate my eyelids with my fingers, but they feel like they're cooked. In my desperation I walk, I hit myself with some object, I don't know what it is, and I fall to the floor. I get up, I slowly extend my arms, my feet. I don't know where I am and where these petrified objects that surround me have come from. I recognize a chair, a bureau, the smoked mirror in Grandma's room. This time I bump into something solid, I suppose it's a door. I take a wrong step and land on a cold surface. I spring to my feet, but

I fall into a hole, I have nothing to hold on to. I clench my eyes, my jaw, I'm sweating. Is this death? I must take it easy, regain control, I understand ultimately this is part of what I came to learn. I control my breathing and think about cutting potatoes into cubes for a vegetable soup, it is my strategy.

When I think I have control of the air entering through my nose and the blood circulating through my veins, the image of my mother dying in bed assaults me and makes me very sad, I begin to cry. My crying turns into an animal howl when my father is shot down again before my eyes; my house is a pile of ashes, the men hanged from the lampposts. I cry until I get tired and my crying is barely a hum. I try to open my eyes and this time they do, as if the tears had dissolved the glue on my eyelids. I try to remember the face of my sister, Gaby. She is still a child, laughing happily in front of her birthday cake. It is nothing but self-motivation, I think. I need to walk again. I stand up and turn my body 360 degrees. It is a landscape from another world, I am in the center of a terrestrial formation that makes a perfect circle. The moon above shines in a crescent like a powerful spotlight. Suddenly I remember the place. I have been here! I think and stop feeling lost. I have been here with my grandfather, with my father! I am in El Pinacate. The place is familiar to me, we came on a long weekend to celebrate my birthday, and with three of my girlfriends from my early youth to kiss each other. I climb the rock wall and reach the top of that granite mass that rises above the earth like an enormous natural sculpture. The view from the top is magnificent. I sit down and contemplate that rocky valley covered with craters of different sizes, it seems sublime to me, it is as if I were seeing everything from another perspective. The celestial body in the sky, now a close circle, provides good light. I remain enthralled, as if I were on another planet.

In this panorama, silence is everywhere. I notice an enormous presence, it is as if for the first time I became aware of the absence of sound, which I associate with a stranded ship, with the fallen black block of stars that I dreamed of a few nights ago. A large ship without flags or chimneys making its way through the Baja California Sea. I am not worried about time; I cannot be dead, I tell myself. Has my brain stopped assimilating the events? I am at the highest point of the crater; it is without a doubt a place charged with energy. I have always believed it; I know it now, I can feel it emanating from the ground; from the grains of fine sand. I am enthralled by its sensitivity; I am facing a vision. What made this landscape what it is? According to the state's tourist guide, El Pinacate is the product of strong volcanic activity thousands and thousands of years ago. Thinking about this, I don't know if I've traveled forward in time or backwards, it's a fact that something has happened, this time I'm conscious of the minutes, of their apparent slowness. I've never been so aware of my surroundings. The energy of the place under the effect of the moonlight is amazing, it suddenly connects me with a figure, it seems dressed in a space suit. I come to the conclusion that it's an alien. Contrary to what one might think, I'm not afraid. At first, we're surprised, he's the one who shortens the distance that separates us and stands about a meter away from me. It's someone I know and don't remember. We look at each other in surprise, I'm still in shock. Those formations, he explains, are fragments of his planet; they disintegrated and fell to earth in the form of meteorites many years ago. It makes sense if you look closely at that valley. He tells me that he comes to visit the site as a tribute to his ancestors.

"Have you lost your father?" he asks.

The thousand images of my father pass through my memory. I nod. The distant sandy hills take on a beautiful golden hue in the first rays of sunlight ... Then I sleep. I go back up the neck of the hourglass, and, immersed in a great peace, I close my eyes.

That afternoon, under Agnes' care, I recovered in bed. The doctor put me on a drip, prescribed a special diet and rest. For several days I did not dream. Agnes kept my secret, not telling anyone about when I got lost in the desert, although she never accepted that she saved my life.

My bone structure never changed, although something happened to my muscles, which became more flexible and stronger; to my senses, which became almost twice as sharp; but above all, to my perception. Not only do I guess things, but sometimes I feel a kind of transformation, when my blood is pumping at a thousand miles an hour and I have the need to run, jump and shout that I am alive, happy to have been lucky enough to get out of the desert and be able to tell it ... as if I were someone else.

31

I look at myself for the last time in the bathroom mirror, my features have taken shape before my eyes. I feel empty inside, hollow. I have washed the blood from my hands. I smooth my hair, put on my cap, put on my sunglasses and take a breath. When I leave the bathroom, I jump over the body of an earless man dressed in a tailcoat floating in a pool of blood. There are more men lying on the floor, blood on the walls. Don Cellucio hangs from a rope on the stage where he has presented singers, magicians, clowns, comedians and scantily clad girls. I stop to look at him, the fearsome boss is now swinging from a rope in his own business with his face bruised and his tongue sticking out like a cow. He's a nobody in this town now. His eyes seem to not believe the last thing they have seen. I do not feel the slightest compassion for that criminal, as the saying goes: "You reap what you sow." Several of his accomplices have their ears torn off as well. "If you live in violence, it will haunt you until it achieves its goal ...," Gaby told me, shortly before my sad, secret departure from Hermosillo, on a very dark night ... More dead people lying on the floor, wreckage. It's a carnage. Chairs thrown over, broken glasses, forgotten coats, women's shoes. Above the silence I hear the sound of sirens. My instinct tells me that I must get out of there as soon as possible. I push my way through more wounded people and finally reach the street. I run toward the pyramid of Cheops. The city of Las Vegas is disintegrating behind me.

PART THREE

There was a lot of activity that morning at the base. It was obvious that it was a special day. We had been assigned to serve as assistants to the assistants; mostly female soldiers, almost all of them dark-skinned and Latinos. The news was that a large group of soldiers were returning from Iraq. Among them was Martina's husband. The news hit me like a bucket of cold water. Neither she nor I expected it. Two months of honeymoon and suddenly the husband showed up, after eleven months of absence. That meant the end of our relationship, the eclipse of our happiness. Goodbye to the trips to the lake, to the movies, to the state capital. Goodbye to the three-day marathons in bed exuding sex, love. Goodbye to the most beautiful woman my future chef hands had ever touched.

The military personnel set up a podium in the middle of the basketball courts and we put in about two hundred chairs or more. There would be a welcome for the military heroes, a parade and medals would be awarded. Toño and I watched from afar. A minute of silence was observed for those who had fallen in action; those who had not returned. There were cries, fainting, hugs and other displays of affection, shots in the air and the trumpet's command. The general of the base—whom I had never seen—gave a speech and welcomed the brave men. The national anthem was sung and finally the band played "Semper Fidelis" to lift spirits.

The night before, Martina had sent me a text telling me of the surprise. It was after midnight, and we exchanged texts for about half an hour. We agreed, it was a tragedy. The news of her husband's return was indeed very bad, so I slept little thinking about how I would face it; whether I should just act crazy and forget the whole matter or continue with the little game in a more cautious way. Ruminating in a bad mood, I had a dream.

I am playing dice, going through a good streak; all my opponents have no features. I throw the cubes, but instead what falls to the table are four half-decayed molars that roll around among the chips. What we bet now are ears.

32

One afternoon, while cutting branches from trees, I met Captain Thomas, and we stopped to talk. The man looked sad, depressed. Without much preamble, he told me; his son Dan had died in a riot inside the prison not more than three days ago. Twelve stab wounds by another inmate, according to the police. In the end, they had suppressed and retaken the prison by force. I felt bad for the man, I gave him my condolences. I agreed to go to his house to see him at the end of my shift to keep him company. When I arrived, he was ready to go shopping; he wanted to get out of the base, see some of the scenery. He had washed the Cadillac, it looked impeccable, it was really a jewel. He used his visit as an excuse and gave me the keys to the car to drive. The seats were leather and as comfortable as those in an expensive lounge, the steering wheel adjusted to the driver's taste, everything was automatic. I felt isolated from the outside when I closed the door. We left the base and headed down the highway toward Macan City, where there was a large shopping center, and the trip was pleasant and full of trees. On the way he told me stories about his son as a child, about his daughter who had always been a princess, about the whole family together. Then, he realized it was not a topic of interest to me and turned on some music, seeming to regain some spirit. When we entered Macan, he made me park in front of a bar where we went in. He warned me; he would not buy me more than one beer since I was the designated driver, he would have two bourbons. We sat at the bar. From the mouth of the bartender and the attitude of the other patrons, we found out that the Falcons were playing against the Patriots, a great game. The captain pretended to know about the game and the series and exchanged comments about the superiority of the Atlanta team, with the guy next to him. They talked about the Patriots quarterback, who according to gossip was gay, and from there they went on to criticize the Bostonians; conceited, classist and hypocritical guys to the nth degree. The guy at the bar immediately became his friend, not to mention the bartender. I didn't say much, and like the rest, I concentrated on the television. In my other life, by this point, I would have already organized a bet with these guys, and I would be making them pay for the drinks. *Twenty to fifteen in favor of the Patriots*, of course. I smiled to myself. *Why had I said another life?* It wasn't an expression I used. I drank my beer as slowly as possible, until the captain finished his second drink. He paid in cash, threw a last cheer to the Falcons and said goodbye to the bartender and his bar companion. We both wanted more drinks, but we had to go shopping.

In addition to a month's worth of provisions, he made me carry a dozen pints of beer and a bottle of whiskey. Once at the base we unloaded everything; he put away what was going into the refrigerator and I separated the bathroom products, the extras he made me settle in a closet under the stairs to the second floor. Beer in hand, we went out to the terrace and sat under the parasol.

"You know what, young man? There are people born under bad luck. That was the case of my dear Dan. I saw him try his best and still fail. I don't know why, and I will never understand it."

"It's sad when that happens."

"In his case, he only made one mistake, a big one, which changed his life forever, letting himself be carried away by anger. Anger can be a bad advisor."

His words reminded me of Chian Ho's.

"All the investment in him was useless; all of his mother's worrying, that investment in dollars ... in words."

I placed my hand on his shoulder: "I'm really sorry about your son, Captain Thomas, I don't know how to express my sorrow."

"Don't worry, boy ...," he said and drank from his bottle. "You know what saddened me more? His sister didn't come to the funeral. I called her, and she said she would come, but at the last minute didn't and made up a story; the snow in Canada, the flights and I don't know what filth ... That's what awaits me the day I die, no doubt, absence."

"Don't talk like that, Captain, you're going to bury us all." I tried to be humorous.

"Mexican bastards, how come you're not scared of death?" He answered me in the same tone, with a somewhat sad smile.

"If it scares us, what we do is not think about it much, or prepare ourselves enough for when it comes."

"Each one of us lives in error, sometimes we would only like to go back a step, just one, but by that time it's too late, there's no going back."

I listened to Chian Ho again. How was it possible that two beings who were so different in space and beliefs sounded so similar? I looked at my watch and jumped in my seat: "Shit! The bus is leaving right now!" I stood up, intending to grab my jacket.

"Wait, man, you can leave in a little while."

"In a little while? the last damn bus is leaving!"

Captain Thomas looked at me for a moment, put his glass on the table and pulled out keys from his shirt pocket. Car keys. "There's no bus but there's a Cadillac outside … is that useful?" he said and threw the keys in the air.

I caught them, two chrome keys attached to a key ring with the word Cadillac in shiny italics.

I first looked at them, then at him with interest. I assumed he would drive me home himself later after the beers, or that he would lend me the car for a night to get home. I never thought he would end up giving me the vehicle and that he would live only one more month after that. I didn't quite believe it, neither his death, nor the gift of the Cadillac.

That's useful. I thought he was drunk and would regret it. Even that he would ask me for it back the next day, but that didn't happen. The next morning I went to his house to prevent any misunderstanding. I thanked him for lending me the car and tried to put the keys in his hand, but he refused. He was a man of his word, and it was mine, what's more, he had found the papers and wanted to give them to me. "Endorsed as if it had been a purchase, because of suspicions… You have to be faithful, boy, if I said I would give it to you, it is yours."

That night, when I got into the car I felt very good. I put on music and drove as if in cotton wool to the cat house. I parked it, checked twice that it was locked and once outside I observed it with pleasure. I was sure that good luck had returned, although I was wrong. Out of gratitude I began to visit the captain twice a week. We drank only three beers because I did not want to exceed my alcohol limit. A couple of times I took him to the supermarket, we went to Ray Charles Plaza to sit, and on a bench, we licked ice cream. You could say that he adopted me. The longest trip in his last days, we made it to Lake Seminole, where we rowed; he fished with an old rod and we drank three beers, because of the limits.

I attended his funeral, his daughter did too, and she did not stop crying the whole day of the service. I arrived late at the cat house. I turned the lock on the door very carefully, it must have been after midnight, and I didn't want to wake my landlady. I entered quietly, I slid the locks and when I turned around a dozen bright eyes looked at me expectantly in the darkness. I stood still for a moment, paralyzed. The watchful eyes began to move around me and suddenly we recognized each other. "You scared me, you bastards," I whispered to the cats, then I pushed my way to my bed."

It was undulating, I don't know if it was because of the effect of the moonlight, so powerful at that moment, but everything before my eyes was moving. I felt momentarily dizzy and staggered for a couple of seconds. Was a mirage possible at night with only the moonlight? Maybe I was in the depths of a hallucination, where everything, including the walls of the crater, moved in waves. I took a step ... another. I am surrounded by thirteen craters created millions of years ago: the result of the impact of a series of meteorites on the face of the earth ... or perhaps it's the alien's ship with all his ancestors inside?

Agnes died laughing when I told her about the man in the space suit.

33

A card from Pedro arrived at my address, the most old-fashioned thing in the world today what with email and Facebook. The truth is that receiving a card in the mail is a whole other experience, perhaps we are the last generation to experience it. I opened the envelope with some misgivings, it must be something serious. The first thing that came to mind was that my good friend was going to be a father, or was getting divorced ... or changing sex, haha! Why else would you send a card?

Damn Pedro. It was all a joke, the image of a pot-bellied crocodile with a balloon that said: "Time does not pass, only for lizards. Happy birthday!" Good fun, but two things, it wasn't my birthday for several months and I wasn't a Capricorn either. I imagined Pedro with a discount coupon for a card in hand. Nowadays there are coupons for everything, including roses and cards. The latter, a whole section of them in many stores still, for decades a big business displaced by the internet. I love them, I've seen everything from the silliest to the highly creative. There are cards for birthdays, newlyweds, mothers, fathers, anniversary, condolence, pranks and blank ones for the very serious moments.

I imagined Pedro buying the card at half price, along with some cigarettes or gum. They say that nobody changes anymore, and I believe in that. Surely, he remembered me, went to buy something at the supermarket, saw the coupon and decided to use it, vile coincidence. The nice thing was the thought. As far as I knew, he was doing well. He loved his wife, had big plans and a job in the government that consisted in washing the city's monuments and sculptures, that is, throwing soapy water on the fathers of the country; heroes mounted on horses and monumental pieces considered artistic or historical in Washington, DC. These statues are not few. A job, as I understood, very hard-fought, not only because of the good benefits, credits and other extras from the city government, but because two checks were received, one from city hall and another from Park Service.

He was married to his girlfriend of several years, the same one he met in Las Vegas, while I was having an affair with Patricia. Lilia, with whom he planned to have children. He was a good family man. Nothing like the drunk and troublemaking Pedro I had known. The green Pedro with the big hangover, lying next to a rather ugly Cuban in a cheap hotel. The Pedro fighting with a taxi driver over an exchange of money on Las Vegas Boulevard. We both shared a house in Ciudad Vice, where he was a waiter, which he had been doing all his life in this country.

The new job was through a relative of his, who had managed to have connections with certain employees of city government. An uncle, who not only owned two Peruvian food restaurants, but also had a good political fang. The fact is that this uncle of his was owed a favor, which resulted in Peter's position. A simple job, he told me. He and another guy drove a truck with large hoses over the historic center of the city of Washington. He had sent me a photo through Facebook, the hose between his legs spraying a jet of water at some general from the time of the revolution. It's a man on a horse and it's as if he were pissing on him, ha! "Peter cleans monuments," was the title. For jobs that we Latinos end up doing, damn it.

I received my friend's card the same afternoon I returned from the base with Martina's smell on my crotch and belly. It was an afternoon full of surprises. Tigrillo had left me a dead lizard at the entrance to my room; it's the way cats say thank you or, better said, help with the food in the house. My sister had sent me a message; she was pregnant and happy. In addition, she and Carlos also congratulated me on my birthday. I don't know where the hell everyone had gotten the idea that it was my birthday. But as it was, I found myself fascinated reviewing the scene between Martina and me, the kisses, the moans. All those coincidences colliding for the better. I caressed Tigrillo on the belly and head, "Thanks friend, for the lizard ... Mmm, it looks tasty." I grabbed the innocent lizard with two fingers and dropped it in the trash can in the bathroom; very discreetly, without letting the cat know I was belittling its gift.

I threw myself on the bed, still not believing it. Martina was the first woman I had fucked in several months. And she wasn't just any woman, but a beautiful, delicate-looking girl, alone and neglected. If all coincidences don't have a meaning or a connection, then why do they happen? Maybe it meant that my bad luck was beginning to fade; the bad vibes were disappearing, as well as the terrible dreams after my revenge was executed ... But above all, that the evil caused by Patricia had stopped having an effect on me. I'm talking about her witchcraft. I felt the change, I began to feel light, free ... Suddenly, I began to float in the bed, to rise, as if I were levitating. At first, I was scared, I put my hands on my sides preparing for the fall, but this didn't happen; I was separated from the old mattress by about nine feet, I rose higher until I was inches from the ceiling. I didn't believe it. I could see the street through the window, the dust on the curtain rod frame, the grime on the bathroom door. I was floating, mind-blown, I'm not lying.

At that moment, I knew that both distance and time were my best allies. I was an ethereal being, I don't know how I had managed to reduce my weight to that of a feather, how I was overcoming the rules of gravity. It wasn't more than ten minutes, but it was definitive. Then I had a certainty; if the roof hadn't been there, I would have been able to leave the property, go around at least to the corner and back without touching the ground. A woman passed in front of the house pushing a twin stroller, a car and a man on a bicycle, the only one who realized that I was floating in the air separated from the bed was a dog, which looked into the window close to the ground, although this time he didn't urinate on the glass, but ran away. I landed as softly on the bedspread as I had risen. I couldn't help but feel my temples throbbing and a certain nervousness. That had happened, no doubt.

I remembered myself lying on the dark granite of the main crater of El Pinacate, in what I swear is a dream, but it was nothing but the harsh reality of the longest night of my life, the most clairvoyant. I closed and opened my eyes again. I'm in my room in Albany, at Mrs. Robbins's house ... the presence of the ocelot in bed brought me back to reality. He said, "Meow," and rubbed himself against one of my legs. My little friend's greeting brought me out of what seemed to be a trance, although I couldn't help but shiver. I grabbed the quilt with my hands, tight, like the anchor of a ship about to go away with the storm. For several minutes I had contradicted the laws of gravity and that made me insecure. Ocelot began to lick his paws, I slowly let go of the bed until I felt safe, I breathed deeply. I smiled. I patted my friend's head and sat down on the bed, the smile on my face still there. Maybe the dice were about to fall in my favor. After that, why should I doubt anything? Although it is true that my first reaction when I left Martina's house was to run and get out of town, in the end I decided to take the bet like a good gambler and stay. I didn't feel guilty, nor bad. We had acted like animals, there was no denying that.

34

The first trip with the Cadillac was to Atlanta. I was already fed up with Albany, with the soldiers and their wives, but above all, with the brusque peasants who preferred to do everything from their trucks. For example, going to the bank was a matter of rolling down the window, typing in numbers and letters; depositing, withdrawing, having a printed account balance and not even saying thank you. Comer, the largest fast-food company on the planet, offers a drive-in service where you order through a microphone and when you get to the window, they have your burger ready and a young woman hands it to you in a bag with French fries and packets of ketchup, plus a large soda, of course. I have tried to eat like this, and I still can't get it, although there are others who find pleasure in driving and eating their sandwich at the same time, languidly looking at the road to the rhythm of their favorite song, in slow motion, staining the steering wheel and seats with grease.

Atlanta turned out to be a fit city. There were a lot of people on the street, perhaps because it was early autumn, and everyone had gone out to do the shopping. There was traffic, slow and heavy, and I didn't come in a cart, but on a steed, even strangers turned to look at "Spirit of Heaven," as Toño had baptized it for its metallic color, in his eagerness to give a name to everything; The TV was Juana, the phone was Paco, his old car was Tatoyo and so on. Once the Cadillac was in the parking lot, I walked around, looking at shop windows, corners, restaurant menus, women passing by me. Finally I went into a bar that I liked. I ordered a beer and ended up drinking three.

On the phone I had messages from my landlady, from Toño, Peter and from a certain Mrs. Highs, who wanted to talk to me. I immediately thought, maybe it was a lawyer with some surprise, some fight. When I receive things like that, I feel like running, closing my eyes and running. I had gotten tired of being the road runner, *beeep-beeep*! Something smelled fishy about all this ... It had to be about money, some kind of blackmail for what happened in Las Vegas. For a moment, it occurred to me that maybe Captain Thomas' daughter wanted the car back, although I dismissed the idea, I had the papers, they were signed by both of us and everything had been legal, even if she wanted to.

Peter greeted me, saying he was happy to be moving into a new house in the suburbs, thanks to a loan, and he sent me his address in case I decided to visit him in Virginia. We had a friendship pact, so we kept each other informed from time to time how we were doing. He had left Washington, DC because it was expensive and elitist; the rents were stratospheric, the food was sky-high. Peter and I were like those deep-sea runners who lag behind for a moment but always finish. Peter was ahead in terms of the number of places he had lived and made a life for himself. The latter was the hardest, because there are new lessons to learn. You leave everything behind, not just furniture, books, clothes but friends too. A homeless man came into the bar to ask for a drink, dragging his terrible stench with him, like the long tail of a lizard. He was already drunk, you could tell, it was perhaps the cause of his downfall. He started asking for money at the tables, but soon someone came and pushed him out. For some strange reason, I sometimes associated homeless people with those World War II pilots who were left on battlefields, with the tips of their planes in the middle of the field, with them inside, about to explode. I saw it in a film, perhaps that's why.

In one text, Martina wanted to see me; the problem was that her husband wouldn't leave her side for a second, and she didn't know how to get away. I remembered her. In short, he was in love, but that was bullshit; another fucked up relationship. Why did I love fucked up relationships? I reproached myself. We had gone to bed long before we even met. Like two animals. Not a porn movie, certainly, but a strange way to bring two people together, don't you think? And I say it's not porn, because the truth is that the whole experience had been quite traditional, me on top of her with the sheets covered. Nothing very experimental; afterwards of course, there was that, but I won't tell you about it because it's private.

I felt jealous of her husband, maybe right now he was in bed with her, doing something he learned back in the Middle East. I asked for a second beer. That meant that I might not see her for a few weeks. The fact that the guy was an abuser infuriated me. He would fuck her and hit her, or the other way around. I squeezed the bottle, what a war hero. But sometimes no one is more to blame than the victim. *Don't fuck with me, buddy, you're not here to criticize anyone*. True, who was I to open my mouth? I had fled Las Vegas to escape the curse inflicted by Patricia. Beautiful woman, although light-haired, with long nails, a big mouth and an incredible sense of survival. Cunning as a fox and evil-minded as a demon.

I remembered her, she boasted of being the survivor of a dysfunctional family, an alcoholic father, perverse relationships and the porn industry, the latter I found out much later, already in the second round. She had learned witchcraft with some black women who had landed by chance in the video company, where she had fallen for the typical modeling, fame and easy money thing, according to her. When I met her, I had already gone around the stadium four times. It was one of those things that puts two people in contact and is called chance, or the collision of two destinies. She took hold of me from the first time we met in the breakfast room. And the second night in her bed, the sex was impressive. She had an incredible vaginal movement; it was as if she could move the muscles inside her body at will and suck. She let you do it, but when she wanted it to end, she began to move inside as if an ancient witch inhabited her ...

A drunk who seemed asleep. He composed himself for a moment, drank the last drops of his drink and barked: "Reality is obscene, it stinks of poop, semen and screams! The world is raw, bloody and cruel!"

35

I meet my grandmother. This time she is waiting for me at the entrance of a ruined hacienda. She opens the gate that's been closed for many years. We enter through an arched corridor. The ceilings have collapsed, we walk on rubble and pieces of brittle tile. Some walls are also in ruins, others are badly damaged. We pass through a red stone staircase that leads nowhere. There is no doubt it was an elegant construction, it preserves interesting details, such as a cross of brocaded metal on the main door, the remains of a fountain and a wall decorated with multicolored mosaics, in what must have been the entrance to the rooms. My grandmother walks with familiarity in the place. We cross a courtyard into a huge nave, which must have been a ballroom or a place for receptions. The floor in this area is made of very fine sand, as if the disintegration had taken place from the foundations of the place. I advance cautiously, afraid that one of those walls will collapse on us. My grandmother stops at an old, rusty, dull brass bed, of large proportions. She sits down on the cherry-colored cover, perfectly laid, and rests her hands in her lap. "Doña Marina," she tells me, picks up the sweater she has been working on and resumes her work with the hooks between her fingers, without paying much attention to me. On the four legs of the bed, there are chickens tied; they cackle, they spin around, they dig their beaks into the sandy floor to get back up. Some scratch, others peck at each other, they flap their wings noisily.

"Take a seat, son," she says, pointing to an old chair, about to fall over. I sit down with caution, knowing that the chair can topple over, but it can hold my weight like nothing else. It is strong, and I am surprised by its apparent dilapidated state. It is afternoon or dawn, there is no sun, so our shadows are not projecting. The sky has a very strong orange color. I cannot understand the scene. Even less, the meaning of the chickens, and if they symbolize something; or just that Grandmother does not want to let them loose, within reach of coyotes and thieves. It is the first time that I am physically in the place, although I have driven by and seen it. It is known as the Antigua Hacienda del Carmen and is located on a detour from the highway to Navojoa. From a distance, it can be seen only as some walls, a half-destroyed dome and a couple of arches. As far as we know, it is the hull of a hacienda from the time of the revolution. Grandmother, without stopping her knitting, raises her eyes and observes me sweetly. A question remains on my lips: "Why have we come here?"

I woke up calmly, without any surprises, unlike at the beginning when my grandmother's dreams began to happen. Fortunately, I don't dream about her every night or even every week; there are periods when we don't communicate. Nowadays, I consider them a dialogue. From all the accumulation of dreams during the week, I set aside my grandmother's and decipher them little by little, until I manage to find the meaning, because they definitely have a particular meaning, I have verified that. The days before Patricia left, I had a dream in which my grandmother warned me, although

I was not able to complete the reading. I missed the part about the sheep slaughtered with stones, the part about the candle on her head.

I yawned big. I sat up in bed. *What did the damned chickens tied by their legs mean?* I went into the bathroom, took a shower and got dressed humming a song. I took the two key chains and smiled. Having a car makes me think about trips and hitting the road. I drank coffee with my landlady, and she told me to make eggs for the two of us. We had breakfast like an old couple, watching television; like a mother and son who can't find what to say to each other. I thought about how I would have liked to spend more time with my mother, watch television with her, walk through the streets of Hermosillo; see her cured of cancer. I remembered her in bed, with oxygen in her nose, with needles in her veins where the serum enters ... Then the damn fire.

36

The four of us went out, Toño with Esther and I with Ana Graciela, the "Maid Easy." We went to the movies and when we left, we said goodbye, each one with their own partner. I liked the girl, but she accepted that she would never fall in love with a man like me, because we represented insecurity and poverty. "Money is everything," she finished. Ana Graciela, a smart, enterprising and ambitious girl. With a boyfriend in Chicago whom she described as a little older. A woman capable of sacrificing anything for money and the "old gringo with an inheritance."

"How many deceiving old men have you slept with?" She didn't like my joke. One thing we did together was plagiarize the recipe of the base's champion and take a picture of it in corporate espionage style; it was very funny. Together, we distracted the arrogant old lady with different tricks, and were able to get into the kitchen. I tried to convince Regina to participate with that same recipe in the annual contest at the base, just to see the faces of the judges. Of course she didn't accept, but she couldn't stop laughing at how we made the old lady dizzy with our racket so that we could keep her recipe for cookies, and the one for chicken in sherry that I still think is delicious. The idea was mine.

The woman kept her recipes written in an old leather notebook next to recipe books, in a corner of the kitchen, an enviable place with the latest in appliances and utensils. That kitchen was in no way inferior to that of any professional chef. With a small, newly acquired twelve-megapixel camera, I took a photo of the two handwritten recipes. For a micro-hundredth of a second, I thought about keeping the whole notebook; it must be a jewel, but I gave up almost immediately after thinking about it, because that was a bit much. Besides, I am not a thief. So, I continued with the plan, took the two photographs and returned the notebook to its place among the other books on the shelf. I noticed a book on Greek food, an expensive one from the look of it; it had good photos, some history. I heard the voices of Ana Graciela and the old lady approaching. I put the camera in my shirt pocket and picked up my toolbox from the floor, all in one movement. I took two steps out of the kitchen and ran into them at the entrance. The woman looked at me a little surprised. *How had I gotten from the bathroom to the kitchen?* She probably wondered.

"I checked the water supply for leaks, but there's nothing wrong with it."

"Thanks," she said, and walked us to the exit.

Once outside we laughed our heads off, kissed each other and in the work cart I took her to the artificial lake at the base, where we fucked in some bushes. We talked and agreed that I would cook chicken with sherry for her and her partners in the house cleaning business, Carmen and Esther, in about a week, on her birthday. We watched the sunset like two soap opera lovers—her words—holding hands.

At that moment I seriously thought, perhaps because of Pedro's influence, that it was time to leave the single life and play house with Ana Graciela. I liked her, she spoke my language. She was sweet and had great maternal potential, despite her defects. As I said, she had two serious ones, the most egregious was being materialistic and the other that she didn't like to read and preferred television. But hey, there's no such thing as a perfect woman. The only trip we made together was to Savannah Beach in her business car, which couldn't go unnoticed because of the red letters on the sides, the trunk and the roof: "Maid Easy. If you need your home or office cleaned, we come to you," was the slogan written even on the inside of the Focus. On two occasions, we were stopped by a couple of potential clients who wanted us to come and provide them with the service.

Ana Graciela was disappointed when, upon arriving at the beach, she took off her clothes and jumped into the water, which was too cold for the taste of anyone who remembers the Caribbean Sea. She came back shivering from the cold and with an annoyed face. I covered her with one of the towels and hugged her. We walked; she collected shells and pebbles, we drew in the sand and built a castle, which was soon washed away by the water. Two days at sea with her, without being able to get into the water, brought me back to reality. She turned out to be tantrum-laden, obsessed with money to the max, greedy and critical. One night she did exasperate me when she insisted on not tipping the waitress; according to her, she had been flirting with me. "Don't fuck with the poor girl, she barely has enough for her damn salary." Making a family, being faithful and everything else, collapsed like the sandcastle. The last night, as I knew it was the last for both of us, I fucked her like an angel. I remember her ecstatic eyes telling me incongruities.

37

"Sergio, how are you?"

"Hi, Terry."

"Sorry if I said something inappropriate last time, I was very drunk and maybe I said stupid things. Just … sorry, man."

"Bah, don't worry. Tequila is like that; it can give you serious surprises."

"Yeah fuck, I had forgotten. Whatever I said was not my intention. Regina said you left the house upset."

"No, not at all, I had a good time. Thanks for the invitation."

"On the contrary, thank you for making us food. You sure know how to cook, bro. It was delicious."

I smiled, grateful for the compliment.

"A little, a little. I would like to study more and be better, I have big dreams." I regretted saying the last thing.

"When you have dreams you have to carry them out, otherwise why dream?"

I remembered his dreams of reaching the Olympics with his basketball team and I felt less bad.

"Wipe the slate clean," he said with a smile and extended his hand to me.

"Of course, man, it's okay." I said shaking his hand.

"You're a good man, you know? Maybe I can tell them apart because I know a lot of bad ones."

He looked sad.

"It must be, in your profession," I answered. "What can I offer you? Water, soda?"

"If you have bottled water, I'll accept it."

"Sure, sure," I turned around and went into the cabin to get two bottles of water from the refrigerator. When I came back, Terry had put his chair in the shade and was looking sideways. I handed him the bottle and pulled out one of the folding chairs used for events, we had about a hundred. I sat down next to him. We toasted with the water. The temperature was pleasant, and the colors of the evening were falling. It was very pretty.

"Hey, in exchange for dinner, or rather, in the same spirit of camaraderie and solidarity, we want to invite you to come with us to the beach. It would be three days, there's a place to stay and everything, it's a friend's house."

"Is it your friend Scot's house?" I asked, anticipating.

"A son of a bitch, right? But no, he's another friend, completely different. He and his wife are going on a trip, and they don't have anyone to leave the dog and the parrot with. Regina offered and so I'm taking the opportunity to extend the invitation. Next week, we leave early Friday and return Monday before noon."

I was going to say no, but his sincerity convinced me. Plus, I hadn't dipped my feet in the sea for more than a month since my trip with Ana Graciela.

"Sounds good, let me arrange something with Toño, my work partner." I extended my hand to him, and we lightly bumped fists in friendship. I looked him in the eyes, Terry was definitely a good man, maybe better than me.

"Make your arrangements."

"Okay, I haven't been to the ocean in a while."

"You'll love it. The beach is less than two hundred feet from the house. The water is cold, so don't get your hopes up, but the place is nice."

"I already know about the cold sea, but the sea is the sea ... *Bacán*, as Peruvians say. And how much do I have to pay for gas? For food, or what's up?"

Terry shifted in his chair.

"No way, nothing, don't worry about it."

"But one more mouth is always an extra mouth, right? Does this place you're talking about have a kitchen?"

"Of course, it's a full house. Why such a silly question?"

"I'd like to help out, going along for free isn't my thing. My father taught me something: 'Everything you have, you have to earn it.' I cook for a living, how about that?"

"Okay, we'd be thrilled, Regina is going to love it."

Terry told me a little more about the house and the owner, another disabled friend, whom he had met in OC at a protest, apparently, he was a millionaire.

"When you're a millionaire it's not a problem to get around in a wheelchair, you know? The beach house is energy efficient and wheelchair friendly. In addition to a pool, it has a basketball court, among other amenities."

"When you're a millionaire you don't have any problems, period."

We laughed. I asked him about the team and how it was doing in the standings. It turned out that it was doing pretty well, second place nationally wasn't too bad. We finished drinking the water in our respective bottles, and afterward, Terry drove away on his motorized machine smiling as he had arrived. He was not only a good man, but one with a lot of courage. I couldn't even put myself in his place.

On Friday morning Terry and Regina picked me up at the cat house. They looked radiant. Regina picked up Tigrillo and petted him. I packed a small suitcase with three changes of clothes, a razor, toothbrush, toothpaste and lotion; plus a new book whose title I have forgotten, and a bathing suit and a cell phone charger. I climbed into the back of the car; they were listening to Bob Dylan—I later learned his name. We didn't talk about anything interesting, and in the second part of the trip, Terry insisted on listening to basketball on the radio. We arrived at lunchtime. The house looked like any beach house today, a high white wall, video cameras and a large automatic metal gate. Regina searched through her bag and pulled out a keychain.

The place was very comfortable and very well designed. It was a one-and-a-half-story concrete house; five rooms with three bathrooms, plus a large living room and a good-sized kitchen. We greeted the animals who were sponsoring our vacation; Clark the dog and Repetition the parrot, who we found saying: "Nice ass, nice ass!" We speculated that the parrot had probably only gotten part of the message, which we deduced could have been "You have a nice ass," or "Nice ass, sweetheart" or "Nothing like a nice ass." Terry explained to us that the friend in the wheelchair, but a millionaire, was married to a former Miss America with a *very* nice ass and big tits, that must be how it was. Regina asked how the millionaire had ended up paralyzed. Terry didn't know the details, only that he had been in an accident in a sports car.

We settled in, each of us free to choose the room we liked. The room I chose looked directly out onto a palm tree growing in a pot and had a door to the terrace, where there was a parasol, a round table and chairs. In addition to an electric grill and a minibar. On the lower level, there was a round pool and a garden. I opened the window, letting in the sea breeze, its smell and its humidity. That night we had pizza for dinner and drank beer on the terrace, looking at the stars and listening to the coming and going of the water. We told each other a little about ourselves too, and I learned a few things. Like how Terry, before Iraq, didn't like basketball as much as American football; that he had been an excellent deep-sea diver and now was only a mediocre swimmer. Two things that embarrassed him were how bad he was at math and how shy he was with women.

He also told us that he was an orphan, although he still had a sister whom he saw only twice a year. In many of those things we were alike, I told him and pointed out the similarity between our experiences. Like having only one sister and being an orphan in my teens, as well as being bad at math, of course. The two things that embarrassed me, particularly, were the hair that grew on my back and being sentimental. Regina laughed about this and, when it was her turn, she told us that unlike us, she still had both of her parents. Although she didn't have any blood siblings, she did have an adopted sister whose life was full of trauma. Also, unlike us, she liked equations, self-help books—which I hated—and biographies. As for sports, she preferred yoga, and the only embarrassing thing was her little toe that had almost no nail. We toasted to the complexes and physical mistakes in unison, "What the hell?"

I felt comfortable and told them how important my grandmother had been in my upbringing; how she liked to use old sayings and metaphors where animals usually appeared to educate us. Also, how she had taken my mother's place, while the other one was slowly dying, numbed by morphine, in bed. Regina took my hand and looked at me sweetly. We drank another round of beers, trying to guess the names of the stars in the sky and the location of the Andromeda galaxy.

Regina was the first to say goodnight; she was tired. Another thing she didn't like very much, unlike us, was driving, she said before leaving. Terry and I talked a little about basketball and baton pong. I told him that I had fallen deeply in love with Samantha, he laughed. I found out she was married to a corporal and was actually Regina's best friend; they both attended a Sudoku club. I remembered Samantha's thighs and got chills. We finished our last beer and went to our rooms.

That night, against my intentions, I didn't dream of Samantha at baton pong with a short dress and beautiful eyes, but of Sonora, of my past...

I'm walking along the beach; the body of a gray whale has been thrown out of the sea by the waves. I approach the animal; it grows huge as I get closer to it. My grandmother is waiting for me, sitting in a rocking chair, knitting the last details of the sweater she has been making for me for some time now. I sit down on the sand next to her and we both remain silent before the dying animal, which resembles a stranded ship. The cetacean is twice the size of a trailer and as tall as a two-story house. It lets out a final snort, moves its tail and dies while we wait for the waves to reach our feet and for time to pass. Like Jonah, I try to enter the dead animal, it has expired with its mouth open, a very bad smell emanates from it. My grandmother prevents me from entering.

The moment I enter that enormous being, I wake up. I'm bathed in sweat.

I stood up and looked out the window. On the horizon the sun timidly emerged from the water. The smell of the sea had activated that dream ... In real life, the dead whale on the beach had happened about twenty years ago. We were on a family vacation. I was walking with Gaby along the seashore when we saw it and ran to it. It was an extraordinary sight for us, but for many others, it was inexplicable. When we arrived, the animal was giving its last thrashing and making strange noises, as if it were choking on all that air. There were a lot of people, some of whom were throwing buckets of water on its skin in order to make its agony less painful. Among the people around the dying cetacean was a woman praying. She waved flowers in the air and murmured a prayer to the sea. The reason why the great mammal had come out of the water, according to an old man, was because it was suffering from either a virus contracted in the contaminated water of the Sea of Cortez, or some poisoning caused by the ingestion of putrefied algae ... I shook my head. Remembering is like teleporting into the past. It's fabulous to have memories! Don't you think?

The proximity of the sea makes me erotic. I masturbated under the shower thinking about Martina. I got dressed and went straight to the kitchen. I made coffee, washed some potatoes and put them in the microwave, as well as some bacon. I chopped onion and garlic, then mixed everything together and put sour cream on top. Separately, I cut tomatoes and celery. Regina was the one who caught up with me, she helped me set the table on the terrace and open the white wine for the mimosas. The three of us had breakfast in complete calm, we joked and couldn't help but complain about how politicians have hijacked the planet and corporations have sucked up all the resources. Regina offered to pick up the dishes and put them in the dishwasher. I entertained myself looking at the pictures and photographs on the walls. Most of them showed Terry's friend, always with some different woman or on board some sports car, motorcycle or boat. I couldn't imagine a guy like that pushing a wheelchair.

After breakfast we went down to the basement. All three of us were amazed. The huge room contained a bar, complete with a counter, a pool table and an electronic ping pong machine. There was also a red loveseat on a soft red carpet. Ceiling lights of different intensity and colors. Terry started playing with the lights and managed to make the room completely green, then blue. Above the loveseat there was a white light, another one over the coffee table. We exclaimed oohs, ahs, boos, wows and made jokes. Terry mimed a blowjob by puffing out one cheek and running his tongue inside, we laughed. We concluded that the owners of the house were quite voyeuristic. We discussed voyeurism. Regina said it was more of a man thing, although there must be exceptions, of course. Not all voyeurism fell into the sexual category, Terry said, there were other kinds; he told us about an officer who loved to watch people die. She asked me if I was a voyeur. I was slow to respond, but since we were among friends, I accepted. I told them about my experience in Las Vegas, when I lived with my wife, who had encouraged me to do it, but that deep down I didn't like it. Voyeurism had made me suffer a lot. Regina said she couldn't make sense of it, although Terry and I exchanged glances. *If men are voyeurs, women are the worst exhibitionists,* I thought.

We returned to the upper floor in an elevator. The house had ramps at the entrance and to access the beach, plus two elevators. It was what is known in real estate jargon as a "wheelchair friendly" house.

Regina and I took off our shoes, went down the stairs and walked out to the beach. Terry turned on the television and watched us from the windows. The water of the North Atlantic was gray, thick and cold as hell, perhaps because a storm was coming. Out of the corner of my eye, I glanced at Regina. Good legs, nice ass, nice waist, but small breasts ...

I reproached myself for my behavior. I was a bastard evaluating my friend's wife. I returned my gaze to the sea, the clouds creating shapes, and I kept myself there, on the footprints that disappeared in the sand. Regina jumped and avoided the cold water, but she looked happy. I thought about her poor husband inside, tied to the damn wheelchair.

"I love the ocean, the fact that it is imposing. Maybe because it makes me feel free."

"In my homeland, we crossed the Gulf of Baja California by boat, then the peninsula. We would walk for something like three days to reach the open sea, the Pacific, which definitely has another color," I said.

"What? My first memory of the sea is my mother and my sister building sandcastles. Every time I come, it is the first thing that comes to my mind."

Regina jumped in the air dodging the cold water on her feet and smiled.

"Last night I had a dream, it happened a long time ago …"

"What was it?"

"It happened when I was a young boy. I saw a whale die. It had been thrown out of the sea. It turns out that at that time, I don't know now, whales came to the Baja California Sea to spawn and have their babies. This whale I'm talking about apparently was suicidal. At least that was the story that ran in the newspapers."

"I thought only humans thought about that."

A group of people passed by carrying folding chairs, coolers and cartons of beer. I looked at them intrigued.

"There's is a small estuary up ahead. People go there to swim, the waves are calmer and it's shallow. Let's see if the three of us can go later."

We frolicked a bit more and returned to the house. In the afternoon, a storm broke out, the sea became choppy. We drank brandy. There wasn't much food in the refrigerator, but with the little I found, I made tapas. Martina offered to go shopping the next day. We set up the chairs in front of the large window and watched the storm develop until nightfall.

"You definitely have talent with food, bro, it was delicious."

"Mm, yes, yummy, thanks for cooking for us," Regina said.

"It's a pleasure."

"Thanks to you, for the work." Terry really liked my food.

"You're welcome, man. Cooking is no problem for me"

"No, but it does take time, I can tell you that since I know a few things." Regina came over and kissed me on the cheek on her way to the kitchen.

The storm intensified and the sky turned dark.

"I enjoy storms, especially if they're like this one; a combination of thunderstorms with tropical storms and strong winds ... Maybe because it never rains like this in Texas," Terry commented.

"Really? You wouldn't believe me, but there can be thunderstorms without water in the desert," I said.

"Where? In Sonora?"

"I happened to see an impressive one one night. Every time a lightning bolt struck the sky, the desert lit up again as if it were daytime, but not a single drop of water fell; the wind, the sound, everything was the same but without water."

"How incredible, I've been told about that kind of storm."

Regina came back with a sweater on, and an extra plate of food.

"It must be scary, right? In the desert," Regina said as she sat down again.

"No, it's like with any other thunderstorm, but it's rare, maybe because we associate thunderstorms with rain so much," I replied.

"What if you get hit by lightning?" Regina asked again.

"Well, it'll fry you," Terry said, and we all laughed. "It's advisable to get rid of any metal you're carrying; like rings, belt buckles, coins, etc. Even shoes. Many boots have metal in the laces. Army boots even have metal in the front and back, to protect toes and heels."

The three of us looked at each other. Apparently boots, night vision goggles, infrared deactivators, the most sophisticated weapons and even satellites, were of no use at the last minute when luck abandons you.

We finished eating and Regina got up, taking the dirty dishes with her to the kitchen. She came back and stood in front of me.

"Sergio, it's my turn to clean and put the dishes in the machine, it's part of the deal … so don't move, okay?"

"If you want, I can help you."

"No, no, no, sir, you enjoy your drink and calm down while I do my part."

"Okay, okay. Cool."

Regina raised her glass and toasted with us: "Cheers, guys."

Terry looked at his watch and said: "The game is about to start, what do you say?"

We sat in front of the big television screen .

"With these screens it's like you're in the stands," Regina commented, throwing herself on the couch next to me.

"True," I said.

Terry turned around with his chair and all, raised his finger high and said: "False ... Nothing, absolutely nothing, is the same as being in the stadium watching the game live. Here you see it, there you live it."

Neither Regina nor I said a word, paraphrasing my grandmother: *God's word, no king can refute it*. The Boston Celtics were playing against the Atlanta Hawks.

"Who are you rooting for?" Terry asked me.

One of my rules in games is to root for the home team.

"The Hawks, what do you think?"

"I thought you might root for the Celtics."

"Never."

"They are champions and famous because they have more money to buy better players."

"That's the situation in sports today, the same thing happens in soccer and in baseball, don't get me started," was my comment.

"Yeah, fuck, *before* the players were from the city, from the team where they played, and they did it for love of the jersey and the homeland, not for money."

"In soccer, all the team jerseys have the name of the corporation that sponsors them in giant letters."

"In a little while the military uniforms will be the same."

"How sad," Regina ended the conversation."

The commercials ended and the game restarted. The Celtics were moving the ball from one side of the court to the other with incredible speed despite the Hawks' strong defense. In three passes they made a memorable score, a ball that went under the basket. I was tempted to place a bet with Terry, but I didn't want to let him lose; only a stroke of luck, or a more risky attack, could save the Hawks from the inevitable; as if written in water.

Regina stood up, yawned and said goodnight to us. She was going to shower and then to bed. She kissed Terry on the mouth and me on the cheek. She looked tired. She stretched like a cat, and I could see her nice ass, her small, tight breasts.

"See you tomorrow, guys, enjoy your game and if you want beer, it's there in the fridge, just don't finish it."

"Good night," we said in unison.

The game was half over and the Hawks' destiny seemed to be assured. I went to the kitchen for a couple of beers. I was craving another strong one, but decided against it when I remembered that we were going swimming the next day and I didn't want to be hungover. Those things are a bad combination. The cameras pointed at the cheerleaders, and we licked our lips, at least I did. I remembered Samantha. I knew that she didn't live on the base and that she came to practice every other day. I also knew that she was married for convenience, and that she was happy with the idea of meeting me. The commentators talked about the plays; the players, the statistics and even the grandmothers and cousins of each one on the teams. A new round of commercials started.

"These sons of bitches, more than sports journalists, are some damn gossips. I mean, who the fuck cares if the captain of the Celtics lives with his girlfriend and his mother? Fuck!"

"It's voyeurism, bro. That's what sells, hence the success of Facebook."

We toasted. I went to the bathroom, came back and sat down. Terry didn't seem to be paying much attention to anything; he was staring out the window into the distance. Suddenly, he turned to me, smiled and as if to cheer himself up, took a big sip from the bottle of beer: "Sergio, as my friend, I need you to do me a favor ..."

"Whatever you want, as long as it's within my possibilities."

"Don't take it the wrong way ..."

"What's it about?"

"I need you to make love to Regina."

"What?" I said and jumped in my seat.

"Honestly."

"Are you crazy? Regina is like my sister; you both are my friends."

"Precisely because of that."

"You don't know what you're saying Terry. You have no idea …"

"I don't know, true, but I can't tie her to eternal chastity; she's a woman, she has needs. It would be cruel of me."

I looked him in the eyes: "Yes, Terry, but that hurts. I know what I'm telling you ..."

He turned the beer bottle over twice in his hands: "Do it for her."

I took a deep breath. "It's sick, it can destroy relationships, not only ours, but both of you."

"We'd have to face it then, when it comes."

"No, Terry, that's not it. You don't know what you're asking me."

"It's a decision we've both made. We've already discussed it, *she* and *I*."

I looked at him incredulously: "Already discussed it? And how are you so sure that I'll accept?"

"We're not sure, but I know you like her, I've seen you watching her, I saw you this afternoon on the beach ..."

This time I looked at him seriously: "What if you regret it later?"

"It's better with someone I know—and it won't hurt her—than with a stranger, behind my back."

"You make it difficult for me."

"It would be a special favor. If you were the huge man in this wheelchair, and I were you, I would do you the same favor without a doubt. That's what friends are for, right?"

"Don't say that about yourself."

"So?"

"The problem is that I've established another kind of relationship with Regina and suddenly changing it, it's going to be impossible for me."

"She's a whole woman; with sexual desires and needs ... I love her, that's why I'm asking you to make her enjoy it as if I were the one doing it."

I drank my beer, all that conversation had made me nervous, a little out of place.

"It's just a little sex, I'm not asking you to fall in love with her, that's *my* role to play."

"Of course."

"Or don't you like her?"

"Regina is beautiful, it's not because of that. Anyone would sleep with her, anyone with a brain and a cock, that is."

"That's precisely why I'm asking you."

"And what about her?"

"She hates cheating. This wouldn't be cheating."

I put the beer bottle on the table and stood up. I said goodbye to Terry walking away toward my room. Before taking the hallway, I said: "Let me think about it. And you, you think about it too."

In the room, I undressed, turned off the light and got into bed. It was a crazy idea. The coming and going of the waves lulled me and soon I fell sleep, although not for long. Around two in the morning I had a visitor. Regina didn't let me protest, silencing me first with her index finger, then with a kiss that was followed by many others. She smelled of soap, of a jungle woman. The sheets fell to the floor, soon we were naked, sweating and rolling around in bed, while the salty sea breeze cooled our backs.

When I woke up, no one was there, as if I had lived a dream. In any case, it was better. I did my routine of squats, sit-ups, push-ups and twists with kicks. I was going to go in for a bath, but I felt like running on the beach. I decided to take the opportunity. I dressed in shorts and a T-shirt. I went out to the living room, then to the kitchen for a glass of water. The place was silent. My friends were probably still asleep. I opened the sliding door to the terrace, went down the stairs and soon I was in the sand making disappearing footprints on the water that came and went. My feet sprouted wings.

38

I came back from running. Regina had gotten up and started breakfast. She looked radiant. We kissed on the mouth, although I moved away early, I didn't want to be so cynical in front of Terry, should he come into the room. It hurts to see your wife sharing caresses with another, I knew that very well.

"I got a head start. Breakfast soon; pancakes, bacon and eggs. I also gave the parrot and the dog breakfast," she said. She was dressed in very short shorts and a loose T-shirt. "It smells delicious. I'm going to take a shower and I'll be back," I said and started for the bedroom.

"I'm in the final touches, so hurry up," she warned me.

When I returned to the dining room Terry and Regina were already at the table.

"Good morning," I said and sat down.

Regina served me coffee and brought me a full plate. I stuck my fork in and stuffed my mouth: "Yum, delicious. Thanks, Regina," I said, referring to breakfast, but also to the night before.

She understood the message very well and winked at me in complicity. Terry threw the phone on the table; something had upset him.

"Bastards."

For a moment I thought he was referring to us.

"I don't buy it, goddamn it! I'm not the same, and not just because of the lack of limbs, but because I've changed over the years ..." He tapped on his phone, indicating a message he didn't like. "Before you enlist, they promise you a job, a career, a future and security. They say they are your family. Once you are no longer useful to them, though, they treat you as if you were a burden, as if you would have been better off dead. They promised me 'legs' and I am still waiting for them."

"Terry has joined other disabled veterans to go to protest in Washington, DC. There are people who have been sent out of the hospital without treatment. We need a more humane system. We can't leave everything to private health and therapy companies. Imagine, once the money allocated for you has run out, they just discharge you. There are colleagues who have not even had their bullet fragments removed. Did you know that? It's disgusting," Regina said.

"It is cheaper and more profitable to give them pills than to do surgery. The whole medication thing is a very long chain of money … There is great disappointment among my colleagues with similar problems, but they are not allowed to speak, and some have even been threatened."

"Like with everything else, if you don't have influence or connections, they put you at the end of the list," Regina added.

"I no longer have any hope that they'll give me the best pair of 'legs,' as they told me. They'll probably give me something they have left over."

"The army is as corrupt as Congress." It was obvious that Regina hated them.

"There'll be a march in less than fifteen days, this time we're going to demand an increase in the pension. There are people who are homeless because they can't afford to pay rent. If you served the country, they should treat you with dignity, don't you think?"

Terry held his head, perhaps he morally regretted having been on the list.

"The senators just increased their salary by twenty percent, the vice president too and what about the rest of the population?"

"They're all disgusting, the worst thing is that we all know it." This time it was my turn.

"It wasn't a war, it was a damn vendetta," Regina spat. She hated them not only because of the scandal of enrichment of certain companies associated with politicians in the government, but mainly because she considered them guilty of Terry's situation.

We served ourselves a second cup of coffee.

"That's how I met the owner of this house, at a march in favor of cities being more, 'Friendly to wheelchair users.'"

"Terry is part of a network of veterans and non-veterans, wheelchair users in the United States and they are demanding their right as citizens."

"They discriminate against us, damn it. The cities are inaccessible to the disabled. Is there a public ramp that allows us to enter the beach? Outside of this house, maybe, but I don't think any other house in the area has a ramp."

"I doubt it too," said Regina, taking him by the hand. "But don't get depressed, honey."

I thought for a few minutes, satisfied with such a delicious breakfast. "The owner of the house is rich, right?" I asked. "I'm sure he has one of those wheelchairs that are so popular in California, do you know them?"

"No."

"Pretend it's a sun lounger, but instead it has four big, wide yellow wheels."

"Really?"

"The guy is rich, or at least he lives very well," said Regina smiling. "Let's go find it. I'll go to the garage at the entrance, you look in the basement," she told me.

I stood up and headed to the basement bar. Ten minutes later, I heard Regina's screams. She had found not one, but two beach wheelchairs, she danced in front of Terry as if she had won something very important. He caught her with an agile movement, and she let him do it. They kissed on the mouth.

"I told you, come on, these rich people have everything."

"Well let's change and go to the beach," said Terry.

"Say no more."

Fifteen minutes later we were in the water; me pushing Terry, Regina riding the waves in a spectacular red, two-piece suit that looked great on her. It was a beautiful morning. We went into the water, swam. We brought Terry in with us, in the beach chair. He certainly had fun, and we all laughed. We tried to build a sandcastle, but it turned out that we were terrible architects, and it fell down when we tried to add a second floor. We came back to the house, bathed and got ready to go to the village to eat. I had a bland pasta. They had salad and beef. Everything had been left on the stove for too long, according to my palate. We stopped at the wine shop. We bought beers and two bottles: whiskey and rum, which we left almost half full later. This time the party was in the basement, with red lights and rhythmic music, which made us dance first and then fuck on the indirectly lit loveseat. The first one to start the game was Regina, I don't know if it was because of the alcohol or something, I just remember Terry silently backing up in the wheelchair and staying in the dark, stroking the scar on his face while Regina and I changed positions several times. We had such a spectacular orgasm that we both screamed. My voyeurism came out, and I showed off. I couldn't help but remember Patricia and all her damn exhibitionism.

39

It was about a month before I saw Martina again. Nothing but a quick encounter at the base supermarket. She had gone to buy some products for Captain Thomas. I saw her pushing a cart with groceries as she turned from one aisle to another and caught up with her. Knowing that there are cameras everywhere in these places, I spoke to her while pretending to pick up a can of vegetables.

"Hi ..."

She was surprised to see me and reacted as if there was someone else beside us.

"Relax. Just pretend we are two customers coinciding at the same shelf. How have you been?"

"Fine," she said dryly, while doing as I did, looking at canned products. Her eyes were covered with sunglasses, and she was wearing a long-sleeved blouse, jeans and boots.

"How's everything?"

"Fine."

"What have you been up to?"

"Nothing much ..."

"Let's talk, don't just answer me with monosyllables."

"What do you want to hear? I've been with my husband, fulfilling my duties as a wife."

"What duties?"

"Those of a married woman."

"Can I see your eyes?" I asked and got ready to take off her glasses despite her refusal. She had a black eye. I lifted the sleeves of her blouse. She also had several bruises.

"No way, no way ... The bastard hit you ..."

"We had a fight. It really was my fault."

"You mean, you deserved it—that's what he told you."

"I started throwing things at him, I knocked over one of his trophies."

"Did he give you that black eye as a damn trophy?"

"Like I said, I deserved it."

"In his world, Martina, you don't deserve that, don't fuck around."

"I have to go ... he's waiting for me."

"Does he also keep track of your time? And what comes next? He ties you up with a chain around your neck when he leaves you at home?"

"I'm leaving."

"We've already talked about this, Martina, you have to report him ... if you don't love him anymore, get a divorce."

She put several cans in the cart and squeezed the cart's bar, nervous, ready to leave. "He would kill me."

"Son of a bitch."

"I have to go."

"How about we meet later, at my house? My landlady is going to cook a recipe that I left her this morning, I'm giving her lessons."

She grinned, in spite of everything. "I can't leave the base."

"Why?"

"No."

"Then let's meet at the golf course, near the lake."

"I can't, he keeps track of my time, too, and ..."

"What a son of a bitch, who does he think he is? You're not his slave."

"Plus there's gossip, very bad rumors. They involve you."

"Like what?"

"They say that you've abused several women, that you're a *Jody-fucked*."

"A what?"

"Someone who takes advantage of the absence of soldiers to get into bed with their wives."

"That's not true …"

"That's what I said."

"And that's why he hit you?"

"Yes."

"How did he know?"

"Someone's been saying that."

"Who?"

"Candice."

"Really?"

"Yes."

"Slut."

"I really am leaving," she said and moved off to the registers.

I was speechless. *Son of a bitch lizard*, I said to myself, thinking of Candice. Maybe it was time to get out of that place. *And what about Martina?* I left the store quite confused; a part of me urged me to run, and the other demanded that I stay. *Am I ready to change my future again?* I asked myself. It wasn't as simple as hitting a direction on another road. *But go where?* It was obvious: I was an intruder here and I was an intruder there. How can people be so happy in one place for all their life? It was a fact, but I continued without a home, perhaps forever … *Jody fucker*.

That afternoon I saw Terry and Regina. I arrived with beers and with Tigrillo in my arms, who jumped up when I entered the house and went to hide under an armchair. Terry couldn't contain his joy; a professional basketball team had hired him. Regina ran to hug me when she saw me and told me the good news. She was proud of her husband. I congratulated Terry, hugged him and opened one of the beers for him.

"Brother, congratulations! This is the beginning of a great future!"

"Thanks, bro, I hope God hears you," he answered.

"A talent scout was following him during the season. He has been calling him for days. They finally reached an agreement today."

"And what is the name of the team?"

"The Braves, New York."

"No, really? Don Terry, that deserves a big cheer. Great, bro!" I raised the bottle high.

"Thank you, thank you ... As you said, eventually something bad brings something good."

"Well, I didn't say that, my grandmother did."

"Well, your grandmother knew some things, no doubt. Thanks to this wheelchair I'm going to be a professional player."

"Without a chair or with a chair, Terry, it was already in your destiny, and it had to happen."

"Fate or luck, call it what you want, I'm just starting to get it all figured out."

"That's great."

"That means moving to New York."

"Better than Albany, right?"

"A thousand times," Regina said. She approached Terry and kissed him on the mouth again. "I love you," she said while cupping his face.

"And when do you leave?" I asked.

"I have to show up for training in two weeks."

"Wow, that's fast."

"Yes, it is."

The three of us raised our bottles in the air, a toast.

Terry went to turn on the music, he looked proud, happy.

I took off my windbreaker and said, "I'm going to prepare a dessert for you, you're going to lick your fingers."

Regina jumped for joy, turned around like a ballerina and ran to the kitchen with me, where we discreetly kissed behind the refrigerator.

"Do you know that women have two hearts?" she said in a low voice.

"One can love a man and live with him, and the other can have a very similar feelings for another, very different man."

"That's called rhetoric."

"Hahaha, call it whatever you want."

I gave her another kiss and pulled her toward me. I squeezed her ass hard in my hands.

"Let's finish the meal," I said and closed one eye. I looked through the door, Terry was still in front of the stereo looking at records. I returned to Regina, knelt on the floor and, pulling her shorts and panties aside, licked her slit a few times. She smelled incredible, intense. From my position, I saw her close her eyes and hold on to the oven handle. We heard Terry's voice from the living room and we both recovered. I got ready to mix the flour with the sugar and the eggs, while she took things out of the refrigerator. I turned on the oven and plugged in the mixer. Between this and that, I rubbed my hips up against Regina several times. She was horny as hell. Maybe because of the good news.

In the dining room, Terry began to clean one of his guns on the table, while Johnny Cash's voice spoke over the speakers about a man dressed in black who is in solidarity with outlaws.

We had dinner quietly. We joked. Regina was one hundred percent happy to leave the base. In fact, she didn't know New York and was slightly afraid, although as excited as a little kid. That's what we were doing when Samatha called to congratulate them. After the usual good wishes, Regina put me on the phone with her. She knew about me; how good I was in the kitchen and about my vintage Cadillac. I told her about her beautiful eyes, how elegant her name was and how good she looked in her cheer uniform ... All of that in public, and later, while we were both sweating on the bed of a hotel, we also said other things to each other. When I hung up, I couldn't contain myself, the great body of that goddess jumping and throwing herself in the air was in my mind, creating an erotic halo over my head, like that of the saints of the 18th century. That night Regina and I didn't have sex, first of all because we weren't as drunk as the previous times, and second, because it was obvious it wasn't a good idea after Terry's big news. But we did the next day in the phone booth. The phone rang again, this time it was Regina's mother. She also called to say hello and congratulate them. Regina went out to the patio, and Terry and I were left alone at the table, with empty plates.

"Text messages are faster than gunpowder," he said, and removed the newspaper that covered the recently cleaned gun, took it and placed it between the two of us.

As you know, guns put me on alert, so I looked him in the eyes, letting him know that I didn't understand the meaning of that movement.

"Calm down, Sergio. Do you like it?" he said, referring to the weapon. It was a black, six-shot revolver with a wooden handle, Ruger brand, caliber .357. Magnum.

"Yes, it's nice," I answered.

"There was a captain in Iraq, he forced prisoners to play Russian roulette with one of these. The bastard enjoyed it when any of their brains got speckled on the walls. He made brothers, friends, neighbors and relatives shoot each other. The closer they were to each other, the more he enjoyed it. He would trick them into thinking they would get away free, that he wouldn't rape their daughters or sisters, or that he would simply give them better food or better treatment. It's a powerful weapon, despite its size."

"I know it, a friend in Sonora had one of these," I said. *Agnes*.

"So you like it?"

"Of course."

"Take it, it's yours."

"How so?"

"You're going to need it."

"No way, what are you talking about?"

"The brotherhood knows about you, son."

"What the fuck is that?"

"Okay, I'll put it to you like this; they say you've taken several women to bed here on the base, even some against their consent."

"What? That's not true, it's fucking gossip. A fucking lie."

"True or not, they're after you. I'm just warning you."

I remained thoughtful for a few seconds.

"And if I take it, what will you have for yourself?"

"Don't worry, I have three more pistols and a couple of rifles."

"Wow, that's quite an arsenal."

"Nowhere near an arsenal, but in my condition, I need *something* to defend myself with when the time comes, don't you think?"

"Of course," I said. I grabbed the gun, checked that the safety was on and put it in my waistband, under my shirt.

Regina came in: "Mom sends her best regards, Terry, and congratulates you, says she's proud of you. I told her I am, too. As soon as we're settled, they'll come visit us. She's excited to come to New York. My dad said he won't miss a single game on television."

"Heh, you should have said thank you, that I love them too."

"I let them know, of course," she said and started to pick up the dirty dishes. "You're coming too Sergio, right?"

"Of course, good friends are never forgotten." I stood up. I put on my windbreaker and baseball cap with the company logo again.

"I can help you pack things ... if you want."

"Of course, we're going to need it," said Terry pushing his chair toward the exit.

We said goodbye at the door.

"Congratulations again, and thanks for the gift," I said.

Terry smiled and we bumped fists.

"Take care and think about what I told you. Maybe it's time to change cities for you too."

"How about New York?" asked Regina, amused.

"I don't think so, it's a very big city for me. I think I'd get lost in the subway." I turned the doorknob and walked down the front steps.

"But are you coming to visit us?" Regina insisted.

"Of course! Oh, Terry, thanks for letting me know."

"Let you know? What are you talking about?" Regina asked. She seemed intrigued.

"You're welcome, you're welcome." Terry gave a small slap to Regina's rump.

Regina walked out with me onto the street and as she kissed me on the cheek, she whispered: "I'll see you tomorrow at your cabin, get ready because I'm feeling like a *lioness*. Oh, and thanks for the cat."

I smiled and said to myself: *Fucking two-hearted women, they're amazing*. I got into the Cadillac and started it up. I put the gun in the glovebox. I smiled, I was happy for my friends, but more so because I would see Samantha in less than eight hours, in front of the public library. I had been well recommended.

Now that I think about it, if I had paid more attention, I would have noticed that two pickup trucks began to follow me.

40

Maybe I didn't want to read the signs, or I didn't notice in detail what had happened. I should have guessed it, when the next morning on the Cadillac's window, pressed by the windshield wiper, I found a note written in black ink that said: "Return the car to whoever you stole it from, you filthy Mexican." I balled up the paper and threw it to hell. *Racism, it never fails*, I thought. I looked around. At that moment I couldn't even imagine that it was the work of the "Slow Death Squad," as Lee and his friends from the brotherhood, made up of retired and active soldiers, called themselves. Some of them mercenaries; others, advisors, all sons of bitches. The kings of torture, I later learned, when it was too late.

The second clue came when two days later Lee's Mustang stopped in front of the maintenance shed with the engine running. When I saw him, I almost ran toward it, thinking that Martina was driving. Fortunately, I was cleaning a lawnmower, so I could see my little queen's soldier husband sitting at the wheel. Did the son of a bitch know about us? Was he coming to intimidate me? Had Martina herself betrayed me after one of the beatings he had accustomed her to? The car was stopped there for about thirty minutes. Of course, I didn't move from my position behind the bathroom window either. That same afternoon, a late-model white Chevy followed me for about forty minutes. In the end, I decided to park near the public library, where I spent the entire afternoon reading until they closed. From there I went straight to the cat house, although I didn't park the car in the same place, but two blocks away.

I put the lock on the steering wheel, disconnected the ignition cables and removed a fuse. As I walked, I paid attention to the entire street, as I hadn't done since my days in Hermosillo; I was surprised to remember how easy it is to put eyes in the back of my head. My landlady was still awake, and we talked; a madman had gone into a shopping center and killed eleven people, including him; she was perplexed. In the kitchen I took a glass and filled it with tap water, she followed me, talking and talking. Among the news in the house was that Santiago, one of her favorite cats, was sick. *It must be obesity*, I thought, although I didn't tell her. I confirmed my suspicions when I saw Santiago come out of the kitchen cleaning his whiskers. He was like some humans, a glutton, a hairy pig. Mrs. Robbins said good night, although she left the television on for me. With the remote in hand, I tuned in up and down the channels, while thinking that maybe it was time to leave Albany. *You are always the same, but you are not always the same*. For some time I had avoided violence as much as possible, as well as strong adrenaline discharges, because they transformed me. I was no longer betting, and more than ever, I had one thing very clear: my goal in life was to become an international chef, to work on a cruise ship and see the world. Of course, I didn't rule out having a family one day.

I had also discovered that revenge is not always satisfactory, and the law is always relative. One of the black cats came over and sat down near me. I felt sad when I realized that I wasn't going to see Martina, Tigrillo, Terry or Regina anymore. That I wouldn't fuck Samantha, the one with the beautiful legs, or Jaire, the fanciful Chinese girl anymore ... Then I made a decision: I would leave on my next paycheck. Maybe I would visit Peter in his new house in Virginia. Maybe I would propose a long vacation to Samantha. I got sleepy and closed my eyes. Although the saying goes, *One can plan, but the architect who designs things in life is the one who executes*. That one, whom no one has seen.

I had one more day, or so I thought; I answered a few calls, met with the manager to thank him and let him know I was leaving and watched soap operas with Toño. I even accepted his junk food. At the end of the day I put the tools back in their place, took a shower and said goodbye to my Bolivian friend, who told me he was moving in with Esther, Ana Graciela's friend, which made him very excited. He also told me that he was thinking of going on a diet, finally understanding what I had once told him after a few beers, regarding poisonous junk food. When I am honest with people, no one can stop me. I congratulated him on Esther, it was always better than being alone. I gave him a hug.

I left the base. My plan was to stop and buy sweet bread for my landlady with whom I had been sharing snacks for the last two weeks. I had planned to see Samantha after midnight, she had sent me a text telling me she had bought some sexy clothes at Victoria's Secret and wanted to show me. She had said,"For your eyes only." I felt a slight erection. The cheerleader turned out to be a boiler, but the sad thing was that very soon I would have to say goodbye to her too.

On Sunday, as a farewell, I would make my landlady and Samantha a big lunch with fajitas, quesadillas and dessert included. It didn't hurt to cook for both of them, maybe I wouldn't see them again, at least in this world. I was thinking about that, when a shot blew out the rear window of the car and made me move the steering wheel from side to side, frightened. The tires screeched on the pavement, and I understood that it was a moment of survival.

The line in the middle of the road became an arrow pointing me to the emergency route. There was violence again, the damned violence that burns forests, souls and cities. The violence that has made history a shame; it was catching up with me ... I looked in the rearview mirrors, headlights with high beams a few meters behind me were trying to overtake me. I opened the glove compartment and took out the revolver Terry had given me. I pressed my foot on the accelerator, new flashes, this time on the sheet metal somewhere behind. The Cadillac, although a little late, reacted and took off. A second car appeared in the rearview mirrors. I put it in overdrive and reached almost 100 miles per hour. Another round of shots; I lowered my head as much as I could in the seat, and it seemed to swallow me. I moved the gear lever, the eight cylinders snorted in unison, although they fell short; the two cars were getting closer and closer, and their occupants fired without rhyme or reason. I entered the highway hoping to run into a highway patrol, but nothing, some trucks, cargo vans, a few cars.

The Cadillac hummed a little, it was as if the years had suddenly fallen on it all at once. Surely in all its life it had had so much demanded of it; despite this, I slammed on the accelerator. I reached max speed. For a moment I thought I would leave them behind, but I was wrong. Once I was ready to pass the next trailer, the bullets whizzed back and forth again. My pursuers soon caught up with me, until they were no less than ten meters away. Then a third pair of lights appeared in the mirrors, evidently this vehicle was even more powerful, as it easily got alongside me and began to ram my sheet metal. Seeing the action, several cars on the road peeled off, and some others began to honk their horns. The shots increased—I could hear them penetrating the Cadillac—the tailgating and the crashes too. It stank of burning tires, of revenge.

A black pickup truck with a large skull painted on the hood had joined the chase; it must have had an engine of at least four hundred cubic centimeters. Like a ghost, it came alongside me and began to push. It was clear they didn't just want to give me a scare, they wanted my head. I shot back at them ... I suddenly felt as if I had descended at least fifty meters under water and was moving away from the surface. When the pickup truck was next to me, I swerved, throwing the truck off the road; if they had the speed on their side, I had the weight of my antique. The pickup did indeed go off the road, but it came back like a damn lion on its prey.

I turned the steering wheel again and we crashed at least three times, we exchanged shots. The bad thing was that I had no more bullets in the gun. The guys in the truck were hitting me, I was on the verge of rolling off the road several times, even though the Cadillac had excellent suspension. I was bleeding from one arm where a ricocheted shot had landed, and part of my face was damaged by the glass fragments embedded there. Those bastards were tough, they weren't amateurs, they were the bastards of the brotherhood. The truck pulled up again, I braked to avoid being within range of their bullets and I hit them from behind. We stayed like that for a while.

A Jeep appeared at full speed firing bullets and managed to get on the left side. I heard a roar and then the Cadillac's engine was dying. It began to throttle; they were using high-caliber weapons. *Why not against the driver?* It was obvious, they wanted me alive, sadists after all. As Terry had said, for these guys death was not enough, they had to make the enemy suffer to the limits of madness. I had read the same thing in one of Captain Thomas' books. I managed to hit the truck again and it went off the road and came back, while my car was losing power and leaving a trail of smoke. A second large-caliber shot blew out the left tire and the vehicle began to skid; I lost control of the steering wheel. Suddenly, I felt the car rise, spin several times in the air, on the way to crash into the ditch, just before the entrance to a bridge. I remember charging to my left side, taking the blow without letting go of the steering wheel and clenching my jaw. The problem in this case, and I realized it too late, was that the situation had gotten out of control and was now bigger than me. The last thing I heard was a loud bang.

I was floating in nothingness, for ten minutes I manage to overcome the laws of gravity. The Cadillac falls into the ravine. For some strange reason I think of the dice, which I throw on the table, and I see them spin in the air in slow motion ...

Instinctively I pressed myself to the steering wheel and closed my eyes.

Grandma is waiting for me like every Friday at Hacienda del Carmen. She looks distressed. Just like last time, she is sitting on the big brass bed, although this time some of the chickens are dead, others are sitting and only a couple are walking in a circle, nervous. Apparently, she hasn't finished the sweater in time, she says. I notice she is upset. I tell her it's not cold and to stop worrying, there is no problem. She shakes her hair. Then, like someone who remembered something, Grandma gets up, takes me by the hand and leads me to the end of that room, where she smears my eyes and ears with mud and clay from the walls. She says something like be prepared, this is just to enter purgatory.

I crawled out of the Cadillac and went to hide under the bridge. It was dark, cold. I felt a tingling on my scalp. This time the blood was my own. I saw myself surrounded by ghosts, dead people and spirits. I shuddered. It was as if the desert had come and surrounded me. I heard voices, the soldiers on the bridge. I began to tremble. My lips went numb, and I bit my tongue, pressing the wound on my arm with a piece of cloth from my pants.

Suddenly I heard their voices closer, it was impossible to escape. It was a fact, they wanted to capture me, and if they had come this far, they would not let me go for anything in the world. I stood up and held a stick from the ground. The best thing was to face them, there was no other way. *The best defense is attack,* I remembered, but I didn't know if it was another of Chiang Ho's phrases or just a line in some movie. I came out of my hiding place between a bush and a rock and stood with the stick raised, ready to drop it on the first person who appeared. And so I did, when a fat man poked his nose out sniffing like a hunting dog. With two blows of the stick I knocked him to the ground and the bulldog fell unconscious. I heard gunshots, ran to take cover under the trunk of a tree and waited for the next one. This time, three of them showed up. I barely had time to disarm one with a blow from the stick and another with a kick, the third hit me with the butt of his gun which sent me to the ground. I jumped up like a spring and threw a punch at my new opponent, but the others had also stood up and one hit me from behind. I tried to run but fell to the ground, where the barrel of a rifle sank into my chest.

"Don't kill him, I want him alive!" Someone shouted in the darkness.

"You fucking filthy pieces of shit, that's how you'll end up, you filthy bastards!" was the last thing I remember yelling at them, in English, of course.

When I woke up, I was tied up by my hands and feet, hanging on a log like a chicken ready to be cooked on a bonfire. I got the chills. I opened and closed my eyes. *Was I about to be roasted?* It was the first thing that came to my mind. I don't know if it was because of the shock, or because someone hit my head, but I lost consciousness again. I didn't know about myself again until I found myself in a metal chair with chains. Without adrenaline, my legs, arms, back muscles and head hurt. I salivated and my mouth tasted like blood. I was chained in a concrete room designed for torture, with all its mirrored glass and an intercom system. I had read somewhere that nowadays they torture you with your favorite song at full volume, for about fifteen days and nights at first, then for months, until you confess. You come out deaf or fit straight for the asylum. These filthy people, when they have you where I was, there is no way out.

In their opinion I was guilty, I had fucked their women, they had gone crazy ... there was nothing to confess. The how? It seemed too much to me, and it was something I was never going to tell them. They were probably going to cut my dick off. Candice's husband came in, I recognized him from a photo I had seen on the cougar's nightstand, the afternoon of our meeting.

"Son of a bitch. You don't even know whose hands you're in," he said. "Your days are is numbered; the minutes of your miserable existence have begun to run."

Maybe it was true, and he wasn't bragging, so ask them for forgiveness—never.

"If it's because of Candice, don't worry, friend, I'm not the first or the only one in the base who knows she has a red babydoll with black hearts, and enjoys anal sex."

The information hit him hard, I saw him change color and choke when he spoke: "How do you know that, son of a bitch? Was it part of the clothes you stole?"

"I didn't steal any clothes, asshole, I fucked your wife," I barked so the others could hear.

The monkey came and hit me in the face, breaking my nose. I spat blood, complained and spewed saliva out of my mouth. I looked at him and smiled.

I heard Chian Ho: *You must prepare to die, before you are about to die.*

Strange relationship that one with Chian Ho. Two men in realities that did not correspond to each other; one working for the Medieval Men cartel and the other, turned into a murderer without intending to be. In the four months that I had the honor of being part of his class, I understood many things related to violence which I didn't know before. Like the reason for my deep depression when I killed the first of my father's four murderers, and the reason for the dreams with my victims; where they set the table for me to sit down to eat and the discomfort that causes me when I wake up.

The guy saw something in my eyes and left the room. Maybe the alien from the desert.

"You old bitches are fucking assholes," I barked at the mirror in front of me. I spat out another gob of blood. I didn't remember how many days I had been there, although something told me it had been several. There were crumpled paper cups on the floor, cigarette butts, wire, remains of insulating tape, urine, fecal matter.

41

I opened my eyes; it was hard for me to keep them open. I felt a very intense pain in my right temple, going down to my eyebrow, where the blood had formed a crust. I breathed deeply, trying to put my thoughts in order. I tried to remember the last events, which derailed like trains. I remembered the car chase, the crashes between the cars, the Cadillac falling off the cliff—with me inside of course—the escape on foot with those bastards behind me, the siege and the apprehension; all in a dizzying succession. The last thing on my mind was when those pigs threw me handcuffed into the back of the Jeep. Everything was hazy after that, like flashes in which I saw myself being dragged through the mud, transported like a deer, tortured by those disgusting people, day after day. How much time had passed since my capture?

I could turn my head. I was suspended in the air, hanging from chains that draped from a beam in the ceiling. My ankles were bound by shackles mounted on the wall below. I opened my eyes again. A very bright light was shining directly at me. I looked down. I was in my underwear. My chest and legs were lacerated, the pain of which added to the general hurt that rose and fell from my being with each breath. Why were those disgusting people still keeping me alive? Surely because they intended to continue the torment and humiliation. From among the shadows I could make out a human figure. It smelled of tobacco. I strained my eyes. Even though I couldn't see well, I knew it was one of my torturers. The guy was sitting at a table, smoking and apparently reading the newspaper.

"Good morning," I said.

The guy turned around a little surprised, perhaps because he thought I was dead. It wasn't Lee.

"Officer, good morning or good afternoon, I don't know." I raised my voice as much as possible, pushing it from my stomach, although it was difficult. I pretended to be somewhat respectful.

The big man put his newspaper aside and looked at me with disdain. On the table there was also a pistol, a pack of cigarettes and two cups of coffee. The truth is that I wanted to die, that's how bad my pain was. For a couple of them I had served as a punching bag. My muscles hurt, and more than one organ. I should have at least one hand or a couple of bones in it broken. I decided to provoke him, to see if he would take his gun and end my suffering once and for all.

"Officer," I said again as loudly as my condition allowed. "Would it be possible to turn off the light?"

He turned around in his chair again and looked at me, I don't know if he smiled: "Where the hell do you think you are, the Marriott?" He blew smoke from his cigarette and shook his head. "What balls, to ask about the fucking light. Ha!"

The guy returned to his reading.

"Fuck it," I said. The longer I lived, the more they would continue torturing me and having fun, and in the end, when I was defeated and I was nobody, or nothing, then they would finish me off, me begging ... It was better to die now. I remembered Chian Ho's words: *There is no such thing as a truce, it's just another form of battle*. Surely the rest of my captors were taking a break or had gone to breakfast.

"Where's the rest of the gang?" I asked.

He pretended not to hear me.

"I'm missing your henchmen, soldier, where are they?"

"They went to their activities, but they'll be back for tonight's party," he said without taking his eyes off the sports page.

Maybe I was still alive because they hadn't been able to break down all my psychic defenses. That thought put me on alert.

"Hey, soldier, are you deaf? Could you turn off the light so I can get some sleep, you bastard?"

He turned his big head again and smiled: "Ha … you think you're brave, or something?"

"No sir, that's clear to me, you're the heroes ... just turn off the light and let me die in peace."

"You're not going to die, for at least another two nights," he said sarcastically and threw the cigarette butt on the floor.

Pigs. They had planned my death. My eyelids fell back over my eyes like two curtains, but that didn't stop me from seeing everything in its entirety. Something was happening to me. Amazingly, I could see the whole room. The three chairs around the table, the dried-up coffee cups on top, as well as the half-empty pack of cigarettes and the gun. I also saw the torture rack in one corner, a metal plate, the chair with chains.

Apparently, I'm in the basement of some abandoned building. There's another table, higher than this one; with pliers, hammers, saws, screws, nails and other hardware in abundance. *In fact, you can be tortured with practically any object, you know?*

I looked at the dried blood on the walls and floor of the whole place, blood that wasn't mine ... A first aid kit with syringes and supplies; a cell and a scaffold the size of a dog kennel; a rancid and rotten smell. I also discovered that I've seen the guy, perhaps in some photograph inside the base, possibly at the entrance to the cafeteria where the photos of the most outstanding cadets, or the bravest, are hung every month.

A few minutes of silence passed, I gathered strength again and said, “Have you heard of parallel universes, soldier?”

“Bah, you can talk all you want, I’m not listening to you.”

This time his response was immediate. Apparently, I had caught his attention.

“If you’re listening to me, soldier … Parallel universes, the things that fit together in two different spaces and times.”

“You talk a lot of shit, motherfucker, we already told you. The captain warned you yesterday while we were pulling your teeth,” he smiled and turned the page.

“You remember my suffering and that makes you happy. Are you proud to be a soldier, executioner?”

“You’re going to force me to torture you a little more, if you keep fucking around.”

Despite the threat, he sounded bored, maybe that’s why he was vulnerable. I feared he was Jaire’s husband, although that would have been pure and simple poetic justice, according to my time with Agnes.

“It turns out that sometimes, these two universes overlap, and that’s when strange things happen.”

My executioner spat on the ground and grabbed his nose. He looked at me. “What the hell are you talking about?”

“Don’t you feel it in the environment, soldier? Atrocities have happened here. People have died and it’s not just you and me. The Aztecs … they called it the Teyollocualóyan.”

“Fuck, shut up! I’m tired of you!” He checked his cell phone and seemed to read something on the screen. He took a new cigarette from the pack and lit it. He crossed his leg.

I fell back into a stupor and closed my eyes. I knew the risk that this implied, and with all the strength left me I focused on opening them again. The presence of my enemy served as motivation and I said: "Soldier, you know that maxim that says: What goes around comes around?"

He put the phone on the table next to the gun. He looked at me with interest, maybe he had heard the phrase from his elementary school teacher or something. This time he crossed his arms. "Yes ..." He spat on the floor. "Fuck, I don't know why I'm even talking to you." He stood up.

Silence took its place again and I focused on organizing my thoughts, on regulating my breathing.

My executioner folded the newspaper in two. He yawned and crushed the cigarette on the floor.

One thing was obvious, I had reached my limit, and I didn't think I could bear any more torture. *This guy is my chance for a dignified death*, I thought. But how could I get him to shoot me? Begging him to do it wouldn't work, offending him probably wouldn't either; he was a soldier, he should have orders and, I supposed, one of them was to keep me alive. I used provocation to try something I knew: "You kick down the door, bayonet in front of you, you and your gang enter that humble house, where you discover a five-member Iraqi family hiding. They look at you petrified. The father and mother speak in a language you do not understand. With a blow to the head with your gun, you force the father to his knees, and you kick the mother, who is in the way. A couple of kicks in the ribs and you knock her to the ground, where one of your men begins to beat her until, in a fit of rage, he crushes her head. Two others take out the enemy, a father and a twelve-year-old son, and shoot them outside the house, while you look lustfully at the two girls of six and thirteen years of age. They cry inconsolably from horrified eyes. Do you remember the eyes? You do remember them, don't you, soldier?"

The incredulous soldier reacted like a spring and staggered toward me. "How do you know that?! How the hell did you know?!" He approached me, his face was white, stunned, like someone who has been caught off guard or seen a ghost.

He grabbed my head. How did I find out such information? Good question. The truth is I didn't know, but it was as if he had told me himself.

"Ah, I know, that bitch Candice told you." He turned from one side to the other, like a caged lion.

I had his attention and his rage. He was younger than he looked.

"No, it couldn't be, because Candice doesn't know about that," he said to himself. "Maybe that bitch Martina? Of course, only Lee would be capable of telling something like that to his wife."

"Don't talk about Martina like that."

"Son of a bitch!" He jumped in the air and spurred me with two punches to the stomach.

"Kill me, faggot, use your gun!"

The sentence stopped him dead in his tracks. It was as if he realized that I wasn't joking, regarding my desire to die as soon as possible.

"Only because I need to keep you alive, bastard ... otherwise you wouldn't have to ask me twice." He let his guard down and spat on the floor again.

I felt pain from the blows, I took another breath and the lack of three teeth hurt me more than ever.

"Kill me, coward!"

"I have plenty a mind to." My executioner took another cigarette from the pack on the table and put it to his lips, this time his pulse was shaking. Then he did something unusual, he took the powerful light and deflected it to one side, slightly, taking it away from my face. That was a relief, even mentally. He put on his military jacket and disappeared.

I visualized Gaby, my nephews, my brother-in-law and the rest of the Alpizars while I was alone. That gave me courage. I remembered another maxim of Chiang Ho: *Every action is a preparation for experience.*

I saw a being in front of me, as if made of smoke, of antimatter ... I recognized it, it was me, without a doubt. A dark being, perhaps my shadow or a projection of myself, who knows? It was as if I saw my back in a mirror or something. I was terrified when this shadow began to approach me, to reintegrate into my body, I closed my eyes, perhaps I was just hallucinating, or it was the product of pain. I squeezed my eyes shut as I felt the shadow grow inside me, materializing. Was it an alien spirit possessing me? When had my shadow abandoned me? I felt as if I had stopped being transparent, it was like coming back to myself ...

The dice fell, six and five. Eleven, a good move for a gambler.

The man returned; he seemed calmer. I noticed his presence. I needed to end this punishment. I took advantage and said: "Soldier, give me a hand, I'm going to go to the bathroom." When I heard my voice, it seemed different to me.

"Pee right there, you've done it before."

"I need to defecate."

"Right there."

"You don't want your superiors to find me covered in shit. It's going to be less fun for you. Then you're going to be the one who's screwed up. C'mon, leave me some dignity."

"I can't let you go."

"You think? The shackles on my hands only, I shit down there," I begged.

"I can't let go of you … they were supposed to be here already," he said, somewhat worried.

"You seem to be a man who likes to gamble. I do. I'll bet you my life that I can't escape, if I lose you shoot me. How about that?"

He sketched a smile: "Impossible."

"One more day, one less day … tomato, to-*mah*-to."

He looked me in the eyes, seemed thoughtful. Maybe my dark humor caught his fancy or something. He came and lowered the chain that kept me elevated a couple of meters from the floor. The pulley turned and I collapsed in that dungeon; with my eyes closed and my arms numb, I didn't even notice the blow to my knees. I turned my body, and when I landed on the ground, I felt relief. It was as if my spine was being rebuilt, my legs were demagnetizing and my upper limbs were being charged with energy. I noticed the blood circulating. It was in my body. My hands responded to my impulses. I felt like a harlequin who on the ground takes on a life of its own. It was only a few minutes, but for me it was more than enough. I felt different, I began to change, I had that certainty ...

A flash in the Sonoran Desert covered that place with sand. A Saguaro tree over two hundred years old shaded me. In the shadow of this enormous cactus I recompose myself, I protect myself from the harsh sun and I sleep. The sand enters through the pores of the walls, the broken glass windows and the ceiling. Asleep, I open my eyes on the brass bed where my grandmother knits me a sweater; instead of chickens, what I find is a floor covered with white feathers, lots of them, forming a large rug. Through one of the windows without glass or frames, I see Mrs. Marina, she calls me. I go out to meet her and she makes me follow her along a path of feathers, to the cemetery where she stops at the grave of her brother Ignacio, who during the revolution used to divine things and give advice from beyond the grave. Grandma sits me on the tombstone, dust rises from the ground around it and when she touches it, it turns into mud, a soft but smelly mud, which begins to smear the area of my eyes and also around my ears and forehead. "So that you can see and hear in the shadows... you will make a trip to the underworld, and you need to be protected." She tells me sweetly, and I let her do it. She is someone I trust blindly; I see concern on her face, an unknown tone, it is evident that she does not want to alarm me, although I know something strange is going on. "Be alert and trust your teachings," my grandmother tells me before leaving me. I open my eyes, the executioner is cutting the cartridge, he is surely aiming his gun at me, and I am in his sights.

"Shit then."

"Take off one shackle at least, so I can pull down my pants with one hand."

To my surprise, he does it, although cautiously. The desire to die is replaced by a powerful desire to survive. Suddenly I hear an echo, it rises from the earth, and I feel how it harmonizes with my pulse, the echo begins to resonate in my muscles, then in my organs, then in my entire being. I am someone.

The pain took a backseat, let's put it that way. The motivation was that MIS, which made my blood circulate at a thousand miles an hour, cauterizing my wounds. Then I thought about revenge, but more about justice; about the power of adrenaline and testosterone, which I managed to concentrate. I opened my eyes and stood up carefully, although with difficulty, but recovered, that's for sure. The executioner indicated the specific area where I should do my business with the tip of the rifle. I was going to pull down my underwear to sit down and defecate, when a current of electricity shook me. I closed and opened my eyes. With incredible ease and just by moving my legs, the chains attached to the shackles came off the wall. With my hands I opened the shackles and threw them like hell, all at an unknown speed. I was on my legs and standing. The executioner could not believe what he had just seen. It took him a few seconds to react, and I took advantage of that to get hold of him and snatch the gun from his hands. We struggled, the MlS fell to the floor and the guy ran for the gun. The executioner took five huge strides in an attempt to reach his target, and when he thought he had done it, I reached the table in two leaps, grabbed the gun first. In a feline movement I raised the barrel and held it against him. The guy stopped dead and made a face of astonishment, wanting to retreat, but it was too late, two bullets pierced his skull, and he fell on his back.

"Son of a bitch. Have fun in hell," I said and got off the table. I sat down in one of the chairs. I turned around. It was as if I could see in the dark. With gun in hand I went to a second room where I found water and junk food, which I gobbled up until I was less hungry. It was like a club; in this second room there was a pool table, a shooting range attached to one of the walls, a sofa and a large flat screen TV. The best thing was to get out as soon as possible.

I returned to the executioner and stripped him of his pants, boots and jacket. I got dressed, although the boots were too big. I picked up the phone from the table to find out what day I was on and where. It was Monday, so the pigs had tortured me for at least five days. I deduced then that the rest of the gang was carrying out their daily activities, including being good fathers and husbands. It seemed I had been their weekend entertainment. I figured that I was somewhere not too remote, although definitely abandoned, some kind of disused military installation. It was almost ten o'clock at night.

I heard the sound of a car and then footsteps outside, with astonishing clarity. I limped toward the exit. With the gun in front of me, I strode up the stairs. Maybe it was because I was used to the dim light, but I could see clearly enough for it being so dark. Maybe it was also the smelly mud smeared by Grandma on her eyelids, who knows? The door opened and led into an abandoned hangar. I saw a pickup truck parked with its headlights on and in the distance other headlights approaching. I rolled on the floor and took cover behind an old, disused water tank. From there, crouching, I ran to a small ramp.

Two of my captors were smoking and drinking beer while listening to the radio with the door of the pickup truck open. I had them in the sights of my gun, but I wanted to see their faces before sending them to the other world. I went around. Covering myself in piles of boxes and empty fuel drums, I approached. I observed them, they looked happy with life; what a surprise those sons of bitches would get. I advanced a bit further, this time taking cover behind a scrap crane until I was less than ten meters away.

I stood up, they didn't seem to notice me, because when I came out from behind the pair of pigs, I barely gave them time to exchange glances. At that short distance I shot them in the legs, both fell to the ground writhing in pain, in shock. One of them tried to draw his gun, but I instantly finished him off with a shot to the head. The other screamed in horror when he saw me, as if he were seeing a resurrected dead person.

"Motherfucker, how is that possible?" he barked, holding his leg with his hands, covering the wound. "You were dead last night, I swear!"

"Well, here I am."

The one lying with the hole in his head was more or less the same shoe size as me, so I quickly took off his boots. He was

Vanesa's husband, Candice's fat neighbor. I walked to the truck, turned off the radio and sat down in the seat to put on my boots. I opened a beer and drank it almost halfway. In the truck I found an infrared rifle, ammunition and a leather jacket.

The big man on the floor was whimpering while he caressed a medallion with two crosses, as if he was committing himself to something. I noticed that the other one was also wearing the same medallion, I leaned over and pulled it off his neck to see it.

"And what does this mean? Same club, family, what the fuck?"

"We were all from the same unit in Iraq; clean-up commandos, search and destroy."

"Thugs, exterminators, that's what you meant, right? I've seen how they work."

"Fuck you, clown, you haven't seen anything!"

I walked up to him, looked at him from my position, took another big sip of beer and kicked him twice in the balls with my new boots.

"Take that, you criminal son of a bitch!"

The man was in pain and clenched his jaws, crying. Then I said: "Do you know what parallel universes are?"

"What?"

"Imagine, you're going to go in, over and over again, to kill the same people in an endless repetition. But from now on, you'll have to devour them afterwards, because the door is locked from the inside and you can't find the key. As if that wasn't enough, the windows have been boarded up. How about that? Imagine that your little daughter, right now as we speak, is about to be raped by three men, they'll do to her everything that you and your brotherhood did to the two little girls in that forgotten village in Iraq."

"What? Eat shit, you bastard! You talk too much!"

"Do you remember the little girl's eyes? The same eyes you see in your dreams, while they beg for compassion. Imagine now, they're not the eyes that sometimes see you from the depths of your nightmares, but those of your little girl. That's the parallel universe."

"Fuck you, I don't know what you're talking about! Ah, I'm bleeding!"

"You're the one who's fucked. Candice, she might cry for half an hour for you when she finds out you're dead, but she'll be ready to collect the insurance and sleep with the first man that comes along as quickly as possible, even before they start throwing dirt on you. Another thing, I'm not the first or the only one who got on your old lady's nerves, there were several, including many of your comrades here."

The guy looked at the dead man, then at me: "You're lying! You abused her when you came to do the damn job."

"Did she tell you that? Think a little, soldier. It's not an activity you do very often, but think. If I had Martina at my disposal, why the hell did I want an old lizard like yours, unless she forced me somehow? And why would she tell her rapist that her soldier husband shoots his clip *way* too fast?"

His pain took a backseat to that logic. He stopped whimpering and gave me a look of hatred, as if he was reflecting deeply on what I had said to him.

"Well, I'm going to wait for the rest of your friends, because tonight is a party night, isn't it?" I finished the rest of the beer and threw the empty bottle in his face. "Have a good time here with your comrade, or should I say, your eskimo brother," I spat and walked to the pickup. "He'll start to stink soon and call guests for dinner. Enjoy it. Too bad there aren't romantic candles and bad music."

I got into the truck, started it instantly. I put it in first gear and skidded off, scattering dust over the two rapists. I accelerated fully. I had to shorten the gap between the rest of the members of the brotherhood. I turned off the lights, I didn't need them, despite it being a moonless night and thick as the breath in a wolf's mouth. I opened the window, feeling the air on my lacerated face. It was a wonderful sensation.

I'm coming out of sleep again. Without shoes, with torn clothes and my fists sore as if I had hit someone, blood on my pants, on my shirt. With a bad feeling and a sour taste in my mouth, I find myself lying in the mud, in a fetal position, trying to keep warm in the morning cold. I am in a forest where there are also palm trees. I do not understand how I got here. With difficulty, I manage to stand up. I am not wearing shoes. I feel momentarily dizzy. I take a few steps; something hangs from my neck. I feel it, at the touch I feel disgust and proceed to take it off. It is a necklace of ears. I observe it in detail; ears, one after another, human ears, strung on a thick metal wire at the height of the lobe, half a dozen of them. I feel disgust ... Why have I taken the ears as a trophy? What dark reason has led me to keep those body parts? Am I going crazy or am I dreaming? Ideas and thoughts collide. Am I lost? At least that's what I think, when a police drone locates me. The spoken portrait matches my facial map and the area of the incident with my location. Little by little I made space in the circle, until my shadow entered, when it was inside, we hugged each other.

42

"The accused, please stand up," said a voice as the judge and the jury members entered the room.

I was accused of the death of four marines, the disability of another and the disappearance of three more. I also faced charges such as assault, breach of trust and lycanthropy, among other more ridiculous ones. The only witness was Candice's husband: Arthur Slack, whom I had forgiven, "although condemned to a wheelchair for life," in the words of his lawyer.

There are a lot of people, some betting that they will cut off my head, and another percentage, that I will burn at the stake. In this theater, where the press is outside and protesters with signs are demanding that I be publicly lynched, I am the criminal. There is no mention of my kidnapping, of the social club with torture instruments, not a word mentioned about the secret brotherhood and no one seems to care about the hangar where the events took place and where I was held prisoner for something like eight days. The only evidence against me is the necklace of ears, since my DNA does not appear anywhere, nor do my fingerprints on the weapons used in the death of the two active marines. On the advice of my lawyer, I have declared myself innocent, since it is only Slack's testimony against mine.

Candice, of course, attended the two weeks during the little theater and spoke to the reporters. She looked stunning, although she always pretended to look like she was guilty and sorry, the bitch. She was the one to blame for all this drama and she was so cool; including the disappearance of three men of whom I personally did not remember anything. When I turned to look at her, she closed her eyes. All because of the damn gossip she had spread at the base. It's incredible how much harm an unscrupulous person can do. I remembered Patricia.

During the trial there was talk of sadism and even cannibalism, although that argument fell apart when my lawyer made them see reason. How did they think I could have eaten three men over six feet tall and weighing something like two hundred pounds? In private, I told my lawyer that I had had sex with Martina, Jaire, Samantha and Candice, of course, although in the case of the latter, I clarified, it had been in payment for her blackmail.

"However it happened, the court will not accept excuses."

I didn't say a word about the other trap, the one set by Vanesa, the fat rapist. Another person I didn't say a word about was Regina, who, by the way, attended the trial with Terry, although I pretended, I didn't know them, as my lawyer had suggested. She was very despondent of course; but I thought I noticed that Terry believed much of what was said about me. I knew it from his look. The most important argument of the defense was that it had all been a matter of jealousy, base passions and deceived husbands acting vengefully, taking the law into their own hands. Contrary to the argument presented by the plaintiffs, I was the victim, and not the other way around. I, who had luckily escaped a premeditated death by trained and expert men. Kidnapping forced deprivation of my freedom and self-defense.

Martina went up to the bench, called by the prosecutor. She looked beautiful, but I noticed she was a bit haggard and somewhat thin. Maybe it was only because I hadn't seen her in something like a month and a half. They made her confess her infidelity, but also her unhappiness with an irascible, violent and abusive man. I told my lawyer about this, and he brought it up at the hearing. When Martina said that she herself had started our affair, there were murmurs in the courtroom. Someone then said that perhaps she was the one who had made her husband disappear. Among the evidence presented by my lawyer, for the case of self-defense, were the photos of my injuries and the testimony of a dentist confirming the forced extraction of two of my molars and an incisor. Another of the aggravating factors in my favor were Slack's contradictions. My lawyer argued that in his first testimony given to the police, he had claimed to hear a deep, cavernous voice, with a slight drag on the l's, which did not correspond to that of the accused. The other testimony where he fell into contradictions was when he referred to me as the tortured one, with whom the boys had had a good time.

My argument was that someone else had entered the room and executed my captors while I was unconscious. Was that so? That when I came out of the basement everything had already happened. I didn't know who or how. Maybe one of the relatives of the many victims of the brotherhood. What about the disappearance of the ten undocumented Latinos reported to the police in the Albany area? The judge, despite the evidence, left the case open and ordered a new, more exhaustive forensic search in a wider radius; where the events had occurred, with the purpose of finding the clandestine graves where I was supposed to have buried my victims. The jury deliberated for two days in a very close vote. One of the arguments of a woman was: How was it possible that a man of medium build, and five-foot-seven-inches tall, could have defeated a unit of Special Forces of the American army?

Someone else evaluated the media consequences; the invincible American army being defeated by a solitary and insecure man of average build. For now, I could be released on bail, although I had to wear an electronic bracelet so I could be monitored. My limits were the state of Georgia, only until the case was closed and a final verdict was given. Upon hearing this, my lawyer and I hugged each other. Attorney Viceaka, a simple and kind man, one of those people who are still in the world and for whom the human race keeps being worthwhile. A brave defender who knew the law.

"Take care of yourself, young man, these people are not going to leave you alone," Viceaka said in my ear.

"What do you recommend, sir?"

"Hide, until everything is over, then leave the country."

I looked him in the eyes. "As you know, I don't have the cash for that."

"Then get out of here, go as far away as possible. Go where no one will be able to find you."

After the temporary verdict, two police officers approached to take me to the municipal detention center, located in the back of the same government building. This time, instead of returning me to the cell where I had spent the entire month during the trial, they took me to a window section, where they gave me a parole certificate and a promissory note, which I had to pay in less than eight days or else my parole would be revoked. At another window they gave me my belongings: my wallet, keys, cell phone and fifty dollars. After that, the police took me to where everyone who was to be released was let go, after providing identification. Another police officer took off my handcuffs. And another one put a tracking bracelet under my knee and told me that I could shower, swim, do anything but try to take it off because an alarm would sound and the police would arrest me immediately. All the detainees were released at intervals. I left with a black man who was accused of robbing some rich people's house, although the only evidence against him was a blurry image taken by one of the security cameras.

Martina was waiting for me outside, plus a bunch of reporters and protesters, who demanded my death. "Death to the Mexican!" I managed to hear before getting into Lee's Mustang; he had been declared missing. "Latinos, go home." The cheap reporters threw themselves at the car. I fastened my seat belt, Martina accelerated and in seconds we were gone from there. We didn't say a word, but we went to an abandoned parking lot, where she stopped the car abruptly. Martina got out of the vehicle, walked to where the pavement ended and a large expanse of weeds and rocks began. She looked worried.

I closed the door, turned the car around and approached her, but not too quickly.

The one who spoke first was Martina: "This used to be the drive-in cinema, maybe one of the last in the country. The economic crisis ended a whole lot of businesses," she said without turning to look at me, arms crossed.

"Martina, I'm sorry. I don't know what to tell you," I said.

"Well, don't say anything, like the first time we had sex. Do you remember?"

"Of course."

"I've never seen a man more silent; it was as if you didn't believe what had happened."

"And I didn't. For several days."

She turned around and looked me directly in the eyes, "I just hope you didn't do what they say you did."

I held her gaze: "The fact that you don't believe me worries me. You're the only person who really matters to me, and when I say this, I'm referring to something more than the scandal and the yellow note in the second-rate press. I'm talking about this moment and the moment that follows it and the next one with you, forever. That is the only important thing for me."

"That's what I want to think," she said with a broken voice and threw herself into my arms.

I hugged her, she smelled good. I realized how much I missed her. I kissed her forehead, her mouth. She kissed me back and held me close.

"Let's go. I have a hotel reservation in Columbus."

I ran my hand over her head and said: "Martina, thank you. I don't know what would have happened without your testimony."

"I wasn't going to send the father of my child to jail, was I?" She broke away from my arms and took a few steps back.

"What?"

"I'm pregnant," she said flirtatiously and ran to the car.

I was stunned. I wasn't expecting an answer like that. I caught up with her, it was all a surprise.

"Are you sure?"

"Of what? Of being pregnant, or if it's yours?"

We got into the car.

"Of both …"

"Why are men always so worried about corroborating who their children are? Don't tell me, now you want a DNA test to prove it?"

I looked at her. I loved the way she made her eyes when she wanted to emphasize.

"No, of course not. But Lee came back like two months ago, right? It's natural for me to ask."

She moved the wheel to pass a trailer: "Just as you know certain things, a woman knows about motherhood and who to make children with. And what if it was Lee's?"

I looked at her profile, I was in love: "Even if it was his I would accept him as my son."

She shook her head and smiled. It was clear that she wouldn't know until she saw him in my arms. Inside I said that a DNA test wasn't a bad idea. She looked radiant to me, that was what mattered in the end. The child's biology was the least of it.

She turned up the radio, and we kissed. In reality it didn't seem to affect her that her husband had been declared missing, maybe because the guy had been gone for a long time.

We arrived at the hotel and didn't go out for the rest of the afternoon. In the evening we went to dinner. The next day we walked on the banks of the Chattahoochee River and later we went to the movies, something we both loved. The movie was somewhere between comical and bad, but it made Martina laugh like she hadn't in a while. She told me herself. I loved her. Once in bed we made plans, we speculated on baby names; Emiliano came to mind, in honor of one of the few decent characters in the history of Mexico. Martina leaned toward Emily if it was a girl, in honor of her favorite poet. We laughed because they seemed similar.

We had a couple of beautiful days, until on the third day something completely changed our plans and the possibility of a life together. First, in my dreams, or half-sleep, if you prefer—since that happened, a part of me always stayed awake at night, just in case—I heard footsteps, car noises. When Martina got up to go to the bathroom, I heard gunshots, and I threw myself on top of her to throw her to the floor. There they were, those wretches, just as my lawyer had warned me. I urged Martina to get dressed as quickly as possible and I did the same, all at floor level and behind the bed. The sniper fired two shots, shattering the mirror on the dresser. I took the gun and went to the bathroom. I opened the window and looked out. There was no one there yet, although I sensed that they were coming. We went out through the window and hid behind some huge trash cans as best we could. A pickup entered the hotel parking lot at full speed, several men got out and two ran to the room we were occupying and entered shooting, using silencers. They came out disappointed and got back into the truck and disappeared as quickly as they had come. The lights in several rooms came on and we heard voices, a siren in the distance; someone had called the police. Several men emerged from their rooms in pajamas and looked toward their vehicles. We took advantage of the moment to leave our hiding place and get in the car, the urgent thing was to escape. We left there skidding, Martina at the wheel, me looking through the mirrors and the gun ready to be used.

"Calm down, Martina, drive slowly, we don't want to draw the attention of the police."

"Sons of bitches, how did they know we were here?" she said, upset.

"I would like to know too. Maybe they know the car."

We remained silent. Suddenly she seemed to remember something: "Because of the credit card I used to pay for dinner last night!"

"How is that?"

"I didn't have the cash to fill up ..."

"You should have told me. I'm afraid they even know more than just where we had dinner."

"How?"

"I'm sure they're using one of their damn drones to catch us," I said, and my skin crawled. That meant that at any moment we could be blown to pieces.

"What are you talking about?"

"Have you heard of those pilotless, super-equipped drones that are controlled remotely and can do things like recognize you, hear you, even bomb you?"

"Sure … but aren't you a little paranoid?"

"Paranoid? That's what they argued when the newspapers began to report that the NSA was spying on the American people. At least two of the members of the brotherhood began their careers in the CIA, and the CIA depends on the NSA."

"It's strange. Lee never told me about the brotherhood."

"It's a secret that only they share."

"It's sad, when you thought you knew the person, the person turns out to be someone else."

I understood, she said it as much for me as for Lee.

"It's strange that being the wife of a soldier, it's news to you that he lied to you, it's part of the training." I was beginning to get exasperated.

"But soldiers are not the only people who lie," the innuendo was directed at me of course.

"Sure, but let's get back to the point, Martina. The brotherhood won't let me get away; it's the way things work. For your information, that's how they caught me the last two times, with a drone."

Martina looked at me incredulously: "A drone? How are you so sure?"

"Because while they were torturing me, I analyzed it, and it couldn't be any other way."

"What if someone you knew told them where to find you?"

"Who? You, Toño, Captain Thomas, Ana Graciela? Don't fuck with me, Martina, they have all the technology in the world and all the information at their fingertips."

"I still think that you're a little paranoid."

"Whatever you say right now doesn't matter anymore. You'll have to go on alone ..."

"What are you talking about?"

"You have to get out of Georgia, go far away, or else they'll catch us both. They're capable of blowing us up on the road, it's that easy. They have my facial map, my DNA and even my damn social security number—the one I had worked so hard to obtain along with my citizenship, the only thing Patricia gave me when we got married."

We discussed this and that.

"It's for the best."

"How are you so sure?"

"I'm fucking sure!" How to explain to her that something deep inside me told me so, that my grandmother had predicted it. I looked her in the eyes.

"Okay … I believe you."

"The next thing is to sell the car or change it for any other, travel alone."

"And what about our plans?"

"Change of plans. I know people in California." I thought of Peter's distant relatives. "They are my best friend's cousins, you can get new papers and an ID with them."

"I don't understand."

"Another personality, another life."

"How so?"

"You will have to live under another name, you are part of the vendetta and there is no other way." We approached a shopping center.

"I don't like this."

Suddenly, I felt hungry, we pulled up to a mall. I figured the damn drone would never dare throw a bomb in a place with a lot of people.

"Go in, let's have breakfast and then we'll talk."

"You talk as if you know everything."

"Not everything, some. Think about it, they know the license plate of the car, with that information they can get everything else."

Martina parked the Mustang. We got out of the car and walked to the mall. Once inside, we went straight to the food court on the second floor. We got on the escalator and as we went up, we admired the artificial waterfall in the lobby. We entered a bar where they served early lunch, it was the specialty. I ordered a beer. Martina ordered a coffee. Since we were the first ones there, they served us immediately.

I picked up my beer and took a long drink, I was nervous. Why did I get so serious when I started to feel cornered? Why the hell did I always get to a point where something like another being took over me? What was the access to that part of my memory that seemed to forget everything? I thought about the charges against me.

"So, we are saying goodbye?" said Martina, bringing the cup of coffee to her lips.

"It's the best we can do, Martina, mainly for you. I don't want to risk you, especially in your condition."

"Do we have to live in fear?"

"With caution. It's easier, that way I can move alone and when you're settled, and some time has passed ..."

"So?"

"I definitely want to see my son."

"I don't understand."

"It's very simple, for the safety of both of us."

"You send me to California to live a false life and you become a fugitive. What does that make our son?"

"Don't insist, don't be foolish." I took a sip of my beer and looked at her, she looked sad, worried.

"Take out your phone," I ordered her. "I'll give you the number of Peter's cousins."

I took out my phone and looked for my friends' numbers. For several years now I had been using card phones, disposable phones whose only advantage is that they are not traceable.

"Ready? His name is Baby Medina, his number is: seven, one, four, seven, two, eight, five, three, seven, six, four. Tell them who you are, that I told you to call him. He knows me. Explain to him that you are my wife, and you need to be incognito. He is going to meet you in person, he doesn't trust phones very much. Ask him for a new social security number and a California driver's license. He's my friend; he owes me favors and he respects me."

We looked at each other: "Have you thought about what I am going to do there? How am I going to pay the expenses?"

"You will have to work, I'm sorry but that's how it is."

"That doesn't worry me, the problem isn't working."

"So?"

"Giving up who I am, Lee's money."

"Martina, don't you realize what's going on? They wanted to kill us last night. They were millimeters away from achieving it. The bullet passed this far way from your head." I opened my thumb and index finger in a pinch.

"Maybe they thought it was you who was going to the bathroom, not me."

"I know those rifles, Martina, and you can distinguish one person from another without problems."

Silence.

"You are asking me to put in the trash not only my identity, but the support of my family. And what about when I give birth?"

The waiter appeared with the two omelets and bread.

"Martina, I know what the change means. I understand losing Lee's pension and the army money, but ..."

"I'm talking about myself, not the army money. It's clear that they won't give me anything until he's declared dead and in a drawer. One of his superiors promised me full salaries once the case is closed."

"Forget about the damn checks, it's the lives of both of you. Only until the baby is born, when you're less vulnerable," I said addressing the fetus in her stomach. I prepared to eat.

A few minutes passed in silence, suddenly she said, stunned, as if she saw herself in the future: "I won't be able to live with another name. I can't imagine."

"Of course you can, Martina, it's just a name."

"It's not just that, you have to start over. It's a way of existing."

"Martina, it's for a while."

"How are you so sure?"

"I'll say it again, I know."

"But I also need my family. What am I going to tell them?"

"No, you can't talk to them anymore. The brotherhood will have their phones tapped."

She took her head with both hands and looked at me terrified: "What, then?"

"You'll have to deal with it alone, without friends, without family. There are a lot of people who live like that. Look at me, I have no problems living in different cities and places, meeting new people and forgetting them."

"You told me that they had cut your roots when you were young, maybe that's why. Then you told me about the fire in your house, about the death of your father ..."

“We all have problems with moving, Martina, with living new lives every time, but when there’s no other way there’s no other way.”

“I can’t get used to it.”

“Don’t worry, you’ll survive.”

“You need to be insensitive to do that.”

“Don’t exaggerate. Maybe just until the baby’s born. Then, when you’ll be less vulnerable, maybe you can negotiate with the military.”

“Negotiate? I haven’t done anything.”

“That you were unfaithful, that you regret it, that you need protection ...”

“How am I going to explain that I disappeared for nine months just like that?”

“By then maybe you can tell them the truth. There has to be someone in the whole damn army who is decent, someone who doesn’t belong to the brotherhood.”

“What if Lee shows up?”

I was silent. I took the opportunity to ask the waiter for a second beer.

“Something tells me that won’t be the case.”

She looked at me perplexed: “Then it’s all true.”

I returned her perplexed look and added, a little annoyed: “Fuck, Martina, let’s start over, maybe it’ll become clear.”

The waiter brought me the second beer.

“How much is true and how much is false?”

“Would you believe me if I told you I don’t know?”

We were silent for a moment. I was slowly sipping my beer and thinking about what to do next. She was watching the people slowly filling up the place, early drunks and young couples having lunch. The sun was coming in through all the windows.

“What if I can’t adapt to California?”

"You will, the weather is very nice."

"What if they find me before?"

"The same old story again. Dye your hair, change your tastes a little, be discreet. It all depends on yourself, if you'd listen to me and pay attention. Thousands of people can, why can't you? Besides, you have two things in your favor, you speak English and you know the system."

"What if I can't, or if they catch me? What if I make a mistake?"

For a moment I thought about withdrawing the bail and pleading guilty. Maybe it was the only solution, so they would leave her alone and therefore our child. Tell the police what happened, at least as far as I remembered. Maybe it was true, and I'd be safer in prison. However, something deep inside me knew that things don't work like that, not in this world at least. Surely the brotherhood must have some little brother in prison, and that one would be the one in charge of stabbing me in the showers.

"The next step is to empty the bank accounts and get rid of the car, auction it off," I said. "On the way here, we passed a lot of used cars. Go back there and trade it, if they don't want to pay cash, exchange it for another one, something that will make it to California. Regarding the money, there should be an ATM right here in the mall, withdraw it. You have to remove the card from the phone and buy a disposable one." I was surprised by my lucidity. "I'll hear from Peter's cousins, so I'll send you a good sum in a few months, don't worry."

She looked at me with eyes I didn't know her for. "So, this *is* goodbye."

I wanted to take her hands, but she pulled them away and hid them in her jacket pockets.

"Yes, temporarily. I'll call you. I insist, buy a disposable phone that can't be traced. We can also communicate by email, from new accounts of course, and fake names. Remember, when we use the phone, they should be short calls and never mention names or other sensitive data. The same when we write on the internet. Use public computers, never the one at home."

"It seems you have experience."

Martina drank the remaining coffee in her cup. "And what are you going to do?" she asked me.

"Don't worry about me. As you said yourself, I'm ready to change my life." I called the waiter and asked for the bill, paid in cash. I said to reassure her: "I will wait for the verdict, that will calm them down. I will remain in the state. I have confidence in my lawyer. Slack does not have a great reputation and has contradicted himself more than once. It is evident, he wants someone to sponsor his legs and his missing ear."

"And then?"

"Well, if I have to face them, I will."

Martina was quick to respond. "It's a very bad idea, I think," she said wringing her hands.

"Which one?"

"Facing them."

"Let it be what God wants, what luck or the numbers on the dice dictate." I caught her hands this time and pressed them against mine.

"Do you still think luck is everything?" She faced me.

"Yes, ma'am. Why we are born in a certain family, city, social class or with certain physical features, it is all a product of luck or chance, whatever you want to call it. Luck is everything, yes ma'am. Many should be grateful for their luck; especially the bastards in power or money."

We were silent for a few minutes.

She looked at me seriously. "Speaking of being born ... so if it's a boy, I'll name him Emiliano, like that revolutionary of yours, and if it's a girl, Emily, like the great writer from Massachusetts. Do we at least agree on that?"

"Completely, darling." I kissed her hands. "Besides, both names look similar and are cute."

She sketched a smile, although she was still upset and worried.

"And what will I tell him if one day he asks about his father?"

"Don't worry, before he can ask that, I'll appear, I promise."

"Are you asking me to wait an indeterminate number of years until you show up at the door?"

"It's not years, months maybe."

"Who do you think you are? What am I? I'm not a nun."

"I'm not asking you to wait like a nun."

"Don't you realize, that's precisely what I got tired of while I lived with Lee."

"Martina, you're a very difficult little queen. Besides, you can always fall in love again, make your life. Fuck the next plumber."

"Fuck you!" She walked away from me.

"I'm sorry, I'm sorry ... come, come. Hey, let's not look bad, we both need not only good luck, but a lot of positive energy to accompany us. We both have a long journey ahead of us." I sat down next to her.

She looked at me with teary eyes and finally gave in: "Okay. You're right."

"Don't cry." I took her by the chin, "Kiss me instead."

We kissed again, this time with more passion. That was a difficult decision. I put my hand on her stomach. For the first time in a long time, I found myself in love, the woman fascinated me.

"Just remember one thing, I love you. I love you both, with all my heart." I had to leave before I regretted it. Martina looked at me with very sad eyes, they almost broke my heart completely. I stood up, "I'm leaving, but we'll see each other later, I swear. I want to have Emiliano, or Emily, in my arms, and you, for the rest of my life. I only have some earrings to fix."

"What earrings? Are you thinking of finishing off all the members of the brotherhood? Cut off their ears and put them on a damn necklace?"

"It wouldn't be bad, they're as dangerous as the Ku Klux Klan, the motherfuckers. But don't worry, that's not what I meant." I leaned down to give her one last kiss on the mouth. She let me do it but made no effort to return my caress. "Don't forget to do what I said. I'm begging you. It's important, this isn't a joke. Okay?"

She looked at me and nodded her head inconsolable.

"I'll call you, send you money and see you in California."

I left some bills on the table with the waiter and slowly walked out of the bar first, then out of the mall where I dissolved into a sea of people, I had to disappear.

The last image of Martina was her sitting in that nondescript bar, under the rays of the sun that filtered through the windows and formed an aura around her.

43

There were Mrs. Robbins, Martina, Regina, Samantha, Candice, Jaire, Muriel, Vanesa and Ana Graciela. Three of them were widows, or that's what they were hoping for. A year had passed since their husbands disappeared and there was no trace of them. According to the forensic authorities, they had literally combed the area of the incident in search of human remains within a fifty-mile radius, but nothing was found, as if the three men had vanished into thin air. The wrecked vans had been analyzed for DNA, but nothing that incriminated the accused, nothing on the weapons except some fingerprints of the victims. There was no case, except for the word of a witness, who was obviously jealous.

The women had agreed to appear in the documentary in the hope that this would unlock the case. As long as their husbands were not officially declared dead, they could not collect the army insurance or the bonuses. Also, of course, for the three thousand dollars that each of them would receive for an hour of interview.

Regarding the case, the most interesting thing according to the producer, was that the accused had turned himself in and once inside the jail cell, he had also disappeared. As if he had gone through the walls or someone had let him escape, or worse, he was murdered in complicity with the authorities. Many disappearances around the same issue, that was the news.

The cameramen and the reporter settled into their positions to continue the second part of the interview, related to the case of infidelity that the local newspapers had been covering for several weeks. Everyone finished their drink, the women returned to their places. They were helped by the assistants, who placed microphones on them and touched up their faces with makeup. The director of the documentary sat in front of the group.

"What do you think about the suspect? Is it true that he was some kind of animal or wild beast?"

They looked at each other. Something made them feel as if they were members of a club; from the moment they started to be interviewed they had already started to be cynical, the glass of whiskey probably helped. "Once he was undressed, he transformed. One could lose track of time, I had up to six orgasms."

"Three, four hours of sex or more were natural for him."

"Yes, he was barbaric, he made me believe that I was some kind of animal, he put me in difficult positions, although all of them were interesting."

"I remember it more like a dance."

"He infected you with music, and he was the rhythm," joked Jaire.

"I still remember, and I get tickles on the soles of my feet, he kissed my toes like no one else. It was very tender," said Ana Graciela.

"I think he was a priest, something like a spirit. Once he touched you, he drove you crazy, you entered his personal temple," commented Samantha, who professed new age tendencies.

"As for me, in addition to other parts, he licked the back of my neck and under my armpits."

"Yes, he was a wild animal, but in a different sense," replied Muriel, who the others did not know.

"Do you think he deserved the death penalty as the public opinion initially demanded?" was the director's next question.

"Not the death penalty, but a greater punishment, instead of being declared innocent in absentia." It was Candice's turn, dressed in a short skirt that showed off her shapely thighs. She sounded resentful, but with a face stretched by her recent operation. "He predicted the disappearance of my husband's daughters, the two girls he had with his first wife, maybe he kidnapped them."

"He was not declared innocent, he was charged with breach of trust and robbery," someone clarified.

"Many of us believe that he didn't disappear, but that he was made to disappear. Please, nobody escapes from a jail cell just like that, at noon, surrounded by police and cameras!" This time it was Regina who intervened.

"He was a very good young man," said Mrs. Robbins.

"I agree. On the contrary, they should give him recognition," Jaire continued with her jokes.

"There should be one of these 'bad guys' in each of the bases," suggested Samantha, who was secretly happy to have gotten rid of her soldier and was now content as the girlfriend of a doctor who was worth his weight in gold. She urgently needed to be officially declared a widow to get married.

"Do you agree that his disappearance is part of a whole paranormal phenomenon?"

"No."

"No."

"No."

"Yes. He used hypnotism with me. I don't remember anything, until we're having sex and I'm sitting on his member. It couldn't have been possible to fall any other way. He used his knowledge to trick people," answered Vanesa, the fat one, as the rest of the women referred to her, particularly Martina, Regina and Samantha, who knew about the rape and hated her for it.

"I gave him money, every time he came to the house. I paid him or gave him some little gift. He subtly forced you to do it," said Candice.

"Once, while we were making love, I touched his back and felt that he had wings. When I had that multiple orgasm, I saw that he opened them and flapped them," commented Samantha.

"And it couldn't be that you were under the influence of some drug?"

"Beyond alcohol and half a joint, that night there were no other drugs involved. Maybe it was the pleasure, but I don't think so. Come on, it's not like it was my first time. He had wings and he flapped them, big, impeccable black wings."

"Don't tell me the guy was a vampire! Hehehe, I'm just finding out!" Regina smiled.

"If he had wings, I don't know and I find it funny. What I do know is that he had a big dick, and he knew how to use it, honestly," Jaire said.

"He left you dry. The best of all was his rhythm, as someone mentioned, maybe because I like to dance. I studied dance for years," commented Ana Graciela.

"He projected your fantasy in some part of your mind, and he integrated himself with it."

"True."

"I didn't say he was a vampire, I said they were the wings of an angel, to me ..."

"We were lucky, all of us ..." Regina added.

"He was an ancient spirit incarnated in a commonplace person, by chance or by luck, as he called it. We happened to meet him in the form of Sergio," said Martina who had not said a single word since the second part of the interview.

"Affirmative."

The camera focused on Martina and zoomed in: "Part of what they say is true, it was a shaman who only appears every few years to do justice."

"How can you be so sure?"

"He told me, he told me everything on the night we conceived our little Emiliano ..."

44

"Grandson, here's your sweater, put it on. I finally finished it."

"How nice, grandma. And it's warm, thank you."

"Make sure to maintain your body temperature, it's important. It's cold where you're going, and winter has already arrived there."